KING OF CODE

CD REISS

Things don't have to change the world to be important.

— STEVE JOBS

PRAISE FOR MARRIAGE GAMES

"*Marriage Games* is one of the most powerful novels I have ever read. CD Reiss gets into the soul of her hero and heroine and never lets go." *Desiree Holt, USA Today bestselling author*

"Through glimpses of past and present, the world of Adam Steinbeck and Diana McNeill-Barnes are revealed in such clarity that readers can't help but visualize the whole picture painted by CD Reiss' pen." ~ *RT Book Reviews*

"I devoured this book; and it devoured me! Spellbinding, swoony, emotional, and mindblowingly addictive." *Katy Evans ~ NY Times best-selling author of Real*

"CD Reiss absolutely blew me away. The characters intrigued me, the story grabbed me, the sizzle thrilled me, and the writing style enticed me." *J Kenner ~ NY Times bestselling author of The Stark Trilogy*

"CD Reiss writes the best erotica I have ever read." *Meredith Wild ~ #1 NY Times bestselling author of the Hacker series.*

"Marriage Games was enthralling! Seriously a fascinating game of cat and mouse. I couldn't turn the pages fast enough." *Aleatha Romig ~ NY Times bestselling author of Infidelity*

King of Code

Barrington isn't a real place and these folks aren't IRL people. If they seem real I've done my job, but it's still a coincidence.

Infinite thanks to the K's for their help with research. If there are mistakes or misinterpretations of coding, quantum physics, the dark web, or reality itself, that's on me.

Print ISBN: 978-1635760828

eBook ISBN: 978-1942833451

4U7H0R'5 N073

AUTHOR'S NOTE

Though there are a few towns called Barrington in the United States, my Barrington is a made-up place. The lack of state or geography is intentional. Barrington is everywhere in America—and nowhere specific. The troubles there reflect small-town concerns many communities share, and it's going to take me a few books to unpack it all.

To that end, I tried to strip the residents' dialect of a specific region, but one might show up. That's unintended.

I want to tell the story of your town, no matter what town or city you call home.

Though I'd love to assure you that I was successful in this (or any) endeavor, I have no way of knowing until it's too late.

I hope you enjoy the book—wherever you're from.

I

Steve Jobs. Bill Gates. Jeff Bezos.

Kings. Emperors. Rulers of kingdoms they built with their own hands. Their own sweat. Nobodies who clawed their way to the top with sheer grit.

Everett Fitzgerald. Even my buddy Fitz is a king.

Rockefeller. Carnegie. Ford.

They changed the world.

I'm about to become one of those guys.

Decades from now, they're going to talk about what I'm about to release into the world. Where I thought of it. What I ate for breakfast. How I got here. I worked harder, thought bigger, drilled deeper. I changed myself from the inside out to get here.

Today, I am granted meetings with kings.

In thirteen days I, Taylor Harden, become a king of kings.

II

There's going to come a day I don't have to fuck in the supply closet.

One leg over my shoulder, the other dropping off the side of the table, naked enough to get the job done, but clothed enough for waistbands and shirttails to get in the way. I hadn't fucked in a bed in four years. I didn't see my apartment for weeks at a time. I'd showered at the gym until we bought the QI4HQ and warehouse, then I put a shower stall in my office.

"Harder," she grunted in the dark. "Fuck me harder."

I gave it to her. A stream of filth left her lips, and I parried with more until we were both reduced to syllables. Then, nothing but the need to get back to work.

We rustled our clothing back on.

"Did you set up the cage?" I tucked in my shirt.

"We made it presentable last night. Jack needed to clean his shit."

Jack. I loved him like a brother, and he could cut code like a motherfucker, but he'd left a Tech World packing slip on his desk when the *NY Times* had done their profile on me. The photo Greeked when it was enlarged. Lucky him.

"Raven, I don't want a repeat of—"

"There's not going to be—"

"I mean it."

"Taylor." Her voice had moved to the door. "Everything's going to be perfect this time. I promise."

She opened the door before I could remind her that I was the one who decided what was perfect and what sucked.

III

"Why four?" Keaton had asked in my studio, years before. His English accent made him sound perpetually disgusted by my arrangements, but he'd insisted on seeing the shithole I lived in so he could feel sorry for me. I'd gone white hat and starved while he'd stayed black hat and thrived. His shirt cost more than my rent.

"Why four what?" I sat in the desk chair in front of my machine. It was the only other chair besides the one he'd bent his six foot four inches onto. He took up half the damn apartment.

"You're naming the company QI4. Q is quantum. I is intelligence. Why four?"

"I liked the way it sounded."

He finished his beer and got up to put his bottle in the recycling. He did it slowly, as if he wanted to fuck with me. He'd been an asshole since high school. Keaton Bridge, aka 41ph4 W01ph (Alpha Wolf if you don't speak 133t), had taught me the art of the dark web, where identities, guns, and drugs were traded in glorious, unindexed chaos.

"Seventy million," he said.

I was glad I hadn't dressed up to meet him because I almost pissed myself.

"But…" He trailed off intentionally for effect.

"But?"

He leaned his ass on the kitchenette counter and folded his arms. "You clean your ass up. You look like a bloody slob."

I ran my fingers through my hair. I hadn't had it cut in months. It was straight-ish when short, but when it got below my ears, it started curling. My beard was short, and my skin was olive but sallow from lack of sun. I'd lost weight, missed the gym for forever, my clothes hung off me.

"At least I don't look like a politician."

"Seventy million," he repeated, reminding me I was in no position to insult his suit. "In Bitcoin."

Oh, fuck him. He couldn't pay me in an underground, digital currency to finance my above-board venture.

"Dude. Come on. How am I going to exchange that?"

"Dude," he mocked me flatly. "I'll help you."

"I'll never get a government contract."

"*We* will. It'll just take time."

"We?"

"I'm tired of living in the shadows."

"Whoa, whoa, I said 'silent partner.' I don't need someone coming in, telling me what to do. Not even… before you even say it… not even the 'Devil of the Dark Web' or, no, *especially* not the devil."

"You'll have control, Taylor. It's all you. I'll never even show up at the office. But my investment will essentially reveal Alpha Wolf's identity, which will serve my purposes and clear the way for the exchange."

I tilted my head right then left as if I was letting resistance drop out of my ears. It was a moment to breathe. I'd expected worse when I asked him for seed money. I'd figured he'd drop a couple hundred grand I could tuck away in expenses while I tried to line up real capital.

Now he wanted to be the capital. Talk about a gift horse. I was looking right in its mouth and wheeling it into the gates anyway.

My phone had encrypted channels with all my primary contacts, including Keaton. As I was walking out of the hall closet after Raven, it rattled as he messaged me.

<Good luck today. Don't fuck it up.>

<You should be here to take some credit.>

<Credit is one thing I don't need.
Keep the receipts off the desk.>

Raven looked great walking into the hall after she'd just demanded I rip her apart with my cock. I had no feelings about her whatsoever, and that lack was mutual. Working sixteen-hour days in the same office meant we fucked each other or didn't fuck at all.

This was why I didn't hire women, besides the fact that they turned nerd IQ points into premature ejaculations. I usually wound up fucking them. But my lawyer had said to hire one, pay her well, and not fuck her. I'd taken two thirds of his advice. Raven had needs, same as I did. She was so anti-drama, anti-emotion, she practically had a dick.

"Check on Jack." I closed the door to the supply closet. "He's a fucking slob."

"The room will be clear."

"It better be."

"Yes, El Presidente." She threw the snark over her shoulder when she was already halfway down the hall.

I went the other way and pressed my thumbprint into a pad by sealed double doors.

A robotic voice came from the speaker. "Name."

A name would have been too easy. None of us used it. I used song lyrics.

"I don't give a fuck, chuckin' my deuces up."

A slot opened, and I put my phone into it. The slot closed. I had a mechanical watch, a Langematik that had set me back twenty grand, which was a deal, I promise you. It wasn't digital, so it didn't need to be checked before entry.

Green light. I burst into the Faraday cage, which was spotless and windowless. The walls, floor, and ceiling were lined with copper mesh that would stop all manner of motherfuckery. The room had no internet. No signal entered or escaped. Not even the drip-drop of electromagnetism from monitors. I'd put copper wire cages around the coding pit and the small factory on the floor below where engineers built the chips and boards.

I'd put full-spectrum lighting on both floors. It dimmed as it went dark outside and projected season-appropriate nature scenes on three walls. The rows of monitors were manned by the best coders on two continents. Three if you counted Giorgo, who had been born in Italy but trained in India. Above them was a huge screen rolling code.

I watched it roll. It didn't look like C++, Java, or anything seen before because I'd rewritten the rule book.

It was beautiful.

I got up on the platform in front of the screen and faced the thirty-three guys sitting at their computers. "Jack!"

He spun around. He was in Silicon Valley chic: a Nirvana T-shirt, jeans, and sneakers. I was the only one wearing a suit, but then again, I was the only one in charge. Fuck Zuck and his sweatshirt and sneakers. I was rewriting the rules.

"That fucking picture better be in your drawer."

He snapped up the picture of his nephew, threw it in his drawer, and slapped it shut.

"Lock it." I didn't wait for him to fuck with the key. "Everyone."

The last five of them turned away from their screens and trained their attention half on me. The usual ADHD cases who couldn't switch tasks easily. I waited. These guys were my people, my tribe. From the least social to the blabbermouths, we understood each other. I knew how to give them what they needed.

"Do not put it past journalists to 'accidentally' open your drawers to look for an emergency tampon. Do not put it past them to look at your cables or 'unintentionally' hit your spacebar to drop the screensaver. Do not think for one second that they didn't bring someone with a photo- graphic memory. Shut the machines down. Name. Rank. Year of hire. How fucking pleased you are with your stock options. If you're not, you're going to have to take a deep breath and talk to Raven."

I got a little laughter. Women scared nerds. Another reason to keep them out of the cage. I wanted my guys to feel safe.

"As a reminder. You can neither confirm nor deny the following." I held up a finger. "The existence of a third quantum logic gate." I held up another finger. "The transverse micro kernel system." A third finger made a W. "Machine code translation circuits." I put my hand down on the railing and pushed off it. "The only thing you can confirm with utmost certainty is that no one currently living on planet earth can hack Quantum Intelligence Four. And that, men, is because you have perfected this thing to within an inch of its life. You know it's going to change the world. Your code is going to be inside the machines of every company in the world, and that's nothing compared to the day we scale and it's in every home, on every phone, in every chip manufactured in every factory in every country. That's you."

I paused to let that sink in and leaned on the railing as if I was whispering in their ears. "After today's announcement, everyone's going to try to get in here. Beware social engineering hacks. We cannot defend against those inside the system. People will hand you thumb drives, cables, whatever. Strangers are going to ask you for your pet's name... which you can't use as a password, but they'll try."

"Who can have a pet?" Deeprak shouted. "We live here!"

Laughter followed. Deeprak could drop a joke. He was as much a partner as Keaton, and he was going to be a rich man.

"In fucking paradise, Deeprak. But you get my point. Don't pick up shit in the parking lot. Beware pretty girls… and boys, David." I pointed at him. "Beware of mail. Cameras. Your own phone can be used against you if you let a girl in a bar put her number in it." I took a pencil out of my pocket and held it up. "If any of you need one of these to write down a number, let me know. Because in thirteen days, at GreyHatC0n, New York, we are going to offer five million dollars to anyone who can get into Quantum Intelligence Four, and you…" I pointed at Joe, who'd never had a girlfriend.

He pushed his glasses up.

"You." I moved to Laurence, who had a weird facial tic. "You." Roger. High-functioning Asperger's. "You." Grady. Social anxiety. "You." Thom. "You." Perry. They all lit up when I pointed at them, and the energy in the room was about to burst. "You're all going to be the sexiest guys in the room."

Cheers. Exactly what I was looking for. I checked my watch, but I knew what time it was. Showtime.

"Gentlemen." I held up my hand, and they quieted. "Shut your machines down. The six of you who are staying, put your smiles on. The rest of you can take a powder. *Wired* has arrived."

IV

Wired had brought seven people. Four women and three men. By the time I was out in the lobby, they'd surrendered their cell phones, Fitbits, and smart watches. They'd submitted to a pat down from security and gone through a scanner we'd bought from the same supplier the TSA used. They'd agreed to use our recording equipment and had already familiar- ized themselves with it.

Mona Rickard scribbled in her little pad. She'd brought her own pencil. It was thicker than the ones we provided. I let it slide when I saw her grip was tangled and unusual. She needed it, and getting a transmitter into solid wood was a project a Boy Scout would have had troublewith.

"Five million," she said, a brown curl bouncing and swaying as she wrote. "For anyone or only people registered at GreyHatC0n?"

"Anyone," I replied. "Worldwide. We'll accept a remote hack. Welcome the attempt, actually. I hear that on the big day, teams are logging in from Râmnicu Vâlcea. That's in Romania."

"Yeah. Thanks. I know. I wrote a piece on Hackerville."

So they'd sent me a girl who at least knew something. Chalk one up for *Wired*.

"The Quantum Four code isn't even based in binary," I continued. "The circuits are built on three-dimensional thinking."

"QuBit. One, zero, random."

"Exactly. When the machines are released to Oracle next year, they can open them up and try to reverse engineer, but they won't. Even the client can't breach it."

"You wouldn't be the first to make that claim."

"If the casing is cracked, the boards self-destruct. They sink and melt."

"And production is here, in California?"

"The machines are made here, on site. We have a plan to scale when we can guarantee security."

The team followed Raven and me to the double doors leading to the Faraday cage. I stopped in front of them and faced the *Wired* team.

"Do you have way to ID the winner?" Mona asked, her diamond engagement ring jogging back and forth as she wrote.

The team got into the elevator as I answered.

"We do," I said. "A masked audit of all compliant commands. Non-compliant are going to look like shitstain on a wedding gown."

I explained nothing. If *Wired* sent anything less than their most technical writer they could fuck themselves. I wasn't wasting my time teaching her how to read metadata. She was going to have to ask one of the guys in IT.

"You have a protocol. And metaphor noted." She looked up and flipped her brown curl away from her eyes. "You're pretty sure of yourself."

"I'm sure about these guys on the other side of the door."

"I hear it's all men."

"I hire the best regardless of gender."

"And all the best had dicks?"

Someone on her team snorted with laughter. The elevator doors opened, and I led the group to the cage doors.

"Google hires all the girls," I said.

"I'm sure." She folded her pad and pencil against her chest and smiled. We saw right through each other, but she couldn't print what I wouldn't say.

"We'll be going into a foyer between the world of Wi-Fi signals and EMPs. Kind of like a lock room in the space station."

"I'm ready if you are," Mona said.

I tapped the panel outside the cage.

"Name."

"I don't give a fuck, chuckin' my deuces up." I chanted the song lyrics flatly.

The door unlocked with a clack.

"Suck on my balls, please," a pipsqueak with the notepad said from behind Mona.

She spun on him like a schoolteacher. "What?"

"I had enough," I added, and Mona gave me a wide-eyed stare. "I ain't thinkin' about you."

Pipsqueak tipped his pencil to me. "Beyoncé"

I winked at him and opened the door. I didn't look back at Mona to see if she'd gotten over it. They piled in. I closed the exit behind them.

"We're ready. Behind these doors is a room sealed against Wi-Fi. There's no internet connectivity. All the electrical outlets route through a secure panel. Quantum Intelligence Four is pure virgin code."

It bleeds when breached.

We said that a lot around the conference room table, but not in front of Mona Rickard.

I opened the doors. My coders stood. On the screen I'd just stood in front of, and on the walls that usually displayed nature scenes, were the scrolls of masked code as it would appear on the Tor site. They were the only light in the room. I laid my hand on the one machine we'd left on. It was in a mini-Faraday and was responsible for the screens.

"What you see here"—I indicated the men in the room—"are the best coders alive today. And on the walls is QI4's code. It looks like nothing because it's masked, and it's going to continue to look like nothing unless someone gets in."

"Which won't happen." Deeprak came from behind his desk with a big white smile. Charming fucker. He'd have no trouble getting laid once he had a minute to wink at a girl.

He held his hand out to Mona, and she was about to shake it when his smile melted like solder on a hot iron. His hand froze between them. I followed his gaze to one of the projections.

The code wasn't masked.

ASCII flew down the roll. Then—

"Binary?" I whispered and stepped toward the wall. There was no binary. QI4 circuits didn't work that way. "Shut it down!"

Scrambling. Clicking. Keys unlocking drawers where safepasses were stored. My glands opened like circuits for sweat, hormones, fight or flight, firing neurons in the face of a breach I didn't have an algorithm to process.

"Shut it down!" The scream rattled the top of my throat.

Jack was the first to have his passkey out, but before he could type in a command, the entire system went dark with a sigh of hard drives winding down.

We all stood in the dim, windowless room.

The air crackled with silence broken only by the sound of Mona's pencil looping over paper, like someone woken in the darkness, writing down the details of a nightmare.

V

TWITTER

@Wired
Ex Black Hat hacker Beezleboy creates
the unhackable system. Until it's hacked.

@gizmodo
That time you bragged about the
unhackable system and someone…

@nytimes
Oracle Inc. may delay system
upgrades in the face of QI4 breach.

@hackerbitch
Beezleboy got pwnd. Always a
fucking pussy. #QI4choked

@git-up
Finally. Someone he couldn't screw
by snapping his bitch fingers.
#tool #douche # QI4choked

@anon_00110001
@hackerbitch
He's the fucking King. What did he make you choke on?

@engadget
Did someone just climb the Everest of exploits?

@hackerbitch
@anon_00110001
Careful – your douche is showing.
 # QI4choked

@anon_00110001
@hackerbitch
Temporary setback. Your most useful skill is tweeting with your legs in the air.
#QI4rulz #stackslut

@shelly-code
@beezleboy363636
That, my friend, is the taste of crow.

@hackeropz
Rumored QI4 hack may be part of a bigger stunt. Don't write off @beezleboy363636 & Alpha Wolf yet.

@hackerbitch
@anon_00110001
080 114 111 110 032 104 097 115
032 114 117 105 110 101 100 032
121 111 117 013 010

@anon_00110001
@hackerbitch
Not impressed by ASCII. Pron is nectar. You can't even get a job that doesn't require kneepads #QI4rulz

@DeadBeefCafe
Anybody seen @beezleboy363636?
Tor's quiet. His account's dead. Is he
hanging from his belt in the closet?

VI

This is how a guy ends up in a windowless room full of computers, wearing nothing but his jockeys. He kicks everyone out. He locks the doors. He looks for code fingerprinting. He spends a long time—the lighting change he programmed tells him it's just about twenty-eight hours—finding nothing. He takes a shower to clear his head. In the middle of it, with soap in his hair, he realizes he could check the core dump for clear text. Rinsing his hair doesn't even occur, and drying off will take too long, so he puts his underwear on while he's walking back to the cage. It sticks to him like a wet T-shirt sticks to tits. He sits down and searches everything.

There isn't much to see until there's a squeak of the door opening behind him, and he spins his chair to see who it is.

"How did you end up…?" Deeprak held out his hands, incredulous over how I looked.

The full-speed-ahead train of my thoughts runs through how I ended up in a windowless room full of shattered computers, sitting in front of my laptop, wearing nothing but my jockeys.

"Your dick hard?" I spun back to my screen.

"Yeah. I'm going to fuck you in the ass if you don't let everyone back in here."

"No one's getting in until we know who did this, or they're going to do it again."

"What the fuck, Taylor?" He pushed a smashed computer with his toe.

I'd trashed four in a deliberate, organized way and couldn't find a chip out of place. Then I lost my shit and smashed monitors against whatever edge I could find. Then I found it. A dongled chip with a quarter inch antenna right in the board.

"The poison pill was in the monitors. Five of them." I pushed the one nearest my foot toward him. A 27-inch screen with a lightning fast GPU. We didn't have the facilities to make our own monitors, so we bought them like normal people.

Deeprak saw it right away and picked up the green board. "Motherfucker."

"Said that right."

"What was it talking to?"

"It had to be transmitted to something coming in and out of the cage. I found a power strip in reception with a receiver in it. Another fucking mail order. Never again."

Deeprak spread the monitor guts on the table next to me and examined them closely. "We're a young office. We had to buy shit to set up. We had to buy a coffeemaker too. We can't open up everything and check for receivers."

"We do now."

"Did they come from the same place? The monitors and the power strip?"

"No. It's a fucking mess. I can't make a connection. Monitors through TechWorld. The power strip was Amazon. The coffee maker was some artisanal company in Seattle."

"You checked the coffee maker?" He stood up from his inspection of the monitor.

"It was clean. Look at this. I'm in the poison pill now." I pointed at a little chip in the GPU I'd hooked up to my laptop, then at the screen.

"Anything?"

"The complete Sherlock Holmes."

"Really?"

"Really. He's fucking taunting me with it."

Deeprak looked over my shoulder. My hacker had pasted the entire library of Sir Arthur Conan Doyle in the comments, and I had to go through every word.

"Have you considered it could be one of our guys?"

"No."

That was out of the question. I paid them well and treated them like princes. They each had a stake in making this work, and they each cared about what we were doing. Whatever it was—worm, virus, hack from God—it had locked me out. I could see the size of the box my life was in, but I couldn't open it. I hadn't connected offsite backups because we were off the grid.

It wasn't anyone on the team. I trusted them, and not a line of code got pushed to the source without me looking at it.

It was me. I'd been complacent. I'd let all their work get destroyed. I'd failed them. They relied on me to lead them, and I'd let them down.

"You all right?" Deeprak asked.

Fuck it. Guilt was taking up time and energy. I was running low on both.

By accident, I laid too much weight on the page down key and forwarded to the middle of a completely different section. I was about to go back when I saw slashes. I hadn't seen slashes anywhere else, then I noticed the digit at the beginning.

9 I beg that y*ou will look upon it*
not as a battered billycock but as
*an in*te/ll/ectua/l/ q*roblem*.*

"Look at this." I pulled the paragraph onto the big screen in front of the room.

Deeprak stood before it with his arms crossed. He was best when he had a problem to solve or a journalist to charm.

"Isolate the odd ones," he said.

I'd already done it.

9gtyue/ll/tn/l/qm

"He needed the q," I said. "So he misspelled problem."

"What if the slashes aren't for the letters?"

"Other options? Numbers?"

"Three Ls?"

"Or ones. Leet style."

9gtyue3tnqm OR 9gtyuetn3qm

We stood in front of the green letters on the black background, arms crossed.

He tilted his head a little.

I paced away and looked quickly.

He looked at it from the side.

I squinted.

As if we had the same neurons, Deeprak and I always thought with one mind. This time was no different.

"Eleven digits. Geohash coordinates," I said. Geohash was a newer version of latitude and longitude that split the world into a grid and gave each box a code.

"God, please let it be Tahiti. I want to go to Tahiti."

We didn't have internet in the cage, but I had a geohash database inside it. I called it up, and the cached satellite picture came on the big screen. All grey. The coordinates were inside a watermass.

"Lake Superior," I said. "Change the three in the second string."

"Done." It came on the screen in a split second, and it was land.

"No white sand beaches." I folded my arms over my bare chest, looking at the pin. The coordinates fell on a big building in a little town in the middle of nowhere. "Where are we?"

Instead of answering, Deeprak contracted the map until the surrounding area was in the frame.

Nothing.

Freeway.

Train tracks.

Farms.

An interstate.

A nameless tributary.

Nowheresville in The Great State of Nowhere, USA.

"Do you think…?" Deeprak said.

"Yeah. I think he left it so I'd come looking for him."

"What are you going to do?"

"Go looking for him."

"Put on some pants first."

I was already out the door.

VII

Fucksville, Nowhere—aka Barrington—didn't have an airport in a one-hundred-forty-mile radius.

That wasn't true. They had a dirt landing strip for crop dusters. I'd passed it on the way. What a shit hole. If I'd chartered something to land there, I would have announced my presence before I even took off.

I wasn't a big fan of Caddys. I drove a Tesla. Caddys weren't a thing in San Jose, but it was the best car they'd had at the airport rental terminal. The girl behind the desk swore by it, hand on heart, eyes rolling with remembered pleasure, and I had to say, though it handled like a cruise liner, it drove like a spaceship.

As I passed into town, the sign said the population was 1,209, but there was a fifth space before the one, as if there used to be ten thousand more people.

The terrain was pre-winter blight. Post exploding fall colors and pre winter sting. Brown, leafless, scrubby. The sky was overhung with grey, but with no discernible clouds, as if a screen of dullness hung between the earth and the heavens.

No way the dude who hacked QI4 was in this town. This was a pitstop on the way to some big reveal that would either be humiliating or expensive.

I was a target. A betrayer. I'd gone from black hat to white hat. I'd created a system to thwart them and bragged about it. I was the Everest of the hacker world. They wanted to get me because I was big, I was a challenge, and I was there.

I pulled into a little parking lot in front of two stores. A restaurant and a grocery store. It was the first commercial zoning I'd seen since passing into town.

When I got out, I had a weird feeling I only got when I went to Scott's Seafood with Fitz. Everyone looked and pretended not to. The room got one eighth quieter. They nudged each other, looked halfway around, pretended to take selfies so they could see over their shoulders.

This was the same—but different. Obviously. Because Fitz and I going to Scott's was normal. My being in flyover central to find a hacker was crazy.

I went up the wooden steps to a restaurant called Barrington Burgers. It was closed. I looked at my watch. It was one o'clock on a Saturday. I cupped my hands around my eyes and looked in the glass door, angling to see through a slit in the blinds.

Looked all right at first glance. Homey little place. Chairs were pushed in but weren't upside down on the tables. Maybe it was dinner only?

Then I noticed the alcohol was gone from behind the bar. The plants were dead. Sugar packets were strewn across the wood floor, shredded and balled in a light dusting in the floorboard slats. Only the white packets were ripped. The blue and pink packets were untouched.

Mice. Rats, maybe. Smart fuckers. I wouldn't have touched that other shit either.

"You looking for someone, mister?"

I turned toward the voice behind me and my god. The prettiest things hid in the most unlikely places. Long, wavy blond hair that reached breasts hidden under a flannel plaid car coat that was cut for men. Jeans. Cowboy boots. No makeup. Wide, full lips with a crease in the bottom one. Angular nose. Freckles. Eyes that went from brown in the center to blue at the outer ring.

She looked away, a little pink in the cheek. Tucked her hair behind her ear. The diamond in her lobe had to be a carat and a half. It looked as real as she did.

"No one in particular," I said. "I was thinking of staying the night around here."

I actually hoped I wouldn't have to, but no one who could hack me *lived* here, and I needed a place to drop my stuff.

"Oh, uh. There's a hotel on Oak." She pointed in a general direction. Her hand was fine, delicate, with white tape around three finger joints.

I took out my phone. She stared at it. Were they still using flip phones in Nowhereville or something?

"Do you know what it's called? I can look it up."

"The connection isn't great around here. You just go right out of the lot.

Go for about a mile and a half, and you'll see a gate onto Oakwood. Take that until you see it."

"What's it called?" I could GPS the name more easily than stare at my odometer.

"Bedtimey Inn? But like I said, the connection's pretty spotty around here." She jerked her thumb behind her toward the little convenience store. "I'm helping out at the grocery. Want to call from there and see if they have any room?"

"I'll just drive over."

She barely moved, but I could tell I'd snubbed her by refusing her offer.

"I'm sure you know what you want." Her eyelids fluttered. Her lashes were blond at the tips and darker at the roots.

Strange looking girl. Beautiful and exotic. Just a touch younger than me. Her nipples were probably the palest pink fading into bronze at the center. Or the other way around. I wanted to know.

It was the wanting that tweaked a thought, a memory, a flash of déjà vu. It tapped a turtle's shell, and though the animal heard the tap, it didn't come out.

"Do I know you?" I asked.

"Um, did you go to Montgomery High?"

"No."

"Do you work at the distro center off the interstate? I sub there sometimes."

"No." I couldn't help smirking. The notion that I was from here, working at the distribution center off the interstate, was ridiculous, and I couldn't hide it. "You just look familiar. But I've never been around here before."

I almost asked her if she'd ever been to Silicon Valley or suggested we'd met at MIT, but why push it? If someone that beautiful had ever left Barrington, she never would have come back.

"Okay." She folded her bottom lip in thought, and I knew where the crease had come from. It was so much sexier as the result of a habit than a genetic detail. "You sure you don't want to call first?" Another thumb jerk toward the little grocery store.

"I'm good."

A shiny blue pickup pulled up in front of the store. She waved at it. A guy in a baseball cap rolled the window down to give us a short wave and a dirty look that may have all been in my head. He looked to be in his late twenties, but hard twenties, with skin the product of sun and tobacco. A hound leaned over his lap and stuck his head out, giving a bark when he saw us.

The girl turned back to me. "Bye, then."

"Bye."

She took two steps down to the lot, blond waves flapping like Old Glory on a fall day.

"Do you have a name?" I called to her.

She turned and walked backward. "Harper."

"Harper." I said it more to myself than her.

She didn't ask me my name but went to the truck, gave the dog a pat, the guy a couple of words, then bounced up to the store. I flipped the key to the Caddy around my finger, watching her. When she disappeared, Baseball Cap opened the car door, watching me. The dog poured out and ran up the steps to the girl.

Harper.

I waved to the guy in the cap. He went toward the grocery store after his dog without waving back. I got in the Caddy and turned the key, but though I laid my hand on the gearshift, I couldn't move until I said in the car what I couldn't say outside.

"Wow."

VIII

Reception was worse than spotty. No hotspot. Data didn't work until it did for five seconds, then my phone would buzz so hard with back notifications I thought the casing would break.

I pulled into the motel parking lot. Two long stories. No cars. Unlit soda vending machine and a snack machine with nothing in the spirals. The office door had a coded realtor's key box on it.

So much for the locals knowing where to find a hotel. I plucked up my phone. No signal, but I could see what had come in. I ignored everything but Deeprak on our cloaked and encrypted message stream.

<How's paradise?>
<By the way, the geohash puts you in the Barrington Bottling Plant.>

"Don't tell me." I scrolled down. "It's—"

<It's closed.>
<OK, so obviously you're in a dead spot. Oracle wants a meeting. We're going to have to resell the whole thing to them.>

"We have to close the hole first. Then GreyHatC0n." I was talking to myself in the front seat of the car. I never talked to myself. I was too secretive for that.

<I'm on board for that, but we gotta fix it and prove it at GHC0N.>

<Agree. Coverage spotty here. Fucking wasteland. Set up Oracle meeting. Call Dan at Walmart. Tap me if anything.>

The crunch of tires on gravel made me look up from my phone and roll down my window. A claptrap Chevy with a rusted-out bottom pulled up alongside the Caddy. At some distant point in the 1990s, it had been either dark blue, forest green, or some shade of grey. The hand-tinting on the windows was buckling and cracking, leaving clouds of transparency on the glass.

The passenger window rolled down slowly, with an uncomfortable grinding noise, revealing the blonde from the grocery store.

Harper.

"Hey," she said. "I called, and it turns out they closed."

"Apparently."

"Sorry. I don't stay in the hotels."

"Not your fault. I should have listened."

She acknowledged my apology with a smile. "I can take you somewhere else."

"Actually." I ended the sentence. I didn't want to ask this across car windows. I opened the Caddy door as much as I could without denting the Chevy and slid out.

She took the cue and got out of her car. We met by the taillights.

"Actually?" The wind caught the edges of her hair, sending blades out in a corona around her face. I gripped my thumbs in my fists. She folded her hands in front of her.

"Do you know anything about the Barrington Bottling Plant?"

She gave me half a laugh that was as good as an eye roll but wasn't. I got the impression eye-rolling was beneath her.

"Why? It's cl—"

"—osed. I know."

"You want to buy it? It's up for sale if you can pay the back taxes."

"I'm not in the market for a bottling plant. I just… you know…" I put up one hand in surrender. "I'm a lousy liar. So I can't make up something plausible, but I can't tell you either."

"Okay?"

"Can you take me to it?"

"Are you going to cut me into little pieces when we get there?"

"Uh, no."

Her eyes narrowed. "Do you intend any harm to me at all?"

"No."

"Are you going to come on to me?"

"No, but if *you* want to come on to *me*—"

"I don't."

"Too bad," I said.

"You really must be a lousy liar."

"Truth is easier. You're safe. Promise. I'll keep my hands in my pockets."

"We take my car."

"Deal."

She pulled out so I could open the door. When I closed it and she smiled, for the second time, I had the nagging feeling I'd seen her before.

IX

She drove as if her Chevy was starving and the asphalt was its single food source. We passed a house in the rolling brown plains every thirty seconds. Some were in worse shape than others, but none looked occupied.

"You have a name?" she asked.

"Taylor."

"Taylor what?"

Did I want to answer that? I wasn't famous (yet). The odds that revealing my last name would endanger me were slim, but I was habitually close with information.

"Why are all these houses boarded? Oh, wait." We passed a set-back two-story with a car in the drive and a dog tied to a tree. "Not that one. But the rest."

She shrugged, flipping her hand off the wheel for a second. "Barrington closed, uh… I guess nine years ago? Give or take, so there wasn't anywhere to work. Folks moved or died eventually. No one's going to buy a house where they can't find a job so… here we are."

A big brick box crept over the horizon, closer than it should have been, as if it had sneaked up on us and whispered, "Boo."

"Why did you stay?" I asked without thinking.

"This is my home."

I was glad she couldn't see my face because my mouth was closed against a ton of shit I didn't say. Like, *you could model anywhere,* or *you're staying for your boyfriend, aren't you?* Which was followed by weirdly compulsive offers to dump him and come back with me. She'd said about ten words to me, half of them questions about whether or not I was a serial killer, yet I wanted to hear her voice again and again.

"Your parents from here?" I asked so she'd talk again.

"My family goes way back. Most left, but my sister and I stayed. I can't really see living anywhere else."

That seemed like a huge failure of imagination.

We got close enough to see the barbed-wire-topped chain-link fence around the factory. The yellow warning signs became visible as the road got rutted, but we were still a quarter mile away. The car rocked, and Harper had to slow down to a less death-defying speed. I opened the window. Vs and Ws of screeching birds headed south.

She stopped in front of a yellow-and-black arm blocking the road, next to a boarded-up guardhouse.

"Okay, you have to drive." She put the car in park. "When the thing goes up, you have to go through fast."

"Okay."

She got out, and I slid over.

She pointed at me through the window. "Put it in drive. You have to go right away. I mean it."

I put the car in drive. She nodded and gave me the thumbs-up.

Disturbing a nest of crickets or cicadas or some other noisy, hopping bug, she reached around the base of the arm and did something I couldn't see. The yellow-and-black striped arm jerked up violently. I went through.

Barely. I hit the gas and sped through. The back of the car was scarcely past when the arm slammed down with a high-pitched squeal.

"Jesus."

Hair flying behind her, she crossed in front of the car, giving me two thumbs up.

Yeah. That deserved a thumbs-up. My life was falling apart, but that had been fun.

She got in the passenger seat. "Great. Take this to the gate. Then we can get out and walk around."

"Can you get me inside?"

I had no reason to go inside, but it wasn't as though I had any idea what I was looking for anyway.

"That's why we're here, right?" Like a tour guide with nothing better to say, she pointed toward a bank of tall reeds to the left. "River's over there. I live just on the other side."

She smelled like ozone, the buzz of the air before it rained, crackling with the pressure of something about to happen as it pushed against the few seconds preceding it.

"Pull over here." She directed me left, around the chain-link fence and away from the parking lot.

The factory was predictably huge. Red brick. Big windows behind steel grates. What had once been graffiti dripped from as high as a kid's arm could reach, as if it had just been melted by cleaner but not wiped away. *BARRINGTON GLASS WORKS* stretched across the top in chipped green paint.

"This thing steers like a bumper car."

"How does a bumper car steer? Pull over by that concrete slab thing."

"It slides when you turn, like it's got no relation to the actual world. And it shimmies left." I put the car in park. "Is this even safe?"

She got out without answering. I rushed to follow her, taking the key out of the ignition as she ran her hand along the length of the fence. It rattled like chains.

"Wait up." I jogged after her. "Where are you taking me?"

"To the back."

"You're not going to cut me up into little pieces are you?" I handed her the car key.

She smiled slightly as she took the key. Just enough to let me know she was considering it.

"So, you came into town in such a rush, you didn't figure out where to stay. Can't tell me why you want to get into an old bottling plant. Got on a snazzy jacket." She whipped around the corner. "Driving a rented Caddy. Those are really nice shoes, and you don't even care that they're getting full of dirt."

"I have money. Never said I didn't, Miss Diamond Earrings."

She stopped short by a gate with a lock. "Tell me what you want here."

As far as I was concerned, I'd been the picture of patience and charm up until that moment. I hadn't pushed her to help me. I'd been nice. I hadn't freaked out half as much as I wanted over the fact that a trapdoor had opened up under my life.

"Are you done helping me?" I asked.

"If you're not here to buy the place?"

"I told you—"

"Everett Fitzgerald's talking about buying it so…" She drifted off as if I could infer the rest.

The Fitz I knew was eccentric, brilliant, two generations from royalty. I couldn't believe he'd ever heard of Barrington Glass Works. Not for a minute. Fitz was in the business of eliminating traffic and solving world peace. Not bottling.

"Since when?" I asked.

"Heard about it a month ago from a realtor in Doverton. He needs it to build the personal helicopters is what we think. He's coming in three weeks to look at it." She glistened with excitement. "When I first saw you, I thought you might be scouting for him."

"I'm not."

She shrugged, clearly disappointed.

"I'm not going to hurt you or the property. I'm not going to buy the plant. I'm not going to do anything you expect. In an hour, I'm going to be a crazy story you tell your friends. Are you going to let me in or not?"

"No."

My patience was held together with scotch tape, and it was getting loose. "Why not?"

"I don't have the code." She tilted her head toward the padlock. It was the size of a box of pushpins and had a row of buttons.

"Okay, you know what? This was fun. But I could have done it myself. I could have driven here with my GPS, parked at the guardhouse, walked here, and been in the same barrel of shit as I am now. No, I would have been better off because I would have had a car. So, no, I don't want to cut you into little pieces. It's not my thing. But my God, if I were a cut-a-girl- into-little-pieces kind of guy, this would be the day I started."

She raised an eyebrow. Daring me. She was *daring me* to cut her into little pieces, which wasn't even on my list of shit to do.

"Let me see this." I got my hands on the padlock.

It attached the ends of a heavy chain, which was wrapped around the poles of the gate. It had a code, which meant it could be cracked, right? I took out my phone to check the Tor boards. Maybe someone had a master code that worked.

No signal.

"Is this the only gate?"

"As far as I know."

"Do you have tools in the trunk? A hacksaw? Stick of dynamite?" I looked at the top edge of the fence. There was a break in the barbed wire. Maybe I could get in there. I hooked my fingers on the chain link just above my head.

"No."

I didn't believe her, but I didn't think tools would do it either. I also didn't believe she didn't know how to get in. There was enough graffiti to account for a hardware store full of spray paint.

"Rebecca or Carlyle would have the key, I guess. She's the realtor over in Doverton, and he does security for everything around here. We can call them if we go back."

"Yeah. No. Don't worry about it."

I took out my pocketknife and pinched out the awl. I didn't have time to pretend a normal way in was going to work, nor did I have the patience to explain a hundred times why I wanted to get into an empty factory.

I lifted the weight of the lock and looked under it. Three pinholes. One bigger than the other two. "Those earrings? They platinum?"

"White gold." Her veil of suspicion didn't obscure her curiosity enough to silence her.

"Can I borrow one?" I asked.

"Excuse me?"

"It's white gold, so it's hard enough that I won't bend it." I held out my hand. "If I break it, I'll replace it. But I won't break it."

She thought for a second, looking me up and down as if scanning my complete character. Either liking what she saw or accepting my shortcomings, her hands went to her ear. When she looked at the tall reeds, her hair blew back. Her neck, her jaw, those earrings. I wanted to mark her right at the base of the curve and the center of the length of her throat.

I didn't even have time for the fantasy, much less charming it into reality.

Two pieces of jewelry sat in her outstretched palm. The diamond post and the backing.

I reached for the post. "Thank you."

She closed her hand before I got it. "What do you think is in there?"

This girl.

"Someone left something for me in there. I don't know what it is, but I'll know it when I see it."

"Who?"

"Someone who wants to screw me. I don't want to be screwed. I want to get him before he gets me, but I have to follow along until I can make a move. Is that enough of an answer for you?"

She opened her hand and let me pluck out the post.

I was extra careful with the post, making sure to push and not bend. The lock popped open.

"So," she said when I handed her back the earring, "you're a thief?"

She couldn't know it was a trick question because she didn't know where I'd been and what I'd done.

"I like to know how things work. Once you know that, you can do anything."

She put the dirty earring in her pocket. I couldn't tell if she believed a word I'd said. It didn't look good for me though. I wouldn't have trusted me if the situations were reversed.

I hooked the lock over the fence and opened the gate. I gestured for her to go in. "Are you coming?"

She held her chin up and crossed through. I followed, leaving the gate open, and we went toward the building. As we got closer, the sheer magnitude of the place got very real. In the vast emptiness, it had looked to scale, but against the size of actual humans, it was titanic. The ware- house windows had survived the closure, some even looked new. The grass and brush were trimmed. We came to a sealed metal door set over a steel staircase to the second floor. The door was painted black. Shiny, as if it was new.

"We bottled beer and soda," she said. "The syrup and soda came from all over, but the glass bottles were too expensive to ship, so we made them here."

"Bottles have been plastic since forever."

"Yeah, the soda went away a long time ago. We did beer, then there was just nothing. All the bottling went to Mexico. The work just shrank and shrank."

"Are we going to have to get past another lock to get into the building?"

"Why do you think I'd know?" She laid her hand flat on the brick that was red in a space between turquoise washes. The touch was loving, as if the building was a pet elephant.

"I have a feeling you know more than you let on."

Her head made a sharp quarter turn. Surprise. Insult. Truth.

"Let's not play games," I said. "Like I said, I'm here to look at something and get the hell out. And I'm sure you have things you have to get back to. So, if you want money to get this over with—"

"I don't want your money."

Of course. Miss Diamond Earrings wasn't interested in money.

"Well, if you want something to get this done fast and get me out of here, just say it."

She wanted something. Something specific. The way she folded her bottom lip in half. The way she wouldn't look at me. There was so much more than simple, stubborn pride at work.

"What time is it?"

I shot my arm forward to hitch my cuff high and checked my watch. It was mechanical and got slow a few seconds every day. She peered over my forearm to see, and I was suddenly embarrassed to have such an expensive thing in Barrington.

"Almost two."

She crossed her arms and tapped her finger on her elbow. "I'm going to take you in because, yeah, I brought you this far and now I need to get going. But first…" She held out her hand. "Your wallet."

"My what?"

"I need to make sure you're not going to steal something or trash the place or whatever."

"No."

I wasn't giving her my wallet. It would take her a second and a half to find out my full name, Google me, and spread the word all over Twitter that I was in Nowhere, USA, a day after the bottom had fallen out of QI4. I didn't want to answer questions. I didn't want to give the guy who'd broken my life any more attention.

In a half second of clear signal, my phone buzzed repeatedly. An hour's worth of notifications were coming in. I had to look at them. They might be a way out of here.

I walked to the gate as if my no had been the final word. It wasn't. I was bluffing.

<I can't find you on the map. Are you in a dead zone?>
<Where the fuck are you?>
<There you are.>
<You're right on top of it. Inside the big building. Factory. Managed by Carl-Ten Security LLC. Let me do some social engineering on it.>

<Cracked gate code already. Need doors. I see keys, not codes.>

On a whim, I asked another question.

<Need intel on girl living here. Mid 20s. Harper. No last name avail.>

<Anything else?>

<Nothing. I got a whole lotta nothing>

The signal dropped. Who knew when it was coming back? What was I going to do now? Go to the hotel in the next town over and try to get into the building legally? By asking nicely? I hated asking nicely.

Harper sat on the metal steps with the toes of her cowboy boots hooked behind the step beneath her. If I was going to be out of here by nightfall, morning at the latest, I needed to find whatever I was supposed to find. The longer I waited, the more I lost control of the QI4 narrative.

My fucking wallet. Driver's license. The real one. Credit cards with the company name. Gym membership.

Fine.

I walked to her. "You can get me in?"

"Yes." She crossed her heart, kissed the fingers that had committed to the cross, and flicked them at the grey sky.

I tossed her my wallet.

She plucked it out of the air. "Thank you."

"Let's go then. No fucking around."

I stood beneath her and watched as she flipped my wallet open and did forensics on it. Jesus Christ.

"Can we go?"

"Taylor Harden. That rings a bell."

"There was a singer with the same name," I lied.

She saw right through it. This was why I only lied through a computer screen. As long as no one could see my face, I could get away with anything. When I was a teenager, the screen had offered me a comfortable anonymity since my emotions showed all over my face. I'd gotten better at controlling my shit later in life, but lies were still hard.

"Platinum card?"

"You said you didn't care about money."

She pocketed the wallet and skipped down the steps. They clanged under her. Her hair swung as she traversed the side of the building and turned around to the backside and a rutted, overgrown parking lot with cracking yellow paint indicating eighteen-wheeler-sized parking spaces. A loading bay.

She clambered up a short metal stair and motioned me to follow. Next to the bays stood a human-sized metal door. She pushed the handle down and opened it.

"You're fucking with me."

"You coming or not?"

I didn't move. She shrugged and walked in, letting the door slam behind her. I pushed the handle down and pulled. It opened. Mother- fucker. I'd given up my wallet without checking all the entrances. Unforced errors under pressure. I was smarter than this, and she was
smarter than I'd expected.

X

An eerie darkness hung over the place. Everything was gone. Offices empty. Halls strewn with beer cans and blankets. Walls dotted with circles of black cigarette ashes. She walked so fast I could barely keep up, but it wasn't as if I knew what I was looking for.

She pushed open wide fire doors into a concrete-floored room the size of a big-league infield. Light poured through the windows. There was stuff everywhere. Crushed boxes. Piles of shredded tarp. Plastic bags. I heard the squeak of rats.

"Here you are." She stood in the center of the room with her arms out.

"Here I am." Wires hung from the ceiling. A few ballasts were left, hanging crooked and bulbless. On the verge of a massive hack, it's easy to get excited and make a mistake. Accuracy is everything. I slowed down and looked at every single object. Every bit of wall space. "Where's the machinery?"

"Sold. It's just a shell. Globalization sucks."

Jesus. As if she understood anything about it.

"That phone you got would cost four thousand dollars without globalization."

"This?" She took out her phone as if it had germs and she had an immune deficiency.

"The complexity of making things can only be affordable with either automation or cheap labor. Trust me. I know."

Pocketing the phone, she nodded, rocking her cowboy boot heel on the concrete. "You know what I know? I know people. I know this town. I know Marty Luman. He's real smart but didn't go to college because he could make a good living here. Now it's too late. I know everyone in the Shover family because the entire town fed them when they lost their insurance and went broke paying for their daughter's leukemia treatments. I know Wally Quinn, who got so depressed when this factory closed that he shot his entire family then shot himself. Everyone who had two nickels to rub together left and took their chances someplace else, and I miss them. I miss all of them. These people are real. They're my friends. This whole town was built around this factory, and when Earl Barrington struggled to keep it open, we all struggled with him. So I don't give a shit about this phone because I got no one to call anymore."

That gorgeous bottom lip quivered.

"What happened to the kid?"

"What kid?" she spit out.

"Leukemia kid? Shriver."

"Greta Shrover died."

"I'm sorry."

"Whatever." She tossed me my wallet. The throw was good, but I wasn't expecting it, and it wound up open and facedown on the floor. I scooped it up. "Are we done here?"

Was I done? What was I looking for again?

"There's nothing to steal, and I didn't bring my bulldozer. So if you don't want to walk around with me, you don't have to."

She turned her back to me. "Fine."

Finally free, I could make short work of this.

I bounded up the steps to the second floor. It was divided into two big rooms. They had less junk than the first floor but were just as useless. I checked every room, every scrawl on every piece of garbage, every mark on the walls. Nothing.

I wasn't worried. Not yet. But I was getting ready to worry.

Third floor. The ceiling was a little lower, and there was no production room. Halls and office after office after office with cots, bags of garbage, broken heaters, a gas generator, a tent, sleeping bags. The stench was distinctly human. It didn't take long to see what had been happening on the third floor, but checking every single room and finding nothing boiled my raw anxiety until the shell of my denial fell away.

I was running out of places to check.

In the back, I found an open elevator shaft.

Up it, I heard Harper say, "Taylor? You all right?"

"No, I'm not all right."

Her head appeared from the first floor. "Why not?"

"Because I came a long fucking way and there's nothing here."

"What are you looking for?"

What would be the harm of telling her at this point?

"A message." I was shouting, and my voice bounced off the walls of the shaft, making me sound even angrier. Good, because that was how mad I was. "A cryptic, serial killer breadcrumb left by a fucker who stole something from me. And I'm not trying to insult you, but you wouldn't know it if you saw it."

"Did you check the roof too?"

"No, I did not check the fucking roof."

I didn't wait for her to answer but stalked back to the hall and up the stairs. The exit to the roof said, EMERGENCY — ALARM WILL SOUND. It was cracked open already.

Slapping the door open, I burst onto the cracked tar of the roof. The grey sheen had melted away, leaving a blue sky and blasting sun. Was the message in the scenery? Walking the perimeter, I could see clear to the horizon. A slope here, a cluster of buildings there, a city far enough away that it was a handful of grey Legos. Harper's shitty non-color Chevy sat on the other side of the fence. Past the tall reeds flowed a slate waterway too big for a stream and not quite a river. A single house peeked over the trees on the other side of it. The top shingles were pocked with newer, brighter patches. It loomed like a haunted mansion with a piebald roof.

What the fuck was I supposed to find?

I checked my phone. No signal. Nothing. What kind of black hole in the center of the country was this?

Fuck this.

I paced to the edge of the roof because even though I said, "Fuck this," with every step, I couldn't leave a single stone unturned. Was I supposed to see something on the roof or in the view from the roof? Was there a basement? Maybe I was supposed to be in the basement? I wasn't leaving until I figured it out. I'd crawl into one of those sleeping bags for the night if I had to.

I wasn't coming back here to do again what I should have done the first time. No way. The next time I got on a plane, I was going somewhere that actually existed with victory in one pocket and the world in the other.

I could see the interstate and a billboard for a topless place. In the other direction, an ad for the closed diner I'd passed on the way in. Nothing. No message on the horizon. None on the roof itself. There was so much graffiti on the walls that I walked right over the spray paint underfoot.

"Hey!" Harper called from the doorway leading to the roof.

I looked at her and saw the red writing at her feet. The foreshortening flattened the scrawl, making it readable.

```
IF (beezleboy cooperates) {
decryption occurs
/*087 101 108 099 111 109 101 046*/
}
ELSE {
engage humiliation protocol
/*083 116 097 121 032 097 119 104 105 108 101 046*/
}
```

As she walked toward me, Harper said, "We should—"

I held my hand up to stop her from stepping on the message, then I put it together and wanted her and a million others to trample the code until it disappeared.

I touched a red letter. It was dry. A pebble had gotten painted on. I put it in my pocket.

"We should go." She completed her thought even though she was distracted by the writing. "It's going to be cold tonight."

"Sure."

"Is this what you were looking for?"

"Yeah. I think so."

"Does it mean something?"

Did it? I knew what she meant, but I asked myself a different question with the same words. Did it mean something? Did I have to obey? Did I have to believe? Did I have to trust?

"The numbers inside the stars are ASCII text. It says, 'Welcome.' The next part is where the guy I'm looking for calls me by a code name I have on the internet. Says... see right here it says *if*? If I cooperate, I get something I want, and everyone laughs at me if I don't. Last line between the stars says, 'Stay a while,' which is real cute. Because the longer I stay, the more likely I am to be an even bigger loser and have the world laughing at me."

"Huh. That's weird."

"He wants me to think he's in Barrington."

"Interesting."

"Do you know a guy who knows stuff like this? Computer code? You might not recognize it—"

"Don't know a guy like that."

"He might be in IT security, or he might be a kid who stays inside a lot and plays video games."

"Nope."

"He could be really young."

She shrugged. "I have to go."

Everything I'd ever built could crumble, and she was shrugging. Great. She took off, not even looking to make sure I was following. Bounding down the steps, hair flying, she wasn't wasting any time. I chased her down the dirty stairways and outside.

"Wait up!" I called.

She didn't slow down, going to the other side of the gate, and she waited there for me as if I was a kid she wished she hadn't taken to the supermarket.

"I'll take you back to your car." She slammed the gate behind me and picked the lock off the chain links. What was her deal? "There's another hotel about twenty-five miles down the interstate. Or the country club in Doverton might have a room."

She knew something. She had to. She was trying to get rid of me so she could… what? Talk to the dude?

"I can't go that far."

"Why not?" She yanked the lock to make sure it stuck and headed for the car.

Because I'm afraid of leaving the geohash.

Because there's something on your mind.

"I have the feeling I'm supposed to stay here."

"Really?" she called over her shoulder before she got in the driver's side.

"Really." I jogged to catch her, putting my hand on the top of the door. "And I'm kind of stuck." I bowed to see in the open window.

She rolled her eyes and shook her head. "Yeah. You are."

She turned the ignition over, and I hurried around the car and hopped in the passenger side. We regarded each other for a minute. Her eyes were a sample of every single iris color in the human genome. She broke our gaze to pull forward and stopped the car at the striped arm.

"Your turn to get the gate up," she said.

I didn't know what switch she'd hit back there or if there were wires I had to cross. I didn't know if there was a key or a code. But I sure as hell wasn't going to sit there and tell her to do it. I wasn't going to puss out on a challenge. Because that was what it was. Flat out.

"Fine."

I got out and looked behind the box. It was everything I'd expected. A tangle of dozens of indistinguishable wires. Worse, they'd been painted white as if on spite. Two had to touch to make the arm go up. Four had been stripped.

She pulled the car up to the edge of the gate. The arm would swing up then down. If I did something wrong and sent it down early, it would land on the car—or her. I was frustrated as hell and a little pissed off at her for daring me to figure out how to do what she already knew how to do, but I didn't want to hurt her or bang up her car.

When I touched two of the stripped wires, the arm buzzed but didn't move.

Mathematically, the presence of four stripped wires made me less likely to find the combination. Three would have made it easier. I would have found the green wrapping, which would have been the ground wire, and eliminated it as a possibility.

I scratched the white paint off one.

Blue.

"Do you need help?" she called.

"No!"

The next wire was blue too.

"I got it," I added.

But I didn't, because the third wire was blue, which should have meant the fourth was the ground wire. But I checked anyway and it was blue as the sky. Either there was no ground wire, or they'd run out of green, or they didn't give a shit and never grounded the wiring.

I touched two more wires and a ball of light appeared. The copper ends of the wires went on fire.

"Do you want me to tell you what to do?" Harper asked from a mile away.

"I said I have it."

"You don't sound like you have it."

I didn't have it. I didn't have it at all, but fuck if I was going to admit it.

"You have to—"

"I said I have it!"

Getting out from behind the box, I stood by the gate and faced the car.

She leaned out the window like a fucking know-it-all. "You don't want me to tell you?"

She was smirking as if she knew damn well I was in over my head. Well, what the brain couldn't puzzle through, the body could correct with brute force.

"No."

I bent my knees and wedged my shoulder under the bar. My guess was that the gate had some kind of broken locking mechanism, which was why it slammed down so quickly. Which meant if I straightened my knees, it would rise with me.

"What are you doing?" she asked. "If you can't figure it out, just say so."

"So." I straightened my knees, and my shoulder picked up the gate. It was heavy, and it hurt like fuck, but it went.

"Shit." She pulled the car forward, but the gate tapped the top of her windshield. "I'll pull back and you can drive…"

Fuck that. I got my hands under the gate and nudged myself back toward the pivot point at the box. The changed angle would bring the other end of the gate a little farther up. It got heavier and harder to move as the pressure from the fulcrum increased.

It lifted and the shitty little Chevy passed through. I dropped the arm. My shoulder was unhappy, but my feet moved fast to get in before she took off.

"You have a really massive ego," she said, getting onto the highway.

"All the wires were the same color. Who does that?"

"Wires?"

"You have a different name for them out here?"

"You didn't see the switch?"

The switch? There was a switch?

"You didn't see the switch." She changed from question to statement.

"I guess I didn't."

She tried not to smile at my utter ineptitude. The force of her will against the strength of her instincts tightened the muscles around her mouth, twisting it into a wave form.

"It's cute the way you're trying to save my really massive ego." I had to smile, and so did she. "But you're going to hurt yourself like that. Go ahead, laugh."

She laughed, slapping the steering wheel. I laughed a little with her.

Just a little.

XI

She had gone into tour guide mode on the way back to my car. This is this, and that is that. Here's where I drank beers with my friends. Here's my high school. Here's Bobby Droner's place. He went to Iraq and didn't come back, etc., etc.

I listened carefully for an IT guy, a kid going to college, a computer engineer, a thief who'd found a way into the liquor store safe, a teenager who spent too many hours in front of video games. Names flew by me, and I caught what I could. But none of them was my hacker.

The only thing that kept me nodding was the knowledge that there would be an end to all this. When we entered a desolate square of empty storefronts and a post office, my phone buzzed.

Note to self: *The dead zone is live when the wind blows from the south.*

<Oracle meeting. Next Tuesday on
the Redwood campus.>

<I'll be done by then.>

<Good. Next. Harper Barrington.>
<Daughter of Earl Barrington. Owner
of the factory in the geohash coordinates.>

That explained the diamond earrings and how she knew which door of her father's old factory to open but little else.

<College records? She's smart.>

<Jack's on it.>
<You all right out there? You didn't fuck her, did you?>

She had her wrist on the top of the wheel, hair blowing across her face. I hadn't fucked her, but man oh man, given the right time and place, a better situation? If my life wasn't in a spray of broken pieces at my feet?

<Nah.>

I had more to say, but the signal dropped and our messages self-destructed, as they were programmed to do.

"Good news from home?" Harper asked at a light there was no point in stopping for.

"Yeah. Hey, where's the nearest hardware store?"

"We just passed it."

I felt for the little red rock in my pocket. "Do they sell spray paint?"

"Yeah. Why?"

I held out the pebble. "I wonder if they'd tell me who bought this color recently."

Her reaction was the reason for the question. Would she look trapped? Would she confess she knew who it was? But as she turned the corner to the hotel, and before I could observe her expression, I saw my car. The conversation about who in town bought and sold spray paint became a big fat fucking joke. My rental car was covered in a red compliment.

NICE CADDY

"Fuck!" I got out and headed for it. The trunk was open slightly, as if the vandal hadn't snapped it closed all the way. Probably broke the lock. This was going to cost a fortune. Big damn inconvenience. I might as well just buy them a new fucking car. I didn't even like Cadillacs.

I noted the similarities in color and that whoever had coded the roof couldn't be the same guy who'd insulted the make of my rental. Besides the obvious subtlety of the roof message and the blunt ignorance of what was on the car, the E on the roof had been done with careful, straight lines. The E in NICE looked like a backward three.

"Wow." Harper had her hands stuffed in her pockets. "This kind of thing never happens."

I opened the trunk.

"Bullshit."

My bags were intact, though shuffled around from the drive. I looked beneath and between them, in the corners and under the carpet.

"Damnit."

My laptop was gone. I slammed the trunk closed and it popped open a few inches, as it was when I'd found it.

"Fuck you too." I cursed at the trunk but it didn't seem insulted.

I muttered obscenities, getting into the driver seat, door open, one foot still on the pavement as I put the key in the ignition and turned. Nothing happened. Not even a *whrr whrr*. Not even a *click*.

Harper got in front of the car and wedged her fingers in the hood. "Can you pop this?"

"You are a cliché of a cliché," I said.

"What?"

Fuck it. I wasn't explaining the word cliché or how the small-town girl who knew her way around a car was so unlikely it was obvious.

I popped the hood and joined her at the front grille.

"Well, doesn't take a rocket scientist to see your battery is gone." She slapped the hood down before I could get a better look. "My friend Orrin owns a garage. He'll give it a tow. Until then—"

"You knew the code for the gate the whole time."

"I'm sorry?"

"You grab me the minute I get into town and send me to a hotel you know damn well is closed. Then you follow me, all surprised, and take me to the fucking factory. And who suggested the roof? You. I was ready to go and then, 'Oh, try the roof,' because you might miss the big, fat fucking message."

I stepped toward her, and she stepped back. I didn't want to be threatening, but let's face it, I did.

"You knew the code to the lock, didn't you? If I couldn't pick it, you knew it."

"I don't know what you're—"

"You know exactly who he is."

"Who?"

The innocent act was cute. Real cute. Once I got to the bottom of this, I was going to fuck the cute right off her.

"Just take me to him, Ms. Barrington."

Her big, multicolored eyes got even bigger, and that crease in her fucking lip got deeper when her mouth opened in surprise. She recovered so quickly I doubted I'd seen it at all.

"I go by Watson."

"Since when?" I glanced at her finger. No ring.

She put her hand in her pocket. "You know my name. So?"

"Explains the earrings. Your father owned this town."

"And?" Her back was against the car, and I was six inches from her. "I don't own anything. The state owns the property for back taxes. And these were my mother's earrings. Sorry if I'm not allowed to have them."

"Take me to him." I was up in her face because fuck her explanations.

"I don't know any guy."

"Fuck you don't."

A car pulled up. I didn't look at it. In my world, cars passed all the time. I didn't look away from her defiant face or her chest heaving under the plaid jacket.

"I told you," she said.

"You *lied.*"

"I did not—"

The wind went out of me. The world got swept into a whirl of color. Pain flashed through my back. A dog barked and growled.

When my vision cleared, I recognized his face. The guy from the truck outside the grocery store. He smelled of cigarettes and wintergreen gum. He pushed me up against the Caddy by my throat so hard that my back was arched against it and the only parts of my feet touching the ground were my toes.

"Orrin." Harper's voice came from my right, about five miles away. "He's all right."

"I don't like the way he was talking to you."

"Yeah, well." Her hand curved around his bicep. "He's from California."

"Aw, shit." He dropped me like a wormy sack of flour. I fell to my knees, rocks sticking in my palms, humiliated. "Why's he here?"

"Car broke down."

"Huh. Well, I can take care of that." He yanked me up by the collar until we were face-to-face. "I'm going to take your car to the shop. Give it a look. In the meantime, you are going to treat this lady like the queen she is. You understand?"

I breathed in the affirmative.

"Where's he staying?" Orrin asked Harper.

"I'll keep him at the house."

"Aren't you nice."

"You know us. We take all comers."

He got in my face. "I'm driving."

"I can take an Uber." This dipshit, backwoods, broken-down *Deliverance* shithole town without decent signal didn't have Uber. I knew that. But even though I kept my mouth shut for a living, I couldn't keep it shut in front of this guy.

He pushed me into his truck. "As far as you're concerned, I'm Uber."

The pressure on my chest disappeared when he let me go, and I found my footing. Adjusted my jacket. Despite all logic to the contrary, my pride was intact. My value was lodged firmly between my ears. I'd been beaten up by knuckleheads more times than I could count. And that was saying something.

"Now that you two are best friends," Harper said, "let's go. I'm getting hungry."

XII

Orrin drove and Harper followed. He didn't say why she followed to her own house and he wasn't taking questions. That was what it was. His dog, a bloodhound named "Percy, short for Percival" licked my cheek raw from the backseat. I scratched his neck.

"You like dogs?" Orrin asked.

"Love them."

"You got any?"

"Nah. I work twenty-hour days. Once things slow down, I'm getting one. Two, maybe. This a bloodhound?"

"Ridgeback. Runt of the litter but can still chase a rabbit halfway down a hole."

"Bet you can," I said to the dog, who ate up the attention, dropping a big slobber on my shoulder. It was all right. A dog knows when you like him, and if he likes you, he lets you know back. You didn't need to decode them.

We pulled up in front of the house I'd seen from the roof of the factory. I knew it was the same from the piebald roof. Victorian with original windows, warped wood, wraparound porch. It was pale yellow with trims in five different colors. The paint was so cracked and dulled I couldn't tell if the color combination had been an attempt at period authenticity or if they'd just used what they had. It would have been worth a fortune in Northern California.

The front yard was well-trimmed, with grass that was green and lush. The rosebushes were flowerless and thorny. The hedges were perfect. Five other cars were parked on the dirt patch to the left of the house, in the shade of the setting sun. Orrin put the truck at the end, behind Harper's car, which was still clacking as it cooled.

"Thanks for the lift," I said.

"You mind what I told you."

I nodded, but maybe I wasn't emphatic enough.

I was halfway out the door when he grabbed my shoulder. "Percy likes you, and that counts for something. But not everything. If I see you get like that with our Harper again, you and I are going to have more than words."

Our Harper? While I appreciated his protectiveness, I was curious about who was included in *our*. "I think that's more than fair."

The dog stepped over my lap and poured out before running up the side porch steps, where a woman waited to pet him. She was in her late twenties, no makeup. Short, curly blond bob. Jeans and an apron.

"Orrin," she said, "you staying?"

"Nah. Mal's cooking."

She eyed me. "You must be Taylor." She held her hand out, and I shook it. "I'm Catherine. You're welcome here."

"Thank you."

"Harper's in the kitchen if you want to say hello."

Behind her, Harper already stood at the screen door. She was diffused behind the ripped screen, wiping a bowl with a dishcloth.

"Hey," I said.

"You made it."

"I thought he was going to dump my body in the river."

"The river woulda killed you if he didn't." She pushed the door open halfway and stood to the side so I could get into what looked like a mud/laundry room.

As soon as I crossed the threshold, I was assaulted by the sound of people. Children. Pots banging. Parents shouting. China clacking.

"What's the occasion?"

She headed for the kitchen, and I followed, practically tripping on two toddlers, one running with a clean fork in each hand.

"Same occasion as always. People need to eat."

I checked my packet sniffer for signal. Nothing on data and no random Wi-Fi.

"We're partying like it's 1999," I grumbled.

"What?"

"Nothing."

We crossed a few rooms, and I peeked into others. They were spotless but bare to the floorboards. No furniture. No rugs. On the walls, between the sconces, were hooks, wires, and pale rectangles where pictures used to be.

The kitchen hadn't been updated since the seventies. Three women and a girl of about seventeen fussed with steaming pots and running water. Harper took a bowl from a woman who wasn't a day under ninety. She had a bandana around her wrinkled forehead and bangly bracelets on her thin wrist.

"Mrs. Boden, this is Taylor."

"Nice to meet you." Her handshake was firmer than I would have guessed possible.

"Likewise."

With her free hand, she pinched the scruff on my chin, which had just grown to a pinchable length. "Oughta do something about this. You look too French Resistance. And they couldn't free Paris without help, you know."

Harper broke in. "Carmen, Juanita, Beverly"—she pointed at each woman then the high schooler—"Tiffany. This is Taylor."

They each greeted me. I repeated their names so I'd remember, and Tiffany blushed and looked away when I did. Harper slapped me with her dishtowel as if I'd tried to seduce the girl, then she stuck her head into the hall before I could deny it.

"All children in the house! Wash your paddies!" She brushed by me. "You too."

A line of kids stomped past on their way to a sink and soap. I stood at the kitchen faucet and pushed up my sleeves. Harper stood next to me.

"This the usual no-occasion crowd?" I asked.

"Sometimes. You staying tonight? You're welcome to."

I didn't know what I should do. I felt trapped, but I wasn't. Not really. There was a hotel and a country club one town over, apparently. They probably had Wi-Fi. I could help Deeprak track down our hacker from there, or I could make some calls to soothe buyers.

I could make it look good enough to stabilize the deal but not fix it. I couldn't walk into that meeting with conviction. I wasn't that good a bull-shitter. My confidence came from doing things perfectly.

"I have a lot of work to do," I said.

True. But also false. I had work, but without a connection, I couldn't do shit.

"Orrin will probably have a new battery in it in the morning." She handed me a towel.

I shook off my hands. She had the loveliest smile. I had to remind myself that I could do both of us more harm than good. She was too sweet. Too sharp. Too blond.

Sideways to the sink, I dried my hands. "Who would take my battery?"

"Thieves?" She washed her hands.

"Very funny."

"Fresh batteries are worth money, which people here don't have a lot of. I'm not condoning it—"

"Or the spray paint, which was just mean."

"Or the spray paint." She dried her hands.

Everyone was out of the kitchen but us.

"Which was the same color as the painting on the roof. I'm thinking it's the same person. Or people."

She looped the towel around a drawer handle. "Even if I knew…" Which she did. I'd have bet my balls on it. "I wouldn't tell."

"Harper, I want you to know, if it's some kid crying for help, I'm not an animal. Actually, I just want to know how he did what he did."

"What did he do? Besides maybe rip off your car battery?"

"He hacked into a system, a computer system I'm developing. Whatever he did, it was really difficult. Really well-timed. The execution was perfect. Guy like that doesn't belong in jail. I'd probably hire him."

I couldn't decode what happened with her face. Surprise opened it a little, and I saw anger and happiness at the same time. Before I could pin it down, it was gone. She kept looking at me, and I kept my attention on her.

"Harper!" Catherine called in a singsong.

"Let's eat." She turned away and went into the dining room.

Dinner had been loud, messy, and pretty delicious in a not-too-complex way. Men appeared from the yard when the food was out. We had stew in chipped bowls. The silverware was real silver, and the water glasses were canning jars. Folding chairs set next to white, plastic picnic chairs around a card table. I remembered most of the names. The kids were lively and well-behaved. Harper sat next to me.

When I was asked where I was from, my answer elicited questions about the weather, gas prices, and state taxes.

What I could gather from them was that the factory closing had hit them hard, but Catherine, who blushed when mentioned, had been the town caretaker ever since.

"I remember when she sold the dining room set we should be sitting on right now," a weathered man named Neil said. "My wife wanted to throw herself on it when they loaded it onto the truck."

"It was so nice." Beverly shook her head slowly. "How much did you get for it?"

"Enough to pay down Phil and Dina's mortgage. And worth every cent." Catherine stood and started taking plates, ending the discussion. "Harper made bonnet cookies this morning. Who's ready?"

The kids clamored to pick up every dinner plate. The dining room descended into chaos again.

"Bonnet cookies?" I whispered to Harper, catching the scent of the air before it rained.

She turned to me, and we were face-to-face in the middle of a crowded room. "There are so many eggs in the recipe. When my great-grandmother was a girl, they wouldn't fit in the bag. She put them in her bonnet on the way home."

"That's nice." I said it to fill space, watching the flickering changes in her expression. I didn't know if I should kiss her or grill her until she revealed who'd hacked me. Maybe I could do both.

Orrin had brought my bags in from the car. Everyone had said it was nice to meet me and left. I turned my back, and Catherine had somehow folded herself into the walls. The house fell into a darkstillness.

Harper led me upstairs, flicking on lights with loud *clacks* from old switches. The steps creaked like nobody's business.

"How old is this house?" I asked.

It was the smallest of small talk. But the house felt haunted, and that seemed like a relevant data point to proving it wasn't.

She stood at the top of the stairs with her hand on the banister. "Nineteen eleven. You look freaked out."

"Me?"

"You."

"I don't freak out. I have nerves of steel."

"Want a tour?" she asked at the head of the hallway. Two short halls went east-west, and a longer one went north-south. All were as bare as the lower level. "There's not much to see."

"That would be great."

"I figure it'll ease your mind." She put her hand on a knob.

"I'm not freaked out."

"Sure." She flicked on the sconces. The room we entered had a cot, a two-drawer dresser, and peeling wallpaper. "This was my room when I was a kid."

"Where do you sleep now?"

She was already out a door on the other side of the room. "This is a linen closet. It's between two rooms. They all are." Shelves. Towels. Sheets. A bulb on a wire. "This was my brother's room." There was a pause where I thought of asking a question, but she answered before I could get a word out. "He's in Yemen right now. It's his third tour."

She strode through the room without stopping, clacking the switch behind her. "My sister's room."

It looked as though someone actually slept there. A half-open armoire had clothes in it, and the sheets on the full-sized bed were fresh but mussed.

"Catherine?"

"Yup."

She continued. We wound up in one of the short halls. A stairway led up to a door at the top. Framed pictures hung on the stairwell walls. I hadn't seen a single thing on the walls yet, and I slowed down to look.

"We keep the bodies up there." She waved me toward her. "Come on."

She blew through old maids' quarters, a narrow back stairway, three more closets, two bathrooms with toilets that hissed and sinks with separate faucets for hot and cold, a library full of books, and the only comfortable-looking chair I'd seen since entering the house. Every room was clean. Every one had the absolute minimum amount of furniture. None had a decorative element that could be moved without ripping off a part of the house.

"The master suite is the nicest." She opened the carved mahogany door a few inches. "You're not allergic to mold, are you?"

"Nope."

"Good." She opened it all the way.

It *was* the nicest, biggest, and it did smell of mold. A chandelier had hung in the center of a ceiling that seemed just a little higher than the rest. It had a mural of delicate flowers preserved under a layer of dirt. The hardwood inlay on the floor was in a chevron pattern, with a wide border of darker wood. Past wide French doors, a balcony looked over the black night of nowhere.

"It is nice. I don't see the mold. I can smell it but not see it."

She pointed at water damage on the wall. "It's worst on the bathroom side. There's a mushroom that grows out of the wall every year."

"That's not mold. It's—"

"Fungus. I know. We have both."

"The mismatched shingles are above this room?"

"Yeah." She opened the French doors to the outside.

"But there's a third floor?"

"Not over this half of the house."

She walked out onto a balcony that I wouldn't have trusted to hold the weight of a kitten. But she did, so I joined her.

The autumn air was cool and breezy. The interstate banded parallel to the northern horizon, invisible until headlights drifted along it like fireflies. Below us, light from the downstairs windows landed in the first few yards of the property. At first, I thought I was looking at a pit of snakes, but it was thorn bushes. Hundreds of branches were tangled together in a mass of sticks and rose hips.

Harper put her elbows on the railing, crossed her ankles, and stuck out her ass. What a work of beauty it was. I had to stop myself from slapping it as I passed.

"How far back does the property go?" I asked.

"To the river." She pointed straight back.

The river, if I could tell correctly in the moonlight, was a little more than an eighth of a mile away, where the reeds and a line of trees broke up the sightline. Above and beyond that was the roof of the factory.

A light flicked on in the house, and my instincts tracked the movement back to the yard and the tangle of thorn bushes. I didn't say anything, but she followed my gaze down below. The bushes took up about as much space as my first apartment in San Jose. The rest of the property to the river was trimmed and landscaped.

"We like it that way," she said. "It blooms in the summer."

"I wish I could see that." I did want to see it. Summer was on the other side of the next year, but I wanted to see it.

"The room next to this one is nice." She jerked her thumb toward another set of French doors on the other side if the balcony. "You should crash there."

My elbows joined hers on the railing. "I'm sorry about before. I was frustrated."

"Next time I won't be so nice about it."

"Really?"

"I can knock a guy's balls so fast he won't even know it until he screams soprano."

I laughed.

"I'm serious. Wanna try me?" She put her hands up and tried to look severe. It didn't work. She rotated her hands, angling the fingers, one knee up, mouth exposing her fight teeth.

I laughed again.

"Don't test me, stranger," she growled.

"Stranger?" I put my hands on hers. "We've shared a meal." I laced my fingers in hers, and she let me. "I've met your family and friends." I pulled her close. She let me do that too. "We broke into a building together."

"We're practically best friends," she whispered.

"The minute I saw you, I thought you were beautiful." I let my lips brush hers, and they crackled with ozone. "I could barely even speak."

"I don't believe you."

Drawing my lips over her cheek and down her neck, I felt the vibration in her throat when she moaned. I didn't want to rush, but I didn't have a lot of time.

She might tell me the hacker's name in the morning, when she was careless, maybe a little ashamed, wondering if she'd see me again.

Which was possible. If everything worked out with QI4, if I found the hacker and got this thing off the ground, I might get involved with a beautiful creature from a foreign land.

"Believe me," I whispered. "I'd never lie about something like this."

My lips found hers. When she spoke, I felt them move. "You're staying tonight though? The car."

She wanted it. Her voice was soaked in it. I could seal the deal in three to five minutes.

"I'm staying tonight."

"Good."

Lips at the side of her mouth, fingers stroking her neck, I asked, "Do you like to fuck, Harper?"

A little vowel sound escaped her lips. I was too close to see her expression, but her voice told me I'd gotten where I wanted to.

"I think you're beautiful. I want to see you naked. I want to make you come with my mouth. I'll make it last a long time." I paused. She didn't pull away. "I'd love to bury my cock in you until you come again. And again. And again."

Her breath fell heavy on my cheek. I pulled back to get a look at her face to see if she was horrified or turned off.

Her lips were parted and wet. Expressive and open. I kissed her.

I couldn't tell if she kissed me back.

She pressed her face into mine, but her lips weren't moving or responding. Not that my dick cared either way. It just knew I was smelling and tasting her. It felt me pull her body into it and burst into a raging erection before I had my tongue fully in her mouth.

Her arms stayed around me, but she didn't move any more than her tongue.

I disengaged completely. I wanted to seduce her, but I didn't want to take what wasn't offered. I'd overplayed my hand. Shit.

"Sorry," I said.

"No, it's fine."

"I misread your signals."

"You didn't!" She kneaded her hands together. Her eyebrows made an inverted V.

I wanted to believe her. On that balcony, she had a sincerity that went deeper than it had all day. Maybe I'd caught her by surprise, or maybe that was how they kissed outhere.

"Well, thank you then." I reached behind the French doors and hoisted my bag over my shoulder. "Can I get into this room from here?" I pointed at the adjacent set of doors.

"Yeah. Sure. I, uh—"

"I really should get to bed."

She got in front of me. "I'll put sheets on it."

I hadn't known her for more than a day, but her desperation surprised me. She didn't seem the type. She was acting as if my attention had higher stakes than a less-than-satisfactory kiss. Of course, I could have been misreading her the way I had a second before. Which she denied. Which meant I wasn't misreading.

The snake ate its tail.

I spoke tenderly and took her hand. In that moment, she seemed too vulnerable for careless courtesies. "I'll do it. You've done enough to help me today."

"It's not a big deal."

"I'll feel bad if you do it." I squeezed her hand and let it go. "The linen closet is off the bathroom?"

"Yeah."

"Okay. Thank you. I'll see you in the morning."

"Okay."

I still wanted to seduce her, fuck her, get the name out of her. That strategy was on life support either way. Outside the strategy, human to human, I wanted to tell her something that was true.

"I meant it. You're really beautiful, Harper."

"Yeah, well… I know." She said it as if I was telling her the sky was blue. No embarrassment or fake humility. It was what it was.

"Hey, uh, you have Wi-Fi?"

"Yeah, the router, the thing with the antenna?" She wiggled two fingers at the sky. "Kind of old and spotty. You can get cellular in the backyard sometimes."

"Thank you."

"Good night."

"Bye."

I went into the adjacent room and snapped the door closed. The door to the master suite closed a few seconds later. I was alone.

XIII

I found the light switch. Two frosted glass sconces hung on either side of the bed, lighting the ceiling and casting the rest of the room in diffused light. It was as bare as the others. I put sheets on the metal-framed twin bed and got in the shower.

It had been a long fucking day. I had no way out of town, and I was in a mansion without a couch. My hacker wanted me to stay, and I was getting the fuck out of here. I'd pay the rental car company whatever they wanted once the battery was in as long as I could get on a fucking flight.

But Harper.

The moments before that kiss.

When her skin tingled under my lips.

She'd made me so fucking hard.

And I was again. Just thinking about it made blood rush to my cock. I ran my hand over it.

There had been something inexperienced about the kiss. As if she'd wanted to but didn't know how and nerves had kept her from going with her instincts. Was she that innocent? When I stripped her down, told her to sit on the bed, and stared at her naked body, would her chest break out in hot pink? When I gently asked her to lean back and spread her legs so I could see her pussy, would she hesitate? When I said I wanted to see her touch herself—

I grunted and came before I could finish the fantasy, shooting my load in the cleft of a cracked tile.

I finished washing myself, put on sweat pants, and plugged in my phone. A cone of lines appeared in the corner of the screen.

Live Wi-Fi. If she was right, it would be on and off.

Password protected. PassCrack, an app I'd developed and sold for Bitcoin donations back in the day, didn't work. WarWalk didn't either. It looked like a simple WEP but obviously wasn't. Weird. Even in Silicon Valley, which was riddled with IT guys, one of those would have worked.

A human sound came through the walls. A woman crying. More than crying. Wailing uncontrollably. I stood. Harper? No. There was a lightness in it. A crispness. Harper was throatier. The cries came from everywhere. Right, left, downstairs. For a second, they seemed to come from the balcony. Then the crying drifted away.

Seduction was out. As much as I wanted to fuck that girl, and I *really* wanted to fuck her, this place was crazytown. The internet made the world small enough to find the hacker from home, without risking my sanity. I could fuck Raven anytime.

Raven's not going to be half as good as Harper.

That was my inner predator talking. Raven was fine. I had to focus on getting Wi-Fi.

I had one last toy in my toolbox. An offline app I had been dicking with when I was bored and missing the old days. I'd developed it to pick stocks, and it had lost everyone money, but repurposed, it was a decent password finder. I ran it.

Boom. I was on. Notifications flowed in.

The crying started again—but closer.

Ignore it.

All previous messages from Deeprak had self-destructed, but the new ones flowed, decrypting with my fingerprint on the device.

<Jack gets a bonus for this.>
<Tap me when you're on.>
<You're on.>

<Everyone in the cage is getting a bonus. What did he find?>

<We should get on voice.>

<Can't. Close quarters.>

<Fine.>
<Harper Barrington also goes by Harper Watson.>

He uploaded a picture. The resolution was shit, but the smile was Harper. The girl in the picture had dark hair. She was a little rounder. Standing on Vassar St., in front of Building 32, with its metal façade that was designed to look as though it was in a constant state of collapse.

I knew 32 well. Computer science. The AI lab.

<Is that her?>

<Harper Barrington's blonde>

<Try this one>

Another picture came up. She had on a knit hat and pinched her bottom lip between two fingers.

<That's her>

Did she have a boyfriend who was studying at Stata?

Well, no, she had the books. *The Visual Disp—* was clearly visible when I stretched the photo.

"Display of Quantitative Information," I said to myself, finishing the title. "That's not even coursework, Harper. What are you doing?"

<Same girl>

I flipped between the two. Yep. Same girl. Take the dark hair out of the equation, and there she was.

I couldn't remember her. I lived in a world where the smartest men in the world gathered and were too awkward to make it with the small percentage of fuckable women. Women had always been easy to get into bed, but I'd never fucked her. Not a blond her and not a brunette her. I was sure I wouldn't have forgotten it.

<Was she there when I was?
I'd remember this girl>

The crying got louder and stayed consistent.

<She was a freshman when
you split>

How many girls at MIT were that hot? You'd think my dick would at least have a little recollection. The photo of her had self-destructed already, but the cognitive consonance of her paired with MIT had imprinted the photo on my mind. It was her. Harper Watson. No bell was rung, except for the Sherlock Holmes story in the scattered code comments of the poison pill.

Watson was a really common name, but the connection was made.

<She couldn't have hacked us.>

I typed the statement but didn't hit Send. He'd ask why I thought that. My answer was simple. I knew all the female hackers with the skills to pull this off, and she wasn't one of them. I sent the message.

NO CONNECTION

The Wi-Fi had dropped. Reconnecting didn't work. I ran the hacking apps and my network protocol analyzer to check for available signal. As a despairing female wail rattled the walls, the packet sniffer did its job.

SCRAMBLER PRESENT

A chill immobilized my spine.

She'd seen I was on the Wi-Fi and cut me off.

No.

The name. Watson. Sidekick? Why not Sherlock or Holmes? Was I reading into it?

Maybe the signal had just dropped.

For all she knew, I was watching porn or checking email. Or could she see my conversation? It was encrypted end to end, but if she was good enough to hack QI4, nothing was safe.

I swung my legs over the bed and went into the hall in bare feet, shirtless, sweat pants hiked up over the right knee but not the left.

The crying was louder in the hall and seemed to be coming from every doorway. Harper had taken such a roundabout tour and there were so few markers that I was lost.

Not that I knew what I was looking for. A sound besides crying. A light in the wrong place. The smell of ozone.

"Ow!"

I picked up my foot, leaned on the wall, and looked at the bottom of my big toe. I plucked out the splinter, but once I started walking again, I realized I hadn't gotten all of it.

"You need to redo these floors," I grumbled to Harper as if she was in front of me and I had the authority to tell her what to do with her house.

Taking my hand off the wall, I noticed I was close to the stairwell up to the third floor. I favored the toe as I climbed quietly. Too quietly. Every floorboard in the house groaned and squeaked, but not the stairs to the third floor. They were as worn as a 1911 staircase and as quiet as if they'd been built yesterday.

She didn't want anyone to know when she was going up here. Because I knew for shit sure, by the time I hit the top of the stairs, that she was behind that door. When I saw the photos at the top of the stair- well, I was even more sure. It was dark, but my eyes adjusted. It was her. Graduation cap. Braces. Clear, dewy skin and freckles. Prom. Satin dress and diamond earrings. Receiving an award. I couldn't see the details of the award, but she was blond again. She was blond in all of them.

I put my ear to the door, pressing against it until the crying inside the walls disappeared and all I could hear was the sound on the other side.

Clicks. Tons of them. She was typing like a fiend.

That was why she had tape on her fingers.

My God. It was her. Harper had hacked QI4.

What was with the kiss that wasn't a kiss?

What about the message on the factory roof?

And the name?

Why change it?

Had she been married?

How had she gotten the poison pill in the monitor?

Was she still married?

More than the name and the comfortable possibility that a man was involved in the hack, the thought of her having a husband didn't sit right with me.

I leaned on the door, listening to the pattern of the keystrokes. No waiting. Straight typing. Not waiting for a response from someone on the other side of the wires.

The spacebar made a different sound. I pressed my ear to the door. How often it was hit told the story. Coding and English had a different spacebar cadence.

A husband belied her tight innocence, and though none of it fucking mattered, I became momentarily obsessed with the idea that she was married. Maybe her rigidity was guilt. Maybe Mr. Watson was in a faraway desert war or making a living in another part of the country. He could be dead.

I forgot to listen for the spacebar patterns. I didn't notice when the keys stopped clicking at all. All I noticed was the change in gravity as its force went from beneath my feet to beneath my head as I fell. I got my feet under me in two steps, tumbling into the room when the door was opened.

Standing straight, I whipped around to find Harper with her hand on the doorknob.

"I knew it!" I said even though I'd known nothing until three minutes before.

She yanked the door all the way open, teeth grinding, throat mid- growl. Her skin was lit by the whitish-blue of flat-screens, and the finger she pointed at me was wrapped with white tape. "Get out!"

"How did you do it?"

"I don't know what you're talking about."

We circled each other like boxers in a ring. Behind her was the door, a desk, three monitors scrolling code, an ajar bathroom door. The monitors were flowing C++, a deep web database for a retailer, and a Tor chat. Following my gaze, she hit a key, then another, and the screens went dark.

"How did you get into QI4?"

She turned back to me, and we circled each other again. "Fuck you."

"Are you married?

We stopped circling.

"What?"

I didn't know what had come over me, and it didn't matter. I didn't care if she was married or not. I needed her to give me my life back.

The utter stupidity of my question forced me to step away from my surprise and hostility. She'd hacked me. Fine. We had work to do. She and I.

But I kept losing focus.

She was that smart.

In that body.

Under a sleeveless ribbed tank, she was braless. Her nipples were rock hard. Her gym shorts rode low, giving me a peek at the smooth skin of her belly. If I kissed it, I'd be close enough to smell her.

"Watson. Harper Watson. Who is Mr. Watson?"

"Wait. Let me just..." Her eyes drifted over my face, down my naked torso, landing between my legs.

I was wearing sweat pants, and I was very, very hard. Of course. The body always betrays the mind.

She crossed her arms, covering her nipples but hiking her shirt up a little. "I'm not married."

"That's good to know. Um, this is a surprise, but—"

"Why? Because I live in flyover country or because I'm a woman?"

"Yes."

"You are fucked up, Taylor Harden. You were always fucked up."

"Always fucked up?" She locked her jaw against another word, so I filled in. "Did I know you from MIT?"

Her eyes flickered. I knew more than I was supposed to, and it unnerved her. Good.

"IHTFP." She unlocked her jaw enough to hiss the campus acronym for *I hate this fucking place.*

"I didn't… we didn't…"

"No. We didn't. I was a freshman. You were fourth year, and you never came back after Christmas break."

I scanned my mind again, narrowing the parameters to the years before I left. Brunette Harper still wasn't there, but the photos hadn't lied.

"You had dark hair. Why?"

"No one takes blondes seriously."

"No one takes… what?"

"I know how it goes in tech. No one takes women seriously. We're unemployable, unfinanceable, useless. And a blonde? All blondes are good for is sucking dick. I've been around Tor sites. As a guy. I know how you assholes talk. I know what you think."

Deny. Set yourself up as an exception.

"I'm sorry." I wasn't. But whatever. I needed to get off the subject and onto more important topics, like what the fuck we were going to do about this mess. "First of all, I want to say… the hack? Wow." I slow-clapped. I couldn't tell if she appreciated my admiration at all, so I stopped. "How did you—"

"Fat chance."

"Excuse me?"

"I'm not telling you shit."

I'd never met a hacker who wasn't a show-off. Telling the community *how* you breached a target was ninety percent of the exploit's fun.

"Harper, you exposed a serious vulnerability. I'm willing to offer you a lot of money."

"Too late."

There wasn't a hacker on earth who didn't want to give the gory details of their exploits. At least none I knew, but they were all dudes. This was another planet.

She just needed a little prodding.

"It was Jack's receipt on the desk. You run it through a sharpening algorithm? So you could see what we were ordering and from where? How did you intercept the monitors? The distro center is Amazon."

Her face didn't change. That told me more than any expression. The effort to not signal acceptance or rejection was harder code than subtly answering without saying anything.

She wasn't telling me shit.

"What do you want?" I asked.

She turned toward the monitors and tapped her fist against her mouth, but she didn't say what she wanted. I got the sense she never would.

"Why did you bring me here?" I asked gently because she held all the cards and her exploit wasn't going as planned. That much I could tell.

"I didn't think you'd come here."

"Why leave the coordinates then?"

"I thought you'd send people, like law enforcement or the news or *anyone*. I thought then everyone would see what's happening here and feel sorry and understand and do something. But you didn't, and now I don't know what to do."

Like a soundtrack, the crying in the walls rose again. It had more of a sad, weeping quality and less of a wailing despair.

"That's not you," I said.

"It's not."

"Who is it? Catherine?"

"She's sensitive. She gets like this a few times a week. Her heart breaks for everyone but herself."

"Who's she crying for today?"

Her throat expanded and contracted as she swallowed. The monitors made her eyes white at the edges. She was thinking, but I couldn't tell what was on her mind.

"Here's what you're going to do, Taylor Harden." Her gaze went over my body again.

My boner was gone, so her gaze lingered just above my waistband. I realized that though her expression was sexual and hungry and I liked sex as much as the next guy, I had no power in the relationship. The feeling wasn't pleasant.

"Go back to your room. Rest up. We'll talk tomorrow morning."

"No. We talk now."

She spun the Herman Miller chair to face her. Twelve hundred dollars new. The most expensive piece of furniture in the house.

"Good night." She sat and swiveled herself in front of the bank of screens.

"Now, Harper."

She acted as if I hadn't spoken at all. With her back to me, she was still and calm. One screen came to life, asking for a password. The others stayed black, and I could see her reflection in them. She was crying, but somehow, she held her body still.

"Close the door on the way out," she said without a hitch in her breath. I'd never seen a woman with such control.

She didn't want comfort. Offering it could only make the situation worse. I had to do what she'd asked. What choice did I have? I opened the door, noticing the deadbolt for the first time. I could pick that if I needed to get back in.

"Taylor?" The sexy, innocent girl who was suddenly more terrifying than any guy I'd ever met. Even crying, she was scary.

"Yeah?"

"I have a scrambler on your cellular data. And you won't be able to get into the Wi-Fi again. I plugged that."

"You're fast."

"Yep."

I had nothing left to say. I wasn't going to stand there and beg for an answer.

When you have no negotiating power, you have to use the only leverage you have.

You walk away.

XIV

My father was a licensed contractor. He'd inherited the business from his father and assumed I'd take it over at some undefined future time. He bought property, fixed it, sold or rented it. He renovated and rebuilt houses if he liked the owners. It wasn't unusual for my father to work Saturday and Sunday, miss dinner, come home with a beard after being gone for days at a time. I'd never met a man who worked harder for every penny he had, and for me and the citizens of our little world, he had plenty.

My mother stayed at home with me and my little sister until she started school, then Mom kept the books at my dad's business and brought us to the office after school and on weekends. She'd always been good with numbers, but at one point, she stopped using the calculator because it slowed her down. Once Dad ascertained that she hadn't made a single mistake, he thought Mom's genius was her most charming trait and bragged incessantly.

Once Mom started working, Dad started taking me to jobs. If I was old enough to hold a wrench, I was old enough to tighten elbow joints. I learned everything he taught me, and I learned a lot of stuff he didn't.

He talked to my mother differently than he talked to me, and his tone with her in the office was different than his tone at home. He spoke to the guys who worked for him differently than he spoke to my mother. When he took me to the bank, his body language talking to the guy in the suit was different than the lady behind the glass.

And always, always, always, he was in charge. My dad had a very small kingdom in the state of New Jersey. He didn't have a big name or millions of dollars in disposable income. We didn't have servants or an army. We were regular people.

But he was a king.

So in sixth grade, when they took me out of St. Thomas and put me in Poly Prep, I was in for the shock of my life.

I had everything I needed, but there were people with more. Much more. People who didn't work as hard. People whose power wasn't *earned* but inherited or lucked into.

A year at Poly cost more than double the national average income. I didn't learn that until much later, but I knew at the time that something was off. The kids at Poly were different in ways I couldn't pinpoint. They didn't really know what their parents did for money and spent no time thinking about it. They didn't know how to fix things and didn't know how to find out. And Dad was different around their parents. Still confi- dent but louder, brasher, less astute.

It was as if he didn't know how to crack their code.

He didn't know how to crack Mom's either.

Just as I was settling in, the stress of the money, the culture, the missed signals snapped her. She cleaned the house. Redid the books from the past two years. Accelerated every plan and activity.

She was manic, and she was everywhere. Bake sales. Theater department treasurer. Substitute statistics teacher.

Then she was depressed, and she was nowhere, and her room smelled of sweaty sheets and unbrushed teeth.

I swore to myself it didn't affect me. I swore I had it under control.

And I did—as long as I was on land.

Gov (short for Governor, I kid you not), my best bud in that first year, invited me out on his dad's sailboat for the weekend. In the first few hours, pulling out from the dock on Wiggins Park Marina, heading down the Delaware River and out toward the bay, the taste of salt and the thrust of the boat put me in high spirits. Gov and I talked about the kids in school, the sights on the banks of the river, and fantasized about the size of the fish we'd catch.

As the Delaware Bay fell away and the dark fists of landmasses grew smaller on the horizon, I grew uneasy. Following Gov, I did some tasks below deck, got ready for lunch, and stayed calm.

But it was out there. I knew it was out there.

Gov and I were in the front of the boat, watching the lap and curl of the water around the tip of the boat. He left me there so he could pee or eat or answer his father's call. With a sandwich in one hand and a can of Coke in the other, I was alone.

Utterly alone.

I didn't have a landmass to orient by. The horizon was an endless circle around a spotless, treacherous sea. The sky was a flat blue, and the boat was nothing, nowhere, the finitely small about to be crushed by the infinitely large.

The sky had weight, and it pressed against my chest. I was being snuffed out of existence as if I were no more than an offensive insect sliding on the curves of a pure white bathtub. I had to get out, but I was hemmed in by the indifferent sea.

Gov said I threw up. Maybe that part was seasickness. The rest was a good old-fashioned panic attack.

I pretended to laugh it off later, but inside, I never wanted to feel that insignificant again.

In Barrington, with the sound of crickets outside, I didn't just think about defeating Harper. I was distracted by the huge, unchanging physical landscape. Human instability. The breakdown of the small while the infinite spaces above could crush me with indifference.

I had to remove all emotion. Breathe. Keep the panic at bay. I had to break down my judgments and preconceived notions so I could see the code and only the code.

What could Harper want? Not a job. She hated me. Money? Capital? Power? Bragging rights? Sex?

She could have had any of those things by asking, but she hadn't asked. I went through her reactions to everything I'd said and done, but I hadn't been trying to figure her out all day. I'd been looking past her instead of at her.

I was rusty.

I kept thinking of her polychrome eyes, her ombré lashes, the crease in her lower lip. The body she'd hid behind a plaid coat was tight and feminine. Her tits alone distracted me for an hour.

And the hack.

When I could get my mind off her body, I went back to the hack.

She'd found her way into a closed system. I doubted it was a social engineering hack. Had to be a pure exploit. God damn. I wanted to hire her, fuck her, kill her, and decode her.

After she released QI4.

I didn't know how long it would take to patch the flaw she'd found, and it was more important than ever to do GreyHatC0n to prove the system was secure. I'd increase the prize. Lengthen the time.

Then I was back to the tits.

The eyes.

The code.
Dad.
How she did it.
When I could get out.
Of course a woman did this.
What did she want?
Crickets.
Tits.
Eyes.
Code.
Time.
Dad.
How.

IF (beezleboy decodes Harper) {
he will be king
/*and the king will own his subjects*/
}
ELSE {
the king will break
/*and the king can never break*/
}

XV

In the kitchen with the sun barely up an hour, Catherine didn't look as if she'd been crying all night. She looked bright and happy. A T-shirt with an eagle and an American flag peeked out from under her apron. She served me as if I was a king, but I didn't feel like one. I felt like a lazy guest.

"So, Mr. Harden," Catherine asked as she poured me a second cup of coffee. I stood by the counter rather than sit in the dining room. "What are your plans?"

I wondered if she knew what her sister was up to or if I was supposed to know that she knew. I wasn't going anywhere without answers, and I needed answers before I got back home.

"I think I'll be taking off this afternoon." I hid behind my coffee cup. "Some house you have here. Harper showed me the master suite." I put down my cup. "I couldn't tell if the ceiling was plaster fresco."

"It's enamel on tin."

The stairs creaked, announcing Harper well before she arrived.

"That saved it from water damage," I said.

"That's what Kyle said."

Harper, despite not crying all night as far as I knew, looked worse than her sister. Hair askew. Eyes puffy. Dragging her feet as if she didn't have the energy to lift them. She didn't say a word to me as she picked up the coffee pot and poured a cup. She drank it black, cupping her hands around the mug.

"Good morning!" Catherine said. "I got eggs if you want some."

"No, thank you." She spoke into her cup, watching me over the edge.

"Good morning," I said.

"Good morning," she replied flatly.

Voice drained of emotion + intense look over cup = Catherine doesn't know what's going on.

Catherine went into the pantry, humming.

"How'd you sleep?" Harper asked.

"Like I was awake. You?"

"Slept like a rock."

Surprise her. Don't let her get her footing.

"Did you enjoy it?" Sleeping was the text. Fucking was the subtext. I put it on the side of a barn where she couldn't miss it.

"It's just sleep." She poured more coffee, avoiding eye contact. "Not exciting."

"What would you rather be doing?" I put another target on the side of the barn. I was getting to her. She put sugar in her second cup. No one did that. People picked the way they took their coffee and stuck to it. What was next? A caramel macchiato? Was she flustered? Or was she trying to tell me something about how unpredictable she was?

Catherine returned with cans of beans. Harper and I looked away from each other as if we'd be caught doing something we shouldn't.

"Can you give me a lift to Orrin's?" I asked.

"Oh," Catherine chimed in, "if you're going that way, can you bring Trudy Givney something?"

"The shop opens at ten," Harper grumbled.

"Perfect," Catherine chirped. "I'll get you an envelope."

Harper's attention lit on a stack of red-and-blue-swirled bowls on the counter.

"What are you doing with Grandma's bowls?" Harper asked.

"Oh, Rebecca can get—"

"No!" she barked. "You're not selling those. Put them back. Put them back right now."

"Harper, we talked about this. They're meaningless objects."

"Put them back, or I'm going to break them!"

Catherine paused while Harper's face went into a rigid adulthood that directly contrasted her threat to smash things rather than lose them. I was about to offer money for the bowls. Good money. Whatever they wanted.

"Here." Harper put her cup down and reached under her hair to her ear. "Take these. Sell them. Give the money to whomever." A quick tug to the other ear got the second diamond out. She handed them to her sister. "I don't even like them anymore."

Catherine took them without a moment's hesitation. "Thank you. It's

Alejandro. They picked him up for shoplifting, and if he doesn't make bail—"

"I know. They keep him in jail."

"He's just a boy."

Harper nodded, and Catherine hugged her.

"I can help if you want," I interjected without thinking. "I have money. Just not here right now."

"We have it." Catherine patted my arm and left the room. The stairs creaked.

Harper poured more coffee with one hand and rubbed an earlobe with the other.

"Do you think that was weird, or was it just me?" I asked.

"You should have seen when she tried to sell the silver teapot." She handed me a cup. "She doesn't get it about maintenance. If she'd sold everything and invested it in something, she could help Alejandro now and his brother in ten years." She blew on the coffee. The surface flickered like a pitching ocean.

"And what you're doing now, bringing me here, that's maintenance?" I asked.

She sipped her coffee, thinking too hard. Maybe she was out of her league too. "I was supposed to be showing the world what was happening here. I wanted Everett Fitzgerald to see it before he came, and I know you know him. I want you to tell him about the bottle works." She shifted her cup around in her palms. "I didn't hack you for personal reasons."

Bullshit. Everything was personal. Even this. Especially this.

"Whatever I do to you won't be personal either."

She smiled and put her cup down. "Want to tell me what you're going to do to me? I'd like to be prepared."

"Exactly what you did to me."

She came to me and put her hands on my chest, drawing them flat down to my waist. "So you're out to ruin me? I like the sound of that."

She couldn't mean what it sounded like. No sane human would go to such trouble to get laid, but her expression oozed desire. So she wasn't sane, and neither was I. My mind was a seesaw with sex on one side and fear on the other. The fulcrum was curiosity. Once it was satisfied, I'd know whether to fuck or run.

I grabbed her wrists but didn't move her hands. "Is that all you want?"

I tried to sound amenable, and maybe I fooled her into thinking I'd believe anything she said, but I listened and assumed she was lying.

"More or less. You were pretty prolific at MIT. All the girls talked about how good you were."

"That's flattering."

She bit her lower lip and let it pop out slicked and wet. "I'm not as good."

"Girls don't have to work as hard."

She tensed like a two-by-four holding up an archway. If I'd had a caliper to measure the rage in her face, it would have stretched open as far as Frieda Gallen's legs.

She picked up her cup and straightened her spine. "We work twice as hard for half as much, and you know it."

"Not to get laid."

She spit out a laugh. Inside it was a long story she wasn't going to tell me. "I worked pretty hard to get you here. I might as well get something out of it."

"You can't get some redneck to fuck you?"

She slammed her cup down, spraying sticky black coffee all over the place. If it burned her hand, she didn't show it, and if the mess bothered her, she didn't take a second to clean it up. Her face went from stone-solid rage to soft humor.

"I ain't never fucked no city boy before." Her accent was overdone to the point of comedy.

Catherine blew in like a ray of fucking sunshine. Harper took her hands off me and wiped the spill off the counter.

"Got it!" Catherine sang, handing Harper an envelope. "She'll be at the coffee shop."

"I can do it later."

"Come on. I'll buy you a hot chocolate." I flicked her mug.

"I have to help Catherine."

"No, you don't," her sister said. "Just go!"

Harper gave me a look of death before she acquiesced. "Let me brush my teeth, then we can go."

XVI

The shitty Chevy went pretty fast for a car that looked as if it had been abandoned in a corn field. The seat rumbled and purred under me even though the plastic upholstery was cut into a foamy yellow wound. I cranked the window open and leaned my elbow out, angling my right-hand fingers to rest on my forehead and chin.

The two-lane blacktop was pretty smooth, but the storefronts we passed were empty, boarded, broken, with sun-faded signs for a diner, a thrift store, fashion, sewing supplies, and pets. The necessities remained. Groceries. Pharmacy. A local bank with a name I'd never heard of. Liquor. A convenience store whose main convenience seemed to be lottery tickets.

"This the main strip?" I asked Harper.

A strand of her hair whipped out her open window. "Yeah. It's shit. I know."

"I didn't say that."

She stopped at a sign, though no one was coming in the other direc- tion. The flapping strand dropped to her shoulder. "It's hard for people to run a business when no one's buying. Sew-Rite only stayed open until last year because Bonny lives in the back. Still does, but she's got no money to put stuff on the shelves." She pulled forward. In a block, we were at the edge of town, cutting a hard right onto a pocked light industrial area.

"Why'd you come back? From MIT?"

"I live here."

"You didn't graduate." It was a question and a statement at the same time. If she'd graduated, she wouldn't have come back to Shitsville.

"Neither did you."

I was sure the situations were different. I'd had enough to live on from a trust Mom had set up in one of her moments of medicated lucidity. It was barely enough to live on, so I'd moved into a San Jose garage to rein- vent circuits. Harper knew the story. Everyone did.

She wasn't going to answer a direct question. She wasn't going to be cornered by an inquisition. I was going to have to stir her until what I needed to know was kneaded into the conversation.

"You going to finish someday?" I asked.

"Are you?"

"I'm waiting for an honorary degree." I joked—but not really. "They only give them to you when you don't need them anymore." I paused as she pulled in front of a corner diner. "Like everything, I guess."

She glanced at me and slapped the car into park. "My father got sick." She spit it out as if holding it back would be permanent. "Soon as he closed that factory, he started coughing, and then it was blood. He could have afforded an army of people to take care of him, but he only wanted Catherine and me. He didn't trust anyone in town. Genny Reardon's a nurse, and Dr. Therro at least could have helped with the medicine, but he thought they'd let him die because he closed the factory."

"Did they hate him?"

"They loved him." She slammed the car into park like a statement. "They wouldn't have let him die. Even though he did. Lasted three months after I got home."

"And you didn't go back? To MIT?"

"Couldn't leave my sister." She opened her door. "Let's go. I'm hungry."

SHE ATE a half-pound cheeseburger (rare) and a plate of fries (overdone) like a hostage. I knew she had food. She wasn't starving. She just had a healthy appetite.

"You have a hollow leg," I said.

"Here you go, hon," Trudy said, setting another pink milkshake in front of Harper while addressing me. "You having anything else, mister?"

"Taylor," Harper said around the last mouthful of burger.

She'd introduced me to Trudy when we'd arrived but made no other conversation about the envelope or what the fuck I was doing there. Trudy seemed to be the same age as Harper, with a little more makeup and several dozen fewer IQ points.

"Taylor, then." Trudy had a thick down-hominess that seemed forced and overdone, but I was starting to think it was genuine. "You staying around, Taylor?"

"No," Harper snapped before I could answer.

"That's too bad. Well, it's nice to finally see our Harper with a member of"—she dropped her voice to a whisper—"the stronger sex, if you know what I mean."

"I—"

"Trudy! Jesus!"

Trudy wagged her finger at her friend. "We don't talk like that in my mother's place. It's just unexpected, and you'd be crazy to think we weren't all wondering about him."

"I am crazy." Harper picked up her milkshake. "The check, please?"

"Nice to meet you." Trudy smiled and went behind the counter.

"Wow," I said once she was out of earshot.

"Forget everything she said."

"I'm wowing at you. You were kind of a bitch."

She slid the half-empty milkshake away. "If she was so happy I was walking around with a member of 'the stronger sex,' she wouldn't have looked at you like you were a meal ticket."

"And what am I to you?"

"Oh, fuck this." She leapt out of her seat and snapped the check out of Trudy's hand.

"Hey, I got it."

Before I could get my hands on my wallet, Harper had put the envelope and a twenty under the check and smacked them both down on the counter. She walked out without looking back.

"Harper!" I caught up with her and wedged myself between her and the driver's side door. "You're upset that I'm leaving?"

"No. I'm not."

"You spent a ton of time and energy getting me here, and now I'm picking up my car. You're upset. Don't lie."

"I'm upset because…" She took a deep breath. "I'm frustrated. Trudy went to school with me. She was knocked up in eleventh grade by Robbie Bonnacheck. She's lived with her mother since then, working two jobs and barely pulling in shit, so what does she do? She gets bored when she's twenty and lets Tim Breaker knock her up with a daughter who, by the way, is really, really cute, but my God… she can't afford to feed these kids. So now? She's twenty-four, and that money is for prenatal care because she's too fucking stupid to take birth control."

"Is that why you don't have kids?"

"I'm different."

"I'll say."

"And you know what really pisses me off? I love her, and I love her kids. I love the assholes who don't even think of using a condom and fuck their own selves up in exchange for ten minutes of… I don't even know."

I was about to say something. Add a little filler that had all the markings of compassion and empathy. I had neither emotion for stupid people or bad decisions, but for Harper, I had it.

"You don't even know?"

Her jaw clamped like a vise. "Just get in."

I got in, and she took off.

"You don't care, do you?" she asked.

"About?"

"Our troubles. You're not telling anyone."

"Can we stop this? Just for a minute?"

"Stop what?"

"The bullshit."

She let that hang in the air as she drove. I tried not to look at her, but it was hard. Even in profile, her expression changed by the second.

Making another left, she drove past an open chain-link fence. The driveway led to a cinderblock garage wide enough for three cars. One of them was the Caddy. A big dog barked. Piles of red-brown car parts hung from a huge shed with a roof but no walls.

"I'm not lying." She parked the Chevy between the shed and the garage.

"Tell me the truth, and I'll make phone calls about Barrington. I'll tweet it out. Everyone will know."

I didn't convince even the most gullible part of myself. She shook her head and laughed.

"Logic error," she said, unlocking the doors. "In exchange for media attention, you want me to admit I'm lying, but if I'm lying, I don't care about the attention."

The fall hurts when a guy's knocked down a few pegs.

She was still lying.

From the garage's shadows, Orrin came out of an interior door with a guy in cheap chinos and a yellow polo. Percy padded behind, happy at his master's heels. The rattle of a chain link snapped me to a much bigger dog making the racket. A ninety-five-pound bruiser was hurling itself at the fence it was trapped behind.

"You just want your shit back," she muttered.

"Well, yeah. I know what I want, and I did what I had to do to get it.

You're a hacker. I can't figure out why you didn't just take the money you needed."

"You mean steal?"

"Yeah. Take. Steal. It's not any different."

She spun in her seat as if she couldn't hold back another second. "It *is* different. I don't steal. I don't cheat. I do things fair and square."

"Are you fucking with me? What kind of moral gymnastics did you have to do to convince yourself hacking me was fair and square?"

"You'd never do something for someone besides yourself. But you needed to get hacked. You're a little shit. You're every problem with the world."

"And now you're no better. Do you miss the moral high ground? Because you left it as soon as you locked my system. Is the weather different down here? Or is it actually the damn fucking same?"

"I am not you. I care about people. All you care about is you. Not even you. All you care about is what people think of you."

"You don't know me."

Of course she didn't. She had no idea what I was thinking or feeling. She'd just made a bunch of assumptions. The fact that all of them were right notwithstanding, she'd built a composite picture out of thin air. I was allowed to get pissed about that.

"You targeted me because you don't like me, but you didn't make anything." Percy's barking got closer, but I had more to say. "You created nothing. You stole what someone else made, and you're holding it for what? What do you want to give it back?"

"I'll give it back." She let that sink in. "When I have what I want."

She crossed her arms, tapping her finger against her bicep. Her nails were naked, and she didn't have a stitch of makeup over her freckled nose. The highlights in her hair had been kissed by the sun, not the salon. So easy to take for granted. So easy to underestimate.

"How much do you want?" I tried to sound nonchalant. People had fraught relationships with wealth, so I never said "dollars," "cash," or even "money" during a negotiation.

"If I was after money, you'd be broke already."

She spoke truth. She could have done something much simpler and more profitable. But she hadn't. I still wasn't sure what she wanted. She kept me on shaky ground, and I was starting to think it was on purpose. She was hacking me, and I didn't have any defenses against her attack.

XVII

At one point, my mother had decided to clean my room down to the plaster. When I got home from school, all my shit was in the driveway, and she was painting the walls.

Clearly, she was in a manic phase. Clearly, she couldn't be reasoned with. I was supposed to let her do her thing and make sure she was safe.

But yellow?

I'd been powerless then too.

When she spoke about yellow paint day, even years later, my mother said the look I gave her broke through the mania long enough for her to stop painting and move to the next project. It was the only thing she'd ever remembered mid-episode.

"If I was after money, you'd be broke already."

After Harper said that, I must have given her the same look, and it must have come from the same place of powerlessness. Because I didn't accept that I was ever helpless, and the existence of a situation where I didn't have choices or options tasted like a mouthful of dimes dipped in shit. I spit it out.

"When I'm through with you, you're going to wish you'd killed me."

I'd broken through her tough-chick performance. She opened her car door and slipped out as if stomping toward the garage was proof of anger, not proof of a defensive position. I got out after her with every intention of driving home some point or another. I'd forgotten what we were talking about, but I was going to hurt her until she cried, and I wasn't going to give the smallest fuck about her feelings.

Which I did.

But I didn't.

Maybe a little.

Two steps in front of me, she turned toward me with her finger out as if she had a point to make and I gave a fuck what it was.

Which I did.

But I didn't.

Not even a little.

"Do it," I growled. "Sell off my code, and I will come after you until this town is a wasteland. Do you understand me?"

"Fuck you."

"Do you un—"

"Hey, Harper." Orrin's voice cut the wind just as Percy got his nose under my hand.

I petted him without thinking. Orrin pinched a lit cigarette between two grease-streaked fingers. Right behind him stood the guy in his fifties with the yellow polo, chinos, and clean hands. Despite the conservative costuming, he was tattooed with clock gears and pierced, his black hair whirling in the wind. His name, Johnny, and a corporate smile of a logo were embroidered over his left tit.

"Hey, Orrin." Harper was all perk and smiles, as if we hadn't spent the last five minutes threatening everything we each held dear. "Hey, Johnny!"

Johnny kissed her cheek, which was more than Orrin had done.

"Mr. Harden," Orrin said.

"Thanks for working on the car." I pointed at the Caddy sitting in the garage. "The hood's still up. Is it working?"

"Just fine."

"They call you Hard-on in school?" Johnny asked, proving that inside, he was more tattoo than polo.

"Yes. Yes, they did."

"You punch 'em? Or did you cry?"

"I fucked their girlfriends."

With every circuit in my brain, I mustered up the will to not look at Harper to gauge her reaction to what I'd said. I had little to gain from knowing it and everything to gain by acting as if I didn't care.

Johnny, on the other hand, whooped a laugh of surprise and delight. He stuck out his hand. "Nice to meet you."

"Same." I shook his hand.

"Welcome to the Capitol of Crap." He swung his arms wide. "Citizens too stupid to leave, and those that left are too damn cowardly to stay."

Orrin shook his head. "Don't mind him. He—"

"We're the salt of the earth's what they say. Them in power, with the money. They stroke us. Jerk us off with some bullshit about how hard-working we are. Tell us we're the real America. Like we're stupid. Them fucks set man against man so we can feel like winners, but let me ask you." He held out his arms and stepped back. "Do I look like a winner to you?"

"Jeeze, Johnny," Harper interrupted. "Can you—"

"If you want to win something," I said, "we can get in a fistfight."

Johnny whooped another laugh, falling into a deep, wet coughing fit. Even Orrin chuckled as we walked back to the garage.

"Well, not too many men alive can shut up old Johnny," Orrin said. "This is a nice car." He laid his hand on the chassis. "Regular battery doesn't fit. I had to order one special, then I called the rental company because they'd shit themselves if they thought an unlicensed guy was touching the engine. Let them know what was happening."

I turned away from the car. Across the road sat a corrugated tin building with boarded windows and a *Restaurant Supplies* sign swinging in the wind.

In the foreground, Harper leaned on her car with her arms crossed, talking to Johnny.

"Did they say when the battery was coming?"

"Tomorrow or next day."

Was that enough time to get Harper to release QI4? It was going to have to be.

"Here." I reached for my wallet, feeling the little red pebble in my pocket as Percy sniffed my balls.

"Sit," I said, and he did. "Good boy."

"Pay me when the work's done."

We shook on it, and Percy trotted back to the garage behind Orrin. When I got back to Harper, Johnny was headed for his truck.

"Am I taking you to the airport?" she asked.

This was her way of getting me to go home and tell everyone about Barrington? That was the exact opposite of what I was going to do.

"How do you know I won't just call the FBI?"

She crossed to the opposite side of the car. "What would all the hackers say if you narked on one of their own?"

"GreyHatC0n's in eleven days." I leaned over the roof of the Chevy. "We have a challenge running on day one. It's worth a lot to me to plug this hole. You could do a bunch of things with that money. Buy furniture for the house." I squinted at her in the bright sun.

"You think I went to all this trouble to buy a sofa?"

"Get help for your sister."

Her jaw tightened, and her eyes narrowed. I'd hit a nerve. She went from pensive to sharp in a split second. Behind her, the big dog *uhf uhffed.*

"Small business loans," I continued, "scholarships for the kids you were talking about. Supplies for the school. Whatever."

She leaned over the other side of the roof, tapping the hollow metal. "I know you don't come from money, Taylor. Not real money."

"So?"

"Money, real money, is about maintenance."

"Are you blackmailing me or asking for a job?"

Orrin watched from the office door. Harper gave him a dismissive jerk of her chin. He went inside.

I placed the pebble from the rooftop code on the roof of her car. "This is the same color as what's on the Caddy. You were with me when the car was vandalized. And maybe this is a town of coders, but it's not. You wrote on the factory roof. So who fucked up the car?"

"Maybe the hardware store's got one shade of red." She didn't even believe that.

"Sure, Harper. Whatever. Or you can tell me what you want? I'll give it to you, and you give me my life back. But tell me something I'll believe."

She laced her fingers together and tapped the pads of her thumbs. So much of her story was in her hands. The nails were cut short, and she'd taped her fingers again, but now I knew why they were wrapped like a hacker's.

"If you want me to take you to the airport, I will," she said.

"If I want you to unlock QI4 first?"

"You'll have to wait."

Progress. Too bad it didn't matter. She was nuts, and I was walking a tightrope with her.

XVIII

My situation was precarious, unusual, unprecedented. I couldn't tell if I was making a mountain out of a molehill or seeing the molehill from so close that it looked huge.

Harper had wondered if I was going to cut her into little pieces because she was imagining me in sections.

My phone was charged, and I got a moment of signal from the balcony overlooking the thorn bushes. Something was getting through the scrambler, or she'd turned it off.

Fuck encrypted texts. I called Deeprak.

"Dude," he said without so much as a hello. "Where have you been?"

"It's her. Harper. The girl from MIT. She did it."

"Why?" His voice cracked. He was exhausted.

"Plight of the working man. She wanted to draw attention to the recession. Whatever. I'm coming back."

"How did she do it?"

Below me, the thorn bushes wove together like a square of steel wool. A bent and cracked white picket fence held the bed to shape.

"I don't know."

"And you're coming home?"

I almost called him crazy before I told him I was coming home for shit sure, but he deserved an explanation. "There's something off here. It's like a cross between *Children of the Corn* and *Wicker Man*."

"Are those movies? I'm more of a Bollywood guy."

"Creepy. It's creepy."

"Oh. Well. In that case, come back. We'll just tell the guys to find another job. Our clients will understand—"

"Deeprak—"

"—why it's so important for you not to be in a creepy place."

Was he shouting? It was hard to tell with his voice so shredded.

"You don't get it."

"I get it, my friend. I fucking get it." He'd never taken this sharp a tone with me, and for that reason alone, I shut up. "You're in a new place with someone who has it out for you. Taylor Harden is a target and feels bad. Boo-hoo. Now get over it. You've had it easy your whole life."

"Wait a minute. I worked my ass off."

"But your head's buried in it. Creepy is working your ass off for *nothing*. You worked your ass off for *something*."

I could have argued, but I couldn't have argued with his intensity. We were going to have a long, hard talk over beers when I got back.

"Fuck you, Deeprak." That was as close to capitulation as I intended to get.

"You too, baby."

The line of the factory roof was solid brown against the horizon. A V of birds headed south along it. If I showed my face in the office without QI4 in one piece, I was going to be a laughingstock. Distance insulated me.

"I'm coming back as soon as I figure this out, and I'm not playing into what she wants. Make sure no one talks about where I am."

"They don't know."

"Not a word to the press. No exposure. Nothing. My whereabouts are unknown."

"Agreed."

I peered into my room. Empty. Door closed. I did the same with the master suite. Empty.

"Can anyone hear you?" I whispered.

"I just got home. I live alone."

Just got home? He'd probably combed through hardware and code for twenty-four hours or more.

"You're working hard for something."

"Make sure of it."

I ended the call just as Harper came onto the balcony from the master suite. She had a disturbingly self-satisfied look that I wanted to kiss right off.

"How's everything back home?" She leaned her hip on the railing, arms crossed, indicating the phone I'd left facedown on the railing with a quick twirl of her finger.

"About as wonderful as you'd expect. I left a full complement of guys with their limp dicks in their hands."

She smirked. "That imagery is so appealing."

"Does it make you nervous, at all? Being out here with me? The guy you're in the process of fucking over? I could pick you up and throw you off this balcony right now. Leave you in the fucking thorn bushes." I'd never threatened a woman with violence before, and the threats came out of my mouth so easily I scared myself a little.

Harper didn't seem half as nervous about it as I did. "Who would unlock your system then?"

"I've cracked harder cases than you, miss."

I was a little closer, my finger pointed right at her like a punctuation mark. She looked away. Now she was nervous. The idea of violence didn't faze her, but the idea of being outwitted went right to the core.

"I didn't think you'd actually come." She touched my elbow, just brushing along it.

The normal reaction to being touched by an enemy would have been to pull away, but her electrical current didn't throw me back. It created a closed circuit between us.

Luckily, my right hand knew what my left was doing.

I grabbed her arm with my other hand and held it there. "What do you want?"

"A lot."

"What?"

"In five years? A house on the lake and a kid or two. Short term?" She put my hand to her chest. I was never going to get a straight answer. She was crazy and fucking gorgeous and too smart for her own good. All those things at once.

I was trying to put all the pieces together. She tilted her head, and I tilted mine. She leaned in a little, and I leaned with her as if I could hear her better. I was curious what she wanted short term because a clue to my fate was there.

"Short term I'd just like to—"

I leaned a little too far, brushing my phone off the railing. I grabbed for it. It bounced off my fingers, twisting in the air, off the back-porch overhang, spinning faster and away into the thorn bushes below.

"Fuck!"

I wanted to choke her, but it wasn't her fault. It had been my elbow leaning too far left.

I ran downstairs, past Catherine puttering in the kitchen, and stood at the edge of the thorn bed. It was bordered by a two-foot-high white picket fence. The thorns went to the top of it and not an inch past it.

When I tried to part the brambles where it looked like the phone had fallen, I was rewarded with blood from two slashes.

Harper was right behind me. "Let me call you!"

"You know my number?"

She slid her finger over the glass. Of course she knew my number. I leaned over the bed.

"Is it ringing?" she asked.

"Fuck!" It wasn't ringing. There was no light. No buzz. No nothing. "Is it ringing on your end?"

She put the speaker on. Half a ring then a cut to voicemail.

"Shit." It had hit the wall and the ground from the second story, but the way it had smacked the porch overhang had probably had an impact.

"Maybe it just shut off when it fell?"

Her optimism was fucking touching. I didn't hold out much hope that it would ever work again.

"I'm gonna hack the shit out of whoever stole my laptop," I grumbled, scanning the bushes for an opening. "They won't be able to buy a pack of gum again." I walked around the perimeter, cursing myself for leaving it in the trunk.

Having circumnavigated the entire area, I crouched, trying to catch a glimpse of my lifeline to my world. The branches were so thick I could barely see an inch into the depths.

"Can we get in there?" I asked.

"I guess I can see if one of the guys can come by?"

"When?"

"Tomorrow afternoon, probably?"

I couldn't tell if she was sincere. Couldn't read her. Didn't know if she was full of shit or if "the guys" weren't available in the morning because no one did anything in a hurry. Didn't matter. Every word out of her mouth was a lie.

Fuck it.

Wasn't like it could ring anyway.

"Tomorrow, phone or no phone, you tell me what you want. I'm not staying around here without clarity on what I have to do to get my code back. If you won't give it to me, well, they can all laugh at me. I don't care. I will walk right out onto the interstate if I think you're wasting my time."

I didn't wait for a cute excuse or a snotty word. I couldn't tell up from down. I couldn't be sure if I'd pushed the phone over the edge or if she'd made sure I knocked it over.

Didn't matter. I was done with Harper Barrington and her bullshit.

XIX

For years, I called her Schrödinger's mother.

Quantun logic is often explained by the simplified version of Schrödinger's paradox. There's a cat in a steel box. You know it's there. You can't see it, hear it, or measure it, but you can show its placement. Is it living or dead?

It's both.

And neither.

A star, an atom, a mother with bipolar disorder—can be measured only by placement or mass, never both. Unsurety, in-betweenness, constant movement, randomness, the potential of all things to be in either one place or another, in one state or another, was the heart of quantum mechanics.

It was also the heart of my mother, who had become more and more unstable as the years went on. I eventually stopped calling her Schrödinger's mother because that would have made me Erwin Schrödinger, who created the puzzle to disprove the physics I believed in.

How's Mom?

Moving constantly.

Should I come home for Christmas?

Dad. Come home for Dad.

I did. When Mom was manic, she buzzed and spun around Dad. Her body was active, and her mind was focused on everything yet calm. When she was down, her body was in one place, usually bed, but her mind was elsewhere.

Harper was volatile and erratic. Or was she? I couldn't predict her any better.

Catherine had told me she was at the distro center working a night shift. My phone had gone over the balcony as if Harper had timed it so she wouldn't have to deal with the repercussions. As if having dinner with Catherine and whomever else showed up (Trudy and her kids, Orrin's wife, another family whose names I didn't remember) would calm me before bed.

I went to her bedroom door, seeing what kind of lock she had. I could open it, but it would be loud. Catherine saw me, and I couldn't seem to disappoint her by breaking into her sister's room.

So I waited until she went to bed, which never seemed to happen.

I watched the moon cross the frame of the window, imagining all the ways I could hack her if I just had my laptop.

Harper came back before Catherine was out of the way.

Harper was making me dependent on her, and someone in the town was in on it. Someone had spray painted the Caddy. Maybe there was an odd-shaped battery in there, but even if it would take a few days to be delivered, I was sure Orrin wasn't going to put it in and let me go until Harper had what she wanted, whatever that was.

Catherine was about ten minutes into shaking the walls with her sorrow when I thought I heard my phone ring outside. It was a little after midnight. I looked over the balcony and convinced myself I could see the phone's dim blue light in the bushes. But the illusion stayed longer than the time a phone would ring, and the sound of it melted into the mix of the wind and Catherine crying.

Piece by piece, I'd lost control over my life.

Right before I fell asleep, I wondered if I was going to die in Barrington.

The next morning, I got out of the shower to a steamed-up mirror. I found a note that only showed up when the mirror was fogged.

102 101 122 122 111 116 107 124 117
116 040 123 124 101 124 111 117 116

Decoded, it said "Barrington Station."

She was lucky I could read octal or she would have been waiting there a long time.

XX

No one downstairs. The house had two states: full of people or deserted. I poured coffee and tried to think clearly.

Barrington Station.

Couldn't Google it. Couldn't locate it on satellite. There was phone on the wall. It was a beige box the size of a bag of coffee with a curly cord. I had no idea what to do with it.

When I picked up the handset, I discovered a clear plastic circle set into the base piece. The spiral cord connected the handset to it.

I had to pause for a second. I'd seen this in movies. Right. Finger. Turn. Wait. No problem. But who to call?

Numbers were scratched on the wall in pen, pencil, a few scratched through the yellow paint to the plaster beneath. Some had names above and some didn't. It was like a living record of every number ever spoken through that old phone.

Car service. Right. They'd know.

I dialed. How people watched that circle tick around every time they wanted to make a call, I'd never know.

"Matt's Car Service," the female voice answered.

"Hi, I'd like a car to Barrington Station."

"Sure. You know that's closed, right? Next best bet is Doverton."

"It's fine if it's closed. That's where I'm going."

"Where we picking you up?" The dispatcher didn't seem to care one way or the other. She was just trying to get the job out.

"I'm not sure of the address." I'd never felt so incompetent. I could practically see her roll her eyes. "The Barrington house. The mansion. It's on a dirt road off… I'm not sure."

"I know it. You'll be in front?"

"Yeah."

"Fifteen minutes."

She hung up. I waited.

AGAIN, I'd done Harper's bidding. Again, I'd come like a dog when called. The cab driver was a Middle Eastern dude with a short beard. Ahmed. He looked to be in his twenties and about five foot five. He pulled over on a nondescript patch of road. A pair of square wooden stakes stuck out of half-buried concrete blocks. The station sign must have been there.

"Barrington Station!" he said.

"Can you wait for me?" I handed him cash.

"I have another pickup." He handed a card over the front seat with the change. I took the card and left the rest in his hand for a tip. "Call and someone will come."

"I don't have a phone with me."

"You got fifty cents?" He pointed at a payphone ten feet in, a relic from the days when people needed to call a cab from the station.

"It works?"

"I know it does. Trust me. Fifty cents. You need two quarters?"

"No. I have it. Thanks. Hey—" I stopped myself halfway out the door. "What if I wanted to go to the airport?"

He laughed. "Airport? Hundred forty miles?"

"How much would it cost?" I didn't ask because it mattered but so he'd take me seriously.

"You call dispatch, okay?"

"All right."

I got out, and the car took off. I was alone in the middle of nowhere. Then I realized she could have left that little note at any time for any reason and I'd chased it like a puppy playing fetch.

The grass was knee-high, and leaves crunched underfoot. The trees were half-covered in red and brown leaves hanging on for dear life.

I walked perpendicular to the road and came to cracked pavement. Following it, a building appeared soon after. Red brick with green shingles, boarded windows, and poured concrete slab, it looked as if it had never been a major station. The archways had decorative stones over them, as if someone, at some time, had given a shit. I passed through the arch, into the station, through to the other side. The slab dropped off into grey gravel that led to rusted tracks.

I went into the station again. The floor was concrete. The walls were painted white under layers of graffiti. A locked door led behind the boarded-up ticket window. I scoured every surface for a message but found nothing.

Outside, I stepped onto the tracks. Facing north, they disappeared around a sharp turn. The fall leaves clicked in the wind, and the grass rustled with the movements of small animals. Rats. Squirrels, maybe. Groundhogs, if they had them out here. The clouds moved across the cyan sky so steadily I could have set my watch to them. Nothing else moved. Nothing else made a sound. I was locked in position, listening for changes as they snapped neatly into the continuity of time.

"It's amazing what you can do despite the obstacles." Harper's voice cut through a daydream I didn't know I was in the middle of. She came toward me from the north, walking on a track with her arms out for balance.

"You really work too hard to make a point."

She wore mirrored sunglasses I hadn't seen before. She dropped off the rail onto the ties. She wore a blue shirt under her open plaid car coat. It was unbuttoned, and her bra was red. The velvet swell of her tits curved into a sweet divot between them. Not too wide, not a straight, dark line. Just right for running my tongue over.

"I figured, since we're stuck together," she said, "we'd make the best of it."

"No. That's not what you figured." I overacted in the reflection of her sunglasses. I had to look *bigger,* but holding my arms out and talking louder didn't change the optics. "You're showing me more despair. I get it, okay? This sucks."

What did I see in her glasses?

A tiny man looking down her shirt.

I hadn't even realized I was doing it.

"Do you remember Lucy Park?" she asked.

"Sure, I do."

Lucy Park had been a sweet little Korean girl I'd done a first-year P-set with. She hadn't had much experience with men before we started it. By the time the quarter was over, she could take my entire cock down to the balls.

"She was a TA in my Calc 2 class. Married. Going for her PhD."

"Glad to hear it."

"She said you taught her how to fuck."

What the—?

The clouds moved at the same speed across the sky.

Calm down.

"We were both adults."

Had Harper dug something up? Was I going to wish she'd done no more than hack my system? Was she trying to ruin my life even more?

"She said you taught her what men like."

"I like grown women. I like them wet, and I like it when they want it. So if you're going to make up a story that I assaulted her, you got the wrong guy."

The line of her mouth curved a little, stretching the bottom crease. Her face was no more than a half smile and two miniature Taylors in the reflection of her glasses.

Crossing her arms, she unbuttoned the blue shirt. Her red bra was simple, unpadded, with a hook in the front. The thin fabric did nothing to hide her hard nipples.

"I was worried this would be uncomfortable." She unhooked the bra. "But that was stupid of me."

"Whoa, whoa."

My hand was doubled and huge in her lenses. The bra fell away. Her tits were round, velvet, crested with soft pink.

"I have something you want."

"Seriously?" Confused, irritated, disoriented, yet unable to keep from looking at her tits. The way they were proportioned against the curve of her waist. The shadow the sun cast on her belly. I stepped back, either to get away from her or get a good look at her. I wasn't sure which.

"You want QI4 back. And I need something from you."

I'd never been plied with sex before. Sex was casual and fun. She was using it to disorient me, and I didn't like it. Not one bit.

I advanced on her, taking her breast with my right hand, closing in on the nipple as I took her mouth with my tongue. I was merciless on her tit and her lips, biting and pinching my annoyance. I pushed my cock against her.

When I pulled away, two of me looked back.

I ripped the sunglasses off her and threw them on the ground. Her blue-ringed irises stared back at me. If I looked close enough, I was in the pupils.

Fuck her.

I abused her nipple, twisting until her mouth opened a little.

Pain or pleasure? Both?

"I don't like being manipulated," I hissed through teeth that wanted to bite her again. "You didn't hack me just to fuck me." Leveraging her hips, I pushed my erection against her.

She shifted so her clit felt me. "Teach me." Her breath was hot and damp. "Teach me how to do it."

I let her nipple go and grabbed the whole breast. I wanted to come on it. Paint it with my semen. Run my fingers through it and shove them down her throat. "Why?"

"Each thing you teach me, I'll release—" She gasped as I moved against her. "I'll release part of QI4."

"Tell me why."

"No."

I bit her lower lip. That lying little crease. She squeaked in pain, and I made her suffer before letting go.

"You have men here."

"I don't want to be fucked like a princess."

I took her chin in a hand still warm from her breast. "Why? You'll waste what I teach you on them anyway."

She pushed me so hard I nearly fell back. Good. She should be mad. She should be as pissed off and horny as I was.

"Now you listen to me." She bent slightly at the waist, as if she was ready to attack. Her tits went from objects of desire to objects of power. "You're going to do what I'm asking you to do. You're going to take as long as you need to. Teach me how to kiss for your boot loader. You'll get your master boot sector back when I can use my hands. Your object code when I can suck a cock. And the source code is released when I know how to fuck."

"You're crazy."

"I am. I'm out of my fucking mind. I'm nuts from seeing my friends die. From my sister crying every night. From these fucking drugs everyone drives a hundred miles to get. The filth in the water and the air's fucked my brain so bad I can't even think straight."

No. Her shouting, her tension, her growling conviction, told me… no.

Yes, but no. I was sure she was telling the truth about the things she saw, and I was sure she was unhappy and upset about the deterioration around her. But she wasn't crazy. I wasn't even sure she was truly as desperate as she wanted me to think she was. Maybe she was three steps from actual crazy desperation and she could see it coming, which would make her smart, shrewd, and very sane. She was what my grandmother would have called "crazy like a whorehouse priest."

I knew I'd deal with the priest; I'd just never thought I'd be the whore.

I held up my hands, stepping onto the track as if standing a few inches taller would make a difference.

The rail vibrated underfoot.

"What you're asking? It's crazy. But you're not," I said. "So I need to know why. I need to know what kind of plan I'm playing into."

"Did you ever need to know a woman's reasons for fucking you? What's the difference now? You do what you'd do if we met in some bar in SanJo. I do what I'd do if I was feeling charitable."

"That's a real achievement in compartmentalization."

The rail tremors underfoot sharpened, increasing with the faraway rattle of an engine.

"Trains still running on this line?" I asked.

"Yeah. Freight."

The tremors increased, and the steady silence was broken by a rumble. She didn't move her shirt down; it stayed bunched above her tits, tangled in her bra.

"They just pass Barrington?"

"At a hundred miles an hour."

I stepped off the rail. I wasn't in the mood to get run down. Standing close to her, she was a few inches taller, but still not taller than me.

"You can hear it," I said softly. "Same as I can."

"I know when to get off."

"Fine." I turned my back on her.

One step. Two. Was she getting off the rail? Was she really crazy? The rumble got louder, punctuated by clicks and clacks.

Basic stopping distance equals velocity squared over two times the coefficient of friction times the acceleration = unknown variables=tonnage, grade, maintenance, which means even best case, the train needs half a mile to—

Fuck this. When I turned to run toward her, she was still on the track. I grabbed her arm and yanked her away as the train came around the turn. I pulled her to the station as the freight train flew by. Without her sunglasses, I could see the determination in her eyes.

I'd lost a game of chicken. The simplest zero-sum game in the lexicon. Too simple for either of us.

"You just proved exactly nothing," I said.

"I grew up here. I told you I knew when to move." She buttoned her shirt without hooking her bra. "But you still felt the need to save me. See? You're not a total asshole. But that's *me.* So let's pretend this is about you and me. Just us. Not about Barrington or the people in it."

"I'm not touching you again."

"Yeah. All right. Sure." She stepped back, swaggering. "You need a lift back?"

Of course I did, and she knew it. But fuck her. I wasn't getting into a car with her.

"No."

"Suit yourself." She left the station and disappeared into the trees, ass swaying like a lure.

A few seconds later, her Chevy pulled out from the cover of the trees and onto the two-lane blacktop. Then she was gone.

XXI

Turned out I didn't have two quarters. I had ten credit cards, a twenty, and an emergency fifty-dollar bill jammed into the corner of my wallet. It was just as well. I had no idea where Harper had gone, and I needed a minute to think before I ran offhalf-cocked.

Walking on the shoulder in the direction Harper had driven, I tried to get my head around her offer.

I'd been pursued before. I wasn't so much of a predator that I only fucked what I chased. But this girl was insane. She'd gutted my life so I'd teach her how to fuck? It would have been easier to fly out to San Jose and shake her little tits at me. Sell those earrings for a nice hotel room.

My mind slid into the possibilities inside a hotel room, and now that I had full visual on the tit situation, I could get really detailed about it.

In every fantasy, Deeprak texted to say there was no problem. We were ready to roll with GreyHatC0n. Without his messages, I couldn't touch her. Not even in a fantasy hotel room.

The route was a single lane in each direction, weaving through a lightly wooded forest. Not much traffic in the first hour. Three cars going in my direction and one coming the opposite way. I didn't put my thumb out for the first hour of walking, and only one truck slowed down to ask where I was going. The guy looked like a traveling salesman in a cheap suit with a passenger seat loaded with fast food bags. I waved him on.

I missed my phone.

How was Deeprak going to contact me to tell me how fucked up it was that I couldn't sacrifice a little sex with a beautiful girl to save the company? How was I going to imagine the incredulity on his face when I told him how hot she was? That under normal circumstances, I would have taken her twelve ways from Tuesday? And she didn't want a commitment. Just a crash course in how to please a guy, with the first lucky guy being me.

Despite the fact that Harper had the keys to a lock I needed opened, she freaked me out. I didn't trust she'd do what she promised.

And it didn't matter.

Man, her body.

And the way she let me kiss her. Like she was receiving the kiss. That was what it was. She was learning it as I did it.

The buzz and rumble of a car coming from behind me woke my mind up to the pain in my feet and the time of day. The sun was getting low in the sky, and I was just going to have to stick out my thumb.

The SUV passed with the driver staring at my thumb and me. Then two more. I must have gotten to a more used part of the road. All the cars had local plates. All the drivers were women. If I was a woman, I wouldn't have stopped for me either.

The forest broke, and I was walking along open plain.

The rumble of a motorcycle cut the air as it passed. A motorcycle with a sidecar. I stuck my thumb out even though the back of a motorcycle or a deathtrap sidecar weren't what I had in mind. The bike stopped. The driver wore a leather vest that should have scared me, but I was tired and hungry. The back graphic said *Lord Of Rust* in old English lettering and had roses twined around the chemical formula for oxidized iron.

Odd. Odd in every way.

The ninety-five pound *uhff*-ing dog was in the sidecar with its tongue lolling. Johnny swung his leg over the seat, and we met in the space between us. His corporate polo was gone in favor of a T-shirt that said, "Horologists Take Their Time."

"Nice afternoon for a walk," he said. "Unless you don't wanna get robbed by a bunch of broke motherfuckers with tattoos."

"You gonna rob me?"

"Shit. I ain't no motherfucker." He smiled to let me know he wasn't offended. "Where you headed?"

"The Barrington place. I'm headed in the completely wrong direction, aren't I?"

He shrugged. "Depends how much walking you're fixing to do. Nobody picking up hitchers these days. Even nice white boys."

"Why's that?"

"Double murder a few months back. They found the guy, but everyone's skittish."

"Was he a nice white boy?"

"Yep. Nice haircut and an Oxycontin habit. Started like a regular robbery then went all wrong. Cops couldn't figure out if the hitcher was a bigger moron than the driver, but there was plenty of stupid to go around that night. I don't know what gets into people. They get a gun and have ideas. Gonna be a hero. Prove something. Shoot a guy who's high on painkillers in the knee and think the pain's gonna stop him from turning the gun back on you."

"Great story. Really."

"I have more."

I looked up the road, then back down it, then at the dog in the sidecar.

"Come on." He clapped me on the shoulder and stepped backward toward the bike. "I'll take you back if you don't mind sharing a sidecar with Redox."

"Redox?"

"Yeah, the—"

"Oxidation reduction process. Dude."

"Kids are gone, so a guy's gotta have hobbies, right? Mine's science." He pointed at me then at the dog. "This here's a nice city boy," he told Redox. "That's a fancy jacket, and it ain't gonna hurt you. Be good."

"Does he bite?" I asked.

"'Course he bites. No point otherwise. Your other option is to ride bitch with your arms around me, but you'd have to kiss me first."

I got into the sidecar. Redox was in the middle of the seat, and from the way he looked me straight in the eye, he had no intention of moving for a white boy in a nice jacket. I squeezed in where I could. Johnny handed me a black military helmet and took off back toward town.

XXII

Johnny made a stop at the gas station, and I got to the register in time to pay for his cigarettes and some beef jerky. He spent a bunch of time talking to the guy behind the counter about off-gassing pipes and toxins. The guy laid his hands over his plaid-stretched gut and nodded. I got the feeling Johnny was like the town idiot, except he was really the town savant.

"You know Harper went to MIT, right?" he said.

"Yeah," I replied. "She's pretty smart."

"We was all proud of her. Then she came back for that fuck of a father. He shoulda croaked faster. Done us all a favor."

"Harper said everyone loved him."

"Feed them enough barbecue, and they'll love you."

"I'll remember that."

He tossed me the black helmet. Redox hadn't budged.

"Is the Barrington place far?" I asked.

"Let's get something to eat first."

"I'm buying."

"Damn right, you are."

He took me across three empty parking lots and a light industrial service road behind an abandoned brick structure. We landed in a dark bar right out of a movie. It smelled of stale beer and cigarettes and sounded like treble-heavy speakers and clicking resin pool balls. There was no sign out front.

Johnny pointed at a seat at the bar and introduced me to Kyle, Damon,

Reggie, Curtis, and Butthead. A mug of beer and a shot of something amber appeared at my elbow.

"You were up at the Barrington place last night." Damon pulled on his long goatee.

"This is the California guy Harper found." Reggie handed me my shot and held up his own. I was apparently expected to drink it.

"Found?" I said.

"Knew each other in college, ain't that right?" Johnny added.

"Those girls pick up strays where they find 'em," Kyle said. "They're all right."

Damon grumbled something behind his beer.

"Crazy broads," Reggie added, smiling as if they were his own special crazy broads.

Kyle shook his head and threw back his shot, leaving wet hair on his handlebar moustache. Butthead, whose four hundred pounds were at least twenty pounds sideburn, shook his head as if he didn't have to say a word out loud. They all understood each other in glances and half sentences.

I threw back my drink. Wild Turkey. Maybe. It burned, but I liked a little burn now and again. I cooled it down with a gulp of cold, pissy beer. It was good, and a new shot was in my hand a second later.

Damon raised his. "To the Barrington girls."

Sure. I'd drink to that.

"What the fuck's that on your wrist?" Johnny asked me, clicking his beer mug on my Langematik.

"Fucking watch."

"How much that set you back? Thirty large?"

"What the—?" someone behind me exclaimed.

"Not telling."

"Oh, shit! He ain't telling!"

Everyone laughed. I didn't think it was funny.

"It was a steal." I wanted to show them I was shrewd. "My dealer found a guy who didn't know what he had, and I grabbed it."

"What you do for a living out there in Cah-lee-fornia?" Johnny stretched out the word to mock it. He was the leader of this crew, at least for the night.

"I'm a hacker." Which was partially true but most easily stated and threatening enough to make my balls look a little heavier.

"A hacker?"

"Holy shit!" Butthead exclaimed. "So you, like, get into people's computers and steal?"

"Yes and no—"

The gang argued about what hackers did, their feelings about us, how cool or not cool the entire idea was, and whether or not hacking made you a man or a pussy.

"Hack me!" Damon took out his phone. With his long goatee and huge holes in his ears, he could have been transplanted into the San Jose hipster scene in the blink of an eye.

"Are you serious?" Butthead tried to talk sense into him, but Damon waved his phone at me.

"Fuck it. Hack me right now. I ain't got nothing to steal. Fuck it. I want to see."

"Nah." I denied his phone. Once I touched it, it was mine.

"Do it, motherfucker."

"No."

"You ain't shit. You mean you can't."

The group went up in *awws* of resignation when I shook my head. They really thought I couldn't. No one had doubted me in years, and suddenly my balls were featherlight.

"Fine," I said, taking Damon's phone. I pressed the volume and home keys at the same time. "Give me that safety pin." I pointed at a row of them on his jacket, and he pinched one off.

"You need the passcode to... oh shit."

I didn't have my own device, which would have cut my hack time in half. But there wasn't much I couldn't do once I was into his phone, which only took a second. Then I downloaded a piece of code I'd developed to do a particularly neat trick. A few taps, and his life opened her legs for me.

"Your One US Bank password is 123123? Are you trying to get robbed?"

"What the—?"

"You have $423.34 in there. I'll leave you the twenty-three dollars. You're welcome."

Voices of amazement and awe, which I bathed in. I was a sucker for this shit. I didn't need or want his four hundred dollars but his esteem. Their esteem. I didn't know them, but these guys made me feel like a king.

Butthead had his phone in his front pocket. I tapped it with Damon's to connect them. It was so easy it was a joke.

"Butthead," I said, "your Twitter password is 'titties,' all lowercase. So's the America First Bank checking and the—"

"I like titties. What can I say?"

"Kyle."

"I know my passwords, thank you." His voice was resonant and serious. What it suggested clearly was "I believe you're a hacker. You can stop now."

I gave Damon his phone. "Do a factory reset and protect yourself, would you? All you guys. Long passwords, all different, numbers, letters, symbols. All right? Stop fucking around."

"Tell you what, California Boy," Kyle said.

Shit. This wasn't going to end well. Nothing that started with "tell you what" and ended with something besides your actual name ended well.

"You beat me at eight ball, and I'll give you my bike." Kyle pointed out the window at a shiny Harley. "You lose, and I get that watch."

It was a fair trade if only the objects were considered. Except I could buy a new watch in a minute, and his bike was probably a bigger invest- ment for him.

"I can't take your bike," I said.

"You think you're gonna win?"

"I know I am."

"Man, you are all balls, kid."

"Might be so. But I can tell the time on the wall. What are you going to do without your ride?"

"Fuck it." He slapped down his empty mug. "Don't care. Come on."

He grabbed the shoulder of my jacket and "helped" me up. Someone tossed me a stick, and I caught it. Chalk came half a second after, and I snapped that out of the air with my other hand.

I really didn't want his bike, and I liked my watch, but I could risk it to give these guys a rude awakening. Because math. Physics. And I was just tipsy enough to not care about getting the shit beat out of me. Loose enough to think landing in the hospital with a pool cue up my ass would get me enough sympathy from Harper to release my system.

Yeah. The shots had gone right to my head. Kyle put another Wild Turkey on the table rail.

"Do you fucking people eat?" I asked.

Butthead shouted over the music, "Johnny! Get Mr. California a burger! And get two for my fucking belly." He turned back to me with a smile. "Yeah. I'm fat, and I don't give a shit."

I took out my wallet and gave him my credit card. "Then get three. I don't give a shit if you're fat either. But change your passwords. Make them longer and put in a number or something."

"You're all right for a California freak." He took the card.

"You're the nicest fat fuck I ever met."

I must have been drunk to say that, and everyone else must have been drunk to laugh so hard. Kyle started the rack. Damon pushed him away and accused him of cheating. Kyle cursed at him. Johnny pushed them both away, said something about even odds of a stripe or a solid falling, and rearranged the balls. Once the rack was set, it was determined that the guest broke. The eleven landed.

"So how you like that Harper?" Kyle asked.

She's nuts.

"Nice girl." I circled the table, doing geometry in my head. I could land the nine and set up the next four shots. I wouldn't take his bike right off the bat, but I wouldn't lose either.

"You stay in the house last night?"

I sank the nine and had a perfect set up for the ten.

"Yeah. Side." I leaned over, took the ten. I wasn't drunk enough to miss the twelve in the side pocket or the setup for the fifteen in the corner.

"She show you Barrington hospitality?"

The balls clicked, and the fifteen made it, but the fourteen wasn't lined up like I'd wanted. Because… what was Kyle talking about? Was he implying I'd fucked her?

"Food was good. Mattress was lumpy."

"She made you forget about that though. That's my guess." He leaned on his cue and winked.

I looked at him over my cue, still sliding it over my thumb. "She's a nice girl."

"Sure is."

I had a lot going on in my life. I was responsible for the employment of dozens of people, and my life's work, the work they'd all slaved over, was being held hostage by a crazy woman who'd threatened to sell it. I was in Nowhere, USA, without a car or a cab. My phone was broken and imprisoned by thorns. I was going to get the shit beaten out of me if I wasn't careful.

But when he implied that Harper was some kind of easy whore, I was ready to tear shit up. I was aware that she'd taken her shirt off in an abandoned train station and begged me to fuck her, but that was me. The thought of her fucking these guys—or any guy, if I was being honest with myself—boiled the bourbon in my blood.

I took my shot, and the fourteen dropped in the corner. "She's a beautiful girl." I paced around the table after the thirteen, which hung on the edge of a corner pocket. "And smarter than anyone in this room." I leaned over and sank it. "Including me."

I was complimenting her to get the guys to talk, maybe tell me if they were in on her plan, but that didn't mean I was lying.

"Me too," Johnny said. "Just saying."

"She's too good for this shit." The thirteen sank like a body over a waterfall, and the cue ball bounced left, tapping the eight. It dropped into the side pocket. "Too good to be stuck here. If I were her, I'd do some desperate shit to get out."

I laid my stick across the table and held my hand out to Kyle. Ruefully, he pulled on the silver chain that made a U at his waist and isolated a key.

"You don't know this town well enough to say that." He snapped off the key. "We're her people."

"That may be so." I still didn't want his bike, but in the seconds that passed, I decided I'd give it to Harper as payment for their shitty rutting. "But she's yours too."

Kyle slapped the key in my outstretched hand and grabbed it tight. I braced myself against what I thought was next. A punch. A flip. Any act of violence I had coming for shooting off my mouth in the backwoods.

"I don't need you telling me what the Barrington girls are." He looked at me closely, inspecting every pore, every hair, every flick of my eyes.

I looked back at him with the same directness, funneling my inexplicable anger in his direction. "What are they?"

I wanted him to say it so I could get this over with. His face cracked, and lines appeared around his mouth when he smiled. It was as if I'd said something that relieved him.

"They're us. That's all there is to it. They're good girls. Good people. And if you respect them, we respect you." He let my hand go.

I put the key on the rail. They'd been baiting me, trying to get me to say something dirty or cruel about Harper and her sister. Fuck them and, also, good for them.

"Who's going to win you your bike back?" I asked.

"One of my people." He tossed the cue to Reggie.

XXIII

In the dream, I was eating her pussy. It was dry, but I was eating that shit as if it was my last fucking meal. Her legs clamped tight around my head, squeezing and squeezing and squeezing, until I said her name right into her cunt.

"What?" Her voice was clear, as if her thighs weren't around my ears.

"Harper." My voice was flat and toneless in sleep.

"You're going to wear it out."

The dream ended. I was left with a headache and a dry mouth.

I didn't want to open my eyes. If I did, I was either in the hospital or in the Barrington house. Maybe I was in Butthead's house. Or Kyle's. Maybe I was lying on the pool table.

But where I wasn't was my own bed or the couch at QI4HQ. Nope. I was definitely still in Shit City and batshit crazy Harper Barring- ton/Watson was right next to me with her freckles and her strawberry-shortcake tits.

"Water," I croaked like a frog.

"Right next to you."

Keeping my eyes closed, I reached to where I'd remembered the night table was in the room I'd slept in.

"You're more likely to knock it over like that."

Damn. That meant I was leaning in the right direction, which meant I was in that same room. Fuck.

"And anyway, that's the wrong side," she added.

Different room? Okay. I reached out with my left hand. My knuckles found cool plastic.

"For the love of Pete." Her exasperation was cute in a psycho kind of way.

The cold container was put right in my palm. It was short. I opened my eyes. Everything was a mad blur except the water container I held three inches from my face. It was a purple-and-yellow sippy cup with clowns biking around the sides.

"You don't have to pick your head up this way," she explained.

I closed my eyes and put the bottle to my lips, sucking on the end like I'd sucked her hard little clit. I remembered it had been a red-painted pebble.

Or not.

That had been a dream. Right.

"Thank you."

"There's something for your headache if you can reach it. Or I can get it for you."

"I got it." I gave up sweet darkness and opened my eyes for real, blinking the blur out. The ceiling was painted in roses. "You put me in the moldy room."

"Closer to the stairs. You were heavy. Butthead's not in great shape, you know."

I got up on my elbows. I was dressed. I knew that much. Ablanket was thrown over me, hiding my dream-induced boner. When I turned to Harper, my neck hurt. She was in a white wicker chair, one knee folded with her bare foot up on the edge. Her arms wrapped around the bend in her leg, and her fingers laced together around her calf. I couldn't read her expression.

"Thank you," I said. That hurt too.

"You still drunk?"

"A little."

"Kyle said you could still hit bank shots better than you could stand."

"It's math." I scooped up the three brown pills on the night table. "I can do that drunk."

"Apparently. You were the proud owner of half the Harleys in town until about midnight."

"I don't ride." I washed down the pills with sippy-cup water and flopped back on the pillow. "They can keep them." I put my arm over my eyes. My Langematik was gone. "Where's my watch?"

"You played nine ball with Johnny. Mistake."

Right. Math + Sobriety > Math/Drunk.

"Those guys are a bunch of assholes. I don't know how you stay here."

I meant it as a compliment, and she read my sarcasm like a pamphlet on guy-speak.

"They're all right." Her voice was bathed in warmth and pride.

"No, I mean, yeah, sure. They're fine. But I can't get the hell out of here, and I don't even live here."

"You should really think about my offer. I'm a great student."

"You're a terrorist."

"I'm desperate. There's a difference."

I moved my arm and looked at her. "Why?"

"Why is there a difference?"

"Why are you desperate?"

She got up, leaned down until her hair brushed my chin, and whispered so close I could hear the wet pop of her tongue on the roof of her mouth.

"You haven't been paying attention."

She quickly kissed me and walked out before I even felt it.

XXIV

I'd gotten where I was from paying attention. Her town was desperate. The guys in the bar last night were desperate. They stank of it. Their jokes were laced with it. They were uneducated, unemployed, and stuck. But Harper had money, beauty, and talent. Maybe the headache was keeping me from seeing what she wanted me to see.

Maybe that was all I had to do. See her problem. Then she'd release my system and kick me out of her fucking house. Maybe she'd marry one of Johnny's kids and make smart babies.

Yeah. No.

Harper didn't need to marry anyone right now.

My reaction was so quick I couldn't question it until I was entrenched in refusal. Obviously, from a completely impartial standpoint, she was too good to be stuck here. I didn't need to want her myself to know that. Staying here and making babies with a guy in a trucker hat was a betrayal of her potential. As opposed to (me) someone with resources (me) and a valid passport to take her around the world (me).

Not me, obviously. I wasn't interested in crazy. I wasn't even interested in a relationship.

But someone *like* me.

The room swam when I sat up, and the knife in my head jabbed hard when I stood, but I wasn't so hungover that pissing in the bed was an option. By the time I'd emptied my bladder, I had my balance back. My eyes cleared, and I could see the wiry mushroom growing out of the ceil- ing. The paint it grew from was probably full of lead. I put my dick away, washed my hands, and tried to walk out. But the mushroom bothered me.

It had a long stem and a small, cone-shaped head. I pulled it, but the plaster put up a fight. A chunk of dusty white grit came off, leaving rocks and dust on the toilet tank. But a string of mycelium stayed attached. I pulled again. Another line of plaster came off.

"Shit." I dropped it and let it hang from the fissure. That was going to bother me more than if I'd just left it alone.

"Mr. Harden?" A female voice came from the bedroom.

Catherine stood in the doorway with her hands folded over her chest. She was so sweet and unassuming in an apron and dress. Like a real throwback to an earlier time. The exact opposite of her sister. I wondered how much she knew about what Harper was up to.

"Yeah. Hey, thank you for putting me up again."

"It's not a problem. I was making eggs. Did you want some?"

"Hell yeah."

She smiled. She liked being useful. I could tell that much. "Any preference?"

"Any way you make them. But if it doesn't matter to you, fried is fine."

"How many? Three?"

I could have eaten a dozen. "Yeah. That would be great. Thanks." She was about to leave when I stopped her. "Catherine?"

"Yeah?"

"Where's Harper?"

"Running errands. Be down in ten if you like your eggs hot."

Catherine had eggs, coffee, toast, and bacon ready on the kitchen table. I washed up in the sink.

"I made a mess in the bathroom."

"What was it?"

"The mushroom was making me crazy."

She laughed. "Reggie plasters over it at least twice a year."

I rinsed, wondering what a person would have to do to make Catherine angry. "I can spackle it up."

"Really? Well, you can see if there're any tools in the shed." She handed me a towel. "When are you leaving, Mr. Harden?"

She didn't sound cruel or rude. Her tone barely moved.

I wiped my hands, wishing I had an answer. "I keep trying to."

The eggs were still warm. I tried not to shovel them, but I was starving.

"I want you to think about taking Harper with you." Catherine sat across from me, cradling her coffee mug.

Did she know her sister was a hacker? Did she know her sister was inches away from ruining me?

"Excuse me?"

"She's dying here, and she won't leave. The longer she stays, well, you know what happens."

She didn't know. She thought Harper was just her smart sister.

"To be honest, I don't know what happens."

"She made it to twenty-five without having kids. Most girls around here start at eighteen. She's going to be an old maid like me unless she finds a man who can match her." Catherine didn't look as if she'd hit thirty. Hardly an old maid. "I think where you are, she might find happiness."

In Silicon Valley, a girl like Harper would get swooped up like a steak in a wolf's den. She'd have her pick of rich and talented men. The fact that what she'd done to QI4 would make her a talent commodity was an oddly secondary concern.

"She can go where she wants."

"No, I mean… you could introduce her around. Be her friend."

My reflection stared back at me from the black surface of my coffee. "I could. But where I'm from, no one really likes me. Right now, my company's under attack, and outside the people who work for me, everyone thinks it's funny, or cool, or they're somehow vindicated. The whole world watched me burn, and now you know what they're disappointed about? Not that my creation crashed. They're disappointed that they won't get to be the ones to take me down. They won't get the glory. Someone beat them to it. So I'd love to help Harper, but if I brought her back with me, they'd hate her too."

"I doubt everyone hates you."

"Believe it. I can show you tweets that would make your hair turn red."

She blew on her coffee and sipped it. Tapped the edge. "She's had a rough time."

"I know."

"When our father died, she was supposed to take time off school and go back. But our mother…" Catherine shook her head pensively. "She took a mortgage out on the factory, defaulted first chance she got, and left with everything. Just. Gone."

"I'm sorry."

She waved as if it was old news. "There was a man involved. Of course. Had been for a while. She was waiting for our father to die so she could leave."

"So you started selling furniture."

She smiled at some foolishness then sighed. "I hear someone has a problem… if all I have to do is give them an antique to sell, I give it to them. That's all they'll take. An object or work. No one accepts a handout."

"It's a big house. That's a lot of problems."

"It is." She gathered the plates and brought them to the sink. "And there are more. Always. The furniture's gone, and I'm running out of projects around here."

I couldn't imagine her sacrifice. Richest girl in town with a father who owned the primary place of employment reduced to poverty by her own mother.

"Do you have tools around? Hand tools? Stuff like that?" I asked.

"In the shed out back. We've loaned a lot out and sold some, but the basics should be there."

"Okay, to your first question, I don't know when I'm leaving. Harper and I have some things to work out."

"What things?" Her voice was all hope wrapped in surprise.

"Just things. Let me fix that hole in the wall first."

XXV

I found the shed to the right of the thorny bed of bushes. It was a rotted-out mess. The door nearly came off when I opened it, and dozens of crickets jumped whenever I moved something. How did these women decide what got attention and what didn't? Was it money? Time? Materials?

The tool bench was tidy but dirty with disuse. Some of the metal jar tops screwed into the ceiling had glass jars of nails threaded in; some were just circles waiting to be used. This had been someone's special place. They'd kept pictures of boats, model planes, vintage cola signs, and wooden boxes that probably held treasures I had the curiosity but not the courage to open.

A hole in the roof had let water in, rusting everything. A hoe with the grey handle. A sledgehammer with the handle half broken off. A pair of pliers screamed in a permanent open state.

I found a box of old scrapers crusted in plaster. I found three containers of joint compound. I could only get one open. After working past an inch of dried crust, I found a pocket still wet enough to use.

Back upstairs, I scraped off the mushroom and plastered over the crack, laying the compound on as smoothly as I could. It stuck and shifted on the cracking plaster, and I ended up with a larger patch than I wanted. Eradicating the mushroom meant ripping out the mycelium, which was probably in the wood on two of the walls and the bedroom adjacent. No one had time for that.

"Taylor?" Harper's voice came from the open French doors.

I checked my watch, but it was gone. Once I was on the balcony, the breeze cooled the moisture on my skin. The sun came in at an angle, and I was a little hungry.

Harper looked up from ground level, shielding her eyes from the sun. Her hair was in a loose ponytail at the back of her neck.

"What are you doing?" she called.

"I'm not leaving until you give me what you took, and the mushrooms were making me crazy. They grow behind the walls. It's… unnerving."

"Unnerving?"

I gripped the railing. *Are you doing this or not?* "Come up here, Harper."

I'd decided. I was doing this.

I pointed toward the doors on the other side of the balcony that led to the room I'd slept in the night before. I did not say please, and I did not ask a question. One of us was in charge, and it wasn't her. Even if she had the keys to my life on the little ring in her head, this wasn't working if she was the one calling the shots.

I washed my hands in the mycelium-free bathroom by my room. No time for a shower.

The stairs creaked. A pressure grew behind my balls because I knew what was coming.

She stood at the end of the hall, hand draped on the bannister. Branches of hair had escaped her ponytail and dropped to either cheek. I pointed at a spot on the floor in front of me. She scratched a spot on her neck, which was unremarkable except for her hand. It looked as if it had been rinsed in light blue paint and scrubbed. The tinge was in the corners of the nails and the deep lines in her wrist.

"Come into my room and close the door," I said.

"You're all sweaty."

"You want to do this or not?"

If I had been trying to scare her, I'd failed. She practically skipped into the room.

"Close the door," I commanded again. She did it. "I want to set the rules right off."

"Okay."

"You won't tell me why you want this or why you went to all the trouble, but if you're trying to trap me into marriage or some shit—"

She laughed derisively. "Yeah. No."

My feelings were not hurt.

Nope.

Not one bit.

"Condoms." I put up a finger. "Every time."

"Yes."

I put up a second finger. "Don't come to me with emotional attachment. I'm not interested."

"Me neither."

My third finger made a W. "This has to be done in nine days. If it's not, I'm leaving, and I'll just deal with the consequences."

"It won't take longer than that. I told you. I'm a really good student."

"All right. Let's get this show on the road."

I dug my thumb into my other palm absently, thinking this might not be a bad way to spend a few days. QI4 would be back, Deeprak would spin it into a learning experience; we'd work on manufacturing our own goddamn monitors and BIOS. I could just go back to the way things were. That alone was enough to give me serious wood.

"Take your clothes off, Harper."

XXVI

I'd never seen anything like it. She *was* a good student. Good like the kid who raises their hand highest, shakes it, bounces, and says, "Ooh ooh!" until they're called on. She dropped her jacket like a bad habit and attacked her shirt buttons with enthusiasm.

"Okay, okay," I said. "Hold up."

"What?" She was frozen with her shirt on one shoulder.

"Slow down." I dropped into a chair, crossing my legs and watching.

She tossed her shirt on the floor. Then her bra. Bent to slide her pants down. Deliberate. Slow. Authentic.

By taking away the cover of kisses and close bodies, I intended to make her uncomfortable. Punishment for what she'd done. Hack my system. Humiliate me. Put everyone on my team in jeopardy. Lure me hundreds of miles away. Use me.

And for all of it, never tell me why.

She was naked in front of me. Smooth and pale, hair over her shoul- ders so I could see her shape from top to bottom, her rounded tits, her curved waist, the bald triangle between her legs. The tiny slit at the bottom was the focus of all my attention. I couldn't have solved for *x* and looked at it at the same time.

"You shaved." I asked a question by stating the obvious.

"Men like it. No?"

"Some do. Some don't."

"What about you?"

"How you keep yourself is your business. There aren't any rules."

"Ah."

"A guy will let you know."

I got near her and let the backs of my fingers run over her nipple. My body pushed up against my mind, saying, *Now now now.* But the moments before the first time, before sex with whomever, they were worth savoring.

She licked her lip and looked at me with an utter guilelessness that was so sexy the pressure to get my dick in her became unbearable. Fucking her would be so easy. Giving her a tip or a trick, nailing her, bending her, and making her come over and over. So easy.

But I had my pride. "Kneel on the bed."

She did it, and I tapped the edge of the foot.

"This is awkward," I said. "You're blackmailing me, you won't tell me why, and I still want to fuck you."

"You're a complete fucking douche, and I still want to fuck you."

I held my finger up to her face. "Keep talking like that, and I might start to like you."

A smile crept across her face. She confused the fuck out of me, but I liked her. I hated her. I was angry at her. I was afraid of her. And still, I liked her.

Letting weight fall against her bottom lip, I leaned into her until I could feel her breath on my chin.

"The moment before a kiss is important," I said. "You need to savor it."

"Okay." Her eyelids fluttered.

"Never rush." I heard her swallow. "Lips first. Keep it loose." I brushed ours together, and she shuddered. I had full wood already. "Light. Gentle to start."

I kissed her top lip then below. She tasted like river water and rain. I flicked my tongue into her mouth quickly, and she gasped.

"Has no one ever kissed you before?"

"Not like this."

"Open your mouth, just a little, and play against me. Make me work for it."

Her jaw moved against mine. I played her lips and tongue, tasting every millimeter, every fold of skin and membrane, getting inside her just a little until I pried her open and owned her.

She groaned into my mouth, laid her hands on my stomach, and brought them down to my waistband. She unlooped my belt. "Is this right? That I'm going for it? Or should I wait?"

"If I wanted you to stop, I'd move your hands. Same for you."

"I'm not good at cues." She nodded and slipped the belt from the buckle.

"You're doing fine."

"When I was a kid," she said, "they thought I was slow. I said weird things. The other kids didn't like me because I didn't relate like a normal person. Teachers hated me because I'd start to answer a question then ask another question they couldn't answer before I finished. They thought I was too stupid to finish a thought. I'd start a sentence in class and get distracted by all the things in my head I didn't know. So I'd just stop talk- ing." She opened the belt and got her fingers behind my top button.

"Don't stop." I wanted to fuck her. Needed to. But I wasn't talking about her getting my dick out. "Telling me. Don't stop the story."

"My grades were terrible. If I hadn't been rich, I would have been special ed. But my parents made sure I was with the 'normal' kids." She took her fingers off my pants long enough to make air quotes.

She popped my jeans button. I took a hard breath. I had to listen to her, or I was going to blow my load.

"I didn't get picked on for the same reason. Everyone was afraid my dad would come down on them at the factory. But one teacher, Mrs. Prescott, she started asking me questions, and when I paused, she asked me what I was thinking about instead of getting annoyed."

"People with high IQs have a hard time socializing."

She made quick work of my fly buttons. "Yes. And that plus everyone being scared of me? That's why I don't know how to do this."

I took her by the wrist and kissed her hand.

"You know how." I put each finger in my mouth, sucking until it was wet.

Her breath got quicker. Her every-color eyes widened.

"When you stroke me, it's better when your hand is wet." I lowered her hand to my cock. That worked. "Gently at first."

The head of my cock felt like a full balloon. I slid my fingers down her belly.

"Spread your knees."

She leaned on me to keep her balance, and I touched the wettest cunt I had ever touched in my life.

Shit. I was going to lose it. I pulled away.

"What?" She looked as if I'd slapped her.

I pushed her down. "On your back."

The best part of sex is the moment a girl's legs open the first time. It's hot when she's naked and her tits are at full attention. But that moment, when a girl shows me where she's most vulnerable…

She lay before me with one hand over her belly and her ankles crossed. I was at her feet, returning her stare.

"How am I doing?" she asked.

"Great." A little pressure on her thighs and her legs opened like a flower.

"So what I was just telling you?" she said.

Her clit was hard and wet, and when I touched it, she stopped talking.

"About you being socially awkward?"

"Yes, I—"

When I slid my finger in her, two things happened at once.

One: she came.

Two: a ring tightened around my knuckle.

I moved with her and yanked out as she was in mid-arch. It was cruel, but I was shocked out of the moment.

She was left in a puddle of skin, breathing heavily, and I knew she was wondering if that was how it was supposed to go.

"You didn't tell me," I growled harder than I should have.

"I was about to!" Her hair looped all over her face.

"You have to tell a guy before you even get your clothes off."

She scrambled onto her knees and put her fists on her naked hips. "Well, that's a rule you don't get a second chance at."

"How are you a virgin?"

"I just told you how."

"Between Mrs. Prescott and MIT, you couldn't get laid?"

Naked and shameless, hands still on her hips. "Have you noticed everyone steers wide of me and my sister?"

The guys had tried to get me to admit I was fucking her, and when I hadn't, they'd seemed good with it. Better than good. Kyle had seemed relieved.

"You got cooties or something?" I asked.

"My father's dying wish was for them to 'protect' us. Me especially. Fact that it was years ago hasn't changed anything."

"Protect you from what?"

"Getting hurt. Casual sex. Pregnancy. We're like prize cows. Damon's been trying to get in my pants since high school. Johnny broke his finger in sophomore year because he caught us behind the grocery store. That was that." She slapped her hands together.

"Every guy at MIT wasn't trying to get you into bed?" I buttoned up. Fun times were over.

"They could try. Sure. But I—" She stopped herself and balled her fists at me.

"What?"

"Nothing."

"I just had my finger in you. We're past 'nothing.'"

She got off the bed and snatched up her pants, finding the waistband. She put them on without the underwear.

"None of them were like me. Bunch of guys who could barely talk to a woman, and when they did, I felt like a redneck piece of trash." She fastened her fly as if she could just as easily have ripped it to shreds. "And stupid me. There was this one guy who was the worst of them." She isolated the collar of her shirt, stretching it as if she was going to put it on. "On the first day, he stood next to me in line in the Forbes Building. One of his friends got in front of me, and I was too timid to say anything. But this guy called his friend a fucking jerkoff and told him to get in line…" She wrestled into the shirt. "No one else talked like my people here, buthe did. I saw him around and tried to be near him, but he didn't notice." She interrupted buttoning the front to snap her fingers. "Then I had to come home."

"Honestly? Can I say something *honestly* without you destroying my life?"

"Sure. Why not."

"If I'd noticed you, I would have fucked the shit out of you."

"Thanks. I think."

"And if you were in SanJo when I staffed… I might have hired you. But the 'wanting to fuck you' thing would have been a problem."

Her jaw tightened, and her face hardened as if she didn't believe me.

"That's not comforting," she said.

"I didn't say it to comfort you."

"You need to fix that, Taylor. You need to grow up and stop letting your dick run the show. It's pathetic."

I'd been told that before, but her disgust sent the message right into me. I was ashamed. Deeply ashamed. I carried my cock as if it was the president of the company, and I didn't make any excuses for it, but now I wanted to curl into a ball and think about all the decisions I'd made because of where I wanted to stick it.

I'd thought I was making sure the workplace was appropriate, but what I'd done was make it safe for the impulses of the least appropriate person. Me.

And… Raven. Of course I'd made sure there was one consenting partner in the office just for me.

Nice leadership. Real nice. I didn't blame Harper for being disgusted.

"Yeah. Well. I guess, when you put it that way, you're right."

Her mouth got narrow and tight, folding hard in the center crease. She opened the night table and took out a pen, biting the cap off as she came toward me.

I let her take my hand and twist it until my forearm was up. She wrote a string of numbers on it while clamping her teeth on the cap. Four digits in, I knew what it was and tried to stay still and quiet until she finished.

4920616d20736f20736f7272792c2062757
42074686973206973206e6f74206f7665722e

"Thank you." I felt ridiculous for thanking her.

She must have felt the absurdity too. She put the cap back on and pulled out her phone.

"I have to go to work," she said, tapping on the glass. "Keep your nose clean." She tossed the device on the bed faceup. The contact was QI4HQ, and it was ringing.

"You had me on speed dial?"

She walked out without answering.

XXVII

I was shaking as I read off the last letter to Deeprak.

"Got it." He read it back to me.

"Close the Faraday cage before you put it in. And assume we're being monitored."

He dropped his voice. His breath had the cadence of a man walking quickly. "Someone's here. He's taller than I thought he'd be. He knows where my mother lives… in Rangpur, for fuck's sake."

That was Keaton. Six-four and as imposing as an all-knowing monolith.

I wasn't surprised my shadow investor had shown up, but I was alarmed. I'd assumed I'd be there to fend him off when the time came. Deeprak didn't have the tools or testosterone to keep Keaton away. "Stall him."

"Easy for you to say. Where did you find this guy?"

"Tor, where else?" I lied.

"Great. Fucking great." He paused. I felt everything he wanted to say because I knew him.

"He's not scary," I said.

Deeprak grunted.

It was my responsibility to say what needed saying with the knowledge that Harper might be listening. I had to take what I knew about her and decide what she cared about. "He's putting on an accent to scare you. Did he mention the MI6?"

"In passing."

"He's not British Intelligence." I couldn't leave it there. Deeprak and I didn't lie to each other. Not outright, though I'd omitted plenty. "Not officially, but..."

But what?

It was a bad time for omissions. And what scared Deeprak might also scare Harper. Not a bad thing.

"He knows people," I added. "He's done... work."

"Work?"

"Work. Just...look, that's Alpha Wolf, okay?"

"*OhGodohGod*. Taylor, what did you get me into?"

Before I could devise a smart answer that would both soothe Deeprak and scare Harper, the voice on the other end got deeper, with an English accent sharpened for maximum impact.

"Beeze Taylor, my little protégé. You're calling from a well-cloaked number."

"Apparently."

"Are you enjoying yourself?"

I sat on the floor with my heels angled against the wood. "Weather's great where I am."

"Where are you?"

"In the United States. I'm not running away with your money. You know that, right?"

"You're too much of a pussy to steal from me. It's your incompetence that surprises me."

"Let's skip the niceties, okay? I'm going to fix this. We're going to be ready for GreyHatC0n. Period."

"Your sidekick's typing something into what appears to be the only working machine in this useless little cage you have here. Could it be a hexadecimal string? How quaint."

Keaton was never the positive and supportive type, but he stood by me when things got rough and was loyal to a fault.

"It's up!" Deeprak cried from somewhere close. "It's booting!"

A cheer went up from the guys.

I didn't realize how tense I'd been until the anxiety dropped off me like a coat. It was over.

What was I going to do about Harper?

The question wasn't a new source of anxiety but a new source of possibility. My thoughts were unfiltered, unguarded. The walls between the compartments of my life fell away, and the impossible bled into the possible.

Take her with.

Stay here

Long-distance relationship
Hire her
Make her fucking president
New division
No sex
I'm the boss
Just business
All sex
Find her something with a friend
Do not let this girl out of your sight
You can have her
You win
You lose.

I could parse it all. Figure it out. Make a decision.

But from the other side of the phone, Deeprak shouted. "Fuck!"

"Oh, dear." Keaton sounded bemused, which I'd learned was a way to keep from getting angry.

I'd seen Keaton angry only once, when he'd found out the FBI flipped me on the credit card hack. I hadn't turned on him, but he'd lost an opportunity. It wasn't pretty.

"What's happening?" My unguarded moment was frozen into a minute.

In the background, Deeprak was shouting *fuck* over and over at a machine-gun tempo.

The phone dinged in my ear. A message.

"Take a look," Keaton said. "And let's be clear—I'm not leaving until I've protected my investment. And you. Even if it hurts."

The phone went quiet. No Deeprak. No white noise from the guys in the cage. Harper's phone received the photo. It was a picture of the cage's big screen. Black but for five words at the bottom.

Enter decryption key to boot:

She'd said she'd give it back in four sections. I should have believed her.

I didn't know how long I sat there with my head between my knees, trying not to cry like a little bitch.

XXVIII

In the end, it was my father's voice that got me off the floor. In my head, clear as day, he told me to stop feeling sorry for myself. No problem ever fixed itself, and this one wasn't any different.

I had her phone in my hands. What more did I need?

Trying to use the same hack I'd used on the Barrington guys, I came up against a solid security protocol. She'd walled off everything so she could make the call for me. I couldn't see what she had on there. I couldn't even see her phone book. I tried to get past it but wound up frustrated.

"Fuck this." I tossed the phone on the bed and got in the shower.

Harper had unlocked the QI4 boot loader. I didn't know what else I'd expected. The agreement was bigger than what we'd done. Teach her how to please a man, not stick a finger in her and make her come in three seconds.

The water wasn't hot enough. I turned the knob. I needed to burn this shit right out of me. Man up. She wanted to fuck. What was the problem? Why even hesitate? I'd used and been used by women since I was in my teens. I'd made deals and exchanged favors. Sure, I'd felt as if I had more power in those transactions, but so what? Harper and I were just another negotiation. This didn't have to be any different.

Which meant what? Three more turns in the bedroom? I could do that. Bang it out by tomorrow. So to speak.

I put on my jacket, brushed my hair, and got myself looking like a sore thumb in this shithole. But I was as far away from crying like a bitch as I'd ever been.

From the top of the stairs, I heard Catherine in the dining room, chatting with other women. Maybe the same crowd as had made dinner the night before. I didn't hear Harper's voice. I backed up and stood at the foot of the stairs to the third floor. The door was closed. I went up and pressed my ear to the wood. Nothing on the other side. Not a keystroke or a breath.

So.

A choice.

Was I Taylor or Beezleboy?

I'D BEEN ENROLLED in Poly for about a week when I realized I didn't fit in. Cliques had already been established, and rich kids were thick with them. Not every parent wanted every kid in their mansion, and not every kid wanted every other kid ogling their seven-hundred-dollar shoes.

I'd thought we were rich. But guess not.

Keeping my nose clean wasn't that hard. At that age, I couldn't get far enough away to see the pattern of class and cruelty. I was back to being a lonely kid, far away from my friends and my neighborhood. Out of my depth and out of my league. My dad told me to buck up, and my mother wouldn't get out of bed. She just cried on the days she didn't have the energy to fix everything.

I was sitting alone in the cafeteria when Keaton found me. He was two years older, but since I'd skipped third grade, he was only one year ahead in school. In maturity, he was at least decade older.

"You're in my JavaScript class." He shoveled down a plate full of string beans. He was the first vegetarian I'd ever met.

"Yeah. I like it." I'd been pushed ahead in math and science and was borderline remedial in reading.

"It's shit."

"But it's easy."

"You want to learn some real stuff, you come to my house on Saturday." He pushed a card across the table. Name. Number. Address on my side of town.

"I'll ask my mom."

He snorted. Didn't say another word to me for the rest of the meal.

XXIX

Hacking is about technology, coding, and knowing people. It's also about the mechanics of the world. Keaton taught me that with few words, and I lived it. I knew how a toilet worked. The physics of chairs. How to make moonshine and beer. The world became one giant hack, full of things that needed to be understood so they could be broken to my advantage.

Once her phone went to sleep, I couldn't reopen it. It was locked tight. Unlike Damon and the guys, she knew how to protect her device from attack.

But she wasn't around, and her system was just up a little flight of stairs.

There's not much to picking a lock once you get the feel for it. There had been an awl in the Barrington shed toolbox, and I had a tie clip I didn't care about, so I bent it open. After listening for movement and hearing nothing, I was in Harper's office in three minutes.

I closed the door behind me. The stairs wouldn't creak, but her windows faced the front of the house. I'd see her shitty Chevy coming up the driveway.

Tapping the spacebar did nothing. She'd shut her system down when she wasn't at it. Good girl.

I hit the power button. The floppy disk drive (yes, the floppy drive) croaked to life, and the fan spun. While it booted, I opened her drawers.

Hackers distrust computers for good reason. We're big fans of pencil and paper with their eternal compatibility and geographical security. Harper was no different. Her desk drawer was full of scraps of paper, analog office supplies, and wooden pencils. A girl after my own heart.

That being the case, I ignored what was inside the drawer in favor of what was hiding under it.

I pulled the drawer all the way out and felt along the bottom panel. Flat wood all the way to the back…until I came to a ridge. Something stuck in the seam between the bottom and back panels. I flicked it with my fingernail, felt it give a little, then got under it and slid out a little green notebook.

Sitting at her desk chair, I flipped through. Calculations and drawings for a tiny circuit I recognized as the poison pill she'd left in the monitor at QI4. Seeing the drawings, how she did it with a soldering iron and a cut board from a cheap cellphone, I started to sweat. My face got hot. Was it anger or embarrassment? Was it the fact that she'd done what anyone could have?

No.

This was special.

She's special.

And she did you a favor.

The pain in my chest should have decreased when I saw the details, but it got worse. The simplicity and scale of the design couldn't have been reverse engineered, and I had to give her credit. With very little to go on, she'd cracked open what I'd sealed tight.

What the notes didn't tell me was how she'd gotten into the monitors or how she'd gotten a signal past the Faraday cage. It didn't tell me where she'd hidden the transmitter that went into and out of the cage often enough to move pieces of data.

Most importantly, it didn't tell me why learning how to fuck like a pro was on her virgin radar.

I brushed my hand under my nose and smelled only soap. I'd washed the sweet scent of her off my fingers.

Taylor Brian Harden
023-56-1029 5/29/88
Camden, New Jersey.
Cooper's Poynt El. Grad '01.
Poly Preparatory HS. '05 MIT '05-'08

M-Julie Kips 078-11-1876
F-David Harden 173-63-1850
Mar 07/12/85, St Paul Episc.
923 N. Jordan Rd. 08103 856-365-2289

Ella Susan Harden 09/05/91
Cooper's Poynt El. Grad '05. Camden HS. '09
Rutgers MBA Bus Admin '13
084-55-6570 Mar. Quentin Mitchell
04/23/13 034-15-2230

Pets - Goldfish - Irving d. 6/99.
Sib. Husky - Jamesey d. 10/02

Fiona Messing '05 Donna Grettin '05
Brenda Svenka '06 Carolyn Borlyn '06
Katrina Yu '06 Franziska Popp '06

She was good. Organized. Tight and unemotional. After the social security numbers of my entire family, the addresses, the names and deaths of every pet I'd ever owned, the women in my life took up pages. Some of it had been culled from interviews and articles. Some from rumor. My family's socials had been pulled from some dark corner of the internet. The picture of me that had been stuck in the pages was on photo paper. Eighth grade graduation. Green cap and gown. An A+ nerd. I flipped to the back.

Grace: Let's hang out this summer. - Taylor

Grace Kensington hadn't taken even one of my calls in the months before high school, but a year ago, to support an opiate habit, she'd sold a bunch of Taylor Harden mementos on eBay in anticipation of my upcoming fame. Photos. Yearbooks. A Christmas card. I'd bid up the price of the yearbook with two fake accounts and bought it for far more than it would ever be worth.

I ripped the page out and stuck the picture back in. I didn't care about my info. None of it would get Harper anywhere. But she had too much on my family. She'd done her work a little too well.

I put the notebook back in the seam and put the drawer back in. I yanked on the bottom one. It was locked. I jimmied it open with a paper- clip from the top drawer.

The computer was finished booting. The monitor was still black, and the boot code flowed up the screen in greenish characters, ending in a C-prompt.

C:\

Old school DOS. Nothing fancy. Not a bell or a whistle in sight. It didn't ask for anything because the user was supposed to know what to enter. How many password fails before the system locked completely? Didn't matter. I could deal with that.

The bottom drawer was full of shit, but I knew what I was looking for. I looked under manila folders full of old bills, a sweater, a half-used box of pens, and found a floppy disk with BSD labeled in blue pen.

I stuck it in and rebooted, holding down F5 until…

Bypassing System Files…

And there it was. I checked the index, added a few programs to the config and autoexec files, and had access to everything. The machine hummed, waking up a more user-friendly OS.

I scanned the files and found one called QI4, but it was just a collection of articles about the system. A personal profile of Beezleboy. I found a subfolder with the incorporation papers and a deeper subfolder with two links to blogs about Alpha Wolf, aka Keaton Bridge.

Otherwise, nothing. Nothing hidden. Nothing protected. I knew where to look for shit a user didn't want found, and she had nothing. None of it. Either she was a genius or… well, there was nothing else to say. She'd left me with a lock I could pick and an empty computer.

Chrome hooked up to the web right away. Worked fine from up here, proving she was scrambling signal to isolate me.

Jesus. She was using an AOL address.

All right. This was pure bullshit.

I found Tor, the most popular browser for the dark web, and opened it. I went to the most recent page and got an eyeful of a Chaxxer conversa- tion between @TheWatsonette and @Flow_ro.

And it was filthy.

I scanned it quickly so I wouldn't get any harder than I already was.

/Your pussy is so wet. You squirt into my mouth when you come./

/I can take your whole cock down my throat. Shove it all the way in until I'm kissing your balls./

/Spread your cunt apart and.../

/I'm ready for you, my Prince./

Oh, fuck that. I couldn't read another word, and so much for not getting a hard-on. I rode a wave of jealousy, then a swell of rage, into a trench of sorrow. She wasn't completely innocent, but she didn't talk like this to me. Not that I would have minded. But I was confused. I couldn't fit all of it into my head. My finger inside her. Her eager sexual authentic- ity. The membrane gently squeezing my finger.

Sitting up straight, I pretended I was reading someone else's account. Some strange woman I'd hacked. Someone I didn't care about.

/You like when I call you a whore./

The chat ended there. She'd left. Which was good because I wasn't reading another word. My pretense shattered.

What was she doing? She didn't have to talk to this @Flow_ro guy, if it was even a guy. Was she looking for achievement points to please him? Was that what this was about?

The reality I had lived with for the past few days was shaken. I had to see her. Touch base. Make sure she was still Harper. Not quite innocent, not quite jaded. Dirty talker, maybe. Ididn't know.

Why didn't I know?

Why did it matter?

It mattered. I didn't have to know why. I only had to know what *was*. Was the cat alive or dead? Why it was in a fucking box was irrelevant.

Voices came from the second floor. I wasn't ready to admit I'd broken into Harper's room, so I shut down and tiptoed to the door, hearing a male and female voice.

"Where is he?" The guy sounded a little pissed off.

"Upstairs. Johnny, leave it be."

"What's going on with him?"

"What do you mean?" Now Catherine seemed a little pissed herself.

"Cath, don't pretend you're not a grown woman."

"Don't ask questions I don't want to answer."

"You want her getting hurt?"

"It's time for you to go."

The voices became indistinguishable murmurs, then the two of them appeared in the front drive, stopping by Johnny's truck to talk. He had on his yellow polo shirt and a blue zip-front jacket that hid his tattoos.

My ride was in the shop, and I was in the middle of nowhere. Was I going to sit around and wait for Harper to come back? Read more of her dirty talk? Putter around the kitchen?

No. None of it.

I slid onto the stairwell and used my tie clip to lock the deadbolt behind me, then I took the stairs two at a time until I was in the front yard. Catherine was coming back toward the house, and the truck was pulling forward.

"Johnny!" I knocked on the back of the truck, and he stopped. Leaning into the passenger side window, I asked, "You going to the distro center?"

"Yeah."

"Is Harper there?"

"I think she's filling in a shift."

"Can you take me?"

He leaned back as if he was trying to see the entirety of what I wanted. "She's working."

"I'll wait." I pulled the handle, but the door was locked. "Look, I don't have a phone. I don't have a car. So if that means I sit and wait, I sit and wait."

Johnny glanced at the clock then clacked the locks open. "I'm not going to be late on your account. She'll likely be on break in an hour."

I climbed in. The car smelled of dog and baby powder. Johnny turned onto the narrow highway. Pictures of children and young adults hung from the visors and rearview.

"Your kids?" I asked.

"What do you want with Harper?"

"Nothing."

Johnny huffed and got onto the interstate, speeding up to the limit. "Your lie stinks worse than a dog's asshole."

"I'm trying to not get my fingers broken, if you don't mind."

"She told you about that, did she?"

"You didn't ask for my opinion but—"

"Sure didn't."

"She's a grown woman. She can make her own decisions."

He didn't talk for a while, and I had nowhere to go with my statement. The long, yellow distro center came up on the right like a giant hunk of cheese in a puddle of parking lot. We slid off the exit toward it. A line of yellow trucks steered onto the interstate like sticks of butter on a conveyor belt.

"I'm not saying I did everything right in my life," Johnny said. "But if I see a bonehead like Damon trying to make time with her, or that asshole Lawrence, you can trust me one thing: I'm stopping it."

He turned down a wide driveway. Two food trucks were parked on either side of the road. One with tacos, one with burgers and fries. Plastic tables and chairs ringed the backs of the trucks. Beyond them stood the yellow guard tower.

Johnny stopped behind the taco truck and unlocked the doors. "I'll tell her you're here."

I opened my door but didn't leave. Not yet. "I don't need your permission, so I'm not asking. I'm telling you that Harper and I might or might not do whatever the fuck we want."

He leaned over so far I could smell lunch on his breath. My fingers ached. I bent them into fists.

"If you do," Johnny said, "you better get her out of this shithole."

Was he demanding I marry her? Jesus, I just wanted QI4 back in one piece and maybe a few spins around her body to get it. I couldn't promise anything except that I *wouldn't* make her or Barrington my responsibility.

"She'll do what she wants." That seemed noncommittal enough while still being true. She would do what she wanted no matter how fast I ran or how far behind I tried to leave her.

XXX

By my calculations, her lunch hour should have fallen around 6:40 p.m.

I sat. I stood. I paced. I kicked cans. A shift came out, lined up, and went back in. I helped the guys behind the taco truck haul the garbage onto a pickup. They gave me a container of pozole and a little white plastic spoon to eat it with.

A horn hooted from the yellow building. For a few seconds, nothing happened, then people started streaming toward the trucks.

Reggie came out in his yellow polo with an ID card handing from a lanyard. I sat with him and a few other guys in yellow shirts and lanyards, talking about baseball and this dude Donnie's garage renovation. When their half hour lunch was up, Reg said he'd tell Harper I was waiting for her, as if it was totally normal for a guy to hang out in the middle of nowhere, waiting for a girl. They gave me a wave and went back through the gate, and I waited alone again.

I checked the time on my wrist, but my watch was gone. I was nowhere, never, without a buoy to navigate to. The only thing to do was wait.

Keaton had led me down to his parents' basement and snapped the deadbolt behind him. We were in a concrete room with a washer and dryer, hanging shirts, and an ironing board. The circuit breaker door didn't close all the way.

"What's your dad do for a living?" I asked.

"Mossad." He smiled a little. "CIA sometimes. He's a quadruple agent. A freelancer."

The look on my face must have been pure horror because that was what I felt. We were red, white, and blue; apple pie; *e pluribus unum*.

Keaton laughed and clapped me on the shoulder. "I'm joking. Man, you should see yourself."

He brought me through the laundry room to his inner sanctum.

"Where's your accent from?" I changed the subject.

"Mother Russia," he said with a thick Russian growl. "I have as many accents as I want."

The inner room was finished with grey industrial carpet and a black leather couch. A huge flat-screen with gaming cubes sat on one side of the room, and on the other was a bank of computers.

"Donna Breckenridge," he said. "Let's talk."

I shrugged, leaning over to look at the ASCII chart pinned to the wall. "Nothing to talk about. We held hands, then she pretended I didn't exist."

"And Ryder nailed you at lunch."

I'd gotten a nasty "accidental" elbow in the ribs that still smarted.

"Unrelated." I ran my fingers over the keyboards. We had computers at school, but my parents couldn't afford to get me a laptop of my own.

"False." He pulled out a chair. "Women are all about getting you to do things. Ryder's in my grade. He's been dating Donna and talking to Jennifer Paige. Donna sees him talking to Jennifer and uses you to make him jealous. Ryder's a dumb twat, so he did what dumb twats do. Gets on you to prove a point. Jennifer gets scared. Donna's vindicated. Ryder's back in her pocket. Done."

He was right. I knew it in my guts.

"You want to get her back?" Keaton asked.

I shrugged. "She's not that hot."

"I don't mean 'get her back.' I mean payback."

My heart hadn't been shattered or anything, but I was curious about what he had on his mind. "Sure?"

"Have you ever heard of the dark web?" He flipped on a computer. The hard drive whirred and clicked.

"No."

"Sit down. You're going to love this shit."

I sat down, and he taught me everything. I loved that shit.

Between the yellow shirt and the direct sunlight, her polychrome irises seemed paler. Her hair had escaped the rubber band. The flyaways looked like gold solder wire.

"What do you want, miss?" I asked nonchalantly from my new home in a white plastic chair. "This is my spot."

"Lunch?"

"I've had the pozole and a burger. Both were good. I noticed the Hispanic people eat at the burger truck by about the same ratio as the taco truck. White people are about a seventy-three / twenty-seven in favor of the burgers. I've seen one black person all day."

"What did they eat?"

"She brought her lunch."

"Can't blame her. This stuff starts to wear on you."

"What are you having?" I asked, standing. "I'll buy."

She sighed. "A burger, I guess. I'm not feeling tacos."

"Tacos? Fuck that. They have a menu that takes up the entire side of the truck. Have you tried the pozole?"

"I don't even know what that is."

I shook my head and leaned down so I could whisper in her ear. "How to fuck is the least of what you need to learn."

She elbowed me. "You're such a jerk. You still haven't apologized for freaking out."

"I'm sorry." I led her to the taco truck. "Now that you know the social norms and I know your fragile condition, I'm sure it won't happen again."

"I guess I can't blame you. I'm a statistical outlier."

"I love it when you talk dirty."

I ordered her the pozole, but I wasn't thinking about statistics or soup. I was thinking about the dirty talk I'd seen on her Chaxxer account, which I wasn't supposed to know about since I'd boot loaded her machine and broken into her room like a thief.

She took the soup with both hands, and we sat down.

"Thanks for the boot loader decryption," I said. "And your phone."

I slid it over to her. She let it sit. Her breath rippled the surface of the soup as she blew on it. "Have you ever heard of the Stockholm Syndrome? It's when a hostage sympathizes with their captor."

"Never had it." I swirled the straw in my hot horchata. "Stockholm's cool though."

"You have it bad. You're thanking me for giving you back what's yours and apologizing for sex I made you have."

"You aren't making me do anything."

She spun her soup around the container, avoiding eye contact.

I bent over the table, trying to get her attention. "Harper?"

She put her spoon on a napkin. A pool of red soup soaked into it. "I know you want to think you have control, but I am making you."

"Does that get you off or something?"

"Not really."

The hooting from the factory whistle echoed over the plain. Break over.

"Shit," Harper exclaimed before shoveling her soup. "I have to get back." She spoke between gulps.

Our time was over, and I remembered why I'd come.

Dozens of yellow shirts lined up to return to work. No one paid any attention to Harper and me at the little table. Now was the time to find out if The Watsonette was an alternate personality or a part of her I hadn't dug up yet.

"Tell me something," I started.

She answered with an *mmm* between mouthfuls.

"How are you going to suck my cock later?"

She froze, swallowed, glanced around for eavesdroppers. I shook my horchata, looking at her over the edge of the Styrofoam cup.

"I... uh..." She cleared her throat. Folded her bottom lip.

"You know why guys like to watch a good sucking? It's our dirtiest part going into a girl's beautiful mouth. She's letting it happen. Making it happen. My dick in her fucking mouth."

She put her pozole down and looked at her phone. She was going to have to run to get to work in time. I needed a dirty phrase or two that matched what I'd seen on Chaxxer, but she tapped on her phone with one hand and folded her lip with the other.

I wasn't fooled by her attention to the phone. She heard every word.

"I'm going to watch," I continued. "As my dick disappears into your face."

She put the phone on the table, glass down. "I've been practicing," she said, eyes finally on me. "With things. My fingers. A Coke bottle. I can get your whole cock down my throat until I'm kissing your balls."

There she was. The Watsonette.

My next move was obvious. Call her a whore and see how she reacted. Did she leave the chat or hang around?

But I couldn't. The word wouldn't leave my lips. "You'd better get back to work."

She tapped the phone with her nails. "I just told my supervisor I ate bad pozole and I'm not coming back."

"And now you want me to put my dick in that dirty mouth?"

"Yeah."

The way everything she said made me smile had to be the Stockholm Syndrome.

"I like you, Harper."

She didn't say anything. Her eyes were huge. Her demeanor was calm, and she didn't say a fucking word.

"I want to know why. Of everything, why this?"

"Ever have a goal, Taylor?"

"Don't get me started."

"I have a goal, and it's through you. You'll live. You'll walk away and be fine."

"And you? Will you be fine?"

She smirked from one side of her face. "Oral and you get the object code back."

"You tell me how you did it. Then you suck my dick, then the decryption code."

I couldn't believe what I was saying. It was all win for me, but I felt as though I'd never bargained for anything as hard in my life.

She leaned back in her chair and crossed her arms and legs. "I like you too."

I crossed my arms, leaned back on cheap plastic chair legs, and crossed my ankles. Now we were fully crossed. No one was going anywhere.

"How did you transmit signal out of the cage?"

She shook her head slowly and stood. "That's not on the table." Scooping up her soup container and my empty cup, she dumped them into the garbage. "Wait here."

She went past the gate and into the parking lot, showing her ID card to the guard as she went. I was alone again. Her Chevy came out of the gate soon after, and I got into the passenger seat. She drove onto the interstate.

"The poison pill had an antenna," I said. "Too short to send far."

"Didn't have to."

I hadn't expected to hear that. As if she could see my discomfort, a smile twitched her lips. Hackers loved nothing more than recounting an exploit. As much as I didn't want to give her the satisfaction of telling me how she'd done it, I needed to know.

"Just tell me. If your exploit isn't part of the deal, there's no deal," I said.

"I never met a guy so unwilling to get a blow job."

"I never met a woman who wanted to give one for your reasons. If I can even figure your reasons out. Which I can't."

She got off the interstate and took a couple more left turns than rights. I was sure she was trying to disorient me, but that was easier said than done. Eventually, she pulled past an opening between two beige-painted cinderblock walls, past rusted hinges and a couple of wrought-iron strips bent into the shapes of an alien alphabet.

It was a place of weird contradictions, like a toy graveyard or an abandoned arcade. Wood rectangles the size of my railroad apartment in San Jose were set in a grid. Brightly painted cracked flowerpots, broken swing sets, a brand new but disconnected screen door. A twist of lead pipes coming out of the ground. One had a valve and spigot.

The fact that I couldn't see it right away after my father taking me to so many job sites was embarrassing. It wasn't until we slowly passed a tractor trailer wheel filled with thriving tomato plants that my brain put the pieces together. We were in an abandoned trailer park.

She stopped in the spotty shade of a tree and put the car in park. "This was my father's last project."

"Looks like it didn't go so well."

"He made money. Trust me."

We got out. It was chilly, fall weather. The trees' leaves hung like laundry from the branches. When the wind blew, dozens fell like brown scrap paper.

She spun a few feet from me and held out her arms. "Ready?"

I wasn't. My dick was, but I wasn't. "How did you get signal out of the cage?"

"Are you sure you want to know?"

"Very sure."

"Then you'll show me?"

"How to suck a dick better than a Coke bottle? Yeah, Harper. It'll be my pleasure."

She looked down slightly. Bit her lip. Prelude to a lie? Or a closely held truth? "You want a lot for not much."

"I want everything. And I'll pay everything for it."

"Yes. You will." She whispered it like a filthy promise.

Fuck her.

Fuck her for being so in control. Fuck her for being so beautiful and intense. Fuck her for fucking up everything. Fuck her for scaring the shit out of me.

I took her by the back of the head and kissed her, not to tell her how much my body wanted to fuck her or how much I needed to get control of this negotiation, relationship, deal, plan, whatever, but to decode her. In the kiss, my anxiety was soothed. Her lips were honest. The groan in her throat told me she had less control than she thought. Her tongue yielded.

She had barriers, but in that kiss, she told me she wasn't a stone monolith.

When I pulled away, she gasped.

"I could spend the entire day kissing you," I said. "But that's not why you brought me here, is it?"

"No. It's not."

Was she disappointed? Yes. I decoded that much as well, and I relished it. I had to do what she wanted. I didn't have to pretend to like it, even if I wouldn't have been pretending.

I undid my belt. "You're going to suck my dick. You're going to take the entire thing down your throat, and you're going to swallow whateverI give you. Is that what you're after?"

"I want to learn how to do it right."

"Don't worry about that. You're going to learn."

Opening my pants, I got my dick out. I was so hard it hurt. She knelt in front of me, knees in the dirt. When she laid her eyes on my cock, I thought I'd burst right there. I turned her chin upward.

"Open your mouth."

She did, just enough to fold the crease in her lower lip.

"So you know how to open your throat?"

"Ahh." She made the noise people made for the doctor.

I put two fingers on her tongue. "Press the back of your tongue down while doing that." I slid my fingers down her throat as far as I could.

Her eyes scrunched shut. Her stomach heaved twice.

"Hold it down," I said, and she got control of her gag reflex. "You really have been studying." I took my fingers out, letting her breathe.

"Thank you."

Why didn't I get the dirty talk? Why did Flow Prince or whatever get it and all I got were the innocent polychrome eyes?

"Tell me what you're going to do."

She opened her mouth and slapped it shut. "I..."

"Yes?"

"I'm going to suck your dick. I hope you like it."

I laughed. Who could help it? Her courtesy was disarming even when it made me question everything I'd seen on her screen. Even when she was holding me hostage.

"Assume I'll like it and say it again. Say it..." I paused, realizing the right way to approach it. "Say what you'd say if you were typing it and you couldn't see me."

She put her hands on the backs of my thighs, bringing me that much closer to her mouth. "I'm going to suck you until you come in my mouth."

"You know how a news reporter says things?"

"Am I too much like that?"

She was, but complaining would get me nowhere.

"Do this. Say it real seductive. Too seductive."

She tilted her head and puckered her lips, letting saccharine syrup mixed with heavy musk fall from them. "I'm going to suck your dick."

I held my laugh in the back of my throat. "Now do the news reporting with twenty percent of that second try."

"I'm pretty sure you know what I'm going to do already."

"You want to learn to do this or not?"

Deep breath. Eyes closed. She put her hand around the base of my cock and opened her eyes to look up at me. "Fuck my face, Taylor. Fuck it hard."

My dick throbbed in her hand, and for a moment, just a moment, I lost the ability to speak. I had to clear my throat before I responded. "Gold star."

"Yay."

Yay? Who made this woman? What cruel god put together the sweetest traits with this level of joyful filth? I'd never met anyone like her. I didn't know if I'd said that to myself before, but I was sure I'd say it again. She was a complete original.

"Put your lips at the tip."

She did what I told her.

"Lick the drop off. The tip and behind it, right here? That's the most sensitive part. Now put your hand around the base. Open. Say *ah* and press the back of your tongue down. Right. Breathe through your nose as long as you can. Open. Good."

I pushed her head down, and she bobbed on me. Fuck. I usually guided a girl and let her guide me, but this was ridiculously hot. She took every instruction, every correction, as if her job was at stake.

"Pull away when you need a break. Lick the sides and start again."

She did and took me deep again. A blade of hair stuck between her lips and my dick. I pulled it away and tucked it behind her ear. I could come in that hair. I could blow into her mouth the next time the wind blew the leaves down, but that would give her all the control, and I had something to prove.

I wanted information more than I wanted an orgasm.

"Put your hand around it." I nudged her head away, and she looked up at me with my dick in her fist. "The signal. How did it transmit?"

"You want to know now?"

"Now."

She rolled her eyes and licked the taste of my cock off her lips. "The poison pill transmitted to an object that went in and out of the cage. A little bit at a time. When the object was outside the cage, it transmitted to a Pwnie Express item in reception."

"We found it. The power strip."

"Right. It had a router in it." She held up two fingers to show me the miniscule size of the router. "It transmitted back to the object and brought information back. Once I figured out how to lock you out, and when *Wired* was coming, I told the Pwnie Express when to encrypt and how to decrypt, and it told the object." She moved closer, and I couldn't help but touch her face. She was a work of art. Her hack was as gorgeous as she was, and both made me angry and humbled at the same time. "The object went in and told your system what to do."

I stroked her cheek with my left hand and grabbed a fistful of hair with my right. "What's the object?"

She put her hand over my left wrist and held it. "Not yet." Defying the force of my hand, she pushed toward me, flicking her tongue over the head of my aching cock.

"Tell me, or I'm making you swallow."

She answered by opening her mouth, and I replied by fucking it.

"I'm going to come," I gasped. But I had to teach her, not just come in her mouth. "A guy should tell you. And you don't have to swallow for anyone else, but for me, because you won't tell me the… you take—"

Too late. I blew it all, and she took it. When I looked down, her face was knotted.

"Swallow."

She closed her mouth and swallowed, shaking her head like a puppy. "Ugh, I hope I can get used to that."

I ran my thumb along the corner of her mouth, wiping the moisture away. She was lovely. "Why would you have to? Who are you doing this for?"

"Myself."

"Really?"

She straightened her hair, and in the instant before she got on her feet, I felt her desire to answer fully and completely. Tell everything. A moment of weakness, maybe. Or I could have been misreading her.

By the time she stood, the moment was gone, and she was a hacker, a terrorist, my captor, and she was withholding information I needed.

"The decryption code." I put my dick back in my pants. It was still sensitive.

She folded her bottom lip, deep in thought. I waited. Zipped. Buttoned. Tucked.

I didn't want to be too transactional. I didn't want to come in her mouth and ask for payment. Maybe I was a bigger pussy than I thought. She was the one who had turned a blow job into a negotiation.

"I didn't expect you to come here," she finally said.

"And?" I fastened my belt. Was my voice hard? Sharp? Too bad. This was business.

"I need to generate it. Let's get back."

We got in the car, and she took off, eating road like a whale eats krill.

"We skipped a hand job," I said. "We need to go back and get that done."

She perked up. "You're halfway there."

"Yeah."

She was right. I was halfway. The point of no return. Too far away from home to quit and too much a stranger in Barrington for comfort.

XXXI

When we got back, she ran upstairs without a "give me a minute" or a "wait here." I was like a piece of furniture in a furniture-bare house. My fingers twitched. I wanted to talk to Deeprak, touch that old life, connect to the person I knew I was. Even if it meant being reminded of my failure to protect my work, I wanted to be the person I'd spent a decadebuilding.

I made coffee and brought up two mugs.

Harper's door at the top of the stairs was open. Was it an invitation?

"Harper?" I put my foot on the bottom step.

She appeared in the doorway above me. "You were in here."

"I was."

"Like what you saw?"

Was she talking about breaking into her room? Or opening her computers? Or seeing her notebook?

"Maybe."

"Coming up here is cheating."

I took a step up and put my next foot above. "Really? You didn't tell me that."

"I shouldn't have to. I can't let this slide."

"What does that mean?" I could smell her. Smell the room. Feel the pressure of her presence on my dick. I put the cups on the bottom stepand started up to her.

"You're going to forfeit getting the decryption today."

"What?" I froze halfway up.

"Play fair."

"I do. You—"

I had some choice words for her as I bounded up the rest of the stairs. Just as I got to the top, she slammed the door in my face. The lock clapped shut.

"Do not fuck with me, Taylor." The door muffled her voice. She was right on the other side. Inches away.

"I'm a hacker. I hack. I get into things. You can't put this door at the top of the stairs and think for a minute I'm not going to come uphere."

"What did you see?"

I didn't want her to know. I had no idea what kind of leverage I had, and until I did, I wasn't telling her anything. "Your room. Again."

"And?"

How much was I willing to give? "The elastic on your panties is wearing out."

"What *else,* Taylor? Do not even think of lying to me."

Do not even think of lying to me? Who fell back on that?

Someone who was fishing, that was who. I was the one with leverage. She had no idea what I'd seen, and she wanted me to tell her.

And the fact was she wanted something from me that I didn't have to give her. So she could hang on to the Harperware decryption for now. At some point, she was going to want me to teach her something else.

"If you need me," I said, stepping down one, "I'll be around."

I hopped down the stairs without hearing a reply.

XXXII

I looked over the balcony at the thorn bed. My phone didn't light up, and I didn't hear it. Even if I got it out of that mess, it would be useless.

I went through the other doors, to the master suite. Flicking the light on, I craned my neck to look at the ceiling mural with its vignette of pink flowers. It looked Victorian enough, but in the lines, I could see a touch of 1980s.

Catherine came to the doorway with a tray. "You didn't come down to dinner."

"I forgot. Sorry."

"Barnard came by to see how you were getting on."

"Barnard?"

"A large gentleman." There were no tables. She put the tray on the floor. "Fuzzy hair."

"Butthead?"

"If you must."

Well, I'd certainly stepped in it. That was what I got for not asking his real name.

"And Orrin called. He said to tell you the battery's coming in the morning. Your car will be ready."

A car. So simple, yet… everything. A car equaled an option. I'd been short on options until just then.

Catherine pulled her cardigan around herself. "We never fixed this room because I didn't want the ceiling ruined."

"You can fix the mycelium without ruining the ceiling. It's tin."

She looked at it dreamily. Harper was her exact opposite. Catherine had rounded edges and a soft voice. Her sister's edges were going to gut me.

"This was my room," she said. "Daddy gave it to me when he and Mother moved to separate rooms. Those flowers? He had them put in for me when I was having a hard time. Look, over here." She pointed toward a dim corner.

I looked at what she told me but didn't see what she saw.

"Those open roses with the leaves up like that? In a V?" she said.

"Yes. It's..." Weird? Off? Not flower-like?

"That's Harper."

I got up on tiptoes as if the extra two inches would help.

"She was always running around," Catherine continued.

I could see it when I stopped trying to make it a flower in my head. The petals of the rose next to her made a skirt that flowed in the wind, and the beige center of the flower was a little girl's face. The more I looked at it, the more it looked like Harper.

"And I was always trying to get her to stay still and read or pay attention or do anything."

The leaves of the rose next to Harper were around her sister, and looking at it, squinting, I saw Catherine's face in the details. She stopped looking up, and I did as well. We regarded each other in the yellow light.

"A lot of things happened in this room. A lot of tears under these flowers," she said.

"I know why you don't want it ruined."

"Do I bother you at night? People say they can hear me cry all over the house."

"I haven't heard it," I lied.

"I keep saying I'll stop."

"It's your house."

"I'm not upset about not having anything left. Or the conditions I live in, compared to what it was. I wish I'd lost it all sooner."

"Why?"

"The thing about money, Mr. Harden, is that it burdens you with expectations. You get this impression that everything you do matters to other people. And it's not true. Everything doesn't matter. Only some things matter, and those things have to be attended. But the rest?" She shook her head. "I'm being cryptic. I loved a boy who didn't have any money. My parents, and this was the only thing they ever agreed on, they found this unacceptable. He disappeared."

"Just disappeared?"

"Without a word."

"Is he alive?"

She shrugged. "I don't know. My father had the ceiling done to cheer me up."

I smiled. I couldn't help it. The irony was unavoidable.

Catherine saw it too. She smiled and waved as if swatting the entire thing away. "I should have taken it down, but I still like it."

"You're a masochist."

"I am. Now. Your soup is getting cold. When you're done, leave the tray in the hall."

"I can—"

"No arguments."

I tried to argue anyway, but she left with a wave.

I didn't eat much. My brain was calculating.

I wasn't halfway home. Not without the second decryption code. Was it easier for me to get the Caddy, go back to California, and deal with my shit? If she wasn't going to shell out what she'd promised, I didn't have to hang around and provide services.

And the ability to leave gave me leverage. I could leave, or I could stay, depending on whether or not she produced the decryption code.

But I was leaving.

The decision to go back to the familiar calmed me until I fell asleep.

XXXIII

In the morning, Harper was nowhere to be found. There wasn't a peep from behind the locked door, but there was a new lock. As if that could stop me.

I'd pick it when I had something to look for in there. I'd pick it so hard it would blow out the jamb.

Catherine was AWOL. Everyone was. The house was cold and empty. I made myself a peanut butter and jelly sandwich and looked out the back window, onto the thorn garden.

A dog barked from the front. I shoved the last bite in my mouth and met Percy on the porch. Orrin got out of his truck.

"Found you," he said. "Your phone's dead."

"Yeah. I know."

"Harper said you were sleeping."

Percy licked my fingers then stuck his nose in my ass.

I pulled him away and stroked his neck. "Where is she?"

"Over at the glass works." He pointed toward the backyard and over the horizon.

It didn't matter where she was anyway. Not at all.

"I'll get my stuff," I said. "And I'll get the car out of your shop right away."

"Came to tell you about the car. The battery was four hundred dollars."

"No problem, I—"

"Then the damn rental car company came and towed it. I didn't have a chance to even get the battery out of the box. And I can't return it. Fucking *policies*."

I was cut off from another route the fuck out of Barrington, and this dude was worried about a few hundred bucks. "I need a ride to the airport. I'll give you the four hundred for the battery and another four hundred for the lift."

Percy barked as if he thought it was a great deal.

"I gotta open up the shop."

"Later, then." Maybe I sounded desperate. I didn't care.

"Might be able to get you a ride tomorrow. Everyone's over at the works, scrubbing down for Fitz. Word is he's coming around to look into buying the works building."

Harper had mentioned him a million years ago, on the roof of that same factory. I knew him I could call him up and tell him the citizens of Barrington were good people but shithouse crazy, if I had a phone.

"I have to go." I'd already turned back toward the house. I was distracted. My brain was sorting through puzzle pieces. Harper. Fitz. Barrington. QI4. *Silicon Valley Magazine*'s "Most Eligible Tycoon of the Year."

"I'll come around tomorrow," Orrin called behind me.

"Sure." I didn't know if he heard my mumbling. Nothing was clicking, but I knew the pieces fit.

I went right through the house and upstairs to pack.

Past the river reeds, maybe a quarter mile back, I could see the top of the factory. Men were up there, five, maybe six, moving in and out of sight. They weren't meandering or fucking around. They had a purpose to their movements.

I went back up to my room, which had a better angle on the factory. The people on the roof moved slowly, bent down, got up. Harper had spray painted code lines up there. A coded message that put me on notice. I was going to be humiliated.

I smiled. I couldn't help it. Fuck her. I wasn't giving her an inch I didn't have to. I was going to get my fucking boot decryption and be done with her.

A female form walked onto the roof. Long, wavy hair, too far away to discern blond from brunette, but her arm went up and touched her face. I could see her, in my mind's eye, folding the crease in her bottom lip.

XXXIV

The factory wasn't far as the crow flew. I had no idea how to get across the river or what other manmade barriers were between the Barrington mansion and Barrington Glass Works. Without satellite or GPS, there was only one way to find out.

Past the bed of thorns, patches of pines huddled amidst a grass flat. From above, I hadn't noticed how well tended they were, with moats of dirt around the base of each trunk. Spring birds chirped. Cicadas screeched. The sky above was a huge dome broken by the receding mansion and the trees I passed. I came to the tall reeds, which were taller than they'd looked from above. A dirt path opened up, and the sound of the trickling river joined the sounds of birds and insects behind me.

There was a smell. A not very river-ish smell. The reeds closed around the path until it was a foot wide, then it crooked hard right, then hard left, onto a wooden bridge.

The river was the source of the smell. I pulled my hood around to my face and covered my nose. A white sign on a rusted chain swung across the entrance to the bridge.

CONTAMINATION ADVISORY
Avoid contact with soil and river sediment. Use soap and water to wash river water and sediment off skin completely.
United States Environmental Protection Agency.

I wasn't going back to the mansion. Fuck that. I went under the chain and crossed. The bridge itself was on concrete pilings, and the whole thing was in pretty good shape. The painted metal rail was worn at the top where people would put their hands, but I kept my hands in my pockets. The wood boards creaked but were solid enough.

The river looked like any other river, not that I'd seen hundreds. The water wasn't brown, and there wasn't a ton of garbage floating in it. The reeds grew tall. A weeping willow bent over the stream on the other side. The tree didn't look good. Otherwise, there was just the smell.

A four-foot-wide corrugated metal pipe ended at the shore. It was dry inside. Whatever had flowed from the factory into the river no longer flowed, but the toxicity remained.

I ducked under the chain barrier on the other side. It had the same contamination warning.

So much for that.

The factory was in my sightline. The graffiti had been reduced to no more than a tinge of color. Some was a light blue wash that matched Harper's fingernails from a few days before. Cars were parked on both sides of the chain link, and the gate was open. Huge twenty-foot dumpsters were lined up against the walls. I jumped when glass crashed from inside one.

A man waved to me from a window-sized opening on the third floor. "Sorry!"

I waved back and went in the same door Harper and I had used last time.

Where there had been desolation before, the place was abuzz the second time. People everywhere. Talking in groups, pushing brooms, dragging black plastic bags, wiping down the walls. I waved to Reggie and Kyle, who were throwing garbage out the window, then I ran up the stairs, two at a time, to where I'd last seen Harper's figure against the sky.

She pushed a broom across the roof, moving red-stained liquid into the drain. She stopped, moved the broom quickly over an area to scrub, then pushed again.

"You're too good to push a broom all day."

"Wrong." She didn't look at me. "No one's too good to push a broom." She swept hard, sending a wave of frothy red water away. The semi- circle right behind the broom was bare for a split second, and I could see how much her work had faded.

I was in her way. The red water lapped against my shoes. They'd be ruined. She pushed the bristles against my toes, and still, I didn't budge.

"Taylor." She leaned on the handle.

"What?" I crossed my arms.

"You're in the way of the drain."

"I'm leaving today."

She tapped the bristles on the tar, keeping her eyes on the little red splashes. "How?"

"I can still get a cab. I can get a lift. I can walk thirty miles to the next train station. You can have one of these guys tie me down. I know at least some of them are in on it. I don't know who, but it doesn't matter. You're trying to brainwash me for when Fitz shows. I don't know if you're going to play on our relationship or try to get in his jock. But I'm out. I have enough problems. I'll get past your lockdown on my own."

She leaned on the handle again, finally making eye contact. "It's just a mess in here."

"Who'd buy it in this condition? Not a guy like Fitz. He's an OCD case about business. He'd only buy a spotless factory in a spotless town."

"So? We read up. We're smarter than we get credit for."

"Good on you. You don't need me anymore." I got out of her way and headed for the door.

"I don't want to sell QI4," she said, and I had to stop to listen to the rest. She knew how to keep me, that was for sure. "It's wrong to sell it." She kept sweeping. "It's one thing to lock it and make you pay to unlock it, but selling it to someone else is just wrong. But I will. I can get a lot of money for it."

Keeping cool was probably the hardest thing I'd ever done. I could barely stand the thought of my code being inaccessible. The thought of it going to someone else made my hands hot. "You do what you have to."

"Bummer though."

"You're going to have to figure out the 'maintenance' part that's so important to you."

"You're bluffing."

She was in control. I'd forgotten that as a kind of survival instinct, but when she reminded me, I was hell-bent on not showing her how much it bothered me.

"Maybe. But you're in a world of shit yourself." The bite in my voice didn't make me sound tough. It sounded like overcompensation. A presentation of aggression from a man with no power. If I'd felt in control coming across the river, I didn't on the factory roof.

"If you finish the job with me, you'll get your system back."

"You already broke one promise."

The last of the red water went down the drain. On the west side of the building, old furniture and garbage crashed to the ground amid the grunts and shouts of the men hauling it out.

"I don't know why I'm here," I said. "I don't understand what you want or why. Why the sexual favors?"

She picked up a heavy bucket that sloshed when lifted. "They're for me, okay? Everything I told you is true. The reasons you were brought here. All true. But the sex stuff?" She went to another patch of graffiti on the ground and plopped the bucket down. "That's for me. I got everything I could out of online bullshit. Stupid dirty talk with strangers. I'm done with it. So yeah, there's a little revenge in there, but that's the deal."

"You know, when you lie, your nose looks like it points up a little more."

She dunked the broom in the bucket and scrubbed the spray paint. "Stay or leave. Let me know what you decide."

She gave no guarantees, no promises, offering around a deal so ambiguous and unenforceable I didn't know where I stood from one minute to the next. I couldn't measure her. She was movement, not mass. All options and potentialities, but no answers.

The sky over the roof was a dome of clear blue, like a ceiling with limits. It promised that if you went high enough, you'd touch it. It lied. It was an illusion of the finite.

I got off the roof before it pressed me into a dot.

XXXV

"You know what they're doing to you? They're setting you up. They're telling you your life might be shit, but at least you're not him. And you, they're telling you he's out to get you. And you two fucking idiots believe it."

I heard Johnny's voice echo through the second floor as I came down the metal steps. He had a hand on a shovel by a pile of debris, and the other hand pointed at one of the Hispanic dudes I'd seen at the lunch area, while he yelled at a guy with a yellow bandana.

"I'm so sick of your paranoid bullshit." Bandana pushed Johnny's shoulder. I'd met him the same night I'd met Johnny, but his name escaped me.

"Who benefits? Ask yourself." Johnny was undeterred. "You? Have you benefitted one bit from thinking you're better than Florencio?" He pointed at the Hispanic dude. "Cos when you do that, he's not gonna rise up with you and crush them fuckers at the bank. He's gonna come against you. You dumb shits are too busy fighting between yourselves to fight together."

"I can't stand this *pendejo*." Florencio grabbed a broom that had fallen on the floor and got to sweeping. "But you're worse."

"You!" Johnny pointed at me.

"What?"

"When you rich fucks talk to banks, you talk about this shit, right? Don't fucking lie."

"No. We just talk about money." I got close enough to see his wrist. My watch sat on it like a twenty-thousand-dollar game of nine ball. Johnny's tattoos were all gears and numbers. I got the feeling he'd known exactly what it was worth when he'd made the bet. Seeing him wear it bothered me. "Nice watch."

"They're out for us." Johnny turned his full attention to me. Bandana flipped him off and dragged his bag to the window. "Make us fight so they can take the spoils."

"You know you're crazy, right?"

"Sure, I'm crazy. Seeing what I've seen will make you that way. They have all the money, but if we worked together, they couldn't stand against us. This 'anyone can make it' bag of shit they sell us keeps us complacent. Makes us blame ourselves. Bullshit. Pure bullshit. Ask anyone here. All worked hard. Now we can't see a doctor. Can't drink the water. Can't give the kids an education. Don't tell us we didn't work hard, and we're not the only ones. And once you see it? Once you see what happened to us, you start to think, oh my God, is that what they been doing to black people this whole time? And yeah. Shit changes, and you go fucking crazy." He pushed his shovel. The debris was heavy, and he put his weight behind it. "Now we're cleaning up for—"

He lurched back, crying out in pain and dropping his shovel.

"Johnny!"

"My back!" He fell to one knee, hand just above his butt. "God damn it!"

I caught him, but there wasn't much I could do.

"Oh, for the love of fuck, John-boy!" Kyle came out of the woodwork and held up his friend. "This is your lazy ass."

"Help me over to the steps."

We guided him over as he grunted and winced the entire way. A woman ran over to help.

"Johnny, you done it again." She had the exhausted impatience of a woman who'd committed herself to a real pain in the ass.

"I'm fine," he complained.

We put him on the step. It was the only place to sit.

"Take it easy," the woman said. "We can't afford you to miss work."

Kyle pulled off his hat and scratched his scalp. "If we want to paint this floor on Saturday, we gotta clean it up today."

"I'll shovel his shit," I said.

"No, no, no," Johnny protested.

"Yes, yes, yes," Kyle said. "Be a nice break from your ranting and raving."

"I'll carry my own weight." Johnny started to get up, but he cringed and flopped back down.

"I tell you what," I said. "I shovel your shit, and you give me back my watch."

He shrugged and shook his wrist as if he really liked my watch and didn't want to give it up.

"Oh," the woman said. "This is your watch?"

"It's mine now," Johnny said. "And California here won't last an hour doing actual work."

I picked up his shovel. "I'm Taylor. This is my watch. And my back's in great shape."

"I'm Pat," the woman said. "Shovel for my husband, would you? He doesn't need another watch. He only has two wrists."

I nodded to her and turned to Kyle. "What are we doing?"

Kyle showed me the piles of shit and where they went. Then I spent the morning pushing garbage across the floor, into bags, and down the chute. Someone brought music. Fights broke out over "angry white guys screaming," "your bumpkin bullshit," and "taco Tuesday tunes." No one seemed to get deeply offended, but the insults flowed equally between everyone. They were joined by a common goal—seduce Everett Fitzgerald with a spiffy factory.

I didn't think Fitz would be moved by a clean floor as much as a cost-effective deal, but it wasn't my job to save them from disappointment. I didn't say much because breathing was hard enough. Shit was heavy, and I had a point to prove. I didn't have the energy to spare on anyone's musical taste.

By the time lunch was announced, I was a mess of sweat and I smelled like a landfill. Card tables and grills had been set out in the parking lot with ceviche, burgers, asada, and hot dogs. Children ran underfoot in a never-ending game of tag.

"Get away from the river!" Catherine roared at one of them, her gentleness turned to fire.

The kid in question froze then spun away from the tall reeds.

"She's got a wild animal inside her," I said to Harper, who had just straddled the bench next to me with a plate of tacos.

"Yeah. With the kids especially."

"Thought you were over tacos?"

"I changed my mind." She tilted her head to get a taco to her lips. Hair dropped over her cheek and threatened to dive bomb into her lunch.

I flicked it back and over her ear. She had the taco in her mouth when her eyes went a little wider in surprise. The gesture was too intimate. I knew it before I got the hair all the way over.

Harper wasn't the only one looking at me as if I'd just shit my pants. I couldn't swear every single eye was on me, but Catherine and Johnny, who was flat on his back in the bed of his truck, had their heads tilted our way.

"Sorry."

She spoke around her chewing. "I'm sorry, actually."

"Really?"

The afternoon wind was picking up, and she pulled another lock of hair out of her mouth before I could.

"Yeah. We have a deal. You put out, and I didn't pay up."

"Way to make a guy feel like a whore."

She shrugged. "You'll live."

"Well, I'm sorry I broke into your room… but not really."

"You know the saying about the snake?"

"The one that bites you because… what did you expect? It's a fucking snake?"

"That one." She faced into the wind, blowing her hair away from her face.

I took the last bite of hamburger. A triangle of tomato fell out and landed on my shirt. Harper took a napkin out of her pocket and wiped me.

"Stop." I took the napkin. "This is the cleanest thing that's touched this shirt all day."

She smiled, chewing a wad of taco in one side of her mouth. She had a charming, unself-conscious efficiency about the way she chewed her food and spoke volumes with her expression at the same time. She was an open book written in a code I was just starting to understand.

I could have watched her eat for a long time, but a cry came out from the second floor.

"Barrington ladies!" It was Damon, who I'd seen in passing by the dumpsters. His tattooed arms leaned on a second-floor ledge, and the sun made two reflective dots on his sunglasses.

Harper shaded her eyes and turned his way. Her body was curved to click into what mine wanted. It was like math. Only exact figures balanced the equation.

"What?" she called.

"The office is locked," Damon shouted.

"So?"

"Did Daddy give you the key?"

The word *daddy* had a venom I hadn't heard all day. It burned with acidic meaning and was thick with leisurely intent, yet it was subtle enough to pretend you didn't hear it.

"I'll be right up!" Catherine called back. She was as sweet as always but with an edge of impatience, as if she was telling Damon not to fuck with her.

Harper sighed as Catherine walked away with a ring of keys. "I'd better go too." To me, she said, "You finish eating."

When she walked away, her ass swayed and her hair flew in every direction. With her curves and the way she moved them, I had no choice but to follow. I could eat later.

XXXVI

Hacking real life was at least as good as finding weaknesses in code. Once Keaton and I had learned how to pick a lock, opening doors became as much of an addiction as building profiles. We'd find a single piece of information about a person, tack it onto another piece we found on a Tor site, grab a birthday from social media, uncover an address from the mortgage rolls. We skimmed just enough to not get caught, only buying things where our marks bought things. I didn't excuse it. I knew it was wrong, but I did it anyway.

Until the pure code hacks, which were sexier, more difficult, and got the most esteem from the boys in the hacker forums.

I hacked my dad first but didn't take anything. The pure rush was being able to do it. I had power over him. In retrospect, that moment where I looked at his bank account without him knowing was the moment I became a man.

Life was a problem to be hacked. It was never about money. It felt good.

As soon as I saw Catherine struggling with the dozens of keys on the ring, I wanted to cut the shit and hack the problem. But Damon, Harper, two other guys, and myself just watched, quickly alternating between impatience, anticipation, hope, and disappointment, in that order.

I knew the lock, and I knew the type of key. It would be a Kwikset with the three triangle cutouts on top. But she went through every single one.

"Come on, princess." Damon's face was clammy, and he kept rubbing his hands on his jeans.

"Hang on." Catherine isolated a silver key. The last one, and it was a Kwikset.

Anticipation, hope, impatience, disappointment as the key didn't turn the lock.

She dropped the ring.

"You are so useless." Damon scooped up the keys and gave them to her.

I didn't know Catherine, but I wanted to punch Damon.

Harper snapped at him before I could react. "There're no loose Fentanyl bottles in there, if that's what you're after."

"Fuck you, you rich little cunt. You don't know shit about—"

He had me at *cunt.* I had the advantage of surprise, pushing my forearm against his throat and his head against the dirty wall. "What did you say?"

The pressure on his esophagus didn't temper his hostility, which was fine with me. I wasn't ready for the apology Harper deserved.

"Who the fuck are you?"

"Taylor." Harper's voice, behind me. Far, far away.

"Don't talk to her like that."

He pushed me hard against the opposite wall.

"Damon!" Catherine, miles away.

"You push a broom and think you're one of us?"

In a split second, Damon and I were locked hand-to-face-to-shoulder-knee-in-stomach-defense-offense-defense-offense. He had worked with his body his whole life, putting me at a disadvantage, but he wasn't just fighting me. He was fighting whatever made him sweaty and shaky.

Damon's friend, whose name I never learned, just lit a cigarette. Catherine and Harper worked as a team, splitting us. I wound up against the wall with Harper's hand on my chest.

I pointed over her shoulder at Damon. "I'll pick this lock if you leave now."

"You pick the lock?" Damon sneered. "Bullshit."

"Get out of here," I sneered back.

"I get it. Money sticks to money. Fine. Fuck it. Pick the fucking lock."

"Just wanted to mop the fucking floor." Damon's friend regarded the tip of his cigarette then flicked off the ash.

I held my hand out for the keys. Catherine dropped them into my palm. I flicked through the club member cards, snapped the thickest one into the right shape, and was in the office in thirty seconds. There was nothing but an overturned desk and empty shelves. Huge windows looked out onto the halfway-clean factory floor.

I stepped out of the way and let Cigarette Man kick his wheeled yellow bucket through the doorway. Damon made a point to brush against me on the way out.

I almost shoved him, but Harper vise-gripped my arm. I snapped out of it.

"You dropped a bunch of stuff." She pointed toward the hall floor.

I picked up my wallet, a pen, and the napkin she'd used to wipe tomato off my shirt. It had fallen open, revealing a row of numbers written in marker.

"You really should pay better attention," she said softly. "You almost threw it away. And I wasn't writing it again."

"Thank you."

"It's—"

"I need your phone again."

She handed me the black rectangle. When it hit my hand, it woke up. I saw the wallpaper. Harper from just below, with her blowing hair, indecisive eyes, and the factory outlined against the blue sky behind her. She looked powerful, confident, the muse for a revolution.

"Oh, the code." She took the phone and hit the glass with her thumb. "Here."

She handed it to me, the photo safely tucked behind the keypad screen.

I wasn't scared. Not that. But something closer to freaked out.

And not at her.

At myself. At how easily I handled her power over me and how badly I wanted her at the same time.

"I'll use the one in the house."

"Suit yourself."

I kissed her without thinking then ran, but I had to make a stop at the lunch tables first.

XXXVII

Kyle scrubbed down the grill with a wire brush as everyone packed up the paper plates and leftover food.

"Kyle, I need you to watch Harper." I told him what had happened with Damon outside the office.

"Saw him leave a minute ago. Probably getting a fix. But I'll keep an eye on her."

"Thank you."

I ran back to the house, pounding over the bridge, through the reeds, past the thorn garden, napkin crumpled in my hand, until I got to the kitchen, which looked like a culinary bomb had hit it. This must have been lunch central. I picked up the receiver and stared at the clear plastic circle.

What was Deeprak's number?

My grandmother had made fun of me one Christmas because I didn't know any of the numbers in my phone. She then recited every number she'd ever learned. By the end of dinner, we were singing the number my mother grew up with. Grandma still lived there.

I dialed. It took forever.

"Hello?"

"Grandma?" She was pretty deaf. I had to yell. "Hi, it's—"

"Taylor?"

"Yes. Do you—"

"What are you doing all the way out there?"

"What? I—"

"The caller ID says you're—"

"Gram. Do you have my work number?"

That's right. I didn't even know my office number.

"Do you know you're on the news?"

I was on the news? I wasn't much of a news watcher and usually picked up what was happening by following media on Twitter. I hadn't seen a TV in the house, and when I'd seen one in the bar, it had been on sports. So, no, I didn't know I was on the news.

"What are they saying?"

"Your computers didn't work."

"They work, Grandma."

"And you disappeared. Your partner. The Indian—"

"He's from Bangladesh." Why did I bother correcting my grandmother? She was close to eighty. She needed to be happy more than she needed to be correct.

"He was on *Morning Joe*. He said you were fixing it, but Maria Bardono didn't believe him. Said you were running away with everyone's money. Said you were a criminal. And I said, that's the last time I watch you, Mr. Morning Joe. My grandson is no thief!"

She was sweet and loyal, but I'd been a prolific thief and digital trespasser since before her dotage.

"When did they say that?"

"Yesterday. But today Joe had a different guy on. Said you fixed it. I liked him, this second guy. Real handsome. Had a nice confidence on him and an English accent."

She had a short memory for boycotts and a sharp eye for authority.

"Was it Keaton? The second guy? Keaton from Poly? Do you remember him?"

"Oh, I remember that boy. Could be. The tall one, right? Are you coming back here? Or going to California? Roger from the deli usually saves me the pig's feet if you want me to make them."

"I don't think I can."

"Just tell me if you're coming."

Talking to Grandma had always been a commitment of time and patience. I was short on both.

"I will. Do you have my work number?"

"Your what?"

"My work number. I know. You were right. But—"

"You always ate them when you were little. You were the only one."

"I know. I'll come see you, Gram. Do you have—"

"It's just pork, I said a hundred times. You believed me."

"I did. And you were right. Do you—"

"Give me a minute. I'm getting the book out. I'll have Roger save them for you. He gets a side of pork second Tuesday of the month."

I banged my head on the doorway molding.

"Just tell me ahead, or that bitch on Chestnut gets them," she said.

"Okay."

"All right. Let me look. These letters get smaller all the time. B. E. G. Harden is H. H. H. Here you are."

She read off the number. I snapped a pencil from a busted mug and wrote it on the wall.

"Thanks, Gram. I'll come visit. I promise."

"You better. I'm going to be dead soon, you know."

"You have another twenty years. Easy."

"Maybe, you little shit." She said it with an abundance of affection and humor. "Maybe."

We said our good-byes, I made promises I intended to keep if I ever got out of the middle of nowhere, and I hung up. I dialed the front desk at QI4. I should have been able to get Deeprak's extension right away, but naturally there wasn't a touchpad. So I had to wait until a receptionist picked up. Then I had to identify myself, prove it, and growl like a lion before they'd give me Deeprak.

"Where have you been?" he asked right away.

"Shithole, USA, with no phone. Do not ask."

Calling the middle parts of the country a shithole was as natural as pissing standing up. Until that moment. In the shitholiest kitchen in Shithole, USA, I stopped feeling a fundamental truth in the word. The people here were all right, and they were mopping a factory floor to keep the town alive. That said a lot about the place. I was going to take that back—but not now. I read the code to Deeprak.

KDQwOCkgNTU1LTEyMjY=

"I'll head down to the cage," he said. "This is base64. Did you translate it?"

I hadn't even thought to look at how it would translate. "In my head? No." I searched for something to write on besides the wall. "I'll do it on a piece of paper if you can't."

"Hang on. I'll do it on my phone."

I heard the sounds of the office as Deeprak walked through it. Ronald's loud conversations about "this girl gamer on Twitch." The hiss of the servers. The bird soundtrack in the hallway. The universal *ding* of the elevator.

I felt something I didn't recognize at first because I'd never felt it before, but when the elevator doors in my office whooshed closed for Deeprak, I realized what it was: I was homesick.

Deeprak laughed and got back on the phone. "You know what it is?"

"What?"

I heard the elevator doors open.

"Our phone number." Deeprak rattled off a string of Bengali when the ID pad asked for his name.

"She's such a fucking card," I mumbled as if I was annoyed, but the truth was she was being thoughtful. She knew I couldn't get my phone. She knew I'd have to use a landline. She knew I wouldn't have shit memorized. So she gave it to me, knowing that I'd be able to scratch out the answer but not knowing I was in too much of a hurry to do it.

"She?" He interrupted my warm feelings. His chair squeaked, and computer keys clicked against the muted stillness of the cage. "Is it Harper Watson?"

"Who? No."

Yes, but no. He wasn't allowed to know about her yet. I didn't want her accused, and I didn't want Keaton flying his ass out here to torment her or scoop her up. Nope. I wanted her to myself. She was mine. All mine.

That makes no sense.

"Jack checked on her. Did you know we interviewed her?"

"For what?"

"The cage. To replace Walter."

My skin tingled. My breath stopped. My brain went into complete shutdown while I tried to remember every woman we'd interviewed.

I couldn't recall a single one.

But how many had been that hot? You'd think my dick would at least have a little recollection.

"I'd remember."

"You were looking at your phone the entire time, but sure. You might remember her score on the coding test though."

The test was a beast, and my guys in the cage were the best. None of them had scored under ninety percent.

"What was it?"

"Perfect. But, your dick."

Was that true? Had I forgotten a perfect score? I mean, yes, I didn't hire women. Very few small operations did. When I was as big as Google, I'd take the risk. Until then, I couldn't afford a lawsuit or an HR debacle. Couldn't deal with a work slowdown when we were hosed constantly.

And the guys in the cage? We didn't have a pill to manage the awkward social reflux.

"What the hell was Keaton doing on TV?" I asked, changing the subject. A group must have gathered around Deeprak. I could hear the guys goofing off.

"He called off the Oracle meeting. Someone traced the blockchain and yada yada—he was unmasked." *Tap tappa* of keys. "Why can't we get you on video?"

"I'm on a landline. And bullshit. He wanted to be unmasked."

A group cheer went up from the other side of the line.

"It's up!" Deeprak shouted. "'Enter decryption code to boot OS.' Like a boss."

"Two more," I said quietly.

I was in two worlds, thinking with two minds. The feel of her body and the comfort of my real life. Getting between her and Damon because she needed me. A way in. A path I was unreasonably afraid of losing.

But I didn't know her. I only felt her in places I hadn't thought I had. I didn't know why she was doing what she was doing. Why she kept me here. Why she wanted me to teach her the fine art of fucking. If she just wanted vengeance for not getting a job, she would have stolen my system and sold the decryption keys to the highest bidder. So there was some- thing more.

And Keaton was making a move. He was loyal and trustworthy, but not always in the way you expected. He'd be the first to do some damage to QI4 in the service of what he thought was the greater good. He'd act unilaterally and inflexibly.

I'd gotten mono in high school. Worst three weeks of my life. While I was laid up, some script kiddie trying to make points doxxed my personal email, address, name, and birthday. His name was Nelson, and he'd gotten the info simply. He knew me personally and just posted shit from the school directory as if he'd cracked my ID.

Turned out that, besides making points, Nelson was a little twisted out. His girlfriend had mono too. She'd given it to me. Or I'd given it to her. We'd never know who had it first.

Once Keaton found who doxxed me, he erased Nelson's ID from the face of the dark web and wiped out his parents' bank accounts, all while I couldn't get out of bed.

I wouldn't have done that, but Keaton wouldn't undo it. He was Alpha Wolf, and his decisions were not under review. A hacker was only as good as people's fears, and if he let shit slide under his watch, he had no way of maintaining respect.

What was he after now? Why was he coming out of his shell? I wasn't there to tell him to stop or to plead for Harper. I was laid up in Barrington with an analog illness, and Keaton was home and assuming we'd been attacked by a hostile entity.

And weren't we?

Wasn't Harper just another bad actor after an exploit?

Why did she deserve anything less than the most painful response? She'd publicly humiliated us, and she needed to be dealt with. Anything less would be a show of weakness.

I jumped when the phone rang. Not with the usual long rings you hear in old movies. This was a quick European *bring-bring* with pauses between.

Back when phone phreaking was a thing, changing the ring was a fun trick to pull.

Ha-ha.

I picked up the handset. "Keaton."

He was in what sounded like a crowded restaurant. "Hello, Beez."

"Dude. You're pulling call data from the office?"

"You're calling from a landline. How convenient."

Convenient because the location wasn't cloaked. Was I being stupid or subliminally intentional?

"Listen to me," I said.

"No. You listen to me."

I would not be shut down. Not after all the work I'd put in. Not after coming this far. But the back door opened behind me, and a gaggle of women entered with groceries. They were chatting, laughing, plopping bags on the counter.

"Barrington?" he said, having tracked down the phone number in five seconds. Fuck.

Catherine patted my cheek then kissed it. "Hello, Taylor."

"Thank you for helping!" Juanita kissed my cheek too.

I was sure Keaton could hear it. Shit, this was embarrassing. Mrs. Boden gave me a wet one. If Harper came and kissed me on the mouth, I was never going to get Keaton to look me in the eye again.

But she wasn't with them, which was strange.

"What the hell is going on over there?" Keaton asked.

I went into the dining room, stretching the cord around two doorways until the coil was pulled straight. "I don't know what you have planned, but you have to run it by me first."

"You're a non-actor as far as I'm concerned. You're taking too long. Did you find him?"

"I did. I'm getting it unlocked. Just—"

I was met with rage.

"You're *asking* for decryption? Waiting for it? Like a patsy. Like a *n00b*. No. We don't wait. We take. This is what you never got. We take what we want and destroy people who get in our way."

"Keaton, I have this."

"So do I."

"How? Can you tell me how?"

"I don't work for you."

That was true. It had been made clear at the outset. Money flowed at his discretion. We weren't partners, but I wasn't the boss either. And now that he had physical access to the cage, it was too late to cut him off.

"I'm not saying you need my permission. I'm querying the exploit," I said.

I heard a car door slam on his end. A luxurious *thup* that shut out noise from the street. "Someone in this company brought a device into and out of the cage. Yes?"

"Yes. It communicated with a loaded power strip in reception."

"Did you find out who it is?"

"No."

"Once I find out, I'm going to grind them under my heel. Then I'm going to make it easy for both of us. You're going to destroy the man who tried to destroy us, then Barrington is going to be thrust into the dark ages."

He didn't have to tell me the gory details. Revenge and chaos were what he did. That was the kind of person he knew. His family's friends broke things for a living. He could fry the power plant, the water supply, or the sewer filtration without breaking a sweat. He didn't have to touch Harper to do it.

"What if I get the codes before you start breaking shit?" I didn't know why it mattered to me that he didn't destroy Barrington, but it did.

"At the rate you're going?"

"You find the mole there. I'll take care of shit here. Like a team."

"Get me the codes. All of them. Until you do, I'm going to protect you. I'm going to do what you won't do yourself."

Could I warn Harper? Would it matter? Without knowing his plan, what would I warn her about?

Why was I setting myself against my entire life to protect her?

"Fine."

I was about to walk back to the kitchen to hang up, but Keaton said, "Taylor."

I stopped halfway between the kitchen and dining room as two teen girls came through with dishes and flatware. They giggled when they saw me. The red-haired one blushed hot pink.

"Yeah."

"Remember why you started this. You wanted to change the world."

The click and scrape of the girls setting the table got far away.

"Are you there?" Keaton asked.

A little girl with one pigtail half out came into the dining room with a big pitcher of water.

Red Hair took the pitcher and flipped the one intact pigtail, saying, "Go fix your hair, muffin."

"I'm here," I said.

The pigtail was half out because the little one had been cleaning the walls of an abandoned factory all day. And why would a child do that? Everett Fitzgerald was coming to town, and they were all working toward a common goal. That was why I cared. I wanted to see if they could do it.

"She sounds young for you," Keaton said.

"That's not funny."

He paused. Keaton didn't fill the air with words if he had nothing to say or if he needed to take a moment to think. "Something's just become really clear to me..."

"I'll call you when I have the next code."

"You were always a sucker for pussy, Beez. I knew one of them would get to you eventually."

He hung up.

The kitchen was in full swing. All four burners had pots, and every bit of counter space was covered with someone hacking away at a vegetable.

I didn't give a shit about Barrington. I didn't care about Harper, her family, her friends, her father's fucking factory. I could have passed a polygraph stating I didn't give a shit about anything but QI4 and a tight circle of people, none of whom were in this little factory town, dammit.

"What's wrong?" Catherine asked.

"I don't care!" I barked the lie that revealed itself more the more I repeated it.

I cared.

God dammit. I cared.

The hustle in the kitchen stopped for a second. Catherine took me by the elbow and led me into the pantry.

"Catherine, really," I said. "I'm sorry. I'm fine. I was thinking about something else."

"Do you need to go home? I can get someone to give you a ride."

I breathed a rueful laugh. I should have asked her in the first place. I'd have been home already. But it was too late. Keaton knew where I was and that there was a woman involved. And I cared.

"I need Harper."

I didn't mean I *needed* Harper. But it didn't matter what I meant anymore.

"I can call her."

I didn't need a nursemaid, and I didn't need favors. Catherine had enough to do without me worrying her about a threat from Keaton. She didn't need to worry about me or my whining either. Harper and I could take care of it.

"No. I'm fine. Never mind."

She reached into her apron and plucked out a car key, dangling it between us. "She's helping Pat at the store for a couple of hours if you want to pick up a few things."

That must have been the store where she and I had met a hundred years before.

I took the key. "All right."

"I'll get you a list."

I was left in the half-empty pantry with its peeling shelf paper and scalloped molding.

Note to self: you're not going to put anything past that woman.

XXXVIII

I felt blinded by my location. The miles between my company and me were almost as bad as the lack of digital communication.

I had to go back to Cali. Had to get out of here. Had to warn Harper. Had to help the company, myself, this woman who was in the process of destroying me. Had to find out how this knot of facts would turn into a noose and leave me swinging on Main Street.

P&J, as it turned out, was indeed the grocery store Harper had been minding when I'd arrived. I wondered if she'd made it a point to be there, knowing I'd be coming in that way.

She had. I knew it as well as I knew my own motivations. She was too smart to leave that to chance.

Pat was behind the counter. Not Harper. I grabbed the things off the list and dropped them on the belt at the only checkout.

"Thanks for helping out today," Pat said as she rang me up.

"No problem. You were there all day too, and you're right back to work."

She shrugged. "Gotta get done if you want your carrots."

"Have you seen Harper? She's going to miss a really nice dinner."

"She's over at our place. Our modem's been on the fritz. She's the only one that can fix it since our youngest went off to school."

"Ah."

"Eleven seventy-two."

I gave her twenty, and she made change.

"I don't have my phone." I took the coins. "And I need to talk to her. So, can I borrow…"

I stopped myself. Asking for a home address was weird enough. Asking so I could chase a woman down was weirder. I'd have to ask to use the store's phone.

"You can just go over there. I hear you're pretty handy with computers too. She might need some help."

"Yeah. True. Hey. I was wondering something," I said, using all my powers of nonchalance. I was pretty sure they were inadequate. "How did you all find out Everett Fitzgerald was coming to look at the plant?"

She smiled, leaning against the counter. "Well, so interesting. Harper told a fancy commercial realtor over in Doverton he was looking for a space. Said she talked to someone she knew from when she was at college who happened to work for him. Fanny connected the dots."

"It's lucky the agent in Doverton had those kinds of connections."

"Fanny knows just about everyone."

I could accept that as the official story, but unofficially, no.

"Did you talk to Fanny?" Too direct. I backpedaled. "I mean, did you send her a fruit basket or anything? It would be pretty cool if it went through."

"Harper took care of it. Those kinds of connections, you only get them in college."

"I'd have to agree."

We chattered aimlessly as Pat bagged. She had three smart children she was extremely proud of. All were away. Temple. Duke. Northwestern.

"You cannot believe what these places cost."

"I can imagine." I'd used the second of Keaton's Bitcoin infusions to pay my student loans. He'd thought it was funny that I still owed people money when I knew how to hack a bank and take thousands in such small increments I wouldn't get caught.

"We couldn't put up anything for tuition," Pat continued. "The house isn't worth squat. Johnny can only fix so many clocks, and the grocery store margins are pretty tight. I don't even want to think about the debt they're gonna have."

I wanted to employ her children without even knowing what they did. I had an impulse to employ the entire town as if it had cast a softening spell on me.

"Don't. They'll work it out."

She gave me directions. I thanked her, took my bags of groceries, and headed over to Oxalis Street. The layout of the town was becoming clearer. The main strip that Harper had taken me past was a few parallel streets from the civic center. Post office. Library. City clerk.

A cluster of houses grew around a closed train stop. Following Oxalis

Street around it, I found Pat and Johnny's place. I parked in front of the narrow, white-shingled house with a porch and a rusted swing in the front yard swinging in the late afternoon sun.

A dog barked, but no one answered the door.

"Who is it?" an impatient male voice came from the end of the driveway.

The drive was grass with two dirt stripes leading to a one-car garage. A circa-1970s Mercedes covered in boxes and tarps took up one side. Benches and tables took up the rest. The carriage doors were open, and Johnny was leaning over a brightly lit table with magnification goggles.

"Hey, Johnny," I said. "Have you seen Harper?"

He stood straight with difficulty, as if his back still bothered him. "Went home. Fixed the wireless and left."

I should have gone, but I couldn't help looking at the table as he laid his tweezers down and pushed the goggles up on his head. The table was lined with butcher paper, and an open clock sat on it. Gears were arrayed all over the table with pen circling them in groups, labeled with arrows, or placed on tea saucers.

"Where's my watch?"

"Close by."

"Johnny, you're pissing me off."

He shrugged. "You took off after lunch. There are guys still there cleaning. The trade was the watch for a full day of work. Not half a day's work for a really nice piece you lost fair and square."

I was going to lay into him. Keaton had made me feel like half a man, and now this asshole was halving the difference again. I wouldn't be taken advantage of. I was lost and trapped and worse for the wear, but that watch was mine.

"You look like you're about to blow a gasket." He got off his chair and buckled from a back spasm. Instinctively, I reached out to help him, walking him to a beat-up green couch.

"Where's the watch?" I asked when he was settled.

"Where I can't get to it right now."

"I want it now."

"Don't worry, Cali-Boy." He shifted until he was settled in the cushions. "Things will go to shit if we know what time it is or not. Fancy watch ain't gonna save nobody."

Maybe he was right. Maybe I shouldn't get a whole watch for a few hours of work, and maybe everything was going to shit. Maybe I couldn't save the world or Harper or myself. But I couldn't use that as an excuse for not trying.

XXXIX

It was getting dark, but I found the way back to the Barrington house easily. Nothing to it. I had the lay of the land already. I drove around the back and put the car where I'd found it.

Mrs. Boden, wearing a different color bandana on her head and the same bangly bracelet, came to the back porch with the red-haired teen.

"About time!" the older lady shouted.

"Is Harper back?" I asked, handing the bags to the blushing redhead.

As if summoned, Harper came through the swinging door, keeping it open so everyone could get past. She looked at me through the screen.

"You coming in?" she asked.

"We need to talk."

"Did the decryption key work?"

The door slapped closed behind her as she came out, and we were alone. The way the setting sun hit her cheeks made her glow, and the strands of gold hair at the edges looked translucent. She belonged on a postcard.

I kept forgetting she was holding me hostage. I kept forgetting I needed to think strategically. I had more at stake with this girl than I'd ever had with another.

"Did you doubt it would work?"

"Not really. I'm just making conversation."

"What are the thorns about?" I pointed at the thorn bed that had eaten my phone and went down the stairs to the yard.

She came after me. "Don't you have these where you're from?" She snapped a dry twig off the end.

"Roses? Yes. Impenetrable, groomed thorn bushes in our yards? No."

"It's not normal to give the gardeners in town something to do?" We walked around the perimeter.

"You are not normal."

"It still blooms in spring. It's really nice. You should see it."

We were at the back end of the yard, where the very top of the factory's roof cut the horizon.

I took her hand, pulling her to a stop. "Harper."

"Taylor?" Her hair flew in her mouth when she turned, and she drew her finger across her cheek to get it out.

What was I supposed to tell her again? That I knew we'd interviewed her. That I didn't give her the job despite her having a leg up on everyone else we saw.

But was I contrite? Accusatory? Was I just going to relay information? What did I want out of her after I told her I knew?

"Thank you for helping today," she said. "If you'd asked me when we met, 'Would Taylor Harden help clean the factory?' I would have said, 'No, not for any reason.' But there you were. Pushing a broom. Scooping up shit. Not being an asshole."

"My watch was at stake."

"Yeah. Whatever. You can say what you want to keep your reputation as a shithead intact."

"I have a reputation as a shithead?"

"You know you do."

I did know it, and I reveled in it.

She faced me and put her other hand out. I took it, holding both hands between us. I couldn't help it.

"Well, you guys are such a bunch of sad sacks I had to help. And let me tell you, every guy in Barrington has a little asshole in him. Trust me. I've played pool with them."

"I want to say…" She stopped herself as if she really didn't want to say. "Let's get together tonight and get you another decryption code. But… saying this is stupid." She bit her lip.

"Say it anyway."

"The sooner you get four codes, the sooner you leave."

I looked at our hands so I wouldn't have to look at her.

"I'm not sure if I want that," she said.

Was she playing some kind of game? No matter how many ways I peeled this onion, I couldn't get to the center. Was she after my heart? Had she changed the fucking rules?

I had feelings for her I couldn't cope with, but if she was going to start moving the goalposts, I would lose my shit. I couldn't do this dance. Not with Keaton walking around the cage like a specter.

I let go of her hands. She was turning my head inside out, and all the pieces were dropping to the ground.

"You have a buddy on Chaxxer." I'd started, so I had to finish. "I saw it on your screen."

Her eyes went a little wide, and her throat moved as she swallowed hard. She didn't have to confirm it. She knew what I'd seen.

"So?" She planted her feet far apart as if daring me to knock her over. "What's it to you?"

"More practice? Like me? The way I'm practice?"

"I like you better."

"Don't sweet-talk me. You've been telling how many guys on Chaxxer how hard you can suck the—"

"Shut up, Taylor Harden! You just shut your mouth."

"A few years ago, we met a guy on the dark web who was a big fan of my partner. He was no one then. Keaton was Alpha Wolf; this guy called himself Beta Wolf. Just for shits. 'Flow' is 'wolf' backward, and if the B in 'bro' is a beta?"

"When did you figure it out?"

"That Fitz was Flow Bro? That you've been talking dirty on Chaxxer? Or that you were the one to get him to come to Barrington?"

She blinked too long, and her expression went slack as if she was looking inside her own mind. Calculating. I could see her making connec- tions, but what connections?

I wanted to know—for all the obvious reasons and one not-so-obvious reason. I wanted to know *her*. Not just why she was lying but how.

"I can sell him a factory," she said. "Or I can sell him a package. A place to make things and a girl who gives him what he wants, how he wants it."

"How did you find out he likes it dirty?"

Her expression changed a dozen times before she spoke. "Does it matter? I hacked him. He's a man. He's a rich asshole from daddy's money. He wants to be worshipped. He wants a few holes to stick his dick in, and he wants to be told he's got powers no one else has. You guys are all alike. You want to be treated as though you're gold-plated. Well, I got news—you're not. Not him. Not you. Nobody. We're all made of blood and electrical currents. All of us. And we all have a code in our neurons where a guy like Fitz can be tricked into doing the right thing. So, yeah. He's filthy, so I learned to be filthy. But it's got to work in the real world. You're teaching me to fuck so I can seduce him. If I can make him love me, he'll buy the factory. He'll hire us. He'll save us."

"You're crazy."

I'd made the observation before, but behind the thorn bush, something else stirred. She was crazy, but I wanted her. My cock pushed against my pants for her. Her insanity was rubbing off on me.

"You can be in or out." She got her finger in my face. "But you're in because I hacked you too."

I grabbed her wrist and wrested it away from my face. "No, Harper. You're crazy if you think I believe it. You're too smart for such a stupid plan."

There wasn't a bit of insecurity in her eyes. How could she be so confident?

I couldn't counter with the facts, couldn't tell her he wouldn't do what she wanted, because I was halfway to falling for her myself.

Maybe that was her gift.

Fuck this.

I was here to get shit done.

Shit was getting done.

Jamming my hand in her waistband, I made a fist around the fabric and twisted her jeans, tightening the crotch. She leveraged herself on my shoulders.

"When he walks away from you," I said, "come to me."

Her button-fly popped open when I pulled the sides apart.

"What are you doing?"

"Free lesson."

Her gaze went from hard to liquid in a heartbeat, and her hands went to the lump in my pants, stroking through the fabric.

Was it real? Was she faking it?

Pushing her pants down, I got my fingers on her soaking-wet pussy.

Can't fake that.

I crushed her lips on mine, tasting her tongue, biting her with a vengeance that made her squeal. I was going to fuck her right there in the dirt. Half dressed, wrestling under the darkening sky, I was going to tear her apart.

She had my dick out, and my face was buried in her neck as she stroked it. There was no expertise in her movements, but the ache in my body responded as if she did everything right.

"Give me your hand," I said, taking it before she could offer it.

I kissed the tips of her fingers, sucked them, left a trail of saliva across her palm. She gasped in surprise and arousal. I'd get to that later. But for now, I took her thumb in my mouth and sucked hard.

"Oh, I didn't..." After another gasp, she finished, "I didn't know that could feel so good."

I put her slick hand on my erection and paced her. "The head's where the nerve endings are. You have to..." She ran her thumb along the back. "Do that."

She watched my expression with her big, multicolored eyes, taking in my every reaction like a learning machine.

She's learning how to fuck someone else.

I'm fine with that.

I wasn't fine with it. The pressure was building as she jerked me off. It got harder to think. The firewall between my jealousy and what I allowed myself to think was under attack. I put my hands on her cheeks and pressed her face to mine until I felt her breath on my lips.

"You don't... ah..."

Say it.

Do not say it.

Do. Not.

"You don't have to do this."

"Should I suck it instead?" Her voice was soft and suggestive.

She'd misunderstood. I could have corrected her, but I was about to lose it. I lifted her shirt and let loose on her belly, burying my face in her neck, her ozone smell, the air before a storm.

"Harper." I groaned it. The longing in my voice was audible.

I'd been jerked off before, but this time I was in a weakened state. Not because of the orgasm. Those were a dime a dozen. Another bit of chemistry was at work. Some new variable had been added to the algorithm.

She pulled away, holding her shirt up so it wouldn't get sticky. Under her white bra, her body dripped where I'd marked her with my DNA. I could only see the top of her head because she was looking down, moving her unbuttoned jeans away.

When she looked at me, her hair was a wheaten nest and her grin was a conspiracy of desire against logic. As if we were in on something together. As if we were partnered on an epic hacking exploit.

That was it.

I changed my mind about everything.

"Stay there," I said, taking a wrinkled hankie out of my back pocket. "It's the guy's job to clean you up." I kneeled in front of her and wiped her off. "Any guy that doesn't clean you off, you get rid of, you hear? He's not worth you."

It was getting dark, but when I looked up at her, I could just about see her face. The wind blew from the direction of the river, covering her like window blinds. She shook her head. The hair came off her face, falling to one side.

"You got that?" I said. "It's things like that that you have to watch for."

"I got it. He wipes me off."

"He worships you."

I kissed her where I'd marked her, running my tongue below her navel, pulling her jeans to her knees. I kissed the fronts of her thighs as she ran her fingers through my hair.

"He worships me."

She was wearing boots. I could have waited for her to get it all off, but I needed to taste her.

"He treats you like a queen." Pulling her open, I got my tongue on her clit.

"Oh my God." Her knees bent, giving me better access.

Without a wall or a bed to lean against, we fought a losing battle with gravity and physics. We fell into a tangled pile on the ground with my head between her legs, her pants and boots still on, her fingers gripping my scalp. We were feral animals, and I wanted to eat her alive.

I reached up to touch her face. My fingers slid into her open mouth. Her breathing got hard and fast, and the taste of her got clearer, sweeter, more raw. I covered her mouth so the people in the house wouldn't run out to rescue her.

She came in the dirt and scraggly grass, pushing my face between her legs as I pushed my hand harder on her mouth.

"Wait. Wait, stop," she muttered behind my hand.

Even when she tried to wiggle away, I kept on, lightening up so it wouldn't hurt, but I wanted another. One for her. One for me.

Her second orgasm flipped us over. My hand fell away from her mouth, and she straddled me with her jeans behind my neck. Her back arched. I held her to me until she stopped moving.

"Please." She was practically weeping. "No more."

I let her go. She shifted back but couldn't untangle herself completely without help. Her jeans had slid lower and were completely wrapped around the boots. My body was between her legs, with one hand over my head and one trapped by the jeans.

"Oh, dear," she said. "I think we're stuck."

"Think of it as coding praxis. One step at a time."

I rolled until I was on top of her, more or less, holding myself up with my free arm. I kissed her cheek then her lips.

She flicked her tongue over my chin. "That's what I taste like."

"Yes. And I want to tell you something."

I'd never told a woman anything like I was about to tell this one. So I paused and considered it. Thought hard. Swapped words around. It had to be perfect, but I kept changing what that meant.

"I think I need to take a boot off." She shifted and stared at the dark blue sky.

"No. You need to stay still for a minute."

She moved her face from the sky to me. "Okay. I'm still."

"You and I." Nothing I'd prepared was right. I threw it all away. "We don't have to be against each other. We can be..."

Be what?

Partners?

Something simply more?

Or less?

I wasn't ready to define what we were. I wanted to define what we weren't.

"You don't have to do this," I continued. "This thing with Fitz. It's bullshit. You're making it up because it's a stall for the real reason."

"What's the real reason?"

"You want me."

"Oh, God, you have to stop believing your own PR."

She bucked her hips, flinging me to the side. I wrestled her back down with one arm.

"There are too many steps." I held up one finger with my free hand. "You come up with the hack of the century to—one—lure me here"—two fingers made a V—"so I could train you to fuck"—I put the W in her face—"so you can seduce a guy into reopening the factory. And that's two steps right there." Four fingers. "You want to tell me how that plan makes any sense?"

"It makes sense." She growled from deep in her chest. "We've tried Congress. We've tried the law. We spent money we didn't have sending people to talk and talk and talk to businesses. We're still dying here. The only thing that makes sense is getting a human man to do what human men do."

I twisted, pulled, held her in place while I bent my body through the space between her legs and her jeans. Kneeling in front of her in the dark, she was an odd-shaped silhouette in the twilight.

I growled at her, "Human men *fuck shit up*."

She rolled onto the balls of her feet and stood, naked between her waist and her calves. The house lights cast a glow on the top of her body while the thorn bed made twisted shadows over her stomach. I could smell her pussy.

"You know what?" she said, leaning over to loosen her pants from her boots. I reached out to help her, but she swatted me away. "My reasons and my sense aren't your business. Your business is getting your code back."

She slid her underwear up, covering her delicious pussy smell. I remembered I was on my knees with my dick out. My first impulse was to lash out at her. Hurt her. Bring her down to her knees. But a little voice mentioned that hadn't worked with her yet and trying it again would be the definition of insanity.

I stood. "You're better than this."

She spit out a laugh and shimmied her jeans over her hips. "Don't sweet-talk me, Taylor. It's not going to work."

But it had already worked. Her tone was more pliant.

"I should have hired you."

"So you remember?"

I didn't, but I didn't want to admit it any more than I wanted to lie about it.

"When I heard you had an opening, Catherine scraped up the money for a flight," she said. "One night in a hotel. I aced the fucking coding test. You made some comment about 'fitting in with the culture' and didn't listen to my answer."

"So this is revenge?"

She walked along the back of the thorn bed, her boots crunching against the dirt path. One side of her was lit by the golden light from the house, and when she turned toward it, I could see her profile.

I couldn't run away. Couldn't fire her or ignore her. I was so angry and powerless the most hurtful things didn't seem hurtful enough. And as much as cutting her down would be the definition of insanity, I wanted to shame her. Cut her down. Make her cry.

"All I'm saying is…" I paused as if hovering my finger over the send button.

She stopped and looked at me, daring me to press it.

Fuck it.

"You don't have to be such a whore."

I don't know what I'd expected. She walked briskly to the house, taking big steps, ran up the porch stairs, and let the door slap behind her.

Her taste lingered on my tongue. I rolled it around with the word I'd used to break her and failed.

XL

Harper wasn't at dinner. I ate with everyone, made small talk, helped clear the table while watching the driveway for her car. I had a beer with Orrin and Butthead on the porch. It seemed like the best vantage point to watch for Harper to come back.

She didn't.

Percy looked at me with sad brown eyes and a drooping tail as if he felt sorry for me. When I scratched his neck, he laid his head on my lap.

"My God, son. What happened to you to make old Percy give you comfort?"

"Did half a day's work in a factory. Nearly snapped me in two," I deflected.

Butthead belched. Orrin laughed. Harper still didn't show up.

The fucking send button. It needed to be locked before a guy called any woman a whore, especially Harper Barrington aka Watson, who was just about as far from a whore as a woman could be.

Or she was a complete whore and I didn't care.

Maybe the question wasn't about her. Maybe the question was about why I thought I had to ask myself who a woman slept with and why. Or why it mattered. Or why some behaviors were good and some were bad, because I'd done some shitty stuff people could get on my ass about.

I didn't know what I thought about anything anymore. I was all turned around. These guys out here? A guy who let himself be called Butthead as a sign of affection and Orrin, who'd nearly taken my face off because he didn't like how I was touching Harper? Were they involved in what she was doing? Did they see some greater good?

I couldn't imagine they'd allow my voluntary abduction, but there were so many moving pieces to this puzzle I didn't think any one human could do it alone, no matter how smart and capable.

"How did you guys find out Fitz was coming?" I asked.

"Fanny the realtor," Butthead said. "Over in Doverton."

"She's pretty connected." I finished my beer. Debated having another. I wasn't pleasantly buzzed. Just slow and tired.

"I thought it was the Badger," Orrin said.

"The Badger?"

"Mayor. He looks like a fucking…" Butthead waved it away as too obvious. "But nah. He stopped bothering to even leave town after we couldn't get Pepsi to move in."

"Yeah." Orrin sipped his beer.

Whatever part in it they had, I believed they didn't know Harper was talking to Fitz on Chaxxer.

"You spray paint the Caddy, Orrin?"

"Why you asking?"

"You were around that day."

"You think *he* did it?" Butthead laughed. "Dude, that was me. All me."

"What did you do with my laptop?" The anger was a transparent wrap around the hope that I'd get it back.

"Harper's got it."

"Did she say why you should do something so fucking stupid?"

His laughter clanged to the floor as if I'd cut a chain of tension. "Nah. Just said it wasn't a big deal and it was a joke on some rich guy. Said to make an E into a three to pretend I was an uneducated rube, and, you know, she kinda got me going. But you're all right. I don't feel good about it."

Apparently, it was okay to victimize some people and not others. People you knew and liked, you left alone. Strangers, especially ones who fit a certain mold, were crimes waiting to happen. I was mad at the idea of a Butthead, a guy whose morals operated on a vector. But to his face I couldn't be, because I suffered from the same relativism.

"How did she know I was coming?"

"Internet." He shrugged and hid behind his beer.

"Same as how she knew Fitz was coming?"

"Told you that was Fanny," Orrin interjected.

"Fuck, Bernard," I said before finishing my beer. "I'm surprised you wrote 'Nice Caddy' instead of 'titties' all lowercase."

"I had to stop myself. Harper's a lady."

I must have been drunk, because I laughed, and Bernard aka Butthead laughed with me. Even Orrin got that look an older man gets when he has to reluctantly admit the kid got off a good one.

I went to bed on my thin little mattress and stared at the cracks in the ceiling. The noise lessened downstairs. Doors opening and closing. Water pipes rattling. Chatter. Children. I hadn't been around that many children since I was a child myself.

When everyone was gone, Catherine started crying.

If Harper came back, the sound of her would have been lost in the chaos. I needed to apologize or tell her it didn't matter or something. I needed to tell her I meant it, and I didn't. We could do this together.

She doesn't have to—

—maybe she wanted to—

—she's not a fuck-for-riches type—

—you don't know her—

—you know she's a decent person who—

—has been on Chaxxer—

—but she doesn't have to—

Around and around it went.

She was gone too long. Way too long. She could have been lying on the side of the road or in trouble or miles away at some rapist's second location.

I got out of bed and started putting pants on when there was a break in the wailing through the walls. I could hear better. A sound from the hall was coming through, then Catherine started again, and it was gone.

Was it clicking?

Pants on, I went into the hall and stood at the foot of Harper's stairwell.

Definitely clicking. She was at the keys.

I stayed at the bottom of her stairs, listening. Was she typing filthy things? Was @Flow_ro calling her a slut? Or a whore? I'd done the same to hurt her feelings, not get myself off. Did that make me a better or worse person than him?

My bones ached. She could be doing anything up there. Re-hacking me. My brain could barely complete a thought except that she was safe at home, not twisted in a knot on the side of the road.

Bursting into her room, no matter the reason, was going to make it worse.

I crawled into bed and let the crickets lull me to sleep. Not even Catherine's crying could keep me up. I thought I'd slept for a few minutes, but when I woke, the crickets were done and the moon had moved across the sky into the frame of the French doors. Catherine had quieted.

A dark figure stood over me silently. The moon caught the blond edges of her hair.

"Harper?"

She didn't answer, but her shoulders shook, and she swallowed so hard I could hear it. I sat on the edge of the bed.

She held out something. It glinted in the moonlight, clattering to the mattress when she dropped it in the space between my legs.

"My watch." I looked at it but didn't see much but a dark circle. The ticking vibrated against my fingers. "Thank you."

"You have to know how to ask Johnny for things."

"Yeah." I put it on my wrist. The ticking was louder than my heartbeat, but barely. "I'm sorry about what I called you. I knew it would hurt you."

"Sometimes I feel like I'm a stranger here. In my own hometown. It's always been that way. Then I drag you here. It's been less than a week, but I have moments with you where I feel like you and I, we're strangers, but it's temporary. Like there's about to be *knowing* between us I don't have with anyone else. And then you're so cruel."

She sniffed. Her shoulders hitched. She pressed her fingertips against the insides of her eyes.

"But I have it coming," she said. "I know I do. I fucked with your life. I'm still fucking with it. You don't owe me anything."

What did she want? Besides returning my watch, was there something else?

"What brought you down here?"

She shrugged, waving in the general direction of her room, her computers, her Chaxxer account. "I wasn't in the mood for bullshit."

"So you came to *me*?"

She coughed a short laugh. "Go figure."

Turning to the moonlight, raising her hand as if she wanted to say things she couldn't, her breathing got thick and shallow. When she blinked, tears were displaced onto her cheeks.

I wanted to ask her where my laptop was, but it could wait. Every- thing that kept us apart could wait. She needed me more than I needed answers.

I leaned on an elbow, swung my legs back on the bed, and held my hand out to her. "Come on."

"I can't." She was fully crying. Not as unreservedly as her sister, but her voice was wet and broken.

"Clothes on. No sex. I won't even get hard."

She laughed a little and stepped forward. "Yes, you will."

"All right. I might get hard." I turned back the covers. "Come on. It's warm."

Tick-tick-tick, my watch counted the time it took for her to decide.

Knee first, then hand, then shoulder and last leg, she crawled into bed and turned onto her back to look at the cracked ceiling and the bald, dark light bulb.

Everything about that was wrong. I put the covers over her and was overcome with tenderness. It overrode all my good sense. All the brain power I'd wasted and some that I'd used. She was the enemy. She had my life in her hands. She was the reason I was trapped. If I wanted to get what I needed from her, I had to keep my distance.

All those things were true.

But in the moonlight, with my body aching and her silent sobs breaking the crust of my hostility, they became false. Her tears spoke to a different part of me. A part I had no control over. A part I hadn't known I had. A part of me that she'd been prying away since the minute I met her.

Tick-tick-tick.

Sure as I was that she was too emotionally guileless to break my guard down intentionally, I was also sure I could put my battle gear on again tomorrow.

She tried to get control of her breath, and covered her face with her hands as if she didn't want me to see her crying. I gently turned her until my face was at her shoulder and we were spoons.

I barely heard her whisper, "You don't have to be nice to me."

"I know." I held her. I knew she was awake from the way her eyelashes brushed my arm.

Tick-tick-tick.

Johnny making that bet while I was too drunk to remember. The gears and watch guts on his table. My dealer getting a "cheap" Langematik from a guy he'd never met before.

"It was my watch, wasn't it?" She didn't answer, but I was sure she knew what I meant. "All this time I thought… my God… it was me. I was bringing the transmitter in and out of the cage."

"Johnny thought you'd notice the watch was slow before we got all the data."

"Who tells time with their watch?" I stroked her arm. I was the weak link. I was the one who'd had to have the sweetest mechanical piece. It was my ego that had brought the whole thing crashing down. "Who else is in on it? The whole town?"

"Just me and Johnny. Butthead with the spray paint. They wouldn't…

they'd freak out if they knew. Johnny's the only one who believes in karmic social justice. That because my father owned this town and destroyed it, I'm the one who has to fix it."

"Do you believe that?"

"It doesn't really matter, does it?" She wiggled and turned around until she faced me. Her hands were folded flat under her cheek. The sobbing had abated. "I used to believe in forgiveness. I used to read Sher- lock Holmes because they were such good puzzles. When I got to *The Blue Carbuncle*—"

"Is that the one you left in the comments? With the geohash?"

"Yes. Did you finish it?"

"No." I'd skimmed for more clues once I knew what they looked like, but I hadn't read for story. Ego again. I'd thought I knew what the hacker was trying to tell me, so I'd ignored the rest. A stupid, sloppy mistake.

"This regular guy steals a valuable gem. It's famous. Everyone wants it. People have died to own it. Holmes says..." Her tongue flicked over her lips, and her eyes went to the side as if thinking. "'Every facet stands for a bloody deed.' He, the thief, hides it in a goose and gets caught. But when Holmes figures it out, well, the guy wasn't a lifelong criminal. He was terrible at it, actually. Holmes realizes there's no use in turning the guy in. He lets him go."

I touched a half-dried tear with my thumb. "He hid his treasure in a goose?"

"Yeah. And Holmes ate it. He broke the spell," she continued. "By forgiving a thief, he changed someone's world."

"So it's not karmic justice or cultural social whatever?"

"No. It's different. Not that it matters. I'm the one who can do what has to be done. But I like to think that my father is forgiven. Someday my family will be off the hook."

"There's no hook, goose."

She spoke again after a few deep breaths. "Then why can I feel it?"

Her shoulders shook, and she sniffled. She was going to cry again, and I couldn't take that either. Crying women scared me. They made me feel as if I was on a boat in the middle of the ocean, sun up at the top of noon, without a marker to know where I was.

But I had to steer the fucking boat this time. There was no grown-up to make it all right. That was me. I was the grown-up, and I had to commit to a direction.

I held her as tightly as I could without crushing her, but I wanted to crush her. Hard. Into a tight ball I could tuck away someplace safe.

"It's okay." My words were stupid and ineffective, but they were all I had. "You're going to be all right."

"I want to accomplish something. I just want to win again, you know?"

Seeing her weep for validation punched a hole in the world. She was brilliant and compassionate. She worked hard for everyone around her. I'd never met such a genius in my life. Things were supposed to be easy for people like her. She was supposed to have the world at her feet. How could this be true? How could it happen?

"I surrender. You're going to win this. I'll do whatever you need me to."

Her nod was so slight I barely felt it against my shoulder.

I was only human. I was ambitious and callous, but I wasn't any kind of sociopath. She'd hurt me, opened me, then asked for sympathy with her body against mine.

Of course I dragged my lips against her throat then her cheek. Of course they sought out her breath and her voice. And when I kissed her, of course I wanted to get inside her.

I didn't want to seduce her. I didn't want to relieve myself and move on. She was neither project nor prey. She was Harper. Just Harper. She had hands that clawed and a mouth that groaned into mine. She had hips that pushed into me when the line of my cock was against her. She took my control and wove it into desire.

"Fuck!" I snapped as I pulled away. "I said I wouldn't."

She was under me, breathing from deep in her chest through parted lips. "Yes, but we can."

She wanted to. She'd said yes. What the hell else did I need? An engraved fucking invitation?

"No transactions."

"Okay," she said with a sharp nod and locked her hands behind my neck. "No trades. Just sex."

"No." I gently took her hands from my neck. "It would be a trade. Every time we touch each other, it's a transaction. I can't. You didn't come down here for that. And I'm not going to pretend I understand it, but I'm fucked in the head when it comes to you. I'm not going to take my fucked- upness about it and relocate it to you." I kissed her because that crease in her lip needed to be kissed very badly.

One of her eyelids drooped a little, narrowing her focus. "You have feelings for me."

"I said I didn't understand it." I got up on my knees and nudged her to her side. "It must be your powers of seduction."

"I'm amazing," she said with a smile.

I fit my chest against her back and pushed one arm under her neck, spooning her again. "You are. Now go to sleep."

I didn't expect to sleep. Sleeping with another person in the bed was impossible—until that night. Her breathing got even and shallow against me, and her shoulder went limp. I planned on holding her until the sun came up, but soon after, my mind went into the weeds then cut to black.

XLI

I was on the boat again, but I was sitting alone on the stern. My watch was ticking as if it was pressed right up against my ear. Sharks circled the boat. I couldn't see them, but I knew they were there, and I knew they were hungry.

I wasn't scared. I was irritated. My tailbone itched. When I reached behind to scratch it, I pulled back a wiggling salmon. What to do with it? If I threw it back into the ocean, the sharks would eat it, and I didn't want that. I had to save it.

I threw it in a water-filled red bucket. It splashed and swam the perimeter.

My tailbone tickled again.

Another salmon.

Plop, into the bucket.

It was crowded in there, but they'd be all right.

But then, another prickled my tailbone.

Still, I couldn't let the sharks eat it. Couldn't. These were my fish. I was responsible for them.

When I dropped it in the bucket, all three fit comfortably, then four fit, as if the bucket grew bigger on the inside but not the outside.

A fifth appeared with no sign they'd ever stop, and the five-gallon bucket increased its interior size.

"Stay still."

Harper's voice cut through my dream. I was on my stomach with my watch to my ear, and the pitching of the boat had been her shifting weight on the bed. She held me down when I tried to turn, and I let her because whatever she was doing to the place where my back met my butt was kind of nice.

"What are you doing back there?"

"Code number three."

"I thought we weren't being transactional."

"We didn't have sex. So it wasn't a transaction." With the click of the pen cap, she checked her work by counting on her fingers and checking notations in a little pad, then she nodded sharply. "Done."

I twisted around. "How am I supposed to see that?"

"Tricky problem." She took her cell from the night table. I was immediately jealous that she had her connection to the wider world while mine was cut. "I can take a picture, and you can call from here. You don't even have to get out of bed."

"No." I said it more harshly than I intended.

"I promise to not post your butt on the internet."

"I'm not worried about that. My partner already located the house when I called from the landline. I don't want him to locate your personal phone."

"You know I'm cloaked, right?"

"Don't test him."

"So how you calling this one in? Smoke signal?"

I stood. "I already called from the kitchen phone."

She followed me down the hall. Downstairs, Catherine hummed to the *whoosh whoosh* of a broom.

I stopped in the middle of the stairwell. Harper couldn't get past me if I didn't want her to, and I didn't. "You don't need to come."

"You're reading the code on your butt?"

"I was going to use a shiny teapot or something. Hack life, Harper. Not just computers."

"I'll make a note."

"Yesterday. About Everett."

"You apologized already."

"It's a shitty plan. But I understand it. It's not about money. It's about maintenance."

"Yes."

"And also, you're cute when you lie. Your nose turns up just a little."

She tapped my nose from the step above and whispered, "You don't know the whole plan."

I was a pawn in a chess game, and I should have been worried about being used without consent. I should have wondered when I was going to be sacrificed. But I was just curious how much bigger this thing was.

She wasn't going to tell me. I would have to play along until I could figure it out myself.

I unblocked her way, and we went to the kitchen together. Catherine was nowhere in sight, but her presence was felt in the hissing coffee pot and the two mugs she'd left in front of it.

I picked up the phone receiver.

Harper ran her finger along my waistband and shifted it down. I was glad she couldn't see my boner from behind.

Deeprak was on the phone in two minutes. "What do you have for me, my friend? It's getting fucked up over here."

"What kind of fucked up?"

An important question since the person holding me hostage was stroking my lower back with her fingernails and it was driving me crazy.

"Your devil investor's AWOL. I liked it better when I could see what he was doing."

"He'll be happy when he gets back. You ready for decryption?"

"Ready."

Harper read the characters to me, tracing each one with her finger.

"124 131 064 040 164 150 145 040 163 160 157 157 156 163."

"Done," she said then whispered, "It's octal, by the way."

"Who's that with you?" Deeprak asked. "Is that Harper Watson?"

In other words, *are you sleeping with the enemy?* Which, technically, I was.

"Can you just keystroke, please?"

She continued, and Deeprak read it back, which I repeated back to Harper in the oldest game of telephone. I decoded the octal in the translations.

I looked over my shoulder as she flipped her hair, inadvertently exposing her ear. I didn't mind the missing diamond. She looked better without them. More naked.

"You're welcome."

She smiled. The octal converted into "Thank you for the spoons," and she was very, very welcome.

"Yeah, no," Deeprak said. "I'm getting nothing. Can I have it again?"

"Can you call it again?" I asked Harper.

We did it again.

"No." Deeprak's voice was soft with dread. "And I'm getting a new message at the prompt."

Standing straighter, I turned to Harper. I must have been pale or something because she put down her coffee cup and grabbed for the phone. I shooed her hand, but she pulled my arm down until our ears shared the receiver.

"What message?" I said.

"Enter decryption code to boot OS, colon, backslash, then this: 'System will lock after two more failed attempts.' Then the prompt."

"No." Harper snapped the receiver away. "That's not right. I didn't put a lock against a brute force attack. I didn't have to. I'm generating codes on the fly."

"That makes no sense."

"Random is built into quantum trinary. Selective decryption is—"

"It's you!" Deeprak shouted "Put Taylor on!"

She gave me the phone. I held it between us so we could both here.

"It's me," I said.

"Have you lost it, brother?"

"I can hear you," Harper said.

"She can hear you."

"This is bad," she said with a shaky voice. "I didn't set that up."

"You've done enough." Deeprak sounded as mad as I'd ever heard him sound.

"Deeps, listen—"

"Keaton did it," he and I said at the same time.

"He's been hooked up to the sys on his own machine for days." Deeprak's cool, sweet charm was dissolving under the stress. Harper leaned away from the phone and crossed her arms, looking into the middle distance and biting her lower lip while Deeprak continued his rant in my ear. "Fucker. Fucking evil-ass motherfucker said he was trying to crack through. He was locking it. Next time, Taylor, get a goddamn *bank* to invest all right?"

"Where did he go?" I asked. It was the last calmly thought-out question I had. My last hope that all this was some kind of mistake Keaton could clear up if he was around. Maybe he was developing a workaround and had to put a layer of encryption over the Harperware to finish. Maybe this was simple. Maybe I could just hold the ocean in a five-gallon bucket if I stayed calm.

"How should I know?" Deeprak's voice shook. "Jesus. Fucking. Christ."

Calm broke under pressure from chaos. Jesus fucking Christ was right. The world went a little whiter, as if it went under an overexposure filter, washing in white and yellow. Details got warmer before my eyes, dissolving into bright fury.

"Know, Deeprak. Know. Find out. Don't panic without a reason. Don't go code black over what you *think* is happening."

I slammed the phone into the cradle. It made a sickly yet satisfying little ring from inside the case. I picked it up and slammed it down again.

"Taylor?" Harper had her phone clutched to her chest like a buoy on the open sea.

"What?!"

"How could he talk to QI4 if it's not binary?"

"My guess?" I leaned into her, and she backed up against the door-frame. "He's hooked up to your fucking poison pill."

As she still clutched the phone to her chest, her pupils dilated just a little as if taking in extra information. Or because I cast her in shadow.

I put my hands up, not touching her, but extending the moment before I did.

I was so mad at her I couldn't even think. I was clouded with hot red rage. It latched on to every emotion I already had, all the affection and warmth, filling all the places where I'd let her in. All the empathy I had for her. My anger found purchase on those and grew to infiltrate anything decent.

Her butter skin. Her lips. Her dark-to-light lashes. Hurt it. I wanted to hurt it so my anger had a place to go. If I didn't eat her alive, I was going to digest myself in my own acid.

And that phone to her chest, like a black monolith from deep space. I wanted to rip it away and throw it in the thorn bed then shred both our bodies wading to it. We'd be one thing. A single monster made of anger, blood, and brutality.

I wasn't even thinking straight. I'd lost a battle with sense and patience. Logic had jumped to its death rather than be in the same room with what I'd let in.

The little boat rocking on the flat circle of horizon. The pressure. The physical compression of my infinite speckness. I needed a lifeline to a point in the distance. Any point. I needed to know I wasn't cut off, because if this went on much longer, I was going to lose my mind.

"Can you get to him? Keaton? Can you—"

"Not without my phone." I put angry emphasis on the last word, filling it with all the blame and regret I could get into one syllable. "Fuck this."

I pushed away with the force of everything left in me that was civilized and decent. It wasn't that hard a push. It had just enough torque to get me away from her, turn me, and propel me toward the back of the house. To the bed of thorns that covered my phone.

"Taylor?" she called from a miles-long tunnel.

I heard her but kept my pace to the back of the house, slapping open the screen door and heading into the chilly, humid late morning. The clouds were low and oppressive. I opened the shed, and the stink of mildew and rotting wood hit me square in the face as if it could stop me. I plucked a pair of rusted, scissor-shaped hedge clippers from a nail on the wall.

When I turned back to the door and tried to walk out, Harper appeared in a goose-down vest the color of rust.

I reared back, almost stabbing her. "Jesus! Harper, get out of the way."

She moved. "I'm sorry," she said as I unlocked the blades. "I'm sorry this happened. I'm sorry it was my pill. But let's figure it out."

"Sure." I gripped the handles, but the hinge was loose and they flopped and waved. "That's great. Positive attitude. I had it all under control but no fucking problem." I tried to twist the little screw holding the two halves of the scissors together, but I couldn't narrow my attention. "Everything. I had everything. Knee-fucking-deep in money. I had the legs of every credit card company wide open, and I walked away to go straight. For this."

The nut came off the clippers and the halves split. I caught one as it fell. I held them by the handles like giant pointer fingers. I must have looked like Edward Scissorhands.

"For *this*." I pointed a blade into the horizon. The direction of QI4. "This useless hunk of code. And if you think it's anything better than useless right now, you're not thinking. It's been hacked twice. Twice."

I held up both rusted blades at the grey sky, and as if in answer, a rumble of thunder came from far away. A raindrop fell on my forehead.

"What do you want?" I asked the sky. The wind picked up in answer. "Tell me what you want out of me!"

"We don't have long," Harper said from a million miles away. "Your phone's going to get wet."

Of course. Because everything was fucked up. Because every single lucky break I'd gotten my entire life, from my first steps off the brick stoop when my father caught me before I smacked my head to the sweet parking spot in front of Anglioni's, was being paid back in spades right now.

And what had my life been but a series of fucking lucky breaks if I couldn't tolerate a few bumps in the road?

It was a lie. All of it was a lie.

I choked out the shortest expression of what flooded me, throwing the blades into the bushes. First one, then the other, disappeared with a rustle as if swallowed by the ocean.

"I am worthless."

"You're not," she protested.

I didn't want to hear it. Not a word of it. I hadn't said it so she could make me feel better. That would have been needy. Taylor Harden was a fuckup and a lie, but he wasn't needy.

Harper stepped toward me as if she was going to hug me or some shit.

I put my hand out like a crossing guard. "Don't. Don't get all girly and squishy on me. Don't expect me to cry on your shoulder while you pat my back and say it's going to be all right. It's not going to be all right. I don't need a fucking hug."

She looked at me as if I was made of shit and chicken liver. "I wasn't going to hug you."

This woman.

"What then?"

She approached again. Came right up to me. Took half a pause and slapped me in the face. "Snap out of it. Everyone's worthless. Don't be such a baby about it."

My wrist went to my stung left cheek. I was stunned she'd slapped me and equally surprised that it had worked. The mantra of worthlessness that looped in my head stopped and was replaced with complete attention to the moment. The situation. The stillness of the air. The faraway rush of the polluted river.

I didn't know what I looked like to her, but I wasn't frightening enough to scare her or sad enough to melt her into empathy. She was waiting like a blank page. I could write whatever I wanted. She was doing that for me. Like the slap in the face, her openness was a gift, and I could open it…or not.

I lived in a world of butting heads and chest-beating, dick-slinging competition.

And here, Harper had slapped me and left herself exposed. She hadn't slapped me to win. She was trying to help me.

"Huh." My utterance was the breath of a pressurized jar popping open.

Her eyebrow twitched with curiosity. She was utterly fearless.

I was so fucking crazy about this girl. I was losing my mind, and I didn't know how much longer I could fight it. I wanted to save myself, sure. But I wanted to lift her up. Show the world what they'd missed out on. Present her like a jewel in a box then keep her for myself.

But I had nothing.

I was a loser.

That wasn't going to do her any good, now was it? She deserved better. She *needed* better. She needed a win, and I was going to get it for her.

I went back into the shed. Adjusted to the darkness of the places under shelves and behind busted doors. Found another pair of clippers that wouldn't even open. Tossed them. Found the best tool for the job.

A chainsaw. The gas gauge was at the quarter-full mark.

"I'm nobody. I'm just a kid from Jersey."

"What are you doing?" Harper asked when I came out.

I yanked the cord. The engine coughed. "We've both been fucked." Yank. *Cough.* "And you want Fitz. I can get you Fitz." Yank. *Cough cough.* "I'll suck his dick myself. But you're not sucking it. Put your last dollar on that." Yank. *Sputter. Cough.* "I lost everything. I'm not losing you."

Yank. *Roar.*

The rain thickened to a fine mist that swirled around the chainsaw blade. Harper had her arms crossed over her tits and her mouth set into a line. I waited a second with the chainsaw held up. She knew what I was going to do, but she didn't stop me.

I reached over the little white fence and slashed at the thorn bush bed. Shards of wood flew up, stinging my cheek as I cut away the branches.

Harper put her hand on my back and pointed at the scraps of tangled shrubbery. She had on gloves and goggles.

I nodded.

She reached over the fence and pulled up an armful of bushes. I cut a crooked umbilical cord and she hauled the bunch away before throwing it to the side.

Space had opened up inside the fence. I stepped over it, into the little circle of dirt, and cut that fucking shit right out of the earth, slicing at the trunks, squinting to protect my eyes. I thought a raindrop fell from my forehead, but when I wiped it away, it was blood.

Harper barely paused, and I only stopped when I had to get the chainsaw out of the way or risk taking off one of her limbs.

"I think you have to go a little left."

I followed the angle of her arm. "Yeah."

I sliced the bushes. We'd gotten about a third of the way to the center of the bed when the thunder was coming less than three seconds after the lightning. The raindrops got fatter. The chainsaw was running on fumes when it hit something hard and snapped the chain. The motor kept on with a *whirr*.

"What was that?" I put the chainsaw down and pulled the tangle of branches away from the hard object that had broken the blade. It was a marble tombstone.

EARL BARRINGTON
1945 - 2010
B/LØX\D FATHER

There was nothing notable about the stone except the chips and cracks in the word *beloved*.

"Harper?"

"I forgot to mention." She was right behind me. "There are gravestones from this point on to the edge of the fence. It's the family plot."

"This your father?" I pointed at the headstone that had broken the chainsaw.

"The one and only. May he rest in peace. Or not. Whatever. Can we keep going?"

"Who added the extra carving?"

"I got a little drunk." She slid the goggles up to the top of her head. Her hair stuck out from around the elastic like a crown. "He was nice to everyone's face. Played at being their pal like a phony baloney, and they fell for it. I'm sorry, but they were suckered." She waved at the factory over the horizon. "Even Catherine. He kept laying people off and dumping the extra work on whoever was left. Long hours. No overtime. They did it with these big proud smiles because they felt like they were special, you know? 'Sure, I'm overworked and got my health insurance cut. And well, of course he fought Fred McGee on his worker's comp. That's just business. But I'm special because I got to stay.' He was a shit. Acted like he was one of the guys. Then he'd throw all his employees a picnic and make it potluck. What a bag of goods." She kicked the head- stone, but the density of the thorns behind it kept it from falling. Not to be thwarted, she rattled her throat and spit on the grave. It dripped then rerouted into the carved letters. "Fuck you. You fooled everyone. You never fooled me."

"Don't hold back, Harper. Tell him how you feel."

She slid her goggles back down. "This is why she let the bushes grow. Hiding my vandalism."

"I like your vandalism."

With a thunder crack, the rain came harder.

"Shit!" we cried at the same time.

The phone was going to get drowned. I crouched, bending to see under the bracken. The earth was still dry—but not for long. Harper got to her belly and crawled forward into it.

"I can see it," she called.

I pulled on a thick, thorny joint, opening the tunnel a little wider. She crawled, disappearing to the waist. Thorns grabbed her vest, shredding it. When I wiped my face with my wrist, it came back bloody. Great. I didn't care if I got a little cut up, but I didn't want Harper to bleed. Not to get my phone.

I was about to tell her to forget it. We'd cut back more or tarp the thing and wait for the rain to clear. I wanted the phone, but I didn't want her to get shredded.

"Harper?"

"So close."

"Come back."

"Almost… ow!"

That was it. I hooked my hand in her waistband and pulled her out. She slid on the dirt, vest shredding, light as a feather, pants moving below her sexy ass. When her head was free, she twisted and faced the rain.

My phone was in her bloody hand.

"Ha! I got it!"

I pulled her up by the wrists and flung my arms around her, kissing her as if my life depended on it. Her scent mingled with the rain as two parts of the same nourishment. Ozone. Water. A life in latency.

She put the phone in my front pocket and got her arms around me. The rain fell between us, catching some of the blood from my cut, going into our mouths. It tasted like copper pennies. It tasted like her. She was falling from the sky.

I could have taken her right on the ground. Let the loose thorns and splinters cut our skin. Let the rain soak our hair to flat masses and our fingertips to prunes.

Not this time.

Bending, I kept one arm around her waist, put the other behind her knees, and lifted her.

"I can walk." Her eyelids flicked against the rain. She licked sky water off her lips.

"I know."

I carried her out of the thorn bed, up to the porch, where she opened the screen door with an outstretched hand and I kicked it open. Squeaking wet shoes left a trail on the wood floor. Up the stairs, I walked by feel and habit. She laced her hands around my neck. I couldn't take my eyes off her.

The goggles were still pushed up on her head, and dirt speckled her cheeks like freckles. She was so perfectly flawed, so precisely herself, the sum total of all the meaningless moments in her life leading up to me taking her down the hall to my room. She was the cement holding events together. The darkness after the lightning and the thickened silence before the thunder.

It was rainy-day dark at the top of the stairs. She leaned hard to the left until I let her go. Once she was on her feet, I couldn't keep off her. Lips first, I pinned her to the wall. She wrapped her legs around me, and I drove against her until I felt her heat. She grabbed at my shirt as if she wanted to shred it, and I pulled hers up so I could get at her skin.

We took unsure, turning steps to the room I called mine, with hands everywhere. I got under her bra. Her hard nipple was like a completed pilgrimage. The pressure at the base of my cock was unbearable, and for the first time since I was fourteen, it threatened to relieve itself withoutmy say so.

"Hold on," I said.

"No, no." She reached between my legs. Thank God the sweatpants cut the sensation, or she would have pulled back a sticky mess.

I took her by the wrist and kissed her hand. The back of it was scraped as if she'd gotten into a fight with an alley cat. "You poor girl." From wrist to elbow, I kissed her wounds to the crack of thunder. "You got scraped up for me."

The wind slapped the balcony door open, unleashing her hair. She touched my face. It stung.

"You look sexy with a little blood on you." She pulled my head down and kissed my forehead.

A feather floated to the floor at her feet. It blew across the worn wood, getting stuck on the bed leg.

I put her hand against my chest. "I want you. I haven't known what to do with how you make me feel. But I feel…" I shook my head. "Like the world is bigger with you."

Her eyelids fluttered, and the tightness of her smile told me she wanted to hide it but couldn't.

"I want to take care of you. Everything is going to go your way. Do you hear me? You're a queen, and everyone's going to know it. No one's going to treat you the way I did ever again."

She put her fingers on my lips. "Hush. You can't promise that."

"I can." I pulled on the shoulders of her vest. "Starting with me, right now."

She put her arms down, and I slipped the vest off her. The shredded back panel leaked feathers. They blew in the wind like snow. I held it up. The thorns had ripped clear through. I closed the window and tossed the vest in a corner.

"Come." I held my hand out and led her to the bathroom.

The light from the window was enough. I pulled off her goggles before I kneeled at her feet and tapped her boot. She picked up her foot, and I slipped off the boot. Then the sock, kissing her instep before moving to the other foot. She giggled.

"Sorry," she said. "I'm ticklish."

"I'll make a note. Arms up."

Standing, I lifted her shirt over her head, revealing a plain white bra that was half off where my hand had intruded. I reached around to unhook it. She winced. I went around her and moved her hair to the front. A three-inch gash was drying between her shoulder blades, and a half dozen little ones surrounded it. Her jeans were ripped at the top of her butt and the backs of her thighs.

"The thorns got you good," I said, going around to her front and slipping off her bra.

"That thorn bush always hated me. It was waiting for the day it could get at me."

"We should cut it down." I kissed between her breasts, kneeling to get my lips on her belly.

She put her fingers in my hair as I undid her jeans. "It's my sister's. It's her way of protecting the family plot. It's nice when it blooms."

I pushed her jeans down slowly, trying to keep the fabric from rubbing where she was hurt. "Step out."

She picked her feet out of her pants, and I pushed the jeans away. I could smell her. She was so close. A big part of me demanded I take her right there, any way she'd let me. But the smaller part, the part that seemed as though it had been dormant my entire life, demanded I take care of her first.

The medicine cabinet was full of shit. Expired, half-used, dried-up bottles of vanity goop, amber bottles of medicine, bandages, makeup. No alcohol. No gentle astringents. I found a brown bottle of hydrogen peroxide and a few loose cotton balls in a Dixie cup.

I sat on the toilet with the bottle and cup between my legs. "Come. Let me see your back."

She stepped forward, spun on the ball of her foot, and swung her hair out of the way. "Thank you."

"I haven't touched you yet." I tipped the brown bottle over a cotton ball. "I might suck at this."

"It doesn't matter."

I touched the cotton ball to the deepest gash. She sucked in a breath.

"Told you." I dabbed around it before going for the raw parts. "I need practice."

"We'll have to get in more adventures."

I stretched a Band-Aid over her shoulder blade cut and worked on the backs of her thighs. "More adventures?"

"Yeah. Like wrestling alligators in Florida."

"We could take a dog team across Alaska."

She got one Band-Aid across the long cut and a circle on a particularly deep one.

"Percy needs to be on the back with us. We can take pictures of him and send them back. Like people do with the lawn gnomes."

I kissed the place where her back met her ass and turned her to face me. "Whatever you want."

"I like the sound of that."

She ran her fingers through my hair, and I took them away so I could see the damage to her hands. It wasn't too bad, but I wanted to heal every wound she'd gotten for me.

"You know what though? I'm going to kibosh the dogs and the alligators and every other animal. Not even a kitten," I said.

"No?"

I put the bottle and compressed cotton ball to the side, looking up at her naked body with my hands gripping her elbows. The rain hadn't let up a bit, but the thunder had gotten farther away. "Not until you swear you're giving up on Fitz. The whole plan. Get him here by getting Badger to promise tax breaks or whatever. Show him how committed you all are. But he can't have you. You're mine. Only mine. And I know you care about this town. I'll give up everything to save it if it makes you happy. But I cannot let another man touch you. Do you understand?"

She didn't answer. She didn't nod or give me a signal. She picked up the wet cotton ball. "Stay still."

"That's not an answer."

She dabbed my forehead. It stung. She moved the cold pad to my cheek then my chin. The pain followed. It was bearable against her not answering.

"Well?" I asked.

"It's complicated."

"No. It's very fucking simple."

She tossed the cotton ball onto the vanity. "Taylor Harden, I thought I could just keep hating you. I figured you'd help me then go away. I swear to you, on everything I love, that you opened a door in my heart and walked right in. If I knew how to unlock that damned door and throw you out, I would. The way you act. The way you treat me. You're too big in there, and it's uncomfortable."

"That's. Not. An. Answer."

She swallowed hard. "There's no one else. Not after you."

She bent her knees and straddled me. I pressed her down against my erection. She swayed a little, rubbing herself against the length.

"Swear it," I said with my lips on her collarbone. I couldn't kiss the entire surface of her body fast enough.

"On a stack of Bibles."

I kissed her mouth between words, and she kissed me between syllables.

"I'm going to be your first." I stood, holding her. She wrapped her legs around me as I carried her to the bedroom. "Right now."

"Yes. Be that."

"I want you to come your first time. I want it to be good."

I laid her on the bed. She was so fully naked. All cream skin and smooth perfection in the light of a rainy day.

"I'm a mess," I said, pulling my sweatpants down. "I should shower."

"If you shower, I'm going to put my clothes back on and make lunch."

Crawling onto the bed, I hovered over her. My dick weighed a ton, dropping against her belly as if her body were a magnet and I were iron.

"You will not."

"Don't test me, Beeze. We were both out there."

My lips ran down her neck, landing on a sweet, pink nipple. "You smell like the roses. I smell like the thorns."

When her back arched into me, I gave up on a shower. I took her breast, her belly, the sensitive places between her thighs with my mouth. I tasted the nectar between her legs. Gently, I circled my tongue at her open- ing, tasting the tight ring I was about to break. She dug her fingers into my shoulders, and I backed off. I didn't want her to come, but I wanted her to be close.

"I hate to do this," I said, reaching for the night table.I grabbed my wallet and flipped it open. "I need to take care of you."

I put the condom in my teeth and tossed the wallet on the floor.

She snapped the packet away. "I got this." She ripped it open with her teeth, spit the strip, and took out the condom. Would she ever stop making me smile?

Yes. When she stroked my cock, she wiped the smile right off my face.

"That's good?"

"Yes." I was lucky to form a coherent word.

I helped her roll the condom on. That was one thing I didn't want a first-timer to be in charge of, though I felt like a first-timer myself. When she spread her legs wider and lifted her hips, I was overwhelmed by her needs and mine.

I ran my finger over her clit once more, then I pressed against her opening. Her lips parted. The rain pounded the windows, and the drops cast moving shadows on her cheeks.

"Say good-bye to this."

"Yesokaygood-bye."

One finger inside. So tight. I was stalling. I didn't know how I was going to last.

"Fuck me," she squeaked. "God, could you just fuck me?"

"Is that how we ask for something?"

"Please. Fuck me, *please*."

My cock throbbed in my hand as I put it against her. She put her hands on my cheeks and mouthed *please* one last time before I pushed forward.

I felt the break immediately, and the arousal on her face twisted into pain.

"You okay?" I didn't move. Couldn't. One stroke and I'd be done for.

"Yeah."

"I'm going to go slow. It's going to feel good. I promise."

She nodded as if she trusted me because she had no choice. "I want to do it right."

"You're beautiful, goose. You're perfect." I could see that wasn't what she needed to hear. "And you're doing it right. Very right."

I moved inside her, taking it slow and easy. I kissed her frequently. Reassured her constantly. When she seemed less pained, I reached between us and touched her clit with my thumb.

She gasped.

"Is that a yes?" I whispered.

"Yes."

"Does it still hurt?"

"Only a little. Oh, God, but not when you do that."

I pushed deep inside her and circled her clit with my thumb. The pressure to come was building, but she had to come first.

Her legs shuddered. Her knees spread wider. Lips parted, letting out a soft groan, eyebrows knotted.

I wanted to take that moment and live it forever. That second before her fingernails dug deep into my back and her spine twisted. But it was eaten up by her orgasm and my need to keep my thumb on her clit.

When she moved my hand away, I leveraged my knees and fucked her faster, getting as deep as I could and letting go.

Nothing had ever felt that good. Nothing except falling on her and burying my face in her neck, drinking in the scent of infinite possibilities.

XLII

I hadn't curled up with a woman like this since the first week of college, before Soo and I had been too hosed to fuck or even see each other outside study group.

When I woke, very early in the morning, Harper still slept on my arm, still naked and probably so sore she wouldn't be able to walk. My phone wasn't broken. It was charging on the chair seat, silent but flashing. I'd woken to the glow half an hour before, but I didn't have the willpower to let Harper go. Somewhere in Silicon Valley, my life was falling apart, and the umbilical cord to that clusterfuck was calling.

I wished I'd put the phone in another room so I could live in a bubble. Just for one full night, I wanted to take in the smell of her, the satin of her skin, the sound of the rain, and the whoosh of her breath.

A man has to make a choice at some point. Either do great things or enjoy half sleep in the rain in the arms of a woman. I'd chosen a long time ago to do great things.

There was always the possibility I could do both. I'd been wrong before. I had been wrong about the type of person behind my destruction. He wasn't a sociopathic criminal, and he wasn't even a he. He was a she, and she was as warm and bighearted as could be.

I had been wrong about my immunity to women like her, if another one even existed on the planet. I thought about that for what seemed like a long time.

"Can you get that please?" she mumbled. "It's making me crazy."

"It's not even on vibrate, and you're facing the other direction."

"I can feel it flashing."

"Fine."

We untangled. She dropped back onto the pillow, and I sat up. The sky outside was opaque grey, and the sunlight said five o'clock. My watch disagreed by four and a half hours. It was nine thirty.

Jesus. I hadn't slept that late in years. And it was before work hours back home.

Still naked, with a streak of blood on my thigh, I picked up the phone. Harper rolled out of bed and trotted into the bathroom, clicking the door shut behind her.

Deeprak had been trying to get me.

<I'm not asking where you are anymore.>
<There's a clause in your contract.
You become incapacitated, control of QI4
reverts to your main investor.>
<It's been triggered.>

"Shit."

I called Deeprak.

"You need to get back here," he said without a greeting. "Now."

"Where is he?" I sat on the edge of the bed. "Let me talk to him."

"Are you kidding? I'm not going in there. He wants to know where you are. Please tell me your phone is cloaked."

Harper came out of the bathroom, naked as a Renaissance painting. Fuck. I'd been doing everything except what I was supposed to be doing.

"Of course it's cloaked. What's he doing?"

Harper kneeled behind me on the bed and put her hands on my shoulders. She rubbed them and kissed the back of my neck. I was crazy about her, but I wasn't crazy. I knew she was listening.

"Once he locked the system? He made phone calls. Dozens. Jack found him on a Tor forum offering to make QI4 boot sector open source—"

"What? No!"

"If anyone could get past the lockdown. There was a feeding frenzy. He's stirring the pot. He's connecting to Wi-Fi and opening the cage in six days for day one of GreyHatC0n."

He couldn't do that. There was no coming back from the system becoming open source. Anyone could use it. Anyone who wanted to be a star could build an OS on it. It would flush everything down the toilet.

"Has anyone talked to him?"

"Once he got off the forums, he was gone. We all tried."

"Don't go code black. We'll fix this." I said it to myself more than

Deeprak. I had to believe it. I had to talk myself out of a meltdown. The OS had been the easiest part to build. Anyone could doit.

"Fix it? Tell me how!" he shouted loud enough to hurt my ear.

"The quantum circuits are still ours."

"Until someone reverse engineers them."

"It's six days until the convention," Harper said.

"Is that her?" Deeprak asked.

"Yes. Have you checked—?"

"Fuck you, bitch!" Deeprak shouted to Harper.

"Deeps, do not—"

"Then fuck you too, bro."

Harper tapped my phone to turn on the speaker. "We fix it the same way I broke it. Does he have a company credit card?"

"Yes," Deeprak and I answered together.

"Does he use it?"

"It's a Grand Cayman bank," I objected.

Deeprak chimed in. "It's totally cloaked."

"Gentlemen." Her eyes met mine and were so clear that if I'd thought she'd need help standing or doing anything, I was wrong. "It was a yes or no question."

"Yes," we answered in unison again, like busted third graders.

"Can you see purchases from the past few days?"

"Raven has that stuff," Deeprak said. "She's probably stuck on 101 right now. She'll be here in half an hour if there's no traffic."

"Do you trust her?" Harper asked. "Yes or no?"

"Yes," I said without thinking.

I didn't have to think. I trusted Raven. She didn't need the job, but she stayed and it wasn't for the sex. She was the only woman in an office of men. She was oft-maligned, the butt of jokes, well-paid, overworked, and underappreciated. Plenty of other jobs waited at other companies, yet she stayed.

I shouldn't have trusted her. She was a woman and an unpredictable entity, but she'd put a lot of faith in QI4. She deserved it back.

"We find out if he's ordered anything online," Harper said. "We can intercept it at the distro center."

"Is that how you hacked our monitors?" Deeprak asked.

"Yes."

"Call us from her desk when she gets in," I said before I could be questioned.

I said "us," not "me." I didn't know if Deeprak or Harper noticed, but I looked at the unintentional pronoun as if it were a wedding crasher.

"Okay?" I said urgently. "Deeps? You got it?"

Deeprak didn't answer. The silence on the other end of the phone was deafening.

"Are you there?"

"Consider this my resignation," he said. "I'm done being your side-kick. I'll get you a letter in an hour."

The connection went dead before I could try to talk him out of it.

Shit. I put the phone to my forehead and looked at the space between my knees. I trusted Deeprak's competence and loyalty completely. Apparently he didn't trust mine.

If I lost Deeprak, what else had I lost? Who would follow him out? How many of the guys were halfway out or fully gone? Was I operating a shell of a company? I didn't even know. Deep's resignation was a deep wound I had to sew up, but I couldn't from Barrington.

"I have to go home," I said.

"I think you do." She rubbed my shoulders.

"This isn't about the system anymore. It's about the people."

"Yes."

"I need to get to the airport."

"I'll drive."

I looped my fingers around her wrist and pulled her into my lap. I couldn't imagine being separated from her for a second. She'd become a part of my life. "Come with me."

She smirked just enough to give away a deep distrust of something so simple because it was simple but powerful. "I'm not letting him smoke me out." She tapped my chin and stood. "He knows where I am, but he's waiting for you to deliver me."

"I can protect you. I got this."

She sucked in her lower lip just a little, trying to keep her face expressionless. Every twitch of insecurity was magnified. "Get in the shower. I'll pull the car around. If we go now, we can take Route 34. The interstate is gross."

She spun on her heel and left the room as if her decision to get on the plane was the last to be made.

It wasn't. She was coming with me. She just didn't know it yet.

XLIII

The airport was 145 miles away. At sixty mph, I had about two and a half hours in the car to let her know that I wasn't leaving her. She was coming with me. I needed her support, her body, and to a large extent, I needed her brain. She was too smart and too devious to leave behind. She was too sexy and warm to do without.

We were ten minutes out of Barrington, with farmland stretching in all directions. I was driving the shimmymobile, swearing I'd get her a new car as soon as I had a minute.

"So he tells her, on his goddamn deathbed, 'Make sure my daughters marry the right kind of man.' To her face." Harper was in the middle of a story about her father. "Then she tells everyone, and they all decide no one in town qualifies as the right kind of man. What kind of self-loathing is that? How much do you have to hate yourself to take orders from a guy who paid his contractors half what they billed? Because they 'didn't do a good job'? And then agree your children aren't good enough for his?"

My phone dinged. It was lodged in an empty space in the front console, and I could just catch the preview in the sliver of visible glass.

It was Fitz. I pulled out the phone.

"At one point, I wanted to fuck someone just to… hey, there's no texting and driving."

She reached for the phone, but I pulled it back. "Nope."

"No. Texting. And. Driving. I'll read it to you."

She was right. But I needed to see the text.

"Easy does it, goose. There's no one on the fucking road."

I leaned the phone on the steering wheel and read it at seventy-five mph. I don't recommend it. Especially if the text freezes the blood solid in your veins.

—Sorry about QI4, bro—

Fitz was a bro all the way, and come to think if it, he was a week late with condolences. He was secretive and eccentric, but he wasn't cheap with support.

—Sailing around Horn of Africa.
Back in 2 days. Talk then.—

Harper had no trouble getting the phone out of my hand at that point. As a courtesy, she shouldn't have read my texts, but I wasn't surprised that her curiosity bulldozed her manners.

The logic and timing took a second to sink in but no more.

Of course, Fitz could have been bullshitting her the whole time. He was a bullshitter and a filthy, kinky fucker, but he didn't have to lie about buying a factory.

Harper tucked the phone away without commenting. The road went straight to the horizon, disappearing into a pinpoint at the end of the earth.

"It was me, wasn't it?" I asked. "You were after me. Just me."

She turned on the radio.

I turned it off. "You went to a lot of trouble to get me here, and it wasn't just revenge. Maybe you told yourself it was. But it wasn't revenge at all. You were after *me*. Say it. Just say it."

"I don't know what you want out of me."

I slammed on the brakes. Blue rubber smoke billowed so thick I was sure I'd blow a tire. The car skidded to the side of the road.

"Jesus, Taylor!"

"You didn't bring me here to help you with Fitz. He's not coming."

"Maybe he lied to me."

"No. No, you're fucked if you think I'm believing another thing you say. You were after me. You knew I was making my own boards. You want me to buy the factory. You hacked me, and you set this whole thing up so I'd fall in love with you. Right? Say it."

"It's not that simple." She took a breath so deep her chest expanded.

"Were you using him to teach you what I wanted? Or to make me jealous?"

"I was in contact with Fitz to get him here, then he went sailing. But I never thought we could get him. We needed an unproven company that was going to have a growth spurt. You were the most likely mark, but any of the other outcomes was acceptable."

Funny how she ran right into talking as if she had a laser pointer in her hand and a PowerPoint presentation behind her. Strategy and tactics. Straight outta Barrington.

"And revenge? Don't forget revenge for not hiring you, right?"

"Unexpected upside."

I leaned over to her and draped my arm over the back of her seat. "Stop. Lying."

"Fuck you." She got out of the car and slammed the door.

"Oh no. Fuck *you*." I got out.

She was walking back toward Barrington. Fifteen miles in cowboy boots. I should have let her go. Just taken her fucking car, driven it to the airport, and dumped it there. But I had a score to settle.

I took her by the elbow and spun her around, letting go as soon as she was facing me. A truck blew by. Gravel smacked my cheek, and she turned away from the road as if slapped.

"Who's in on it? Catherine?"

"Never."

"Johnny. Butthead? Who else? How did you get them to clean up the factory? Tell me. Is it the whole town? Are all of you in on it?"

Eyes on the ground, toes pointed inward, arms crossed, her body language was guilt. The white heat of my anger was directed at her and back at myself for falling for it. The rage burned through my tenderness but didn't consume it. And that made me angrier.

"You know what? You're right." I held up my hands. "It doesn't matter."

Leaving her, I walked back to the car. Another SUV went by so fast the car was lifted a little from the ground. Fuck these assholes. Fuck this town. Fuck Harper Barrington. The Watsonette. Goose.

She didn't make a sound behind me. I was going to leave her on the side of the road. Let her figure it out.

You're not leaving her anywhere.

Maybe not. Maybe I was going to turn the car around, put her in it, and leave her at Pat's grocery store, where I found her. And I was never going to see her again. I was going to leave her there and not even kiss her. Then I was stealing her shitty car and leaving it in long-term parking. Because—

"I can't let you leave," she said from behind me. Closer than I left her. She was a stealthy little goose.

"Good-bye, Harper." Three steps from the trunk of the car, I waved without looking. Just to hurt her. Just to pay her back for the lies. I wasn't leaving her on the side of the road, but I still wasn't done with the lava burning my guts.

The car's lights flashed, and the horn tooted. All the locks clacked.

I spun around. She had a little handmade remote control in her hand.

"I'm sorry," she said. "I can't let you go."

"Are you out of your mind?" I was in her face in three steps.

"We have to fix QI4 from here." Her voice was steady as a boat on a mirror-flat sea. "I can't let you leave. You'll never come back."

"You know what kind of parasite kills the host?" I picked up a rock from the side of the road. She could lock the doors all she wanted. "An extinct one. If I don't fix this, I can't buy your fucking factory." I lifted the stone, tossing it up a few inches and catching it again as if I were Mr. Nonchalant.

"I know, but—!"

I threw the rock through the passenger side window, then I reached in to unlock the doors. They clacked. She ran to me and grabbed my arm, hair blowing all over her face when a truck passed. She had a desperation I'd never seen before. Putting my hand on the door latch, I kept my face hard and cold, or I was going to be her bitch, and I was no woman's bitch.

"You can't leave," she cried. "Please. I love you."

In a flash of a second, I went from a stretched, bursting bag of hot rage to a brittle shell around an empty cage. My brain went dark. Neurons stopped firing. My heart flatlined for a beat while I absorbed the shock. She was the first woman to tell me she loved me, and she'd caught me in the defenseless state between coherent thoughts.

As if sensing an opening, she put her hands on my chest, looking up at me with her blue/brown halo eyes. I filled my lungs, my heart thumped, neurons fired. She wasn't lying when she mouthed it again.

I love you.

What a brave little psycho she was. What a reckless woman. What a fierce and sensitive warrior.

Somewhere in the conflict of my admiration, a voice cut through.

You're not leaving.

I was leaving. I was taking the car and going back home to salvage what was left of my life. Her love was irrelevant.

You're staying.

I could come back. I could deal with this whole Harper mess later.

You're staying with her.

The voice was correct. I was staying. Every other bit of coding in me resisted what I knew was true. I was staying to make her happy, and I wasn't pleased with the choice. I'd been perforated between what I'd wanted before I met her and what I wanted after, then she'd ripped me in two.

I grabbed the hair at the back of her neck. She closed her eyes and sucked air through her teeth. She went liquid.

I pushed her against the car, grinding my erection into her. "You love me?"

"Yes. From that day in the cafeteria that you forgot. And over the conference room table when you ignored me. All the other reasons, they're real, but they're not true. I hoped you'd help us in a hundred ways, but that's not why I hacked you. I told everyone here something half-true and you something half-true, and I had my own truth. I know I'm crazy. The whole time I was trying to make this work, I knew I was out of my mind. That has to count for something. It has to because I'm admittingit."

I lifted behind her knee to change the angle of her body so I could press against the heat between her legs. She groaned and dug her nails into my arms.

"Say it."

"I brought you because I loved you."

Pushing harder against her, I demanded more because I believed it. For once, what she said had the ring of truth. For once, it was exactly what I wanted to hear.

"Again."

"I loved you."

"I'm going to show you what you love. What you want to keep here. I'm not going to fuck you like you were a virgin yesterday." Another hard thrust. She squeaked. "You're getting fucked like a woman."

"Do it."

I opened the back door and flicked away the few shards of glass that had flown that far. She bent to sit in the backseat. I got in and closed the door, crawling over her like a predator.

She put her face close to mine, but there wasn't going to be any kissing. Kissing was for women who didn't hold me hostage.

"Show me your pussy." I unbuckled, unbuttoned, unzipped.

"I think we can hack the system back," she said, wiggling her pants down to her knees. "If you have his number on your phone."

"He's not keeping anything on his phone." I fisted my cock. All my frustration flowed into it. "Turn over. Show me your ass."

She paused. Started to turn. It was tight in the backseat. I couldn't straighten all the way, and she had no room to flip comfortably.

"What's the way in?" She asked it without irony.

I turned her over the rest of the way. Her waistband was right above her knees, and her ass was oval and flawless, with a dark, fuckable seam in the middle.

"I have to talk to him." I put three fingers inside her. She was wet. Very wet. "That's the only way in. Friendship." I twisted my hand and pressed my thumb to her clit. She groaned. "You like that?"

"Yes."

"You like three fingers in you?"

"Yes. In the meantime, we can look for a kill switch. Or a flaw in his lockdown."

I pulled my hand out and slapped her ass. "He doesn't do flaws." I put my dick to her opening, letting it hover there while I spread her thighs apart. "We have to persuade him to unlock it."

I shoved myself into her hard and deep. She let out a long sound of surprise and pleasure.

"I'm going to fuck you like you fucked me." I twisted her hair in my hand and yanked her head back. "And you're going to take it."

"Yes."

She couldn't finish the question when I thrust into her so hard I thought I'd break her. But I didn't. She looked over her shoulder at me. I pulled her hair until she looked forward.

"This is mine," I said, fucking her hard and fast. Pulling her hair to keep her still while I pounded her.

"Fuck yes. Yours."

I bent over her and put my lips to her ear. "This is what you get for keeping me here. Now I own you. Your tight little cunt is mine. You happy now? You wanted me to fuck you like an animal?"

She grunted. She was so hot. I put my fingers in her mouth so I could feel the vibrations of her groans.

"Answer me. You want it like this?"

She couldn't talk with my hand in her mouth, and that was part of the pleasure.

"Touch yourself." I slammed her as if I could snap her in two.

She let go of my arm, leaving a line of red marks, and put her hand between her legs.

"Make yourself come."

I held back the explosion that built inside me and watched her back arch. She went stiff and tense, yelling in a language that didn't exist.

When she moved her hand away and took panting breaths, I pulled out of her and kneeled, facing the side window.

"I think we can backdoor him," she said.

"It needs a social engineering component. Turn around."

She turned halfway. I took her by the hair again and looked her in the face. She was dewy and loose. Her tongue flicked over her lower lip.

"You're going to suck my cock now. Any objections?"

"No."

"Open your mouth."

She did it, and I pushed her head onto my erection. She took what she could, and my hand demanded more. When I let her off, she sucked air.

"Is he on Chaxxer?" she groaned.

"Yes, but you aren't anymore. Finish sucking me."

Looking up at me, a mischievous smile crossed her lips as if she'd just had an earth-shattering idea.

"What?" I asked, thinking she had a hack on her mind.

"Nothing." She went down on me, sucking like a champ, using her hand with just enough expertise to get me off and just enough clumsiness to be one-hundred-percent Harper.

I didn't correct her. I wanted her exactly like this.

I came in her mouth with the back of my head on the backseat window. She took it like a good girl, looking up at me again with that mischievous glint in her eyes. When I was done, she closed her lips and swallowed.

She straightened her back, and I pulled her up. I wasn't squeamish about kissing a girl after I came in her, especially Harper, who deserved to be kissed long and deep and without a second of hesitation.

I thrust my tongue past her lips, holding her head as if it was precious, and I tasted the sharpness and felt the thickness of bathroom cleaner. "Ugh!"

When I pulled away, she started laughing. She still had a lot of my cum on her tongue. It dripped off the crease in her bottom lip.

"Fuck!" I said, reaching into the front center console, trying not to close my mouth or open it wide enough to drip all over me. I found a napkin and spat into it, then I wiped my mouth and let myself laugh. "You're in trouble, goose."

She was still laughing. I couldn't help but smile with her. I pulled out another napkin and held it in front of her mouth. She closed it and tried to swallow but couldn't stop laughing long enough to gulp.

"Okay, come on." I held the napkin under her chin, but she was holding her belly and laughing. Tears streamed down her hot, pink cheeks. I had to control myself enough to wipe her face. "Stick your tongue out."

She managed to do it, and I wiped it down with the napkin.

"Oh, my God." She ran her wrists over her eyes. "That was… oh, my God. You should have seen your face."

"What was it?"

"It was like…"

She made a face that crossed horror, shock, distaste, and wounded pride, and we both fell into laughing fits. She fell into my arms and made the face again. Then I made the face, and she shook her head because I'd gotten it wrong. We were cracking up and trying to form words. Failing.

"Okay, seriously," I said. "Can I pull your pants up?"

She was lost in it. She seemed to be making up for a few years' worth of missed laughter in the backseat of the Chevy. I pulled up her pants, and she arched her back so I could get them in place.

My mouth tasted like Mr. Clean, and she delighted the fuck out of me.

XLIV

"That's it?" I asked from behind the shower curtain. "You think he's going to fall for that again?" She was using the closed toilet as a chair.

"You fell for it last time. Not him."

"Thanks for the reminder." I stuck my head under the water.

"Anytime."

"But he knows your exploit probably better than you do at this point."

"The problem with you guys is you think it's not going to happen to you. You think you have your bases covered. The more direct we make it, the more likely we are to get through."

"You think he ordered something from Amazon, coming through your distro center, and he's going to bring it to the office and just roll in and out of the cage with it? Because he didn't learn from me?"

"He doesn't know it was your watch that had the transmitter."

Her voice was clearer, louder, with a more defined echo. I opened my eyes. She was naked in the curtain opening.

"You like what you see, goose?"

"I like what I see." She stepped into the shower, getting under the faucet as if she was entitled to the flow. "Why is this freezing?" She turned the temperature up.

I soaped her shoulders, running my hands down her back. "The distro center's going to be a red flag. It's a loser."

She turned to face me and bent her head back to soak her hair. "Don't worry about the distro center." She pressed her lips together and shut her eyes as water poured down her face.

I ran the soap over her. Her body was slick and soft, with hard places at the bones and nipples. "Worrying's my job."

She opened her mouth to get water in it and closed her jaw so it came out in a gentle fountain. It was the kind of unthinking, unplanned gesture we all made in places where we were used to being alone.

"Worrying isn't a job," she said, opening her eyes. Her lashes were black and stuck together like thornless bushes, and one particular water droplet was centered exactly around a pale freckle on her cheek. I rubbed it away. It was too perfect.

"Your plan has so many holes it could drain spaghetti," I said, pushing my dick against her.

"That sounds delicious."

"Are you wondering what it's like to fuck in the shower?"

"A little."

Taking her by the backs of her thighs, I pulled her up and leaned her back against the tile. "Fucking in the shower is as American as apple pie." I held her slick cunt against my length.

"What do I have to do?"

"Spread your legs around me."

"Like this?"

"Tell me what you want. Say it exactly."

She sucked in her bottom lip. "I want you to put your dick… no, cock inside me. All the way. I want it to hurt a little bit when I feel you hit the end. I want you to do it hard so I can feel everything."

"Let me hold you up. And use the wall as leverage. You ready?"

"Yep." She looked down at where we were about to be joined.

She was slick when I thrust inside. Two strokes to get the whole thing in. I grabbed under her thighs, holding her up and keeping her legs open and still. She was still looking between us.

Her curiosity was so hot. I looked with her as I pulled out and went back hard.

"Like that?" I asked.

"Yes."

"God, you're in for it now."

Holding us together, I fucked her as hard as I could, using my body to rub her clit when I was deep. I wanted her to come without my fingers. Just my cock and us and the dripping hot water. To get the most friction, I pulled her to me until she couldn't see between us. There would be another time for her to watch our bodies couple.

In the shower, we were better positioned for a fingerless orgasm. Her mouth opened. Water dripped from her nose onto her lip.

"How's it feel?"

"Yes." Her voice cracked on such a short word. "More."

I gave it to her so hard I grunted with the force. I wanted to crawl inside her and live. Peel her open. Surround myself with her.

Her throat let loose a series of short *ahs*.

"Are you going to come?"

She nodded. I didn't slow down or speed up. I wanted her there.

"I can't hear you," I said.

"I'm going to come."

"Look at me."

The effort to keep her gaze on mine and her eyes open was all over her face. I held her by the jaw to keep her toward me. Always thrusting. Always pushing. Something in me was loosening. The valve was turning, and when it spun, it was going to fly open.

I couldn't come inside her.

But I couldn't stop before she had hers.

I thought about anything. The exploit. Qubit structure. Her name in base64 encoding.

The muscles of her face tightened.

"Look at me," I demanded again to keep my mind off my pending explosion.

Her eyes narrowed to slits but stayed open. I wasn't going to last. Her back tightened, straightened. The muscles in her thighs tightened. She cried out to her creator, scratching the skin off my back more effectively than a thousand thorns.

When she removed her fingers from my skin, I pulled out and held my cock. It was lubricated and swollen. "Jesus, I—"

The valve blew, and I came on her belly, jerking myself like an adolescent. By the time I was done, the shower had mostly washed her clean.

"Thank you," I whispered.

"No, thank *you*." She turned off the water.

She tried to get out, but I blocked her. "I mean it. Thank you. Not for the fuck. I mean, yes, thank you for the fuck. But thank you for…"

For what? I put my fists against the tile and lowered my head. Our feet comingled in the draining tub.

"For kidnapping me."

"I didn't kidnap you."

"You did."

She slapped my shoulder playfully. "Did not."

"Well, whatever you did, it was worth it."

"We'll see." She dodged me and stepped out of the tub.

"You're a once-in-a-lifetime person, goose." I followed her out.

Taking a white towel out of the cabinet, she let it fall out of the fold. "Yeah. Sure."

I took the towel away and wrapped it around her. "I can't explain what you've done to me. I want to take care of you and hurt you at the same time. I shouldn't trust you, but I do. I'm willing to crash to find out if you're trustworthy, and I don't care if you're not. It was all worth it to have you. Everything was worth it."

She stepped on my feet, and I lifted her to kiss her.

XLV

The trick was to get past Keaton, who would have protections on his devices. I was sure he had scripts that he'd coded himself and never released, making them impossible to test.

The sun set at a deep angle through Harper's third-floor window. She was in a tank top and shorts, her butt in her desk chair and her feet on her desk. I'd moved a few boxes of circuitry to stretch out on a beat-up love seat. In the previous hours, she'd looked through the exploit apps on my phone, I'd looked over her shoulder at code, we'd searched Tor for pieces of usable malware, and finally, she'd sat me at her desk so I could look for Keaton on the dark web.

Letting me fuck her was trust. Coming back into town with her was trust.

But probing each other's devices, especially knowing what we knew about each other, was intimate beyond imagining.

"Can we plant a transmitter on Deeprak?" she asked. "You'd have to refuse his resignation and make nice first."

"I don't want to get anyone else involved. He and I fighting works right now. Keaton's got a thing about revenge. If we break him and he comes after anyone, it's going to be me."

"Or me."

"Yeah. No."

"He's going to find me," she said. "I'll deal with it."

She thought she was strong enough to survive anything, but I wouldn't leave her long enough to test the theory.

"I'm not trying to scare you, because none of this will happen," I said.

"Oh, this should be good."

"He's loyal. That doesn't make him a nice guy. He has this code he lives by. If you're in, he'll kill for you. If you're out, he'll kill you."

"'Kill' meaning commit actual murder?"

"Mostly cyber stuff. I don't know if he's capable of actual murder, but he knows people who have the same code. They all live by it. And the rest of these guys? I've met them. I can't say for sure they haven't buried any real bodies."

She'd gone bedsheet white. "I'm the enemy."

"No. Not yet. Just trust me. I'll take care of it."

She cleared her throat. Nodded.

"So." I changed the subject. "We transmit from inside the cage. And he takes the transmitter in and out, like you did with my watch?"

"Yeah."

"How are we going to get him to fall for that?"

"What's he keep in his bag?"

"His bag? Lunch?"

"He brown bags his lunch?"

"He's a cheap motherfucker. And he's picky about his food. He only uses this one kind of mustard made by French monks. It's disgusting. It tastes like asshole."

"But he wouldn't carry a whole jar of asshole mustard in his bag."

I leaned back, stretching the backs of my knees over the armrest. What did he carry around? What had I seen him take out of the leather bike messenger bag? Laptop. Keys. Wallet.

She tapped at her keyboard so fast and hard it was no wonder she needed to tape her knuckles. "I don't know why I didn't think of this before."

I got up and looked over her shoulder, brushed my lips along her neck, then looked again. She was inside a deep web database.

"Is this the distribution center?" I asked.

"Yeah. I cracked it months ago. We don't need his credit card. Do you know his home address?"

"He's not going to just order stuff from Amazon, goose."

"Yeah, that's what everyone says. What they don't know is half the small businesses in this country run fulfillment through four major distro warehouses. One of them's right off the interstate." She pointed north. "Unless the owner's writing addresses in Sharpie at the kitchen counter. Can I have an address?"

I gave it to her. She tapped it into fields faster than I could speak. Nothing came up.

"Wait." I rubbed my eyes, trying to remember the address he had everything forwarded from.

"You're very cute when you're thinking."

"And when I'm not thinking?"

"You're dazzling."

I kissed her and gave her Keaton's forwarding address.

A recent order came up under Lupine Alfa. What my friend and silent partner had in malicious intent, he lacked in imagination.

"British hand cream and deodorant," I muttered. I couldn't believe she was right, but there was the order—in full color LED. "So much for being an international man of mystery."

"It's at the distro center now. Shit. Stuff to California goes out on the night shift because it buys them an extra day. Turning of the earth and all. I'm only scheduled for a morning on Tuesday."

She and I were silent for a minute. She stopped typing and tapped the table.

As calm as I'd been on the surface, I'd been covering a deep well of panic that this town, this house, this woman was a snare designed to hold me squirming forever. The panic revealed itself in its decline. I was still unnerved. Still anxious. But as I leaned on the desk and looked over her shoulder with my arms on each side of her, I could see a way out. The tunnel was long and dark, but at the end was the tiniest and dimmest of lights.

It was the possibility of a social engineering hack that let some of the anxiety go. Hacks always revealed themselves in time. It was Harper. Her partnership. Her knowledge. Her loyalty.

I put one of my thumbs over her tap-tapping fingers. "I say the hand cream."

"I say we have room in the deodorant container." She crossed her fingers over my thumb.

"Both then."

"We need to work fast. I can only hold it in distro a few hours before there's a flag. Everything moves out in twenty-four hours, even if it's five-day delivery."

"I'm not going to have time to fuck you, am I?"

She turned to me with brutal efficiency in her eyes and sex on her lips. "Not if you want to get this done, Beeze." Back at the computer, she opened a field and dropped down the delivery time. "Johnny's on the night shift. He can do the switch. It should be in his mailbox in… I'll upgrade the package delivery now."

"No," I said. "He'll notice. And he's a cheap motherfucker."

"You want to wait an extra five business days?"

"Split the difference."

"Fine." She put him on four-day delivery.

"I code," I said. "You make me some pretty transmitters."

"You think I'm going to let you sit at my machine unsupervised?" she purred.

I kissed her neck. I could die happy with my lips on her jaw, tasting her passion and her panic. "Yes. I do."

She sighed, and with that sigh, she surrendered.

XLVI

Catherine didn't ask questions when Harper sent her miles away to get the nearest deodorant stick that matched Keaton's taste. Harper said she'd done plenty for her sister without asking questions.

The hand cream wasn't as accessible. There wasn't a jar of Moxie's shea butter at retail in a one-hundred-mile radius. So Harper filled out a form saying the distro center's jar was broken, buying us another day. Johnny would grab the unbroken jar from distro and deliver it the next night before his shift.

"We do it all the time." She waved at me as she got off the phone with Johnny. "They log everything, but if it breaks, you fill out a form and it's done."

"Fucking criminals. All of you."

She locked her hands around my waist. "You mad, bro?"

I kissed her and returned her hug. "Yes. Raging mad we have to finish this before I can fuck you again."

She pushed me off her and picked up the legal pad that had our notes and flowcharts. "Let's get 'er done."

Though we'd conceived the plan without words, we'd worked out the details with lists, on paper so nothing was missed.

We would place tiny transmitters, much like the one Harper had built for my watch, into Keaton's toiletries. One or both would (hopefully) end up near his cell phone, where it would keylog from his Tempest emissions. Every tap on his phone would be transmitted to us. He might not bring his phone into QI4's Faraday cage, but we'd have access to his laptop through the Bluetooth connection and could figure out how he'd put a layer of encryption over Harper's. Then it was a matter of time before he connected his laptop to the poison pill. Which would give us access to QI4.

A hundred variables bounced around the plan. This was why I didn't like social engineering hacks. They were too dependent on human behavior, which was unreliable as shit. Openings in code were openings in code. You could depend on code to do exactly what it said. No more. No less. That was the beauty and downfall of pure code.

Harper's machine was safe when I coded what we were planting on the transmitter. She showed me her QI4 hack so I could use pieces of it, and I was lost. It strung together pieces of what she assumed was there, looping them together like a drawstring bag and tying them tightly with layers and layers of encryption and exploitation code she'd designed.

"You really wanted to get me," I said, scrolling through it.

"I guess I did." She reached up to the top shelf of her closet for a clear plastic box. The muscles in the backs of her thighs tightened when she went onto the tips of her toes and just touched the bottom of the box, slip- ping it half an inch forward.

I got behind her and grabbed the box with one hand and her waist with the other. "How long did it take?" I shook the box before I gave it to her. It was full of circuitry scraps.

"Lot of hours. But..." She shrugged, embarrassed. "Anger's a motivator, I guess."

"No shit, goose." I kissed her forehead and gave her butt a little spank. "No shit."

"You really forgive me?"

I hadn't used the word *forgive*. It was too heavy and serious. Too high on itself. It meant something had been broken.

In her little room, with her in my arms, I didn't have to forgive her for what she'd broken. By smashing her way into my life, she'd made it whole.

"I have no choice," I said. "I love you."

We didn't have time to fuck, but we had enough time to kiss as if the future was a done deal.

XLVII

Out in the deep parts of the country, the horizon's different. It doesn't disappear behind buildings or get lost in a haze of light and particles. It's not a line graph of mountains. It's cut straight all around, like an ocean of land, and at night, it's marked by the line where the stars end.

"Why don't you get Orrin to fix the steering on this thing?" I asked.

It was hard enough to keep the shimmymobile on the road in daylight. With visibility at zero outside the cones of the headlights and the wind whipping the plastic we'd used to cover the window I'd broken, I'd almost run into a ditch more than once. She took deep breaths whenever the car went wide, digging her fists into her sweatshirt and tying her face into knots. It was cute and unnecessary.

"He won't take my money. I won't let him do it for free, and if I go to another mechanic, he'll never forgive me. And I like it that way. It's like a horse I tamed myself."

"You're all crazy. Down to the last one of you."

"You've mentioned that. Pull over here. I see him."

I didn't see shit until she pointed toward the right and the headlights caught a flicker of reflective red. His truck was parked behind a bush between the road and the train tracks.

"I love the whole cloak-and-dagger thing you guys have going."

"Yeah, well, if Pat knew, she'd have a fit."

"She'd be right." I pulled up in front of the bush and cut the engine. I'd never known stars could be bright enough to see by, but there was a lot of shit I didn't know.

The deodorant with the transmitter was in a paper bag at Harper's feet. We'd opened the deodorant from the bottom so it wouldn't disrupt the seal and put the transmitter under the base. The other transmitter was in Harper's pocket, protected by clear kitchen wrap.

Harper pulled down the plastic over her broken window. I turned on the dome light. He leaned his elbows on the top of the door. "Well, hello, Mr. Harden. Harper. What happened to the window, here?"

"Taylor happened."

He shot me a dirty look, and I shrugged like a man driven to madness.

Harper handed him the paper bag. "The order number's on the inside of the bag. Do you have the jar?"

He looked at Harper, then me, then back at Harper. There was only one interpretation for that look. *What the hell is this guy doing here?*

"He's all right," Harper said, holding out her hand.

"First, you're going to tell me what you're up to."

"Trust me." She took the jar from him and spun the cap off.

"I trust you. And I like the gentleman in the driver's seat well enough to shoot pool and throw back a few. But trust is a different thing. I'm not risking my job for some rich, excuse the term or don't, asshole. No offense."

"None taken," I said. "But you put the plant in my watch. So consider this more of the same."

"That's what I thought." He dropped the bag back in Harper's lap, stepped away from the car and into the darkness.

"Johnny!" Harper opened the door.

I reached over and closed it. "Stay here."

"Why? What—?"

Grabbing her wrist, I gave her my full attention for two words. "Trust me."

I grabbed the bag with the deodorant and got out of the car, where the road slanted away. I almost fell. Gravity pulled the door closed. As I went around the front, Harper's face went to stone as she shut off the dome light.

No dummy, that girl. She could see us and not be seen if the dome light was off.

No dummy. Unexpectedly smart.

Why unexpected?

Say it.

To yourself, you can say it.

Say, "I always assumed pretty girls weren't that bright."

"Johnny!" I called, running into the bush. I found him with the clack of a zippo and the pin light of a cigarette. "Hold up."

My eyes adjusted to the starlight. We were right next to his truck. He leaned on the bed.

"I'm holding up." He held a pack of cigarettes out for me. I declined. "Good move. These fucking things killed my mother." He took a drag as if testing mortality. "You want me to do you a favor. I know I don't have much to lose, but it's all I have."

I leaned on the cab. He had a house. His wife had a barely profitable business. He had kids in school and a truck. No, it wasn't much. And who was I to jeopardize it?

I had no right to ask him to do me a favor, but I had no other way to save myself. "Tell me how to make it worth your while."

The smoke billowing from his lips was blue in the starlight. It dispersed when he shook his head. "I helped Harper with… what did she call it? Her *exploit*. A few of us did. Desperate people take risks. It was a stupid idea, but you showed up, right on time. It looked like it was work- ing. You, then we were going to work on the Irish one. Fitzgerald. Then Catherine says you're holed up in a room at their place. I had to practi- cally tie Butthead down."

"Why?"

"Because she's ours. We protect her and her sister, and they protect us. That's how it goes. And now I'm seeing… I don't know what you got going on with her. I'm not making assumptions. I mean, I know well enough. It's your intentions I can't seem to figure out."

"My intentions? What were your intentions bringing me here? You talk like you're so clean. You ruined my life so you could squeeze me. And for what? You think I have some endless well of cash? I'm nobody. I'm ten years away from buying a factory."

He threw his cigarette down and smashed it with the ball of his foot. A car passed, casting moving bush-shaped shadows across us before fading away.

"We'll be here," he said.

"Why?" I only said one word, but a lecture's worth of questions was inside it. Why stay if it's so miserable? Why risk everything for a town that had abandoned him already?

"We got nowhere to go. I wanted my children to raise our grandchildren here, but they're in all corners of the country. Maybe three times a year Pattycakes gets one to show up. Maybe. My daughter, did you know she's an artist? She can't ever come back here. For what? So she can be alone? There's no opportunity here for her to be more than a mother, and she can do that anywhere. My son, the one in law school? Who's he gonna represent here who can pay him? I raised them to do better than we did. I didn't know that meant I'd never see them. I miss them. I miss my children. And you can buy that factory and hire all of us at twenty-five an hour, but my kids aren't coming back. It's me, my wife, and this town. It's all I got."

That was that. I couldn't offer him his life or the company of his children. His home wasn't a place; it was a time in his life that all the money in the world wouldn't bring back.

"I'm sorry." I didn't have any words of wisdom.

"Things were supposed to get better." He seemed to speak to the dirt, the stars, his broken heart.

Jesus. I was turning into some kind of pussy. What was the difference? There were winners and losers in this world. We sank or we swam. Complaints were for whiners and failures. Change. Grow. Learn. Get it right the hundredth time if you had to.

I felt the truth of all of that, but I couldn't say it out loud, even in a supportive, managerial way. It meant accusing Johnny of not trying hard enough, not getting lucky enough. It meant accusing him of being complacent, which wasn't fair even if it was true.

My worldview was having a head-on collision with the world.

"I got you." I switched the brown paper back from my right hand to my left and held the right out to shake. "Harper and I will figure it out."

He clasped my hand and shook it. "Sorry I went girl on you."

"Speaking of girl." He let my hand go, and I pointed at her shitty car. "Harper."

"Yeah?"

"I'm not playing around. I love her. You don't have to believe me, but it's the truth."

"You take care of her then. She's the gem of Barrington. You can't break her, but you can lose her if you know what I'm saying."

"Sure." I started back for the car, but Johnny came for me and grabbed the paper bag.

"I'll see what I can do," he said. "No promises."

"None expected."

He got in his truck and turned the ignition. The rear lights turned the greenery black and the ground red.

Harper was behind the bush.

"Is he taking the jar?" she asked when Johnny's truck pulled onto the road.

"I don't want to use him." I passed her. "We'll figure something else out."

I got into the driver's side, and she slid in next to me.

"What happened?" She slammed her door closed.

"Life happened." I turned the ignition. "It's one thing to risk your job for your own good. But this isn't for him or Barrington. It's for me. I can't ask him to lose his job for me."

"Get out." She pushed my shoulder as if we were fighting on a playground. "I'm driving."

"Fine. You drive this shitcan."

"It's not a shitcan. It's a choice. Like you giving up."

She had to scream the last part because I was already out of the car.

Note to self: this was a girl who didn't like to change plans.

"Officially," she said when I got in, "we are not speaking."

She wasn't cute when she was mad. I'd have been crazy to minimize her ferocity. She was formidable, and it was a massive turn-on.

"Unofficially," I said as she made a U-turn to go back to Barrington, "I'd like to kiss you."

"Fuck off."

"Is that a smirk? Are you smiling?"

"Smiling doesn't mean I'm not mad."

"Letting Johnny off the hook doesn't mean I'm giving up."

She let that hang between us on the empty road, and I didn't follow up. I watched the starry horizon change and let the *thup whup* of the seams in the road lull me. How many days had gone by? How many more until Keaton turned the boot code into open source? How long did he have to crack the rest of the Harperware? We had no time, and we had too much.

Five days.

Code laced like a drawstring bag.

Harper turned down the tight little dirt road to the Barrington house. The car did shimmy less when she drove. When I bought her a new car, she probably wouldn't know how to make a left at all.

The contract.

The contest.

The con.

She stopped in front and cut the engine. Didn't get out. Didn't open the door. Said nothing. We sat in the dark together, listening to the grass crackle.

My chain of thought wasn't disrupted.

Cut the cord.

To the anchor.

And drift toward the horizon.

The lights went off on the bottom floor and clicked on upstairs.

Catherine wouldn't cry tonight. I didn't know how I knew that, but I didn't question the truth of it.

The system is closed.

Until it's not.

Then…

"GreyHatC0n's in less than a week," I said.

"If you want to go, you should go."

"You know how Bitcoin works, right? The information blockchains?"

"Yeah." She slid down in her seat in a resigned slouch. "Transparency creates honesty. If everyone can see the transaction history, it can't be falsified, et cetera."

"Documentation of every Bitcoin transfer ever made is available on the blockchain. What everyone sees becomes the truth."

She faced me. "Yes?"

She was so beautiful I didn't think I could ever live without her. I was so far ahead of myself I was living in two mental time zones.

In one, she was mine.

In another, I'd lost her and everything I'd worked for to the consequences of my bad decisions.

"If I tell everyone the contest is on, then it's on, whether Keaton wants it to be or not. He has to unlock it, or he looks stupid. He looks like he's not in control."

"If *you* tell them? How are you getting online?" She spoke softly, as if there were more on her mind than the elegant social engineering of my plan.

"You're going to have to turn off your signal scrambler. If you dare."

"I dare."

I opened the door, and the dome light went on. She squinted.

"I want you to win it, goose."

XLVIII

TWITTER

@Beezleboy363636
None of you bitches are ready for QI4.
#GreyHatC0n #QI4

@hackerbitch
Look who's back. Still pwned?
Change your handle to
@BreachBoy. #QI4choked

@Beezleboy363636
Five mill says you can't get in.
But bring what you got.
#GreyHatC0n #QI4 #IT_Solid

@git-up
You patch that RU hack?
Nyet? I got money on you shitting
your pants. #tool #douche # QI4choked

@anon_00110001
Bro. You find the dude who hacked

you? You fuck him good? Or did 41ph4_W01f break his kneecaps? #BeezeIsBack #QI4rulz

@J0k3r_K1Ng
Oh, shit. It's on.
#GreyHatC0n

@BeezleBoy363636
Wasn't a dude.

@anon_00110001
Bot? AI?

@BeezleBoy363636
Girl. Female.

@hackerbitch
ALL HAIL KARMA.

@anon_00110001
Yeah… no.

@shelly-code
And you haven't literally died of shame yet you fucking sexist douche?

@BeezleBoy363636
Can't talk now. Eating crow.

@hackerbitch
(dies)

@anon_00110001
Dude. Seriously?

@BeezleBoy363636
Bump in the road, people. You need to have a little faith in the early fail.

@shelly-code
I'm buying tickets to #GreyHatC0n
just to see you eat shit.

@engadget
The QI4 Challenge is back on. bit.ly/4nfw8rfS

@Wired
EXCLUSIVE: Sources say QI4 code still on lockdown but ready for a 5-million-dollar exploit. bit.ly/7bfw9sfW

@gizmodo
Show us the money. Five-mill challenge to hack QI4 is back.

@hackeropz
Buckle in. #QI4 @BeezleBoy363636 & @41ph4_W01f are mid-stunt.

Just like I knew he would, Keaton came on a private thread like a gopher popping his head out of a hole.

<PRIVATE @41ph4_W01f>
What the fuck are you doing?

<PRIVATE @Beezleboy363636>
My damnedest to get QI4 back on track.

<PRIVATE @41ph4_W01f>
I HAVE IT.

<PRIVATE @Beezleboy363636>
I've secured my end. Just make sure it's unlocked in time. Out.

XLIX

I leaned back in her chair. She was on the love seat with her feet tucked under her, watching the hacker forums and Twitter blow up.

"It's happening," she said, eyes big. Was she pale, or was it the light?

"Hell, yes. And Keaton's going to have to go along or eat his shirt. He's got pride where most people have sense, so I'm pretty sure he'll go along."

"I don't know if I can."

I spun the chair to face her. "What? This is easy. You hack in. Then you get the five mil and do whatever you want with it. Pay the taxes on the factory. Buy everyone Oxycontin."

"Not funny."

I dropped to my knees in front of her, wedging myself between her thighs. She put her arms around my shoulders.

"What are you so nervous about?" I asked.

"This is so big."

"You've done it before."

"That was different. I locked it from the outside. I didn't get in and crack it. I got QI4 to run my code. And I got a ton of lucky breaks. This time, once I decrypt—"

"*Your* encryption. Harperware."

"I'll be up against everyone. The best."

"You know how to talk to QI4. You're already ten steps ahead." I leaned forward, elbows on her thighs. I wanted her to know I was serious, but I couldn't touch her. She needed to believe it without the sex. "I built this to withstand the attack. I'm not worried about anyone at the conference. Just you. And you can take that money and pay the back taxes on the factory. Then you can sell it, give it away, break it up into luxury condos if you want."

She turned her hands over in her lap and rubbed her palm with the ball of her thumb as if she wanted to change the lines of her fortune. "He won't let me win."

My phone buzzed.

Keaton. Right on time.

I squeezed her hand and dashed down the stairs, picking up when I was in the only enclosed, private space I could think of. The kitchen pantry.

"Hello."

"I don't know if you're a genius or an idiot." Keaton was as calm as ever. "Baiting me to unlock QI4 like that?"

"I'm not baiting you."

"Describe what you're doing."

"Letting everyone know the hack is fixed and we're going on as planned."

"Is it? And are we?"

"It is. Once you open it up, we'll decrypt the lock. The flaw was in the supply chain. That's rectified with line inspections. We are a go."

"What about the hacker? Who are they? That house you called from—"

"I can't reveal that."

"—is occupied by women."

"I promised to keep it secret."

"What does she want? She humiliated us for a reason."

"Relax. We opened it up for hacks to test it."

"In a controlled setting." Keaton's voice shredded in his throat. "That was the deal. This was an attack. A direct attack timed for the most attention. It was meant to kill the demand for a product that was set to revolutionize computing. And we do not sit still for it."

There was only one way to deal with Keaton when he had vengeance in his voice. Calm authority.

"We are sitting still for it because we see the big picture. We don't get revenge because we're butthurt."

"We will discuss this when I see you."

"When are you unlocking it?"

"When I see you." He hung up.

Harper was outside the pantry door, looking more frightened than I'd ever seen her. If she was scared, I wasn't doing my job.

"They say Alpha Wolf is a military contractor," she said. "They say he's a sociopath."

"They say a lot of bullshit."

"He already knows I'm here from the landline call."

"No. He knows I'm here—and possibly the hacker. If we cloak right, and we will, he won't know you and the winner of the challenge are the same person. Once he unlocks the system, we'll open up the Harperware. He won't find you."

She didn't believe me. Not one hundred percent. Twenty percent. All I had to do was fill in the other eighty. I took her hand and led her back to my bedroom, where we wouldn't be interrupted.

"Do you know why I took Keaton's money?" I sat on the bed and took her hand.

She stood between my legs. "He offered the most?"

"No." I counted on my fingers, index to pinkie. "It was in Bitcoin. He's Alpha Wolf. It gave me dark web credibility. It gave the impression I was watching hackers as much as they were watching me. Which…" I made a fist and dropped it. "That's half the story. The other half is weirder."

"Oh, I'm intrigued now."

"Let me tell you a story. I was once a teen hacker who grabbed what he could. I could have gone the rest of my life like that, until one day, Keaton and I cracked Luhn's formula. I was conflicted about it, but Keaton was already setting up a route for secure wire transfers. Then the FBI ended up in my parents' living room."

"I didn't know that." Her eyes widened, and her posture leaned forward slightly. She held onto the edge of my shirt as if she didn't want me to leave until I finished the story.

"They took me to a secure interrogation room where I told them it was me, all me. They knew someone else was involved. Someone with ties to US Intelligence."

"Keaton?"

"Yes, but no. Maybe his parents. Point being I didn't flip on him. I said it was just me. And because I hadn't taken anything, I could convince them I was white hat. Which made even more trouble. Because then I had to *be* one. They tried to recruit me, and you know, I thought, sure. What- ever. Could be cool. But my mother didn't want anyone to decide anything for me at that age and flew into this…" I pressed my fingers into my eyes and let out a nervous laugh. "God, she could be scary when she wanted to be. She had a constitutional lawyer in the room in two hours. They fought hard, man."

"They were going to forgive the other exploits?"

"If they could take me to Quantico right there, yeah. After two days, the lawyer cut a deal. Show them how I turned the credit card company's formulas against them, stay clean, and stay available if they needed me. I covered for my friend. My father never spoke to me again. The FBI comes around every once in a while with some easy shit to help with and a job offer with shitty pay. But Keaton's walking around because I didn't flip on him, and that counts for something. He owed me, and he still owes me. If he finds out it's you, I'll call that favor the fuck in." I kissed her just enough to let her feel me. "You're safe. I'm going to fuck you every day between breakfast and lunch. Then I'm going to eat you for dinner."

She turned to straddle me. I slid down so my erection met the damp crotch of her pants. I pushed her against me, and she let loose a breathy *ah.*

"That's it?" she asked.

"And teach you how to think in quantum trinary."

"I already hacked quantum trinary."

"Without that poison pill it's going to be ten times harder. I can help you. There's plenty you don't know about QI4."

"That's cheating."

I moved her body against the length of me. Hotter, wetter, harder. My dick wasn't going to stop until it was inside her. "You want to win or not?"

"I want to win."

I pulled her T-shirt over her tits. The tips were hard and pink, bending under my thumb, salty on my lips. I yanked on her waistband.

"Off." She stood and pulled her jeans down, and I took out my cock. "Turn around."

Hesitantly, she turned her back to me. Stroking her ass with one hand, I got a condom out of my wallet with the other and cracked the package with my teeth. I spit the edge and rolled it on.

"Tell me…" I guided her onto me and put downward pressure on her hips. "Tell me how much you want to win."

When she was all the way down to the base, I reached around and opened her legs.

"Ah. God," she groaned. "I want to win."

"Everything. You want to win it all." I moved her up and down slowly.

"I want to win it all."

"No matter what it takes."

"Yes. I'll do whatever it takes."

My hands ran over her inner thighs and landed between her legs. I opened her, exposing her clit to the air. "Fuck me, goose."

She moved faster. "Like this?"

I touched where our bodies met and rubbed her hard little clit. "Like you mean it. Fuck like a winner."

She took two more slow strokes, and I ran two fingers over her pussy.

"Yes," she said as if understanding for the first time. She moved her hips hard, deep, in a quick rhythm.

I kept a hand between her legs and took a fistful of hair in the other to steady her. She slowed down when she started coming. I tightened my grip on her hair.

"Win, goose."

She sped up through her orgasm. Her guttural *unf*s went with the rhythm of her thrusts until I gave in to the pressure and came right after her.

She collapsed against my chest, and I held her steady, staying inside her as long as I could.

"You're going to get everything you want." As she turned to face me and put her arms around my shoulders, I held her on my lap. "You're not going to know what to do with yourself. Success is trickier than failure."

"You going to help me with my success problem?"

"Once I solve my own, yes."

She laughed a little. Just enough to keep steady on my lap. She put her head on my shoulder, and we stayed like that for a while.

I'd been called a genius and a game-changer, a harbinger of the future and a once-in-a-generation mind. I'd walked in the halls of power, met with titans of industry, had my name mentioned in the same sentence as historical figures.

Yet holding this woman was the greatest honor of my life.

I was losing my once-in-a-generation mind.

L

The first time we came downstairs together during daylight hours, Catherine was on the couch, facing the rain-soaked windows with a blanket over her legs. She glanced up from her sewing or needlepoint or whatever the fuck long enough to say hello, then she looked back down. I caught a little smirk. I didn't know if it meant she approved or if it just meant she knew.

"There's a pot of soup on the stove if you're interested," she said.

"Thanks!" Harper bopped off to the kitchen with her ponytail swinging and her ass swaying in a pair of little pink shorts. She already had the lid off the soup when I joined her.

"Bleh," she said, putting the lid back on. "Chicken."

"You don't like chicken soup?" I took the lid off. It looked fine to me. "What kind of person doesn't like chicken soup?"

"She puts peas and carrots in it. Frozen. It's gross."

Catherine's voice came from the doorway. "If you want to chop carrots and shuck peas all day, you're welcome to."

"No thanks. Complaining's easier." She lifted a corner of foil from a covered plate. "Is this cookies?"

Catherine slapped her hand. "For church."

Then she turned to me, and I was caught between guilt at looking at Harper's ass and the awareness that her pussy was still on my lips.

"Are you coming?" Catherine asked.

"Uh, where?"

"Church," Harper said, getting the spoons out and knocking the drawer closed with her hip.

"Sure." I said it without thinking. I wanted Catherine to like me. I was fucking her baby sister in her house and eating her food. Saying yes was the least I could do.

Harper's reaction was immediate. "God, no!"

"God, yes," Catherine said, opening a cabinet. "It won't kill you. And now you have to go, or Taylor's going to have to listen to the sermon without you." She pointed at an empty shelf. "Where are the bowls?"

"We can use the white ones," Harper said, opening another cabinet.

"Harper," Catherine scolded, "did you hide them?"

"Maybe."

"I told you I wasn't going to sell them. Where are they?"

"Can't we just use the white ones?" She handed me three white bowls and the spoons.

"Where are they? I need to know you trust me."

"It's—"

"Tell me." Catherine's voice dropped an octave. "Where are they?"

Harper cleared her throat. Catherine crossed her arms. I stood there with a stack of bowls in one hand and spoons in the other.

"They're gone," Harper whispered.

"Where?"

"I'll tell you later."

Later? Later meant "when Taylor can't hear" as far as I was concerned. I put the bowls down and held my hand over the soup pot so she couldn't open it. "Now is good."

Harper crossed her arms and ankles, rolled her eyes, and put her tongue in her cheek. "Johnny pawned Taylor's watch and so I got it back. It's not a big deal, and if you make a big deal about it, I'm going to knock this soup all over the floor." She snapped up the spoons. "Do you want to eat or not?"

I moved my hand from the pot, and Harper slid a ladle out of the drawer.

"Those were really expensive bowls," I said.

"He's a lousy pawn broker. And I might have had a bracelet I didn't like hanging around." She pressed her lips together as if holding back what she wanted to say, then she said it anyway. "I couldn't get your laptop back. That was a straight sale."

"My laptop?"

Catherine gasped. "That was Taylor's?" She held her hands up, looking me with raised eyebrows and a half-open mouth, the words "I didn't know" written on her tongue.

"It got sold to a guy in Florida."

I didn't care about the money, and I was way past needing it to break a hack. But if the wrong person found out it was mine and they took enough time and energy, there was QI4 code inside I didn't want to fall into the wrong hands.

"Tell me you cleared the hard drive."

"I nuked it." Harper looked me in the eye when she said it, and even though I believed her, she held up her right hand. "Swear. It was clean. And I'm sorry for that and all the other things."

"Is that the last of it, goose?"

"What other things?" Catherine asked as she sifted through a rack of envelopes.

"The other things. Now." Harper bumped me with her hip. "Get out of the way."

I moved and let her ladle out the soup. She did it carefully, making sure we each had the same.

Catherine looked up from stuffing the envelope.

"You better ask for forgiveness at church," she said, licking the flap. "For whatever it is."

"I will." She lowered her voice. "I'll make it up to you. I don't know how, but I will. If I have to sell my own machine, I'll give you back what I took."

I was silent. An inconsequential speck on a tiny boat surrounded by continuous horizon, humbled in the sea of her generosity. I'd felt that insignificant before, but for the first time in my life, I didn't fear it would crush me.

We ate the soup, I tried to teach her some tricks coding within QI4, but as soon as I got to anything she couldn't learn on her own, she put her hand on my dick. I used my last condom on her. I didn't mention the bowls or the watch or the mystery bracelet she didn't like. I'd buy her bracelet and her grandmother's bowls back and raise her up on a throne for her selfless kindness if it was the last thing I did.

LI

After showering and finding my best shirt laundered and ironed on the doorknob, I got into the passenger seat of the shimmymobile and let Harper drive me to church.

She pulled up in front of the grocery store where I'd first met her.

"What?" I asked.

"Condoms. Go."

I started to get out but stopped myself when she made no move to join me. "Are you blushing?"

"Shoo," she said, checking her face in the rearview.

I kissed her pink cheek and went into the grocery store. I was the only customer, and Pat wasn't working. A bored girl sat behind the counter, reading a full-color newspaper with red headlines. She cracked her gum as if it were her job, and maybe it was.

Produce took up the center aisle. Tomatoes. Bananas. Oranges. Apples. Iceberg lettuce. The basics. Five other aisles of prepared foods. The personal bullshit section was all the way in the back, and there wasn't a birth control method in sight.

"Hey," I said to the girl at the register.

"Hey." She smiled and closed the celebrity rag. "Sorry. Not much else to read around here."

"Yeah. I hear you." I jerked my thumb toward the back wall. "I was looking for condoms."

"Trojans? Sure." She got up from her chair. "How many you need?"

A billion. "Twenty-four pack would be great."

"We don't have any ribbed in a box of twenty-four."

"That's fine."

She peeked her head up. "We do have the ultra large, if you need it." Her voice was thick and syrupy.

I leaned on the counter. "Do you know I can get my whole arm in a regular size without breaking it?"

"But it's tight, right?" Her eyelashes fluttered. They were fake. So much effort to work in a grocery store. "On your arm, I mean."

"I don't need to show off."

She stood with a twenty-four box of regular lubricated. "Fourteen ninety-nine." She rang it up as I took a fifty out of my wallet. "You're staying at the Barrington place?"

The bell above the door rang. It was behind a wall of chips, so I couldn't see who had come in. Did I want to answer truthfully in front of someone I couldn't identify? Or at all?

"Can you break a fifty?"

She plucked the bill from my fingers. "There's a bedroom with a painting on one of the ceilings." She opened the register and made a production out of checking the bill's authenticity. "Have you seen it?"

Not everyone who had ever seen the painting had fucked Harper Barrington. It seemed like a safe truth. "Yes."

"My uncle Reggie painted it." She flipped the fifty under the drawer and counted out the change.

"Is that the same Reggie with the trucker hat? And the reddish hair?" How many Reggies could there be in a small town? Plenty. The Reggie I'd met didn't seem like much of a pink peony kind of guy, but hell, I'd been wrong before.

"That's him! He worked so hard. Showed us all the sketches he did before. I was twelve, and I thought he was the best artist in the world."

"It's a nice painting."

"Uncle Reg sold paintings sometimes but nothing as big as that ceiling. Mr. Barrington paid him five thousand dollars. It was, like, wow. That was so much. I thought Uncle Reggie was famous and rich, but he never painted another big room like that." When she handed me the change, she touched my hand. "I'm glad it's still there. I thought it must be gone by now."

"Still there."

"I'd love to see it again."

I folded the money and put it in my wallet. "I'm sure Harper or Catherine would show it to you."

Harper's voice came from behind me. "Oh, please." She stepped out from behind the wall of chips and smacked her hand onto the condom box. "Cynthia saw it at my birthday party in last December. Remember, you were smoking weed up there with your boyfriend?"

"Oh, right!" Cynthia faked a memory jog.

"Right." Harper picked up the box as if the shame over the condoms was nothing compared to the desire to shove the box up her friend's ass.

"Nice to meet you." I pulled Harper out of the store. Once we were in the parking lot, I took the box from her. "What was that about?"

"She's a famous boyfriend stealer."

"Okay, one"—I held up a finger—"I'm not your boyfriend. I'm half of your binary pairing."

She pushed me so hard I had to take a step back or fall over. "You're the one to my zero?"

"I'm your mate. A boyfriend can be stolen. A mate can't." I held up a second finger. "Two, she's not my type."

She crossed her arms and leaned on one hip. "Is there a three?"

"Three." I made a W.

"Knew it."

"You need new friends if you can't trust the ones you have."

"Did you text the kettle to tell him he was black, Mr. Pot?"

I laughed. She tossed me the box. I caught it, and we went to church.

LII

Keeping my hands off her in the house of God was no easy task. Everyone turned when we came in, and by the time we slid in next to Catherine in the third row, people had stopped singing to stare. Harper held her head high. I nodded to Kyle, who nodded back as if he approved. Butthead wore a black shirt that pulled at the buttons. Orrin nodded but didn't seem to appreciate my wave. Johnny wasn't around, but Pat didn't even look up from her book.

"I didn't know there were this many people in town," I whispered.

"Shut up." Harper handed me a booklet.

"I feel like I'm on display."

"You are."

"Do I look all right?"

She looked at me. Really checked me out, up and down. "Very fuckable."

She said it loudly enough for the older lady in front of us to shoot a glance over her shoulder. Catherine subtly whacked her sister with her hymnal.

The song ended, and everyone sat.

"What are you doing?" I whispered while pretending to follow along with the readings.

"Praying." She elbowed me, eyes on the reading.

I tried to focus on my booklet but couldn't find the words. Harper sighed and flipped the page, pointing at the right place.

"Thanks," I muttered. I'd missed half of it already.

We didn't get two more lines into it before her hand was on the inside of my thigh. Turning toward her, I let her know she was out of her fucking mind by moving her hand and twisting my face into a scowl.

She was unfazed.

"Praise be to God," she said with the rest of the congregation.

Another reading started. More words. More songs. Harper kept trying to rub against me, and I kept trying to stay churchy. I had a boner that barely fit in my slacks, and at some point, we were going to have to stand and sing. There were about a hundred fifty people in the room with their heads bowed over Corinthians. If I got up now, all those heads were going to unbow themselves. I was going to have a tent in my pants for the Virgin Princess of Barrington, the girl the entire county had protected because they loved her dead father.

"Praise be to God." The congregation's voices rose in the dead, flat tones of churchly responses.

Shit rustled and banged as people stood. Harper put her hand on my ass. I moved it. She did it again even while singing the first verse of the song.

It was arousing, sure. I wasn't made of stone. But it wasn't normal or smart. And yeah, Harper wasn't normal, but she was fucking smart. She was using me as a fidget toy for a reason.

"Can you show me the bathroom?" I kept my voice low but audible so we had a public excuse to be out of the room together.

Of course, Harper got flirty as she pulled me out of the row, practically skipping down the center aisle. We exited into a courtyard with a fountain and gardens of dying flowers.

Once the door shut behind us, I took the lead, guiding her around the back of the rectory to a narrow space between the building and a fence. The ground was scraggly and weedy. A kid's yellow sand bucket lay on its side three feet from a broken orange shovel.

She went right for my belt.

I pinned her wrists against the wall. "What is wrong with you?"

"Nothing."

"Everyone sees you grabbing at me."

"So?"

"So you and your dirty little mind belong to me now, but the people in this town think you belong to them." I let her wrists go. "You have to let them get used to you not being sweet Miss Mary Jane."

"Fuck them."

She took me by the collar. She was aggressive, passionate, as intense as any woman I'd ever met, so I let her wrestle with my damn shirt. I put my arms around her and drew her close.

"I feel free," she said in a low roar that went right from my ears to my spine. "I feel like I can do whatever I want. Really be myself. God, Taylor, I know I trapped you, but you turned around and saved me. I'm free, free, *free*. I feel so… God, I feel so good. I can do anything."

She could, but not because of me. Because she was Harper and brilliant and crazy enough to try the hardest things because she saw the big picture. I kissed her, pushing my tongue past hers to touch the core, throb- bing Harperness.

Pulling her shirt and bra up in one motion, she revealed tits that made me ache. "Fuck me. Right here. At church. Before they finish with communion."

She laid her hands on my crotch like a kid in a candy store. Not just any kid. A kid who had never tried candy her whole life then gone bananas at her first taste.

"Harper. Goose."

My tone got her hands off my pants, but she unsnapped her own fly. "Beeze?"

"You're a little crazy."

She slid her hand past her panties, wrist deep. "I'm so wet."

"I bet you are. And you're reckless."

She groaned. "I can't even think. I want your dick all the time. I can't sleep I want to fuck so bad. Is this normal?"

I leaned into her until I felt her arm move out of her pants. I grabbed her elbow and pushed it back down. "Nothing about you is normal. Go ahead. Make yourself come."

"I should?"

"Show me how you look when I'm fucking you. Move faster. Three strokes on your clit, then back to your pussy, then… yes. That's my goose. I love it when your mouth opens like that. I want to bite that lip."

I took her lower lip in my teeth and sucked on it. She exhaled, hot on my skin. Her nipples were hard, and when I pinched one, she nearly came off the floor.

"Hush," I warned her.

She came quietly, frozen in a muted cry, leaning on me to keep from falling.

I took her hand and sucked on her wet fingers.

Music came over the courtyard then voices.

"Shit." She stood straight, whipping her hand from my mouth, and buttoned her pants.

I laughed and helped her pull her shirt down. "You didn't care in the damn pews."

"Pressure's off, I guess. Do I look presentable?"

I took her hand. "You look like a nice girl from the heart of America."

"Let's go around the garden side. Then we can fade into the crowd."

Holding her hand, I let her lead me through the slit of space and onto the brick path leading to the garden.

LIII

Dirt tasted the same in Barrington as it did in Camden. I'd eaten more than my share of the ground in elementary school. I'd been thrown down, stepped on, had my face pushed into asphalt, grass, dry soil, snowpack, and puddles. By far, the puddles were the worst.

"Uncle!" I shouted before I spit the dirt. There had to be five guys on me, and if any of them weighed less than two hundred pounds, I'd have eaten the football under my stomach.

"Give me the ball," Kyle grunted.

"Fuck off!"

"No cursing on Sunday!" a female voice came from the sidelines.

Hands tried to flip me and strip the ball, but what I lacked in body weight I had in tenacity.

"Ref!"

The whistle blew, and the reverend's feet came into view. He was youngish and wore combat boots with his collar. "All right, guys. Get off him. That's a touchdown!"

Once the weight was off, I rolled off the ball.

Butthead helped me up. "That was some run, brother."

"Thanks." I brushed myself off.

The rest of the team high-fived me and clapped me on the back. Orrin's two high-school-aged sons and his father. Damon's brother. Pat's half brother.

"Butthead would have blocked for you, but he's too fat to keep up with you," Orrin said after he gave me a clap.

"You're pretty quick for an old man," I replied.

A can of beer had materialized in my hand. It was ice cold, and it still tasted like chemicals and bad breath. By unspoken agreement, the game was over. Or there had been an agreement beforehand, years ago, when these boys learned to play park football from their older brothers and fathers.

"What do you mean you never played football?" Damon said from across the food table. "You wear dresses too?"

Trudy shot him a look. I couldn't tell if they had something together, but he seemed less aggressive around her.

"I'd shut it if I were you," Orrin said to Damon. "Darcy'll flay you before you have a chance to say another stupid thing."

"Who's Darcy?" I asked. "Do we need to disarm her?"

"Him," Damon grumbled.

Trudy poked him. "She's my sister if she says so, and if you want me to be nice later, you'll follow along."

"Whatever you say." He didn't look convinced.

"Try the mushroom salad." Orrin pointed his fork at a bowl of canned mushrooms with unidentified beige squares. "My wife made it. Everyone loves it. Go on. It's going to be gone in ten minutes."

"My Orrin's too nice." A woman in her forties with poufy brown hair and glasses I hadn't noticed before patted his arm, and he kissed her on the lips.

"He is," I said as she put a scoop of mushrooms on my plate. "Thank you."

"Uh oh," Harper's voice came from my left. She had a plate with a burger and potato salad. "He's going to want to bring a five-gallon drum home to California now."

I got out of the table line to stand next to Harper. "Is it good?" I whispered.

"Try it."

I forked a couple of mushrooms and stuck them in my mouth. I didn't chew. I didn't think I could. My tongue rejected the super-sweetened, ultra-salty, rank buttbuds completely. I stepped out of earshot and Harper followed.

"No good?" Harper asked around a mouthful of burger.

I swallowed without chewing and gulped the beer. Shook my head hard.

"Is she getting them from your bathroom wall?" I kept my voice low.

She covered her mouth so she wouldn't spit her burger.

I poked at the slippery beige cubes. "What are these little things? Chopped asshole?"

She couldn't laugh. She couldn't swallow her burger. Her face was red.

"It's really not that funny."

A tear fell down her cheek.

I wasn't the funny guy. I'd never gotten a girl because I could make her laugh. They all said they wanted a sense of humor, but I'd gotten by all right without one.

Watching Harper get ahold of herself while I tried to find another mushroom joke in me, I wondered how I'd gotten the girls I had. Around her, I was different.

"You gonna eat that, mister?" A voice came from below, where a little girl of about five stood in a dirt-rolled dress, wielding a white plastic fork.

"This?" I pointed at the potato salad.

"This one." She pointed her fork at the mushrooms.

I hadn't known that many kids, but rumor had it they generally didn't like mushrooms.

"Here." I gave her my plate. "You can have it."

Her eyes went wide, and her mouth opened in joy.

Catherine rushed over. "Lori!"

"She's all right," I said. "Really."

"If you turn your back on your plate, she'll take it."

"She asked politely." I jerked my head at the girl, telling her to get out of Dodge before the narcks got her.

A mistress of subtlety, Lori ran to the table with the other kids. Catherine watched with longing in her eyes. She touched her nose as if it had suddenly filled up.

"Hey," Harper said to Catherine. "Snap out of it."

"Sorry." She smiled, and I remembered I hadn't heard her crying behind the walls in the past three nights. "Wally!" She ran to the children's table, where a kid had barbecue sauce all over his shirt.

"She's like Momma Barrington," Harper said.

"I haven't heard her in a few nights. Or have I just been distracted?"

Harper wiped the last of her burger across a palette of condiments. "She got a letter from her long-lost love."

"The guy? The one who left?"

Romantic? Sweet? Fucking crazy?

"She told you about him?"

"Not much. But that's…wow. Good for her."

"I know." She neatly placed the rest of the burger in her mouth then chewed with one cheek so she could talk. Her every move was graceful and efficient. Mostly, every gesture was honest and part and parcel of who she was. "Been years and boom. He's coming."

"When?"

"Friday. Had to squeeze it out of her. She really doesn't tell me shit, if you want to know the truth. I had to threaten to kick Daddy's grave over before she told me."

Catherine kneeled in front of Wally's shirt as he wept, and a woman in a sleeveless denim shirt who looked just like the barbecue-stained kid ran to them with a roll of paper towels. When his mother reached him, Catherine stood up, getting out of the way.

She backed up, looking wistful, longing. She looked just like Harper, but a little taller, older, with unruly hair. I never wanted Harper to have that look on her face. As if she accepted a world of things that would never be.

"We have to fix her room," I said.

"Excuse me?"

"Her long-lost love is coming, and her room is moldy."

"It's not. It's… wait. You mean the master suite?"

"She can't bring what's-his-name into some shitty bedroom. Come on. While you're mastering qubits, I'll do the walls."

"You?"

"I'm from a line of contractors. And the guys'll help. Where's your romantic spirit?"

"It's my sister. I don't want to think of you creating some romp room for her."

"I've been banging you right under her nose, and she hasn't said shit."

"To you, she hasn't."

I got between her and the eyes of the town. "What did she say to you?"

She shrugged and wiped her mouth. "My sister's not exactly a chatterbox, if you haven't noticed. She has a way of asking how I slept that's pretty much asking how big your dick is."

"What did you tell her?"

"I said, 'He's hung like a watermelon, and he fucks like an animal.'"

"You said that?"

"No, dork. I said 'fine,' but I said it as if I was talking about your dick, and I know she heard what I was thinking because she blushed."

I pinched her chin between my thumb and the bend of my index finger. "Let's get back and make some noise while we can."

She took my arm, and we went back home.

LIV

Once, when we were on a demolition project, my dad had told me that mushrooms are never just mushrooms. In the case of the Barrington master suite, he was right, as usual. The mushroom in the bathroom had eaten the wood behind it, and the more plaster I removed, the more mush- room appeared. There was an entire ecosystemback there.

The day after church, I woke up early, went to the shed to get the sledgehammer with half a handle, and called the lumberyard with an order. My phone was jangling and beeping with messages. Media. Employees. Friends. I reassured my mother, who was worried after the call with Gram, and texted a couple of friends. I didn't want to talk to anyone else. I wanted to fix the damn bedroom.

Harper picked up a shift at the distro center. I kissed her before she left as if I actually lived there with her.

The moment the sledgehammer touched the plaster and I started breathing lead dust, I let the physical activity take over. I was sweaty, stripped down to my undershirt, filthy everywhere. I'd dug sneakers and jeans out of my bag, moved and covered the bed with a tarp I'd found in the shed, and made a really loud, big fucking mess.

"Oh my Lord!" Catherine was at the door in a robe and bare feet.

"Good morning."

"What... what are you doing?"

"Don't come in!"

"But—"

"There are nails."

She bent at the waist, peering into the room. Half the walls were down to the studs, and mold, mildew, and fungus had left much of the busted plaster black on the back side.

"You won't have the mushroom again. The mold isn't safe to breathe."

She looked at the ceiling.

"And that? I looked behind it. It's clean."

"I want to say something." Her voice was as grave as I'd ever heard it. Not black in its tone but a serious shade of grey.

"Yes?"

"I own a gun."

"Okay?"

"I know how to use it."

"Cath—"

"Don't let anything happen to the painting."

I nodded slowly. "Yes, ma'am."

"And thank you," she said more lightly. "It'll be nice to sleep in here again."

She walked away without saying more.

By the time I got the last bit of plaster down, a flatbed from the hardware store arrived with a dumpster in tow.

Butthead got out of the truck with Florencio from the factory and Jorge, who came to the door while the other two slid drywall off the bed.

"Where you want it?" Jorge asked.

"Dumpster in the back. The rest of it can go upstairs."

He called back to the two guys in Spanish. They pulled the flatbed around back. I followed it.

"The dumpster should be right under that balcony, right there." I pointed up at the master suite.

The three other men looked up.

"That the room with Reggie's painting?" Butthead asked.

"Yeah."

"What are you thinking of doing?"

"Fixing it."

"Who? You?"

"Me." I slapped his chest and went to help Jorge unhook the dumpster from the flatbed.

He called out to Butthead. "You gonna help us, or are you gonna chitchat like an international man of leisure?" Jorge's thick accent made his command of the language funny, and he seemed to know it.

Generally, pallets of drywall sheets were raised into an open window by crane, but the windows weren't big enough, and the balcony doors couldn't be used without risking the railings. I didn't want to warn Catherine that her house could be destroyed before the first nail was driven in, so the supplies had to be brought in via the stairs.

We worked out the route around corners and up stairs, padding the corners and moldings.

I jumped up on the flatbed to help Florencio with the top slab of drywall.

"Oh, Jesus. Is Cali-Boy's going to pick up heavy things now?" Butthead hauled himself up.

"The store ain't payin' worker's comp if you blow something, man," Florencio said to me with a grunt. "Trust me on that."

"I'll keep your broke ass in mind when I visit you in the hospital," I said.

We carefully turned the drywall sheet on its side.

"Who's doing this with you?" Florencio asked as we angled the panel through the back door. "Better be somebody good."

"Just me."

"Come on, man. Nobody's stupid enough to do this alone."

"That's me. Nobody."

It took him a minute to get my joke, and he only acknowledged it by shaking his head in irritation. We were angling a seventy-pound sheet of drywall around Victorian-sized doorways.

The stairs were narrow, and the boards were wide and heavy. Jorge turned out to be Juanita's husband, and Florencio made it a point to let me know he was single and Jorge was an idiot to have gotten married. Butthead said that not having any options was easier, but I didn't believe him.

Covered in dust and breathing heavily, the four of us stood among the piles of debris in the master suite. I showed them the black mold on the plaster and the damage to the beams that had to be scraped away and reinforced.

"What's the ceiling?" Florencio asked.

"Enamel on tin," I answered. "The mold couldn't damage it, but I don't know what's going on behind it. You might be back with two-by- fours to replace beams."

"Dude," Butthead stated, punctuating a final word. "You are not doing this by yourself."

"What the fuck is this?" Jorge picked up the half-handled sledgehammer. "You didn't even order a new handle?"

I opened my mouth to answer, but I had no excuse.

"And, wait," Butthead said. "You did all this with that?"

"Don't you assholes have somewhere to go?" I said defensively. "I have shit to do. Come on. Get out of here."

They had a clock to punch, so they left me alone to bag old plaster and throw it off the balcony into the dumpster.

"Do you know how loud that is?" Harper said from the door. She had on her polo and lanyard. The bright yellow set off the fact that she looked exhausted.

"So? You don't have neighbors."

She ran her fingers over the lath. "Three days to GreyHatC0n."

"Three days until you win five mill."

"I'm going to enjoy taking your money."

"It's my partner's. If it was mine, I'd just give it to you."

"I wouldn't take it."

She put her arms around my waist, and I held my hands away from her. "I'm a sweaty mess."

"I don't care."

My shirt stuck to me when she laid her cheek on my chest. I flipped my gloves off behind her back.

"Lead paint. Seriously. Mold. You're breathing it."

"So are you." She didn't let go, which made the next part of the conversation more difficult.

"I need something from you."

"What?"

"The decryption for the object code." She pushed me away, but I kept her close.

"Keaton has to unlock his."

"It's an act of good faith to give him your code first. I think we're past me teaching you how to fuck anyway."

"Very past."

"Keaton's been nagging me about it. I almost wish my phone was still in the bushes. But he has a point. They really need to check it over before we open it."

She took a folded-up scrap of paper from her back pocket. "I figured you'd need it." She handed it over. It had a teddy bear in a Santa hat on the top and the code written in blue pen.

4e 2d 2e 20 6d 20 2e 2d 2e 20 4d 2e

20 4e 20 6e 2d 20 2e 40 4d 20 2e

"Hex?"

It wasn't a message when decoded. Just nonsense letters and punctuation.

She put her hand over it. "Nope. Don't decrypt it yet. It's for after. You'll like it, I promise."

"You're asking a lot."

"I deserve a lot."

I put my thumbs on her shoulders and pushed her away. "Be naked when I get out of the shower."

She tried to kiss me, but I wouldn't let her. Her ass was so sweet as she walked out that I had to slap it.

I took a picture of the code and the Santa bear, then I called Keaton. "Hey, Keat."

"I preferred when you were the face of this company," he said. "Everyone's asking for you."

"Where are you?"

"New York. Where you should be. Now. Immediately."

I was knee deep in moldy plaster and promises. I couldn't leave the house looking like a construction site, and I couldn't leave Harper to hack QI4 alone. "Can't. Still stuck."

"I will send you a car."

"No. I'm doing something."

"I don't want to be here. This was not the deal. It's your job to talk to the media and the stupid people."

"Just be dark and mysterious. Brood and growl."

"Tay—"

"I have the object code decryption key."

I could practically hear tires screech on the other side of the country.

"Now, listen," I said, walking onto the balcony. Below, the thorn bush still had our path to the center cut through it. "I can give it to you at 8 a.m. on Thursday. But I know you want it unlocked now."

"You should too, don't you think?"

"I do. I need you to promise me something first."

"I'm starting to wonder where your loyalties lie."

"In more than one place."

"That's not possible."

"Promise you won't come after the hacker."

For a few seconds, all I heard from his side was the indistinct voices of a public place and his breathing. I assumed he was thinking about it. Barrington had made me into a civilian.

"I promise nothing," he said. "But thank you for the code."

"What?" I looked at my screen. The picture of the paper was on it. He'd hacked me, the motherfucker. He'd used our cellular connection to hack my phone.

"I hope to see you Thursday," he said and hung up.

LV

Her upstairs room was actually a little suite with a full-size bed behind a door. She'd been as naked as a jaybird when I got upstairs, and we twisted around the sheets for a while, fucking as if our lives depended on it.

I thought about going to New York then pushed it away. Then considered it again. I could leave for a few days. I could come back and finish the bedroom. Come back to her. She'd be here. It wasn't so long.

But no. It wasn't that simple, if I was being honest with myself. Even after she cracked QI4, I was convinced I wouldn't come back to Barrington.

I shut my phone off, and she set up her center monitor to pick up TV, opening the door so we could see it from bed. She even had a remote she'd built from an old TV version. Answering a few messages, I knew tension was building for GreyHatC0n. I knew everyone was in New York, working their asses off to get it set up, and I was in bed with the enemy. I had a twinge of guilt that stayed with me even after Harper brought up a bowl of grapes and put her knees on the bed.

"Is today Monday?" she asked.

"Yeah."

She muted the TV signal. Crickets. Rustling grass. The hiss of her processor fans. The squeak of the weather vane turning in the wind above us. In the spaces where it all went silent, I could almost catch the sound of the river flowing.

"Do you hear it?" she said.

"Hear what?"

"Catherine cries on Mondays."

"I didn't realize there was a schedule." I took the grapes and put them on the night table before gathering her in my arms.

She twisted my wrist to look at my watch. "She should be going by now. I know she's in her room. I heard her in there on the way back up."

"Maybe she's not sad today." I turned the sound back on. Commercials. I didn't even know what we were watching. "We should throw her a party."

Harper sat bolt upright, back on her knees in a ribbed tank top that rode up, exposing the space between her tits and her pajama bottoms. "Oh my God!"

"I was joking."

"Her birthday is Thursday. I almost forgot."

"Harper. We have—"

"And the room? Is it going to be done? We can make that a big gift! We can invite everyone!"

"GreyHatC0n starts Thursday," I said with the flat affect of fact.

"So? It's still warm enough for the backyard. Maggie can make a birthday cake."

Harper dropped to her hands and knees and put her lips on my chest. I got hard before she even moved down.

"Who's Maggie?"

"She lives over on Dandelion Road."

I twisted my fingers in her hair as she got closer to my dick. "Every time I think I know everyone… oh, you little tease."

"You'll meet them at the party."

"You have to crack my code, and I have to be on the phone to make sure you don't. Or that everyone sees when you do. And the drywall…"

She ran her tongue from the base of my cock to the tip.

"We don't have time to plan a…"

She sucked lightly on the back of the head.

"Ah, that. Perfect."

Not much could distract me from my cock disappearing into her face. Not the news, which contained the usual reports of everyday malfeasance, faraway violence, and maps with overlaid swirls of cloud cover.

Except Keaton's voice from the television.

"*Quantum code was just a theory.*"

I sat upright so fast Harper nearly choked.

"Sorry."

I didn't have to apologize. She wiped her mouth with her wrist and stared at the screen with me, watching the stone-cold confidence of Keaton Bridge.

"In three days, it becomes a reality."

The black ball of the mic popped out of the frame while the female reporter asked the question. *"We understand the system was hacked just eleven days ago?"*

"It was an encryption overlay, and it exposed a flaw in our supply chain. The system itself hasn't been touched. It is still the most secure system in the world. We challenge anyone in the world to hack it."

"What if there's more than one hack? Will two people get five million dollars?"

His knowing smirk could have frozen the deep blue sea. *"Sure. Why not?"*

"You do not have ten million dollars, you fuck." I didn't realize I'd said that out loud.

"He's showing how confident he is," Harper said.

"He's going to bankrupt himself."

She leaned into me, and I put my arm around her.

"He believes in it. And you," she said. "He's handsome."

"What's that supposed to mean?"

"Are you jealous?"

"No. Fuck that."

The reporter had broken from Keaton to talk to some of the attendees outside the con, make some partially informed comments about hacking, and come back to the "biggest challenge prize ever."

"He's a criminal," I continued. "And I think he was wearing makeup."

She pulled away far enough to look at me. "You *are* jealous!"

"Just saying." I pulled her closer so she wouldn't see that, yeah, I was jealous.

The reporter took up the center of the screen to close out.

"She's a total fluff-piece reporter," I said.

"Yeah, she does the after-the-weather stuff."

"She's not a tech journalist. It's insulting. I mean, it's one thing to not know shit. It's another to be proud you don't."

"The QI4 system will be online from 8 a.m. to 8 p.m. Eastern this Thursday. Get your keyboards ready! The IP address will be posted on the QI4 website. The prize is awarded worldwide for any..." She made a show of looking at a piece of paper. "Invasive malware, adware, worms, DDoS, virus, or Trojan horse." She put the paper down. "But according to everyone I've spoken to here, only a zero- day exploit will work."

"And can you help us non-tech people? What is a zero-day exploit?" The guy

in the left-side box smiled as if he knew damn well he'd forget the answer to his question before he finished his second Cosmo.

"It's a hack invented from scratch, and apparently they're worth five million dollars. So you better get to work!"

I shut off the screen.

"You should go to New York," she said.

"No."

"Why not?"

"What if you need me?"

"You need to get over that right now. I'm not asking you for help. And you have your codes. Did he open the system?"

"Yes."

"You need to go. This is a big deal for you."

She was thinking of me. I didn't deserve her. Brushing her hair away from her face, I wanted to crawl into her skin and love her unpredictable, brilliant soul from the inside.

"What kind of attack were you thinking of doing?" I asked.

"I was going to just put something in the comments to taunt you."

I clamped my lips together. I didn't know how to do the hack she wanted, one where she'd be able to edit the code, but I knew the mountains she'd have to climb because I'd built them. I could have easily defined those obstacles and cut her work in half.

As if reading my mind, she put her hand over my mouth. "Don't. Even."

"Mmph."

She took her hand away.

"You can do it," I said.

"I just locked your system. I didn't crack it. This is a code-only hack. I can't plant transmitters in your office. This is the real shit. I want to do it."

"Do you promise to let me know if you're having trouble?" She started to object, and I held up a finger. "Not right away. But if you get to the end and you haven't done it."

"Can I just suck your dick now?"

"I don't know how to hack it. If I knew, I would have built a way to avoid it. But if you're close, I can tell you what you're up against. It's still up to you to figure out."

"Lie back." She pushed me down and straddled me.

"When you get in there, you're going to be shocked."

She shifted down until her mouth was on my dick again. "I won't be shocked. I'll act bored." She ran her tongue along my length, curling it around the curve of it.

"It's different down to the motherboards."

"So you say."

She took me down her throat and sucked on the way out. I wasn't going to be verbal much longer, so I just spit out the last sentence I could.

"I want you to win."

LVI

Thank God for Barrington, USA.

If I'd had two solid days to hang, tape, and spackle drywall and another half a day to paint it, I still wouldn't have gotten done in time. That became apparent a few hours into the project.

But Barrington showed up. Men who knew how to "do things" came and went through a revolving door, picking up pieces of the job bit by bit. They kept the site clean, did a better-than-average job, took the sink and toilet out so we could hang behind it, and went to get more stuff so often I started to wonder how much fell off a truck on the way to the distro center.

As far as my time went, I was useless forty percent of it. Calls kept coming. My coders, double-checking and rechecking that the system was correct. Keaton complained about my absence. My mother called to see if I was excited. The venue called to make sure they had enough broadband for the traffic.

Harper stayed locked in her room, working. Late at night, we fucked and collapsed.

The morning of the party, Harper got out of bed before the sun came up.

"Hey," I muttered. "It's not even five in the morning."

"It's ten after five." She kissed me gently. "You need to get a watch with a battery."

I slid back in the bed until my back was to the wall. "Are you ready?"

"More than you. You haven't even painted yet."

I grabbed her, pulled her onto the bed, and rolled on top of her. She giggled when I tickled her.

"Stop."

"Take these pants off before I rip them off."

Laughing, she pushed me away. "Taylor! Really!"

"Really?"

She made her voice steady and solid. "Really. I just… I want to be at my best, and I want to be on the forums early in case anyone has any genius ideas. I don't want to get behind."

She rolled over to get away, but I grabbed her by the wrist.

"Taylor!"

"One second."

"We're not having sex now."

"No sex." I let her go and sat on the edge of the bed.

"You won't even get hard?"

"I won't. Give me your hands."

She held them out. Her right index and left middle fingers were taped. I kissed each of her palms.

"These hands are going to do good work."

"Yeah, yeah." She tried to pull them away, but I yanked her back. Her hair crisscrossed her face.

"You have two minutes, goose."

"Fine."

I kissed every one of her finger joints. "No typos from you. Noslipping off the keys from you. No cramps from you." She giggled, and I continued to address her hands. "All of you will show up for work two Mondays from now, whether you're counting money to five million or not." I pressed them together and looked at her. "Your brain has to show up too."

"You're hiring me?"

"Yes. I'm sorry it took so long."

"Taylor."

"Name your price."

She put her hands on my face, one on each side, as if she wanted to hold me still. Even as skin pressed against skin and her warmth mixed with mine, her face was down a long, dark tunnel.

"Harper? I mean it. You're coming on with me."

"You're hiring me because you're sleeping with me."

"I got to know you because I'm sleeping with you."

Her hands fell down to my shoulders. "Did you ever want everything to be fair?"

"Sure." I pulled her down so she straddled me. "But it's not. Nothing is. You were born brilliant. That gives you advantages. Take it up with God."

"God didn't make me sleep with you." She bit her lip as she did a grind into my erection. "Even though I see Him when I do."

"You get credit for good choices." I pushed my hips into her and pulled her down. "You want to see God before you go upstairs?" My fingers ran up her shirt, finding a pebble of a nipple. When I gently pinched it, she tilted her head to one side, parting her lips. I had her. "I'm not going to beg you to let me lick your clit."

I got on my back and spread my arms. When she got up, I thought she was leaving, but she peeled her pants off.

"You drive a hard bargain," she said, crawling over me.

"Wait until you work for me. I'm a real pain in the ass."

She didn't answer in the affirmative. She didn't answer at all, which didn't bother me in the moment.

In the moment, I wanted to taste her as she kneeled over my face. I wanted to suck her hard enough to get her close then let her hover on the edge until she exploded over me, grinding on my mouth.

She came so hard she almost rolled away. I had to hold her tightening thighs down so my tongue could reach her, and even then, she tried to get away.

LVII

"I'm fine! Go away!"

It was ten in the morning, and Harper hadn't moved from her desk. When I poked my head in, she was bent over the keyboard, tapping lines of code or scouring the Tor forum that was put up just to share theories about QI4's GreyHatC0n challenge.

"Are you hungry?" I asked.

"Go away." She turned away from the screen, a deadly focus in her eyes. "I'm not kidding."

The system had gone online right on time. Jack had developed an app for the team that counted the number of break-in attempts and fails.

ATTEMPTS: 34,989
FAILS: 34,989

At times, the attempts column was higher, and my chest twisted, hoping it was Harper. I bolted up the steps twice, but the app caught up a few seconds later, and I got back to painting Catherine's walls with the rest of the guys.

She'd chosen a warm off-white that looked good with the ceiling mural and a pure white for the moldings. We finished right before lunch.

"Harper," I said after I knocked.

"Go away!"

That was my cue to open the door obviously. "Your sister is going to see her room finished. Do you want to come—"

"No." She didn't stop her fingers for even a second.

"It's important."

"Not now," she hissed. "She knows I'm busy."

I'd done a lot of coding in my day, and there was nothing harder than tearing yourself away when you were on to something.

ATTEMPTS: 89,084,172,651,097
FAILS: 89,084,172,651,097

The guys from the cage were on a chat inside the app, discussing the numbers, considering updating the app to count DDoS attempts separately, and crossing their fingers until they broke.

Two guys were missing: Keaton and Deeprak. Keaton was an antisocial shithead, but there was a big hole in the conversation where Deeprak should have been.

Juanita and Mrs. Boden called gift time, blindfolded the birthday girl, and led her down the hall.

"Is Harper coming down?" Pat whispered to me.

I gave her the official excuse. "She's not feeling well. Trust me, you don't want her coming down."

Juanita removed the blindfold, and everyone shouted, "Happy Birthday!"

Catherine stood in the doorway with her hands folded at her lips. The room stank of paint, and the floor wasn't done, but she looked happy. Really happy.

"Don't touch the walls," Kyle called. "Not yet."

"Thank you," she whispered, turning into the crowded hall. She held her hand out to me. "Taylor."

I took her hand. "Let me show you what we did."

I showed her the smooth walls, the moldings, the way the painting was completely intact, the updated bathroom, the place where the mush- room used to be, and the reglazed French doors to the balcony. The barbecue smoke from the backyard obscured theview.

"That's all we could do," I finished. "But the floor needs to be done, and you need new pipes and a rewire."

"Can I sleep in it?"

"Paint should be dry by tonight."

Her cheeks turned eighty-five shades of pink, and she looked at the floor. She hugged me and got pulled out of the room by one of her many, many friends.

"Chris is coming tomorrow," Pat whispered to me as Catherine went into the hall.

"Is that her old boyfriend's name?"

"More like secret love. Only love, if you ask me."

ATTEMPTS: 127,054,836,201,916
FAILS: 127,054,836,201,916

I kept my attention on the third-floor window through conversations about cars and sports, a smattering of politics, and gossip. Harper's excuse for not being there floated without trouble. In a way, it was the truth. She was indisposed, trying to save everyone from the changing world by disrupting the tools of the change.

When she got in, would she cheer? Would I hear her from the ground? Would she text me? Call out the window? Announce to everyone? Keep it to herself?

I went upstairs with a plate of mushroom salad and a burger. "Open the door, Harper. You know I can pick this lock."

It clicked, but she didn't open it. When I did, I found her working. Almost all of her fingers were taped. The roll sat next to the keyboard, its brown core exposed, hanging on to the last inch of white tape.

I put the burger down and looked over her shoulder. "A Plone CMS. Good idea but—"

"Shut it!" She spun toward me, cutting me off with the look of death on her face. "First of all, you're seeing about ten percent of this script, and second of all, I'm doing this fair."

I stole a kiss. It was supposed to be a short peck, but I kept it going until she yielded, just a little.

"I'm going."

She had four hours.

LVIII

The sun got lower on the horizon. The challenge was going to end about half an hour before sunset, but I still kept my eyes on my inaccurate watch. Jack had updated the app with the countdown, but they couldn't figure out how to isolate the DDoS attacks, so the numbers were exponential.

ATTEMPTS: 389,491,610,776,287
FAILS: 389,491,610,776,287
T-MINUS: 02:12:34

Party guests came and went, their jobs and kids determining how long they stayed. I met so many of them I lost track. They shook my hand and thanked me for saving the mural.

I'd had no idea what the house meant to Barrington. Kyle and Johnny were talking by the thorn bushes, waving their arms at the thorns and shouting words drowned out in the white noise of the party. Pat and Jorge shook their heads at whatever suggestion Johnny offered up. Reggie and three others I'd just met listened but didn't seem to have much to add.

They cared about the house as if it was their own.

Harper's not leaving.

She was leaving. Maybe we'd have a long-distance thing for a while, until she figured out how to put the five million to the best use. I could take it.

I was walking toward the thorn bushes to see what the argument was about when I got a message from Deeprak.

<You're almost there.>

<Two hours.>

<When are you coming back? You can write your own ticket.>

<… >

I looked up at Harper's window glowing blue from the screens.

<You are not a sidekick.>

<I hope you keep that five million.>

I didn't. I wanted Harper to have it, even if it meant my own failure. I started to type a bland response. Something on the order of "We'll see." But Deeprak shot back a message.

<You're going to need it to pay me.>

<Yes, dude. That's… >

I laughed at how excited I was to have him back. I'd almost agreed to pay him five million dollars.

<too much, TBH, but I'll promise this: you get paid the same as me. Salary and bonus.>

<I want a team. >

<Yes>

< My own projects.>

<Yes>

I heard something from Harper's window. A clap and a shout.

ATTEMPTS: 710,887,019,611,003
FAILS: 710,887,019,611,003
T-MINUS: 01:54:12

I might have been mixing the sounds up with something else, or misinterpreted what I'd heard, but I bolted up the stairs and poked my head through Harper's door. She'd left it unlocked.

"I'm not coming up here again."

Silhouetted against her triple screens, she shook her hands out at the wrists until they blurred. "I'm fine. I think I might have it."

"Really?" I stepped into the room fully.

"Yeah. It's… I'm not going to explain it yet. It's a combination. Zip, then boom, then right under."

"Can I see?"

"Not until it works."

"I love you, Harper."

"I love you. Please get out," she said absently.

There was something nice about that. To be loved habitually. Thoughtlessly, almost. Being so deep in her heart that she could say she loved me without thinking too hard about it.

I closed the door behind me. She had this. It was happening. She was going to get the money, save the factory, and who even knew? Stay in Barrington? Run it? She'd have to turn a shell into a manufacturing business. QI4 didn't have the capacity for an operation like that. We had neither the money nor the demand yet.

So if she ran the factory, she couldn't work for me back at QI4HQ.

But she had to.

I couldn't stay in Barrington. She had to come back with me. And she wasn't working for the competition, which was everyone at this point. From retailers to software giants to hardware manufacturers, we were about to disrupt all of it, and she couldn't work for any of them. She was mine. I'd found her. She was going to sit next to me every goddamned day to share her beautiful mind at work and her beautiful body at home.

"Hard-on!" Butthead called upstairs. "You got someone here!"

"Me?" I stood at the top of the stairs and pointed at myself.

"You know another Hard-on?"

Before I could answer, a man in black jeans and a jacket stood next to him.

Keaton.

LIX

I hadn't seen Keaton in the flesh in a long time. He kept to the shadows, where he was comfortable, disappearing in crowds, hiding where anyone could see him if they looked.

In Barrington, they watched him in clusters. Young girls giggling and pretending not to look. Groups of men puffing out their chests or singly standing between him and their wives. The primal posturing was unconscious and pretty much standard operating procedure whenever Keaton was in a room full of strangers.

"Nice to see you," I said when I got to the bottom of the stairs. "Just passing through?"

"On the way to certain victory." He held up a bottle of Dom Perignon. "Do they have buckets of ice here in… where are we?"

"Barrington." I took the bottle, and he followed me to the kitchen.

"Well, hello." Catherine wiped her hands on her apron.

"Catherine, this is my partner." I coughed back his name. I didn't know how he wanted to present himself outhere.

He held out his hand to her. "Marcus."

"Welcome. It's so nice to meet a friend of Taylor's."

I held out the bottle. "Do you have a bucket?" I asked before she could mention Harper. I had to tell her he was here. Had to warn her to stay upstairs even if she won it all.

Especially if she won it all.

"Cathy!" a voice came from outside. "We need you!"

"I'll take care of it." Mrs. Boden plucked the bottle out of my hands.

"Dom. Nice stuff. Real nice. Had it once in Paris when I was in nursing school."

"You lived in Paris?" Keaton asked.

"After the Second World War." She slid a silver ice tray out of the freezer. "I cut more metal out of muscle than a butcher at a hunting ground, but I needed 'more training' to practice in the States." She smacked the ice tray on the counter.

Keaton crossed his arms and leaned on the counter. "Paris after the war must have been—"

"Complicated." She pulled the lever on the tray, releasing the shattered cubes.

Keaton could talk to old people for hours, especially women. Where men tended to clam up as they got older, he found women gave less of a shit about who thought what as they greyed and made more interesting conversation.

He wouldn't ask about Harper, and even if Mrs. Boden mentioned her, it would be in an innocent context. I backed out of the kitchen. All I had to do was get up the stairs and tell Harper that no matter what happened, she had to stay in that room. Cheer into a pillow. Celebrate her first hours of victory alone, or my partner would figure itout.

Then shit would get really random, really fast.

A hand gripped my bicep and yanked me away. Keaton had broken Mrs. Boden's magic spell long enough to grab me and pull me into the backyard. The discussion around the thorn bushes still raged, but with Catherine at the center of it.

Keaton let me go and held up his phone.

ATTEMPTS: 1,032,234,165,777,029
FAILS: 1,032,234,165,777,029
T-MINUS: 00:43:34

"I don't understand what happened to you," he said, pocketing the device. "What you're doing here. Why you dripped the decryption out the way you did. I checked everything in your past. Even called your mother—"

"You called my mother? Are you fucked in the head?"

"Excuse me? She was a part of my childhood too. In any case, she says you have no connection to this little town as far as she knows. I found your rental car trail. Not pretty. Intercepted your wireless bill. No calls. No data usage. Found some activity at the lumber yard, a few drinks at a bar in the middle of a parking lot. It's not much, but you weren't even trying to hide. Not really. I couldn't figure out what your game was. How you were trying to screw me. Then it came to me."

"Taylor!" Butthead cried from the porch. "Did you not give your friend a fucking beer?"

A small, hard projectile came toward me at speed, nothing more than a displacement of air in the near-dark. I reached my hand out and caught the can of beer without realizing what it was until I felt the wet cold against my palm.

I handed it to Keaton. "Just hold it. You don't have to drink it."

Another launched then slid off my fingertips and succumbed to gravity with a groan from Butthead.

"I'm dying to hear what came to you." I picked the can out of the dirt, faced away from my partner, and cracked the top.

Orrin pulled a silver canister from the back of his truck. It looked like a keg in the twilight, but it had a hose on it. Behind him, Damon lugged two red gas containers.

"What are they doing?" Keaton asked.

"No fucking clue." I slurped the carbonated slurry and made a face.

"They bottle that shit in Mexico," Damon said as he passed with his gas cans. "That's why it tastes like piss."

"They used to bottle it in the factory over that way," I said to my partner.

Ignoring my recommendation, he took a swig of the beer. "I was trying to figure out your game. Then I thought, maybe you aren't playing a game. Maybe you were being honest. Stupid, probably. But honest. The only way to know was to come here, look you in the face, and ask you what the fuck is going on."

The porch lights went on. They didn't illuminate much, but the way this conversation as going, I preferred the twilight.

"What's going on," I said pensively, looking toward the side drive, where Harper's light fell onto the trees. "It's stupid."

"You found the hacker. Obviously. And you're protecting them. Don't deny it. I thought, up until a minute ago, that they were related to this girl."

"Which girl? You assumed there was a girl. I never said shit about it."

"Please give it a rest. There's a little…" He held his beer hand up at me, tracing the shape of what he wanted to say. "Softening around the edges? And it explains a lot. Why you're protecting her friends. Why you stayed here. Why you weren't hitching on the interstate to get home. Why we got the decryption in pieces. She's really got you on a leash."

The suggestion that I was on a woman's leash was meant to get a reaction out of me, but it didn't. What made me tense up was how close he was to the truth.

"She's not related to our hacker."

With a manner calculated to minimize my reaction, he held the can to his lips and stated a fact as if in passing. "Because she is our hacker." He swallowed with a gulp. "And you love her."

Deny, deny, deny…

I hid behind a sip of beer, looking away from the light so he couldn't see me. I couldn't tell too many lies. I couldn't even go direct opposite because lies in direct opposition pointed 180 degrees directly to the truth.

The drink went down like a pair of loaded dice. "You're fucking crazy."

"We know that's true. But you're a shitty liar."

She was going to win, and he wouldn't let it happen. He wouldn't turn over the money because he'd never believe I didn't help her do it.

"Maybe."

"Maybe?"

Fuck it. Fuck the shit out of it. Fuck it to hell. If I was going to bring her back and make her a part of my life, I was going to have to love her in front of the world, starting with my childhood friend.

But I didn't have a plan to hide QI4's hacker in plain sight. So I could talk about me but not her.

Don't forget who he is or what he is.

He was loyal to me, not Harper. Not to anyone I was protecting. He could act like a normal friend when it suited him. Ask normal questions. But when it came to business, the alpha wolf would shed the sheep's clothing in a heartbeat.

"She's not why I stayed. She's why I'm coming back."

"Is she here tonight?"

I looked at everything but the light coming from Harper's room.

"She's working."

He laughed in disbelief. "Anyone that good doesn't *work*."

Orrin was spraying the contents of the silver container on the thorn bushes. Damon was at the end of the path Harper and I had hacked, dumping gas on the bracken. Orrin's participation made me think whatever they were doing might not be a bad idea, but even the wisest men get a little reckless after a few beers.

"I lost," I said. "She played me, and I lost."

A gaggle of children ran past us like a wave crawling onto the beach.

"If you lose," Keaton said, "I lose. And I don't lose."

A whoosh, a burst of light, and a blast of heat came from my right. I put my arm up in an inadequate gesture to guard againstit.

The thorn bushes were on fire.

Keaton barely squinted. The children cheered. The adults around the bonfire whooped and hollered. Damon got close to the flames, an unlit cigarette dangling from his lips. What a knucklehead.

"Once this is over," he continued, "we'll deal with her."

"No," I said. "We won't. We're going to drop it."

"Oh, Beeze." Disappointment dropped from his lips. "You can be the doormat. I'll take care of it."

I was going to throw him off by calling in a favor, but that was playing by his rules.

His rules, our rules, the rules of the underground? They didn't scale.

"You won't. Let me tell you why." I faced him so he paid attention to me, not the fire. "If you want to go bigger, go better, go more public, this hacker mafia bullshit has to stop. We're going to be under scrutiny like never before. A thousand people might care about whether or not we get revenge, but a few million are watching to see if we keep our noses clean. Don't fuck this up with petty bullshit."

He nodded slightly. I could never read him before, but that changed in the firelight. His code scrolled across his face.

He was afraid of the big time. He didn't know the rules.

"If we walk away from tonight with a secure system," he said, "I'll walk away from retribution. I won't indulge in 'petty bullshit.' If we're still a struggling startup in twenty-one minutes, I'm burning her down."

He held up his phone.

ATTEMPTS: 1,332,871,552,921,972
FAILS: 1,332,871,552,921,972
T-MINUS: 00:21:04

If Harper lost the challenge, she'd be mine.

If she won, he was going to hunt her down until he found her right under me.

I didn't know what to wish for. Both options were losers.

If she won, we were over. For her own protection, I would have to shield her by leaving her behind.

The threat hung in the air like lead. What was Harper waiting for? The last minute? To ensure no one followed her into QI4, was she waiting for the last possible second?

Twenty-one minutes and counting. That was how long she was mine because she was going to crack it. She was too good not to.

The fire hit the back side of the bushes, catching on the gasoline and whatever Orrin had sprayed. The flames rose to the height of the house. Harper's room on the third floor was on the front and side, but if the house caught, she'd be stuck up there at the top of a single staircase.

"Who in the hell thought that was a good idea?" Keaton sipped his beer as if he was watching a movie.

He seemed awfully calm, but everyone was backing away. We were in the moment when a fun thing turns into a dangerous thing. That moment when decent, relatively intelligent people start to wonder if the method they'd implemented to clear yesterday's bad idea was becoming today's tragedy.

And Harper was a sitting duck. Stay back here and try to put it out? Or run upstairs and grab her?

Nineteen minutes.

I stepped forward. Water. The green garden hose wouldn't do much, but if I doused the house? Would it deter the flames from taking the whole thing?

Leaping for the hose, I twisted the valve. Water shot out of the seal between the threads and the nozzle, but it held.

A man came from the back door. I didn't recognize him, and I would have dismissed him as yet another Barrington citizen I hadn't met yet, but he stood out in a jacket and slacks.

He carried a fire extinguisher canister in one hand and the hose in the other.

"Chris!" Catherine cried.

"Stand back!" he shouted, jumping off the porch and spraying the flames.

With those two words, Orrin jogged to the shed. Kyle ran for his truck, which was parked in the back and blocked in by what must have been Keaton's black Mercedes.

I doused the porch, sending Trudy and her friends running.

Orrin and Kyle retrieved fire extinguishers, and the thorn bush bed was reduced to a smoking mass of brambles in no time. I loosened my grip on the nozzle, and the flow slowed to a drip. I couldn't let it go. I wasn't ready to drop the safety net.

Reggie was the first to laugh. Then Kyle. Then Trudy and her friends.

"You." Johnny, who I hadn't seen, pointed at Orrin. "I expect better from you. This was some bonehead shit if I've ever seen bonehead shit, and I've seen some boneheaded shit in my day. Je*sus*."

Damon was blind with laughter. Orrin had his head between his knees, and his shoulders shook with it. I stood there with the hose dangling from my fingertips.

Keaton's voice came from just behind me. "People in dark times do dark things."

"I didn't see it coming."

"Tension's released for now. Danger's like scratching an itch, isn't it? Life's shit until you try to make it worse."

I dropped the hose.

Laughter had taken a backseat to deep breaths and relieved chattering. With a red fire extinguisher, Damon fogged the smoking center of the thorn bed using the path Harper and I had made, a lit cigarette drooping from his lips.

Catherine, who had the most to lose from the foolish attempt to clear the bushes, had her back to the scene, her hands balled into fists and placed on her hips. Chris, the guy in the jacket, stood lover close, brows knotted in irritation.

That must be the guy. A day early, and it didn't look as if it was going well.

I hung up the hose and realized I hadn't dropped my beer.

Fuck it.

"Waste not." I tipped my can toward Keaton and drank.

He slid his thumb along the glass of his phone. "They created the worst danger they could then avoided it," he said, turning the display to me. "Just like a certain technology disruptor."

ATTEMPTS: 2,007,911,945,365,018
FAILS: 2,007,911,945,365,018
T-MINUS: 00:00:00

I stared at the numbers.

They were the same.

Every digit matched.

And time was up.

The chat from the guys was in all caps with strings of exclamation points.

"You did it, you crazy bastard." Keaton was happy. Joyful. I'd never seen him with a genuine smile that wide, but when he clapped me on the shoulder, he was a proud big brother.

My heart was on the third floor of a house that had almost burned down.

Had she stopped because of the fire? Had she simply not made it? What had happened? I'd thought she had it. She'd thought she had it. What had gone so wrong that everything had gone right?

"No one got in," I muttered, checking my own phone. Same numbers. Same time. Same chat thread.

WE DID IT!!!

WE WON, WE WON, WE WON, WE PWNED THEM!!!

CHAMPAGNE AND A BLOW JOB!

"You're their leader," Keaton continued. "Do you have something to say?"

"Yeah." I looked at the trees that had been lit by Harper's window, and they were dark. "I do."

Gentlemen. We are now the
proud owners of Silicon Valley.

The responses poured in, scrolling faster than I could read.

You're the KING!!! Motherfucker!

Pwned!

I'm pissing myself.

Keaton's trunk smacked shut, and he walked toward the porch with the rest of the case of Dom Perignon. He was a cheap motherfucker until he wasn't.

Dude, THANK YOU!

I'm calling Deeprak, man.
I MISS THAT CURRY-EATING FUCKER.

HAIL TO THE CHIEF!!!

I had to go to Harper. We had to make another strategy. Figure out another way to get her the win she needed. I had to deal with the guys fast and go to her.

Deeprak's coming back. If you're interested in being on his team, fill out a form with Raven.

The responses were fast and in the enthusiastic affirmative.

YESSS!!!!

Deeprak's return wasn't exactly what I'd wanted to talk about. I didn't want to get so wrapped up in their joy that I brought it upstairs to Harper. She didn't need to see that.

Guys.
Keep it together.
Make sure the cage stays closed. Celebrate now, take a few days off. Monday, we need to analyze the attempts and see who got close. Then we need to act like they breached because the next person will.
And as a company, we're going to do better. We've already made the best product in the world. We need to be the best company in the world.
See you Monday.

I LOGGED OUT. Took a deep breath.

She was my queen, but what was I king of? Technology? History? What was I supposed to do with that shit? I couldn't live off people's adulation. But her? I could eat and drink her. She was made of the food of life. She nourished me.

My job was to nourish her in her time of crisis.

I hopped up the steps to the porch and was about to run through the kitchen when I saw the black blur of Keaton out of the corner of my eye and heard the *pop* of champagne.

My mind was up the steps to Harper's door, but my body had stopped walking before I hit the other side of the room.

Keaton was indeed popping the champagne over the sink, though he hadn't lost a drop of foam. Harper stood next to him with paper cups pinched between her fingers, four to a hand, tape on all the joints that had taken the worst beating.

"Hey," I said. "I was just…" I pointed upstairs.

"I felt better, so I came down," she said. "Your friend told me what happened. Congratulations."

She wouldn't look at me. Just at the champagne falling. I needed to see her face. Read her expression. Hear her words.

"This guy you're talking to, right here?" Keaton filled the little cups as he spoke. "Taylor Harden. You're going to tell your grandkids you met him, and they won't believe you."

Mrs. Boden swooped in holding three cups in her bent fingers. She pushed her bangly red bracelet farther up her arm. "Just a splash, young man."

"To remember Paris," Keaton said, moving the flow of bubbly to her.

Harper paced to the backyard with her four cups in hand and her face down. I tried to follow, but my business partner put one hand on my arm and held up his champagne cup with the other. Mrs. Boden put champagne in my hand.

"That's the girl?" He didn't wait for me to confirm. "She's stunning."

"I know."

I didn't want to be with the man whose support had made tonight's victory possible. I wanted Harper, who'd almost crushed that victory once and who, by all rights, should have beaten me on the second try.

He held up his cup. "She's victory number two tonight. Well done."

I didn't tap my cup to his. She wasn't a conquest. She wasn't a tool for disruption or a mountain I'd climbed.

"Harper!" I went outside after her. My paper cup disappeared from my hand, and I let it go. I didn't want to drink champagne to celebrate. I wanted to drink Harper's disappointment to relieve her of it. I threaded her fingers in mine. Her skin was ice, and her taped joints were rigid. "I'm sorry."

"It's fine." She still wasn't looking at me.

"No, it's not."

"It was fair."

Fair.

Fuck fair.

Fair was a pipe dream. Fair was different for everyone. Fair couldn't even sit at the same table with justice.

I pulled her close and snarled in her ear, "What's the point of it being fair if the outcome is wrong?"

She pushed me away, gently at first, harder when I resisted. "There is no wrong. There's only what is. Don't make this about something it's not."

"It's about us then. It's a speed bump. It won't stop us."

"Taylor." With a little shake of her head, she took a hammer to the crust around my illusions. Just a tap. I felt the vibrations from inside, but the shell didn't crack.

"Come home with me," I said. "Work with me. We'll find a way to save Barrington. Together."

The party was hitting a fever pitch around us. Damon had a near- empty bottle of Dom in one fist as he pounded his chest with the other. Harper shot out a laugh.

"Harper." My tone was sharp.

"What?" She was sharp back, eyes focused on me, her chin a degree or two higher. The little crease in her lower lip was shallow from tightened muscles beneath.

"This is important."

"Okay, so?" She went from frown to smile with a glance at Damon, who was pretending to put out a smoldering patch of bush with invisible champagne. He was getting big laughs.

"I'm trying to tell you something, and you're being entertained by the biggest jackass in town."

"You know what? Stop trying to tell me things."

She walked past me to Trudy and a few girls, brushing me aside as if I wasn't even there. No. Worse. If I'd been invisible, she'd have had a good reason to turn her back on me.

I was less than that. Smaller. More inconsequential than a man she didn't see right then.

The insistent pressure of my insignificance crushed air from my lungs, weighed my shoulders. It bore down with an exponential force of gravity.

I couldn't continue to exist.

"Harper!" I yelled with all the air my squeezed lungs could hold.

Conversations stopped. In the periphery, faces turned my way, but the person at the end of the tunnel of my attention didn't show me her face.

No moment would happen after this one. There was this. Only this. Then a short, painless blinking out before the void.

The only way out was the tunnel.

I chased her to the end of it, touching her shoulder, curving my fingers, pulling.

"Get off me!"

She kicked me down the tube. It was dark, and the only sound was sucking.

"I love you." Grappling for the edge.

"I know. And I'm sorry about that." Her voice had a clang, as if she was talking inside a soda can.

"No. You love me."

"I'm sorry, Taylor. I don't. I used you. I did a shitty job, and I didn't get what I was trying to get. But that doesn't make me your charity case, and it doesn't make you one of us. It makes you done, just fucking done around here. Go home."

"You're lying. I can see it in your nose." I must have reached for her again, even though I didn't remember making a decision to, because she slapped my hand away.

"I've *been* lying. This is the first time I'm telling the truth. I don't even like you."

The pressure of the air coalesced around my arms in the shape of fingers and hands, gripping, pulling me away.

"You sold the bowls to—"

"I didn't want to owe you anything." She was a little flustered, raising her voice and jamming her hand at the air between us. "I didn't want you to have a reason to come back here."

"You're mine."

"No, I'm not." Her creased lip quivered. Was she crying? Was it sadness? Guilt? Tension? Or did she love me?

"You belong to me. I didn't even exist until we met. I wasn't a man before you. I was an idea. I don't want to be an idea anymore. I want to be real. I can't be real without you." What the hell was I saying? "And you? Living half your life in the shadows? No one in this place knows you. They have no idea what you are. You're going to live and die a stranger."

"Fuck you! This is who I am!"

I couldn't see anything outside her. Couldn't hear anything but her denial. "No, it's not."

If I could just grab her the way she liked, by the base of the back of her neck, pulling the hair tight, she'd be mine. She'd realize I gave her something she needed. She'd know she loved me.

I went to make that grab, hand out with fingers in tight hooks, snarling to take what was rightfully mine.

Someone moved in front of my vision, cutting off the sight of her. That tunnel between us was my breath. I was pulled and pushed in a dry riptide of forces. I fought as if I was drowning. My feet went from under me. I kicked, struggling for the surface.

I knew people, men, were taking me away. Physically. They were increasing the distance between my and Harper's bodies, but the proximity of my attention never wavered.

"Harper! You're mine! No matter where I am! You're mine!"

She was the bowl of the sky above, and I was screaming for her in a glassy ocean.

A loud *hup* preceded the darkness.

LX

My hand hurt, but I kept pounding the window. The back doors were locked from the outside. The keys weren't in the ignition.

The men watched me, lined up between her and me, facing the black Mercedes like a wall between us.

I knew she was out there. Waiting? Sobbing? Laughing?

Keaton got in the driver's seat and started the car. Flinging his right arm over the front seat, he backed out of the driveway. "I've never seen you like this."

I put my cheek on the cool window to keep my eyes on the yard. The wall of men broke up. In a flash of blond between the side of the house and the edge of the car window, I saw her run toward the back door.

"Let me out."

"No."

Was that the last time I'd see her? That flash of blond hair jogging to the back porch and out of sight? Was that the end of the script?

I snapped the door handle. Still didn't work.

Keaton swung onto the road and peeled out as if he was being chased. He wasn't.

"What is wrong with you?" he asked.

"How much gas do you have?" I leaned over, figuring if he had to get gas soon, I could get out.

"Always full. Have you lost your mind? Is this what happens when you succeed? You turn into a raving lunatic?"

I threw my body against the back of the seat, sliding down until my knees hit the front seat.

"You went code black back there." Keaton jerked his thumb in the direction of the house we'd left behind.

"She's trying to protect me. She thinks she'll drag me down."

He turned for a split second to look at me, then he put his eyes back on the road. "She said this? Or you're making it up?"

"I know her."

We blew by the gas station and got onto the interstate. A yellow stick-of-butter truck went by, and the distro center slid in and out of view. As I got more distant from her, I got more distant from myself, moving at seventy-five miles an hour and as stagnant as wet summer air.

"Okay, let me explain something to you," Keaton finally said. "Women are not subtle. If they're not one-hundred-percent crystal clear, it's because they don't know, not because they're being elusive or enigmatic or call it what you will."

The bar where I'd lost my watch came into view and left my sight in an instant.

Gone.

I checked the Langematik. It was wrong. I went for my pocket to check it against the phone. I came up with a piece of paper. I opened it. The last code.

4e 2d 2e 20 6d 20 2e 2d 2e 20 4d 2e 20
4e 20 6e 2d 20 2e 40 4d 20 2e 0d 0a

Hexadecimal. But random—no message because the text decoding left so many dots and dashes.

N-. m .-. M. N n- .@M .

"You were stupid to trust her," Keaton said. "Have a tantrum over that."

Stupid? How could he say that? He didn't know her.

I was drained of the ability to be offended.

He'd never had much to say about women until that day. I was the one with the deep distrust I'd never admitted to until I trusted the wrong woman.

"Never trust a woman who hacks you." Keaton pointed upward as if the truth came from God.

I nodded. She had been wearing tape when she held out four paper cups of Dom Perignon. "Yeah."

"But you didn't help her get into the system."

"She wanted to do it fairly. On her own."

He shook his head. "Fucking myth. No one does anything on their own." He made eye contact in the rearview. "That saved her life. I swear to you. If she'd gone in, after what she already did, I would have made sure this entire town burned."

The will to resist him couldn't overcome my exhaustion. I didn't have energy for arguments, even in my own head. I only saw my mother's old car against the backdrop of Jaguars and Mercedes in the Poly parking lot. The feds letting me go if I just showed them how I'd used Luhn's formula against the banks. Having a best friend with the money to invest in my ideas.

I ran my finger over the paper with the last code.

Dots and dashes started with two. I was an idiot. And a bunch of even numbers should have been enough to clue me in to the fact that the message was *all* dots and dashes if I just broke apart the larger numbers.

2e 2e 2d 2e 20 2d 2d 2d 20 2e 2d 2e 20 2d 2d 2e
20 2e 2e 20 2e 2e 2e 2d 20 2e 20 20 2d 2d 20 2e

It was so simple I broke it down in my head.

..-. --- .-. --. .. ...- . -- .

A simple request in Morse code.

Forgive me

I pressed my knuckle to the window where the land met the darkening sky and whispered to myself, "I don't know what to do."

Fields sped by, the perpendicular rows visible one at a time then disappearing into a bicycle-spoke blur. I was the hub of it. The tiny center of a circle larger than the circumference of the horizon.

LXI

Steve Jobs. Bill Gates. Jeff Bezos.

What does it take to change the world?

Mostly luck and a support system and timing. Secondarily, a person's talent has to fit into the surrounding puzzle of the era, their opportunities, and the willingness of the people around them to smooth the path. Most pieces don't fit on all sides, but when they do, the entire world hears it all click into place.

I didn't feel guilty for being a guy who could make things work with quantum theory at a time when quantum theory was ready to become things. I hadn't turned down favors or hands up. I'd had plenty of both.

Rockefeller. Carnegie. Ford.

Even Fitz seemed to know already, instinctively, who he worked for and why.

Luck + opportunity + talent + other people. There were no shortcuts. We ascended the throne because we fit the puzzle on all four sides.

Decades from now, they'd crown a new ruler. I'd be no one or a myth or forgotten. I might be a footnote or an afterthought. It didn't really matter.

What mattered was my life now.

What mattered was the wrong question anyway.

Who mattered?

That was the question. Who mattered?

A woman who wouldn't speak to me. I was a footnote to her.

Her name was Harper.

LXII

I emailed her once in a language I could write and she'd understand.

```
<script>
var person = {firstName: "Taylor", love: };
var person = {firstName: "Goose", love: math.random};

IF (Goose: love> 0) {
execute phone call = 669-353-2280 ;

ELSE IF (Goose: love < 0) OR (Goose: love = 0) {
execute memory = thorn bushes ;
execute memory = lessons ;
execute memory = spoons in bed ;
execute memory = taste ;
execute memory = voice ;
execute memory = laughter ;

THEN
execute phone call = 669-353-2280 ;
</script>
```

When I didn't hear back, I texted. I messaged. I found a stagnant Twitter account and DM'd it. I wrote the entire thing in Sharpie and sent it in an envelope.

She never responded.

LXIII

SIX WEEKS AFTER GREYHATC0N

SHE WAS BRILLIANT. She knew it too. She wore I-don't-give-a-fuck pumps and told me exactly what I was doing wrong.

"You rolled out the software before you had the capacity for hardware. You disappeared at a critical time for the company. You let a bunch of media take pictures of that monochromatic coding team you got in there." She leaned forward when she spoke, elbows on the table, fingers laced together.

Her last employer had said she was "bossy," "demanding," "shrill," and lastly, after a few drinks, "a bitch."

"I have an HR director," I said, mimicking her posture. "I have a media person and a business manager. You're not here for any of those jobs, so your observations may be correct, but they're not useful."

"This is my fifth interview—and my first one with just you." She indicated the empty room, the shut blinds, the closed door. "What do you want? I was COO of RKD for four years. It started smaller than QI4 and wound up ten times the size."

Interviewing men was easier. I had a better sense of them from a handshake and a nod. We spoke and read the same language. I felt crippled talking to this candidate, but I had to go through whatever this language barrier was. I couldn't go around it anymore.

She was the best for the job. End script.

"Can I be frank? About your reputation?"

"Oh, here it comes." She leaned back in her chair.

"I'm traveling a lot. So is Keaton. Deeprak's around, working on the monitor design."

She shifted her jaw to the side a little in defiance, as if girding herself against what I was going to say. I'd run it all through my head. She thought I was going to question when she intended to start a family, whether or not she was going to be "a bitch" when I traveled, or if she could handle all the testosterone-flinging.

"You have a reputation as a maverick," I continued. "A DIY hands-on outlier."

Her face changed. She hadn't expected me to go there.

"They needed a shark at RKD before they got rigor mortis."

She smiled.

"We're growing fast. You know, we talked about it last time, we just secured a huge infrastructure investment."

"And rumor is another's coming?" She raised an eyebrow.

She kept her ear to the ground. I liked that.

"The rumor is right." I wouldn't have told her that unless she was hired, and she knew it. "We're different, but I want you to bring here what you brought to RKD. We don't have time for timid or CYA. I want you to make mistakes fast and fix them faster."

She held her palms up in a half shrug. "I don't know how to be any other way."

We shook on it.

As if reading the vibrations in the air, Raven came in with paperwork. "So glad to have you on board, Ms. Friar."

"Gwen, please."

Raven turned to me, every word loaded with things she knew that no one else did. "Mr. Harden, Mr. Fitzgerald is on the way to the airport."

LXIV

FOUR DAYS AFTER GRAYHATC0N

I WAS OBSESSED WITH HER, and four days after I got back, Raven caught me at it.

To the world, I was completely in control. I took interviews, accepted adulation and awards. I met with real bankers about real money, not Bitcoin. When I went out, I brought my mother or my sister because I was obsessed with Harper Barrington and no other woman would come close.

I attacked the obsession in my off hours as if it was a second job. Harper's daily movements. Harper's internet presence. Harper's past. Harper's thoughts, feelings, and emotions.

Raven caught me hacking into Barrington Christian High School my second day back.

"Who's that?" Raven asked as she sneaked up behind me. I had Harper's third-grade picture on my screen.

"Niece." I closed the window, lying as if I wasn't the boss. Maybe because I was tired and it was after work hours. Maybe because no one else was in the office.

She'd brought things to sign. New hires. Resumes to look over. Checks. Invoices. A flood of the mundane.

"Taylor," she said.

"Raven."

"Are you all right?"

"Not really."

"Can I be honest?" She sat across from me as if I'd asked her to.

"No. Please. God, no."

"You're a mess." I almost objected, but she got her first words in edgewise. "You're in this office more than you've ever been. You shut windows like a kid caught looking at porn. Your traffic is almost constantly—"

"You're monitoring my traffic?"

"I monitor everyone's. It's my job. And the activity on yours shows certain patterns."

"Patterns?"

"You're hacking."

"That's my job."

"Who is she?"

I hadn't been in the mood, and I would have loved to shut her down, but I couldn't. I'd changed, and I couldn't just tell her to mind her business. "Rave, what we had—"

"Was convenient. We were friends, as much as Taylor Harden could be friends with anyone. And as a friend, I'm telling you, you're a mess. You have dark circles under your eyes. You haven't brushed your hair in two days. Do you want me to go on? Or do you want to tell me?"

"Neither."

It was late. I'd just seen a young, fresh third-grade genius I eventually loved. I wanted to go home and stew. I was still raw from being dragged away in a rented Mercedes. I slid my jacket off the back of my chair. "I owe you. For putting up with me. For staying professional when I wasn't. For everything."

"I was horny," she said. "And I was coming off a bad breakup. Yes, I can sue your ass from here to Disneyworld. But you got lucky this time."

"Turns out I'm a pretty lucky guy."

"Don't push it."

"Thanks, Rave."

I'd been on my way out, but she had to get a few more words in as she collected the checks and papers off my desk. "Did you know there are cameras all over the distribution center outside Barrington?"

"Excuse me?"

"Live feed. Deeprak and I were looking for you, and we came across it."

"Thanks."

Again. I'd gotten one foot out the door when she spoke up.

"And the Barrington post office is using Windows 3.1."

"What?"

"Just saying." Her smile hadn't been joy. It had been pure mischief.

"Motives. Spill," I said.

"You guys with your underhanded crazy 'exploits' and the way you see things other people can't. It's always been intriguing. When I was working with Deeprak to figure out what was going on with you, I… well, it was fun."

"Fun?"

"Yeah. Fun. And I want more."

Her breathing was sharp, and her face was flushed as if she was turned on—but not by me. I knew when a woman wanted me, and she'd moved on from my body to my knowledge.

"Have you heard of Chaxxer?" I asked, pulling a chair out for her.

This was going to take a while.

LXV

We couldn't get into Harper's wireless. She was too good for that. She'd never open a phishing link or download anything unknown. The only way in was around.

In the weeks between secretly partnering with Raven and before my flight with Fitz, Harper had been doing the following things:

1. Turning away the most appealing Chaxxer profiles Raven could come up with.
2. Lurking, but not participating, in dark web hacking forums.
3. Quitting the distro center.
4. Buying groceries with her credit card.
5. Applying to college.

We'd tapped into every security system in town, from the distro center to city hall to the police dash cams. I tracked her credit card to see when she pumped gas, then I watched her do it on station's security video. Raven suggested we tap into the wireless at Barrington City Hall to see if anyone had taken phone video of the council meeting. I showed her how to breach it, and she learned so fast I could barely keep up. She would have been a formidable criminal.

Harper was at the city council meeting to discuss the sale of the factory. Someone had indeed taken video, and it was automatically uploaded to the cloud, where I watched it so closely and so many times I dreamt about it. She was tiny, but it was her. When she pinched her bottom lip, I inspected the video for signs of tape on her fingers. There was none. When she raised her hand and stood to speak, I could hear her clearly but failed to read her mind.

She and Catherine were going to meet Fitz at Barrington Glass Works.

She didn't know I knew that.

LXVI

It was easy to sleep on Fitz's private jet. The whole thing was designed for rest and work. Raven was already dozing, and Deeprak was pounding away at his laptop as if he was playing Whac-A-Mole with the keys. Fitz's team buzzed around a set of blueprints.

I wasn't tired, so I listened to Fitz practice his speech. I never mentioned the identity of the girl he was dirty-talking from his sailboat. The Watsonette was mine, and as far as I was concerned, she was talking to Flow_ro to get to me. End.

"Overpopulation is the single greatest problem we face." Fitz was putting on his "TED Talks voice," which was infuriating in close quarters. Good thing he was my friend, or I would have punched him. "Why? Not because we're running out of space or oil or ways to dispose of our waste. But because there's one resource people need to live that depends on an environmental balance that's being disrupted right now. Water."

Fitz was about to continue, but I interrupted. "That's the longest sentence ever."

"It's two sentences," Fitz said, pointing at the screen. "Look. There's a period right there."

I should have been sleeping, but I was too nervous. "You can't just make one sentence into two by putting a period before a conjunction. That's a bullshit fake period."

"It tells me when I need to pause." Fitz had a manly face despite the red hair, but when he was full of shit, he sounded like a teenager trying to get away with something.

"You paused after 'but,' not before."

"You think your speeches are so perfect?"

"My speeches are awesome." They were. I'd pitched QI4 hardware and software all over the world, selling triple our projections, building the choke on supply I was counting on.

"Then why don't you do it?"

"Because you need the practice."

Fitz knew I was lying and closed his laptop.

"Ladies and gentlemen," the pilot called over the intercom, "we're starting our descent. It's a short strip, so if we don't make it the first time, don't panic. We should be landing outside Barrington safe and sound in eleven minutes."

LXVII

If I rubbed my palms on my pants one more time, I would leave sweat marks. I clutched a handkerchief instead, switching it between my right and left hands like a fucking neurotic. When I'd met the prime minister of the UK, my palms were as dry as her sense of humor. When I'd asked Fitz if he was interested in a partnership an hour after he got off a sailboat, I was half-drunk and easygoing. I'd taken calculated risk after calculated risk in the past month and never lost sleep over it.

Now, in the limo with Fitz, Deeprak, and Raven, my body was in complete revolt.

I wasn't able to eat, and I felt as though I wanted to puke. My mouth was dry, and my skin was wet. I couldn't sit still.

"Keaton's meeting us there," Raven said, swiping her finger across her phone. "They want to know if we need anything."

"We" included Fitz's team, who rode in the car behind us. They'd seen the factory floor, drawn the plans, moved the money, negotiated the zoning, and brought in the utilities at the speed of Everett Fitzgerald's signature.

"Water," Fitz said, projecting without shouting. "The coming water shortage is a global risk that must be addressed immediately. You, people of Barrington, are at the cusp of rev—"

"Cusp?" I asked. "You're really saying 'cusp'?"

"What's wrong with cusp?"

"It's weird," Deeprak agreed. "'Edge?' Can you do 'edge'?"

"I can't. It needs to be cusp."

"It amazes me," I said, "that you can invent and commercialize a system that combines hydrogen and oxygen molecules but you can't replace the word 'cusp.'"

"When you buy me out," Fitz said, "your speech can have all the words that make you happy. But at this moment, it's my signature that got us the money to buy this monstrosity, so I'm—"

"I paid the back taxes."

"Oh my God," Raven said. "Here we go."

"I'm going to use the word 'cusp,' the word 'boondoggle,' and I might throw a 'natty' in there to pretend I'm English." He straightened his jacket cuffs. "Actually, since you'll be squatting on half this property, you should give half the speech."

"Squatting?"

"Until you pony up."

"And you get the hell out."

The plan was for H(two)O to develop the commercial water creation system in half of the Barrington space then move to a bigger location as the operation expanded. By then, the theory went, QI4 would need the entire building. I'd buy him out—with a shot in the arm for interest.

"Keep it clean on your side," I said. "It's mine."

"Squatter."

"Guys," Deeprak interjected, "really?"

I could see the roof of the Barrington mansion as we pulled up to the gate in front of the factory. The arm was up, and the parking lot was full. Bickering with Fitz had passed the time, but as soon as I was forced to pay attention to my location, my heart started pounding again and I had to switch my handkerchief to the other hand.

The car stopped, and the door opened immediately, as if someone had been waiting.

"Holy shit," Kyle said when he saw me. He was in a cheap suit jacket and jeans like the rest of the welcoming committee. "Does she know you're here?"

I got out, straightened my jacket, then straightened his tie. "No."

She doesn't know.

Because she doesn't want me.

And she hasn't answered my letters.

Or calls.

And she doesn't need me.

The air brought me back a month to her ozone scent. The memory of infinite possibilities.

"I think I ought to tell her," Kyle said.

"Aw hell!" Butthead's voice boomed, and I was almost knocked over in an embrace before I realized who it was. "Where you been?"

"All over," I said. "Trying to figure out a way to buy this shithole so you can get a decent suit." I flicked his tie.

"Harper's gonna flip."

Was she?

Was that good or bad?

He was smiling, so maybe it was good?

I was the only one with an unplanned, dedicated two-man greeting committee. The rest of the party, including Fitz's team, was already being guided by what I'd have called "everyone else," which included Damon, Reggie, Juanita, Pat, and Johnny, looking like a sourpuss even from behind.

"Why didn't you tell us you were coming?" Kyle asked. "We coulda set something up."

"Told the sisters at least," Butthead broke in.

"You don't like surprises?"

"Man," Butthead said, "the last time we saw you…" He shook his head.

I patted him on the shoulder. "I'm not going to flip out on you again."

It was a statement. Not a promise. I had no idea what I was going to do when I saw her. I had some words I'd put together. Nothing with random periods or the word "cusp," but something just this side of begging.

The yard was clearing out as people went inside. There was going to be a ceremony, a handover, a lunch with handshaking and greetings, and last, a speech where Fitz promised a ton of shit I really hoped he could deliver.

The events would take all afternoon, and I couldn't wait that long. My need to see Harper broke through my worry over what she'd do.

"Where's Harper?" I asked.

"Funny you should ask." Kyle ran his fingers through his hair.

"Yeah," Butthead added. "Today of all days."

Between the shore of seeing her and the bank of not seeing her was a river. I was getting pulled away in it. "Guys. Where is she?"

"She had to go today—" Kyle started.

"Or she wasn't going to make the…" Butthead snapped his fingers at Kyle as if he couldn't remember but his friend might.

"Trimester—"

"I think they're on quarters."

"Semester, maybe?"

"Where?" I shouted.

"Stanford," they answered together.

"Who the hell gets a midyear acceptance to Stanford?!"

From their shrugs and expressions, they had no clue.

"Is she there yet?" I could take Fitz's car back to the airport right then and haul ass to Stanford.

"Leaving today."

"You might catch her." Butthead pointed over the reeds toward the Barrington house.

She was here. I could run. Catch her. Bury my face in her neck in the next ten to fifteen minutes.

I grabbed Butthead's cheeks and kissed him on the lips.

"Jesus," Kyle laughed.

I heard Butthead behind me say, "Is that blueberry ChapStick?"

But I couldn't answer because I was already on the path through the reeds. Four steps from where the toxic stink began then hopping the chain, hauling ass over the bridge, through more reeds, trees, grass—Jesus, was it always this far?

The thorn bushes were gone except for a few charred rose bushes around the edge of a little family cemetery. I didn't have time to take in more than that. I threw myself against the back door.

Locked.

"Harper!"

Down the steps and around the side. I pulled on the screen door and yanked the handle of the wooden door.

Locked.

"Harper!" I looked up at her room, backing to the other side of the side drive. No light, but it was afternoon. "Harper, are you there?"

Her car was in the front, but she was flying out, so she wouldn't take her car. Everyone was at the factory, so she couldn't get a lift.

"Harper!"

Gone. Was she gone?

Up the front porch to the door. Locked, of course. I pounded on it. Jammed the doorbell repeatedly.

They didn't even lock the doors on a regular day. Why were they locked now?

Because she was inside.

That was why.

I leapt off the porch and stood in the middle of the front yard where I could see a third-floor window. "Harper! I know you're in there!"

A green-and-white car came down the driveway.

Car service. And luck of all luck... a Middle Eastern dude with a short beard leaned out the window.

"Hey," he said. "I remember you. Going to the airport this time?"

"Ahmed."

"Yes, yes. I can help you with your bags."

He started to get out, but I put my hand on the door.

"Listen"—I took out my wallet—"I need you to wait at the end of the driveway, on the main road." I gave him two hundreds.

He took them. "How long?"

How long would it take to know if she'd come back to me?

I was sure I'd know right away.

"Half an hour."

"Okay." He rolled up the window and backed out.

"Hey!" a voice came from above. Harper, leaning out the window from the waist, the heels of both hands on the sill. Golden hair draped on either side of her face. Thrust forward like a woman who wanted things and was going to find a way to get them. "Stop!"

Ahmed had closed his window all the way against the early-winter chill and didn't hear her. Or two bennies had made him hard of hearing. Her eyes swept over the front yard, and she saw me.

I tried to look confident and attractive. Like a guy she'd want to come back to or a guy she hadn't wanted before but maybe, just maybe, she could want now if she was interested in a man who felt humble and insignificant most of the time.

"Hi," I said.

She went back in the room and slammed the window closed.

That wasn't an answer, and I needed answers. I stood on the porch between the steps and the door. I would wait for half an hour. Then Ahmed would return. She'd see him and have to go through me to get out.

I'd let her go—but not without trying to stop her first.

Half an hour didn't pass. Sixty seconds went by before the door opened. She stood on the other side of the screen. My Harper. Even seeing her veiled by the screen, my purpose was clear. She was the last piece of my puzzle.

"Taylor, did you send the cab away?"

"It's nice to see you."

The screen was a sensory barrier. Did her cheeks flush? Did she swallow hard? Take a breath?

"It's..." Her hand went to her lower lip, folded it, then snapped back. "I want to say it's nice to see you too."

"So say it."

Her lips disappeared between her teeth. "I knew you were coming."

She wasn't supposed to. My involvement had been hidden so she couldn't avoid me.

Which was exactly what she'd tried to do, wasn't it? That hurt. I had to call Ahmed and get him back, but…

"How?"

"I hacked you."

"Of course."

"And I found out you bought the factory too. With Fitz."

"That was a secret."

"Why?"

Why indeed. She was still behind the screen door. I could have punched through it and ripped it to shreds. I could have ripped it off the hinges.

"Come out here, and I'll tell you."

"No." Her answer came before I even finished the sentence. She snapped the lock.

"If you knew I was coming, why did you hide? All you had to do was answer an email and say, 'Sorry, I still don't want you. I never wanted you and never will.'"

One of her hands pressed against the screen, going white, bubbling like the bottom of an eggshell carton. "I couldn't." Her voice cracked, and she pressed her lips between her teeth again. "I saw what you were doing, and I knew why. I knew you bought the factory to reach out to me, but Taylor, I'm not for you." She choked back a sob. "I'm always going to be connected here, and you're going to…" She couldn't finish.

I went to the door.

"No!"

I stepped back. "Harper, please…"

"I'm going to drag you down. You'll never be what you want as long as I am who I am. I'm a loser. You're not. My God…" She was fully crying, and I couldn't get near her. "Please tell me you didn't blow everything on that pig of a building. You can't lose it all for me."

"Open this door."

She just sniffed, crossing her arms.

Fuck it.

I pulled the screen door handle. Once. Twice. The third time, the little lock snapped apart the jamb and the door swung open.

The screen had hidden the extent of her anguish. Her face was red and slick with tears. Her shoulders slumped. I went to put my arms around her, but she dodged me.

"I'm protecting you, you dumb shit!" she choked out.

Halfway in and halfway out of the house, I knew something for sure that I hadn't known before. Maybe it was her vulnerability or the weakly guarded posture or seeing her with fresh eyes.

"You got into QI4," I said. "You won the challenge."

"Don't be stupid! You would have seen the breach."

"You were close. Close enough to know you could."

She didn't answer but cried harder.

"You backed off."

I was right. She didn't look at me. Didn't shake her head or wave her hand to deny it.

"Why?" I asked.

"I wanted you to win."

She took a folded piece of paper from her pocket. It flopped halfway open to reveal the code I'd mailed to her.

"This?" She held it toward me like a weapon. "I read it every day, and I remembered everything you ever said to me. I used you again. This code gave me the confidence to apply out of here." She opened the paper and read from it. "'Execute memory = thorn bushes ; lessons ; spoons in bed ;' God, Taylor, the spoons… when I needed you, you were there, and I threw you away. I said, 'Don't call him, don't call him.' Because you forgot the last *IF* function. If call script runs… if I call you and you come to me, you fail. Do you understand? There are things bigger than us. And if I'm with you, you won't have those things."

"Harper." I put my hands out and went toward her. "Harper Barrington, you are working with so much bad data." I got closer. She didn't back away. "Sorting it out is going to take me a lifetime of loving you."

"How are you breaking me down?"

"I'm irresistible. Can you come here, please? Admit defeat, and let's get on with it."

She fell into my arms as if she couldn't hold herself up for another minute. She shook and cried while I held her as tight as I could. We collapsed on the foyer floor together. I wiped her face with my crumpled cotton handkerchief. She took it and wiped her nose, holding it close as she leaned back on my chest.

When the car came around front, she was just about slowing down.

"Are you going to Stanford?" I asked after Ahmed tooted the horn.

"I got an early decision for fall."

"That's in eight months."

"I figured I'd get a job." She looked up at me. "I just couldn't face you."

"You're lying." I touched her nose.

"No—"

"All the schools in the world? Stanford? It's in my backyard."

"Your damn ego."

"You wanted to be near me."

"They accepted me. No one else did."

"You applied because you were hoping to see me. You know it. I know it. You would have been in QI4 reception before the year was out."

"I'm not working with you. You're a jerk, and I'm getting a business degree."

I kissed her forehead. "Can I send the cab away without you?"

"Yes."

Gently, I got up to deal with the car. She sat on the floor with her knees bent, wiping her face and pulling away the hair that had stuck to her eyes.

"This smells like you," she said of the handkerchief.

"I'll wash it."

"Never."

Outside, as I approached the cab, I could hear the celebration and announcements at the factory.

"Thanks for coming back," I said, leaning in the open cab window.

"You need me?"

"Nah."

"Let me give you the money back."

"Keep it," I called over my shoulder.

When I got back in the house, she was standing by the staircase. Her elbows were bent, and her head was tilted a little forward. Her weight was balanced on the balls of her feet.

She looked ready to spring.

The innocent sexual enthusiast was gone. She was a fearsome and majestic animal.

We leapt at each other at the same time, lips crashing, hands clawing, fabric ripping. My tongue ran along hers, tasting salty tears and sweet hope. Our fingers explored places that hadn't forgotten each other. She was soft, yielding, insistent, and when her hand touched my cock, skin to skin, I pulled away before I exploded.

"Harper."

Her hair was a nest, and her voice was practically a growl. "What?"

"I love you, and I always will. But I'm only going to fuck you if I can keep you."

"If you don't fuck me now…" She pulled off her shirt. "You can't keep me."

My brain was hardwired for those bubblegum-topped tits. I bent her back and sucked them. Not sticky sugar. Salt and sex and the blood rushing through my veins.

She leaned back too far and fell against the wall, pulling me down with her. We wrestled with her pants, tearing her underwear, working my clothes away just enough to get my dick out.

When I slid two fingers inside her to make sure she was ready, she gripped my shoulders, opening her mouth and throwing her head back.

"God," she said through her teeth. "Fuck me. Please."

I thrust my dick inside her, and she squeezed me tight.

"Look at me. I want to see you."

She gasped over and over, and with each thrust, she was more mine, spreading her legs wider so I could go deeper.

"Say you're mine," I demanded.

"You're mine."

I pounded her hard for that, and she shouted in pleasure.

"Say I'm yours, goose."

"I'm yours. I'm yours."

With those words, the pressure became almost unbearable. She tightened around me again and let out a long howl, arching her back for me. I held her down while I let go, exploding with her.

We stayed on the floor for a minute, just breathing together. When the wind blew the right way, the sounds of the ceremony drifted over the house, churning with the sounds of our breathing, the pops of our kisses, and the warm words of our love. Her home was settled. Her family had the chance they needed. She'd made her own decisions, and I'd made mine. We'd succeeded, failed, and come full circle back to each other.

Our boats were lashed together, swaying on the endless sea. We were dots, specks, insignificant blinks under the weight of infinity.

I was not afraid.

EPILOGUE

She wanted to get there early, which meant I had to fly back from Virginia early to bring her. I was relieved, actually. I wanted to see how Deeprak was doing with the monitor display production line before Keaton came in to see the protos.

"You could have met me there," she said with a wheeled crate banging down the stairs behind her.

"What's the fun in that?"

"Okay, well, fine then." She slid the crate next to luggage, boxes, and storage containers. Her eyes lit on each one as if she were counting.

I tucked a length of hair behind her ear. "I had your classes checked. Your stats professor—"

"What kind of checked?"

"Asked around town." I held up my hands in innocence. She'd made me promise not to have her professors hacked to collect old tests and data on grading. "She's looking for tenure. So if you need to make trouble—"

"Taylor!"

"It was totally aboveboard."

"Don't check on people for me!" She hit my chest to make her point.

She meant it—for the moment. But I was going to keep asking around for her until she was on her feet. And probably afterward.

A car crunched and rumbled down the driveway.

"Don't eat at the campus café." I picked up a box. "They failed a health inspection this summer and passed just a week ago. That's not about a person, so you can't get mad."

"I'm going to eat at your place." She grabbed the handle on a wheelie suitcase. "Did you send the factory car?"

"Yes. What's in here?" The things in my box shuffled when I moved.

"Nothing. I thought the factory car was a Mercedes?"

The top flaps of the box bent. I could see inside. "You're taking a box of cables?"

"I always need cables."

I dropped the box and bent to see inside one of the containers. "This is full of circuit boards and..." I popped the top off it. "Coding manuals? Harper."

"What?" Her arms were crossed. I'd agreed to not interfere, but she was making it hard.

"Did you bring a toothbrush?"

She pointed at the smallest bag, which was tucked under a foyer table.

In the month since her birthday, a lot had happened with Catherine. She had enough money to buy furniture for her beloved house.

"My clothes and stuff are in there," Harper said.

"All your clothes are in that tiny thing?"

"Can you stop? Please?"

"Goose—"

"Don't 'goose' me. Just..." She stepped back and put her hands out. Her face scrunched. "I'm scared, okay?" I shut up while she took a deep breath. Then another. "I'm scared no one's going to like me and I'm too old, and I'm scared I'm not smart enough."

"Seriously? You're smarter than every last one of them."

I peered past the front curtains at the Range Rover sitting at the end of the drive with the engine running. I couldn't see past its tinted windows. Ahmed, who we'd hired as the factory driver, should have gotten out by now.

An ugly feeling brewed in my gut. Something was wrong with this picture.

"What's with Ahmed? Is he sick in there or something?"

Harper was still on the same train of thought. "I'm afraid I won't fit in. I'm afraid they'll find out about us and think I'm coasting."

"You're going to coast because of your brain. Not because of me." The Range Rover was still idling. "Maybe we should take the Caddy," I said, referring to the car I'd bought her to replace the shimmymobile.

Harper came to the window with me and bent back the curtain.

"Maybe someone's looking for the factory and got lost? Used to happen all the time."

"Stay here," I said, opening the front door.

The porch creaked under my weight. Something wasn't right with this car, and I needed to get between it and Harper.

The car locks clacked. Harper was right behind me as if I hadn't told her to stay inside. She was going to be a real pain in the ass to take care of.

The driver's door opened, and a woman stepped out. Mid-twenties in a black suit and stilettos. Red lipstick. Black hair two inches above the tits. She didn't carry a bag but a leather folder in her manicured fingers.

A guy who looked like a Ken doll got out of the passenger side and buttoned his jacket.

If Harper sensed what I sensed, she didn't show it. My goose stepped in front of me as if it was her house, which it was, and as if she was perfectly capable of greeting newcomers, which remained to be seen.

I put my hand on her waist to stop her. It didn't work.

"Hello?" Harper said.

"Hello." The woman had a deep, throaty voice and an air of entitlement I recognized from dealing with empowered people.

"Afternoon," the Ken doll replied.

"Can I help you?" Harper crossed her arms.

"Are you Catherine Barrington?" The woman asked.

"I'm Harper, her sister."

"Harper." She smiled wide and almost… *almost* genuinely. The guy just stood next to her. He seemed wildly competent in his silence. I just didn't know what he was competent at yet.

"If you're looking for the factory—" I said.

"No." She cut me off, eyes landing on me as if I was what she was looking for. "You must be Taylor Harden."

"Who's asking?" Harper folded her arms as if she was ready to stand between me and an army of Range Rovers.

The woman smiled again and walked to the edge of the steps. She took a flat wallet out of her breast pocket.

"I'm Agent Cassie Grinstead. FBI." She flipped it open with her fingers and held it up so we could see the ID card and badge.

"Agent Ken Romig." He held up his own little wallet and I had to check to make sure his name was really Ken. It was.

"What do you want?" Harper sounded as if she was about to tell the agents to get the hell off her property.

The agents flipped their wallets closed and put them away in perfect synchronicity before answering. I realized it was because they knew they might need their hands free.

I got in front of Harper. I didn't think they'd start shooting, but she was on her way to Stanford to start the life she always deserved and nothing, not these people and not the federal government…were getting in her way.

"Well?" I asked. "What can we do for you?"

Cassie answered.

"We're looking for Keaton Bridge."

</book>

THANK YOU FOR READING! I hope you enjoyed Taylor and Harper.

Catherine and Chris's story is told in the novella *White Knight.* I put a chapter in the back if you want to check it out.

Keaton's story is told in the standalone *Queen of Rust.*

<acknowledgements>

/*The following is not a code language that makes any kind of sense. I made it up and I just think it looks cool*/

{Amy VoxLibris} = (early beta, great notes, tonal adjustment)

{Jenn} = (contents of fridge/availability, support = moral and functional, encode term = "the things")

{Chanpreet Singh} + {Emily Smith-Kidman} = (fast oops detection > releasing a mess/saved, !)

{Jana Aston} = (seed idea/inspiration, eye of eagle, pulls writer out of secret shitstorm)

{Mandy Beck} = (seed PM, support)

{Cassie} = (nonvar = editor > perfection)

{Devon} = (you > great)

{Penny Reid} = (thank you for the lantern)

{Cameron} = (having you = relief)

{Kevin and Louisa}= (SSBjYW5ub3QgdGhhbmsgeW91IGVub3VnaA==)

/*That being said — There are so many people who contribute to the writing of a book, there's no way I could thank them/you all. Please forgive me if I've left you out*/

</acknowledgements>

1

WHITE KNIGHT

I haven't edited this, so there are a billion typos. I love this chapter so it'll probably be the same but I reserve the right to change anything about it before final publication.

I hope you enjoy it!

CATHERINE AT SIXTEEN

AT THE DOVERTON COUNTRY CLUB, there was a boy who worked on the grounds. He had sun-coppered hair and strong arms. In the summer his skin was a burnished russet that made his blue eyes otherworldly. All the girls at the club giggled over him. They were mostly from Doverton, but he and I were from neighboring Barrington. The town bore my name because my father and his father before him had owned the bottling plant, and that was what you did back then. If you created the town and made it thrive you named it after you. Fifty years later, it was still named Barring- ton, we still lived there, and the folks in Doverton called it Trashington.

The town's reputation bothered my father a little...but my mother? When she heard some of the Doverton Ladies of the Court hadn't invited her to a cocktail brunch because she lived *over there*, it drove her over the edge.

"Don't you give them a reason to call you trash." She sat across from us in the limo. Harper and I got dressed in our whites three times a week for tennis lessons. Dad worked at the plant, and mom didn't drive. "That's the first thing." She pointed at Harper. "When you hit them with your racket that's exactly what you're doing. Giving them a reason to look down on you because you're a Barrington."

"I didn't—" Harper's defense was irrelevant.

"If they only knew. We could buy and sell all of them."

"She didn't call me trash she said the topspin reduced the travel distance when in fact the spin vector—"

"Harper!" Mom cut her off again. "No one wants to hear a lady talk nonsense."

I wasn't thinking of my sister or how she must have felt when mom said stuff like that, which she always did. I was thinking of myself and how I was so much more of a lady than my little sister.

"Look!" Harper pointed out the window. "There's that guy again!"

I slid over to her, and there he was. The boy with the rippling tan skin who worked the grounds, biking up the hill in his shorts and backpack. No helmet, bronze hair flapping away from his sweaty face.

His name was Chris. He had a ready smile and full lips that tasted like salt and cola.

Mom tisked. "That boy. He's going to get himself killed. I don't know how his parents allow him to take a *bicycle* twenty-two miles to the club."

"We should give him a ride!" Harper exclaimed, eyes wide with a brilliant idea.

"Heavens, no!"

As we passed him, he waved when he saw us. Harper opened the window and cupped her hands around her mouth.

"Use a lower gear uphill! It increases gain ratio!"

"Thank you!" he said with a smile, and flicked his gear changer. I got away from the window as mom took Harper by the shoulder and pulled her to her side. The driver closed and locked the window. We rode the rest of the way in silence.

***

The first time I'd seen Chris, I was leaning on the court fence waiting for my coach and he was trimming the grass edging on the other side of it with a weedwhacker. I heard it and felt the pricks of cut grass on the backs of my calves. I stepped away from it.

"Sorry, Miss."

"It's all right, I—"

My voice hadn't drifted off or gotten lost. I didn't swallow the rest of the sentence or forget what I was saying. The final words never existed. Everything before I saw him was fake, and after that moment my life became real. Like Dorothy walking out of her black and white world into a three-dimensional colorscape.

My life wasn't divided into the years before that moment and the time after because he was handsome or strong. It wasn't because he was charming or interesting.

It was because he was mine.

He'd known it too.

My coach had come soon after. I never hit so hard or so accurately. I astonished the coach, but I wasn't surprised. I was sure everything I'd do from then on out would be right and true.

When I'd finished my lesson, we found each other like magnets. We didn't say hello or introduce each other.

Wide-eyed, he'd said, "Did you feel it?"

"I did. I did feel it."

We stole behind the pro shop to marvel at what had happened.

"What was it?" I asked when he closed the door.

"I don't know." He touched my arm. It felt like two planets had been on separate trajectories for light years finally collided and melded. I stared at his hand, and when he tried to move it, I put mine on top ofhis.

"Have you felt it before?"

"No. But I still kind of…it's still there."

"Yeah. Me too. I'm…" What I was about to say had felt so trivial I almost skipped the step. "I'm Catherine."

"Chris," he'd said as if waking from a half-dream. "My name's Chris Carmichael. I have to see you again."

I could. I had to. I had no choice. But I couldn't agree before Irv, who owned the shop, burst in with a clipboard. He had a huge round belly, crooked teeth, and a soft spot for Barrington kids who needed jobs.

He froze when he saw us.

"Carmichael," he'd said. "Get out to court seven and take care of the trash." His eyes flicked to me, and back to Chris.

"Yes, sir."

"And young lady?"

I held my chin up. I was an heiress and a club member.

"I believe you don't want your mother to hear back about this. So keep it quiet."

I didn't realize at the time that he was protecting Chris, but later, after I realized it, I was grateful to him. Though, in the end, no one could protect Chris but me.

***

Behind the courts, between the locker room and the club, there was a shortcut for members and an artery for the grounds staff. Behind that was a quarter-acre patch of grass between the fence and Route 42 which stretched between Doverton and Barrington. The entire patch of grass was visible to the road, but there was a tree in the middle of it. A mighty oak with horizontal branches thicker than most tree's fully-grown trunks.

When Chris had a minute and happened upon the right piece of wood, he'd nail chunks of two-by-four or one-by-four into the trunk. He told me about it behind the pool house and in the hidden corners of the parking lot. I didn't know what he was talking about until he finished toward the end of summer as he led me through a hole in the fence.

"Where are we going?"

"Just over here." He put his hand on the lowest block, at waist height. "Put your foot on this. I've tried it already. It's safe."

I dropped my bag at the base of the trunk and he helped me balance as I got my tennis shoe on the bottom foothold. My hands found the ones above, and I stepped up. At the second step, I pressed the back of my skirt against my bare thighs and looked down at him.

"You'll need two hands to climb," he said.

"I think you should go first."

"You're wearing shorts under your skirt. I can't see a thing."

The shorts protected my bottom from view while I ran and spun on the tennis court. But they were still really short, and he was getting a longer look.

"Do you promise?"

"Swear."

I decided to believe him, and climbed the tree until I was fifteen feet off the ground, on a bough thicker than three telephone poles.

I straddled the bough and slid back so Chris could fit. He straddled facing me. I could hear cars on Route 42 and the *pock pock* of tennis balls hitting the court, but all I could see were leaves, branches and mottled sunlight all around.

"Do you like it?" he asked.

"I love it."

He licked his finger and chalked one up for himself.

"Did you decide about college next year?" he asked.

I shrugged. I wanted to get out of Barrington. Spread my wings. Meet new people and learn new things. But Chris couldn't afford to go.

"Did you check out the financial aid booklet at the library?"

"There's no point."

"Well, then I'll get an associates from Jackson County. I won't have to move and—"

"You have to go." He grabbed my hands.

"How are you going to leave your mother?"

"She'll be on her own soon."

Chris was an only child to a mother who had been too obese to leave her bed. In the past year, she'd made him proud by losing 150 pounds. Not enough to be comfortable, but enough to move around the house.

"I'll wait for you."

"No." He got distressed whenever I suggested I'd slow my life down for him. "I'm the one who's going nowhere in life. I'm the one who waits—"

"No, I do not—"

"Yes you do." He squeezed my hands. "Look at you. You can be anything you want. Go be it. That's all I have to say. No. I have something else."

He looked over my shoulder, then back to my face. I knew him enough from our summer together to know I needed to wait.

"I'll catch up with you," he continued like he always did. "I promise I'll follow you anywhere."

I almost lost my mind in his eyes. Almost agreed with him. I could do anything but I didn't want to. I wasn't Harper with her big dreams and bigger brain. I didn't have ambitions or a career in mind. I figured I'd inherit the factory and keep it going, or not. What I really wanted was a house full of people who depended on me.

"I'll think about it," I said because I wanted to make Chris happy for a moment.

"When do you have to be back?" he asked.

"Mom thinks I'm volleying with Marsha."

He brushed my knee with his fingertips. My skin felt like it was melting underneath them and I became very aware of the hard trunk between my legs.

"Marsha's in the pool house with what's-his face."

"Charles."

He leaned into me. "What do you think they're doing in there?"

Marsha was a tramp and everyone knew it. Maybe I was a tramp too. But no one knew, so it wasn't the same.

"Stuff."

"This, maybe?" He ran two fingers inside my thigh. Sensation rushed behind them, to my knees, and ahead to the soft place between my legs. We'd kissed plenty in the back room of the pro shop and the utility closet, he'd run his hands over my shirt. but he'd never touched me like that before.

"Maybe," I gasped. I thought I shouldn't let him run his hand up my other thigh. I should stop this right there. He was going way too fast.

There were *steps* and he wasn't honoring them. But that made his touch even more explosive. My body didn't expect the speed of his advance, and it reacted by opening up all the way.

"Oh, my God." His eyes were wide and his lip was stretched behind his top teeth. When he let it go it went from white to deep pink. "Look at you. I can't believe how sexy you are."

My face tingled. Chris wasn't much more experienced than I was, but he was so open and honest about what he was doing and what he wanted that his words made me blush.

His index finger brushed the edge of my shorts.

"Can I touch you?"

I throbbed when he asked. The ache inside me was almost painful in its need.

But was it too much? Would he think I was a slut? My legs were already open, by design. Wasn't that already an invitation? I could have swung both legs to one side, but I hadn't taken the modest posture.

In the pause after his question, he kissed me, pressing his thumbs into my inner thighs. He was inside me, his tongue in my mouth was such a sweet violation. I wanted more. All the more.

I picked his hands up and put them on my chest. Lips locked, he ran his thumbs over my hard nipples as I reached back, under my shirt and unhooked my bra.

He broke the kiss. I came forward to put our mouths together again, but he leaned back. "Show me."

I would have preferred to kiss while he felt my breasts so it would feel as though I was in thoughtless throes of passion. It would feel less mindful. If we were putting thought into it, pausing and stopping, appreciating every act, then I had no excuse.

Chris gently pulled at the hem of my shirt.

He didn't want mindless. He wanted to see every second. I knew my nipples were hard under the sports bra and he was looking right at them as if he was savoring the sight. His relish shamed me and made my skin tingle at the same time.

In the choice between shame and the tingle, I made my choice.

I pulled my shirt up over my breasts. The bra lifted. He ran his hands along the underside before he pulled the bra up.

He sucked in a breath.

"These are spectacular." He bent the hard nipples before he gently squeezed them. The feeling shot right between my legs as if connected by an electric wire. My back arched and my consciousness hid behind a wall of pleasure.

The bough went from under me, and his hands got tight on my rib cage.

"Whoa, there," he said, keeping me from falling.

"I'm sorry."

"Don't be. Just remember where you are." Every so tenderly, he pinched my nipples again. It hurt a little, but the pain was part of the plea- sure. "Can you put your hands behind you? On the branch?"

He guided my arms behind me. My shirt fell back down, but once I was secure, leaning back against my locked elbows, he drew it back up. I was exposed to the sky.

"Next time, I'll do it your way." He pushed my chin up so I was looking through the branches at the clouds and ran it down my body. "I'll go up first so you can lean on the trunk."

"Yes, okay."

Both hands landed on my breasts.

"I like it when you agree."

He kissed my sternum and twisted the nipples.

I groaned.

He twisted a little harder. "Do you like that?"

"Yes. Yes."

"You smell like roses." He sucked one nipple and hurt the other in a way that brought pleasure to the surface. I was filled with blood, my insides bigger than my outside, stretching my skin to thin translucence.

"More," I gasped, the word falling out of my mouth like a piece of gum I'd forgotten about. I didn't even know what I was saying. I was losing my mind as he worked me over. Blind, deaf, dumb. My whole body was wedged between his fingers.

My face was toward the sky, a curtain of dappled orange from the daylight on the other side of my closed eyes. A frame of white hot shock-waves flickered in my vision, and something broke in me. I stopped thinking, breathing, feeling anything but him as the world pressed in on me and I pressed out into the world.

"Jesus!" he said when I finally gasped and opened my eyes.

"Oh, my G—"

"You *came*."

Sitting up straight, I put my hands over my face. I was ashamed. I'd done that, in front of him, from nothing.

"I didn't think I would!"

When I took my hands away and saw him looking at me, I yanked my shirt down.

"It was awesome!"

Awesome? I wanted to die.

"Catherine!" Harper's voice came past the fence. Chris looked at his watch, but I didn't need to see it. Three p.m. had come and my bra wasn't hooked. I reached behind me and grappled with it.

I had to get down and Chris was in my way. He'd made me come right here, outside in a tree. I was ashamed and nervous, and he was pulling my shirt down to cover me. He was beautiful with his blue eyes and the wavy fall of hair over one side of his forehead. He was inappropriate. Unsuitable. Dangerous to my future, whatever that was.

"Hey." Harper called without shouting. As if she knew I was close by.

Chris climbed up a branch to get out of my way, indicating his hand-made staircase, then putting his finger to his lips.

Harper had her face in the hole in the fence, looking at the bag I'd left at the base of the trunk.

"Coming!" I shouted, scuttling down.

"There you are!" She came through the hole. "Mom said to go to the car. Hey!" She pointed to the tree. "Were you climbing?"

"No." I slung the bag over my shoulder.

"That's really cool." She looked back at the hole, then back up the ladder pinching her bottom lip until it creased. I slapped her hand down. (*Chris and Catherine need to solidify what they like about each other very efficiently and this has been going on a long time)

"Stop bending your lip like that. It's going to stay that way." I took the hand I'd slapped before she had a chance to bend her lip again, pulling her to the break in the fence. "And don't even think of climbing that tree. It's not even safe." She went through first, and I followed. "I'm telling the grounds crew it's there before someone gets hurt."

My muscles didn't relax until we got to the car and I knew Harper hadn't seen Chris up in the tree. If anyone knew the way he touched me and the way it made me feel I'd die. Literally die.

NEW BOOKS

King of Code | *White Knight* | *Queen of Rust*

The Submission Series

Submission | *Domination* | *Connection*

The Corruption Series

Spin | *Ruin* | *Rule*

Standalones

Forbidden | *Hardball* | *Shuttergirl* | *Secret Sins*

The Games Duet

Marriage Games | *Separation Games*

CPSIA information can be obtained
at www.ICGtesting.com
Printed in the USA
BVOW09s0732270917
495654BV00006B/4/P